The Witherspoon Legacy

The Witherspoon Legacy

G.K. Sutton

Copyright © 2008 by G.K. Sutton.

The cover photographs are by Joseph Routon, used with permission.
The author's photograph is by J. O. Love, used with permission.

Library of Congress Control Number: 2008907334
ISBN: Hardcover   978-1-4363-6381-5
            Softcover   978-1-4363-6380-8

All rights reserved. No part of this book may be reproduced or transmitted in any form or by any means, electronic or mechanical, including photocopying, recording, or by any information storage and retrieval system, without permission in writing from the copyright owner.

This is a work of fiction. Names, characters, places and incidents either are the product of the author's imagination or are used fictitiously, and any resemblance to any actual persons, living or dead, events, or locales is entirely coincidental.

This book was printed in the United States of America.

To order additional copies of this book, contact:
Xlibris Corporation
1-888-795-4274
www.Xlibris.com
Orders@Xlibris.com

DEDICATION

Praise God, from whom all blessings flow;
praise him, all creatures here below;
praise him above, ye heavenly host:
praise Father, Son, and Holy Ghost.

Isaac Watts (1674-1748)
(preferably to the tune *Old Hundredth*)

Foreword

Yes, I hate that word as much as many of you. You may skip this portion entirely, as I am wont to do. However, it is a necessary evil for informing the discerning and curious reader of certain trivia.

Firstly, although I have been promised that the disclaimer is found elsewhere, I want to make sure that it is clear that all events and characters, and most of the places described, are purely the product of the author's imagination, and any resemblance to actual events, places or persons, living or dead, is coincidental. Being from a small Southern town, I can not emphasize this strongly enough, to discourage any friend or neighbor from wrongly surmising I have singled him or her out to immortalize or massacre, as the case may be. And heaven forbid that anyone think I am in any way indicting the Episcopal Church or its clergy, which I love dearly. The music and composers are, on the other hand, not fiction and are very real, and all worthy of praise.

Secondly, despite my best efforts and those of my victim editors, there are bound to be errors. This being my first published work, I respond to my anxiety by continuing to edit myself after submitting the manuscript to someone else, until the version being proofread by the editor no longer resembles the current version. One thing the reader may notice is the occasional absence of a diacritical or accent mark. I made a conscious decision that in typing my own work I would rather be excoriated for the occasional absence, than to try to insert the mark, only for it to become some gobbledygook when formatting and style changes inevitably occur during the printing process. My friends can tell you that many of my iniquities are premeditated.

Lastly (because you are bored already), but most importantly, there are people who should be thanked, many of whom I will inevitably forget. I apologize to those. Thanks be foremost to God for his unspeakable gift, and for all other gifts he has given me, including the existence of whirlpool baths and showers, where I can escape the phone and other distractions and brainstorm scenes. Thanks to those who make the dream and the dreaming possible: David, Tim and my friends at PipeChat; those who suffered through reading the drafts—Nicholas Russotto, Kitty Sims; Sand Lawn, who always makes me feel my writing is worthwhile; Canon John C. Fowler and Richard Thornton, who forced me to take up the pipe organ (although, contrary to rumor, guns were not involved); Dr. Lawrence C. Maddock, whose Christmas cards always remind me of my love for literature; my long-suffering husband and supporter Rick, and my parents and family. Many thanks to Joe Routon and J.O. Love, for providing me the photography, for being fellow organ aficionados, and just for being friends.

Chapter 1

"'I am the resurrection and the life, saith the Lord; he that believeth in me, though he were dead, yet shall he live; and whosoever liveth and believeth in me shall never die . . . . For none of us liveth unto himself, and no man dieth to himself . . . .'"

Although the sky outside was a brilliant blue in the Indian summer sunlight, the interior of the cavernous church seemed dim, like a theatre. The burnished mahogany-paneled wainscoting of the narthex wound its way into the nave and absorbed the light, climbing up the walls to a chest-high scrolled fascia, where it was stopped dead in its vertically-climbing tracks by a richly painted stenciled border, at which point pale taupe-green-toned stuccoed walls dominated.

The choir and high altar, in stark contrast, were bathed in a warm ethereal glow. The outside sun emitted a wash of pure light, which flowed in from the twin flanking dormers over the altar, and lit up the buttery-colored walls and imposing east altar window in glorious bloom, the cross and Easter flowers depicted therein fashioned by some long dead immigrant apprentice of Tiffany. The altar window was flanked by cascades of exotic white lilies. The room reflected the style described by architects, sometimes condescendingly, as 'country Gothic', with repeating motifs of pointed arches framing the altar, doorways, windows and ambulatory. Completing the framing of the altar were the twin organ chests, the great facade pipes towering as sentinels, majestic and imposing.

Once one's eyes became accustomed to the lighting, it was apparent that the church was packed with mourners, all facing the high altar and the coffin before it in the main aisle. Along with a full choir in attendance, the chancel flowed with clergy and acolytes in solemn procession, reflecting the light off their pressed and pristine albs and surplices. The colorful side windows, with matching intersecting tracery and bejeweled stained glass, and sans the customary depictions of apostles and martyrs, reflected darker and dappled hues, casting grotesque and sinister patterns of light and shadow. The organ blazed forth, commandingly filling the space with aural accompaniment.

In the center of the somber pomp and pageantry stood one man, tall, lean, without an ounce of spare flesh, his bearing regal and seemingly disdainful, his facial features aquiline, drawn and severe, his eyes green with golden glints, cold and appraising. Although he appeared outwardly calm during this most Solemn Mass for the Dead, he was inwardly reeling, bewildered and seething that God had dealt him the ultimate checkmate. Here he was, Stephen Marks, a bishop and ultimately aspiring to succession for the office of presiding bishop, surrounded by his minions and accoutrements of office, the trappings of his status, his cope on his shoulders, his mitre and staff on the holy altar, and priests and acolytes in attendance, so close to completion of his ambitions and dreams of vengeance.

Meanwhile the unrequited love of days gone by, the object of his carefully laid plans, lay still before him, her eyes closed in death, her lifeless form cold in resplendent beauty, albeit aged, more than he recalled from memories past, now forbidden to him forever. Instead of returning to this place, his one-time home town of Mainville, in glorious conquest to gloat, to bask in his worldly successes and to consummate a final phase of his long-awaited strategy while enjoying the homage he felt overdue from others, he had somehow missed his cue, becoming instead an interloper as he presided over the last rites of burial for the woman who had spurned him years ago. Any triumph he had planned to experience had fled, as he was faced with a surprising and overwhelming impotence to fulfil his desire to see her finally vanquished before him. In her death he ironically became the vanquished.

He had long designed and imagined his confrontation with her, and had convinced himself that nothing would prevent its coming to pass just as he desired. Although he had been informed that she was terminally ill, he had tarried too long in coming, and was now denied the opportunity to accomplish his mad fanciful secret lust to bring her to her knees, to view an anticipated look of regret from her for what she had denied him, and to wreak his revenge. Instead, her letter and copy of her latest will delivered to him just prior to this service were her parting shot, mocking him even as it delivered a piercing blow through the calcified armor over that part that once was his heart. The pages in her unmistakable handwriting with their gravely imponderable news produced a chilling jolt, leaving him gasping in speechless shock with their implications.

As he went through the motions of the service automatically, the procession, the lessons, the homily delivered by the rector, all became a blur. He could not concentrate on the task before him. Scenes from his past, recollections of regrettable events, imagined vistas of roads not taken, the wheels of his planned revenge already set in motion, kept flitting through his brain, tearing at the fabric of his concentration and churning inside him like so much cement in a mixer.

Added to this were novel pangs of loss and overwhelming remorse, combined with anxiety regarding the meeting on the morrow with an auditor from the Presiding Bishop, an episode colliding with the current events to create a feverish intensity of apocryphal proportions in his overworked imagination. The news imparted by the deceased's letter cast a final twist of chaos and unreality threatening the fruits of the carefully conceived conspiracy, creating a gaping wound to the man for whom conscience had been all but forgotten these many years in his acquisition of power, prestige and wealth.

At the conclusion of the *Sanctus* he continued with the Eucharistic Prayer, repeating by rote the old familiar language of oblation, redemption and sacrifice. "And although we are unworthy, through our manifold sins, to offer unto thee any sacrifice, yet we beseech thee to accept this our bounden duty and service, not weighing our merits, but pardoning our offenses, through Jesus Christ our Lord."

His voice broke into a sob. Quickly recovering, he dared not look up, feeling the watchful eyes of others upon him, but resumed without further incident.

In the period of silence following the Lord's Prayer, he involuntarily glanced up and met the eyes of the organist. Her accusatory gaze held his for a grim moment. In that instant the Fraction of the Host in his trembling fingers sounded as cue to the preface of the *Agnus Dei*. As the sound reverberated, his epiphany was complete. He divined in horror the organist's identity, and was certain that she must be able to read his face, that the self-assured façade, the brocade, velvet and satin of his costume were an indictment exposing his crime instead of emoluments of his rank, and that she must be fully cognizant of his true self.

He was filled with self-loathing and shame, emotions alien to him. He wondered with growing terror how many others in the congregation of his home town, all currently a sea of faceless figures in the darkness, were privy to the knowledge of his pact with pride, violence and greed. The realization turned his gut into lead.

Feeling cold beads of perspiration beginning at the roots of his hair—one of his vanities being that his carefully groomed hair, while now gray, was still mainly residing on his head, and his hairline had receded barely perceptibly—and succumbing to a tremor as pain and terror shot from his chest throughout his body to his fingertips, he forgot to partake of the Body and Blood as he shakily motioned for the priest at his right hand and the chalice-bearer to take the wafers and wine to serve the remaining clergy, acolytes, choir and congregation.

Mumbling that he was feeling unwell in response to their quizzical stares, Marks stumbled and blindly made his way to the sacristy, where he weakly closed the door and leaned heavily against the nearby counter, breathing as if he had just run a 5K marathon, his heart racing, the beats colliding with each other in frenzy. He recited to himself, "Get a grip, get a grip," like a mantra, his eyes closed for several moments as he coughed and fought the exquisite pain whirling within him.

"Bishop Marks!"

Hearing the voice as though it was an indictment from the Deity himself, and turning toward the sound, Marks gasped, staggered and fell.

PART ONE

Chapter 2

Amanda Childs completed the final E major chord of Healey Willan's *Agnus Dei* from the *Missa de Sancta Maria Magdalena*, and smoothly transitioned off the organ console as her assistant slid on, engaged a combination piston silently and began the improvisation and introduction to the communion anthem. Playing for the requiem of her dearest friend was almost too much to bear, but Amanda had wanted to make sure Marjorie Witherspoon's farewell from this earth was as Marjorie herself would have wished it. Besides, the physical and mental activity gave her something to concentrate on in order to stave off the inevitable sorrow and loneliness she felt.

For one second her eyes met Bishop Stephen Marks' during the Fraction, and she stared at him, her golden green eyes flashing with rage. Why is he here? she stormed silently, her mouth drawn in a tight line, her jaws clenched, her bearing unconsciously regal. As much pain as he had caused Marjorie in the past, it now seemed the height of cruelty to allow him to preside over her friend's funeral. The moment of anger helped steel her against the grief.

Amanda had made arrangements for her assistant to complete the service so that she might rid herself of her organist's vestments and proceed to the graveside service. She hated to leave early, while the choir was still to sing the Faure and Stanford, but the choir was well familiar with the music without her conducting, and both pieces evoked too many bittersweet memories. Being situated near the altar, she gratefully knelt at the railing, her usually slim and straight form slumped from the weight of sorrow, as she tried to shut out the familiar strains of the beloved anthem and received communion proffered by a deacon. She attempted to pray, but words would not come. For a moment the overpoweringly sweet fragrance of the lilies, the blur of faces, wafts of perfume, the memory-evoking music, the rustling of pressed linen, the sea of black and white forms, the lights and shadows, almost overwhelmed her, and she faltered. Now is not the time, Amanda reprimanded herself severely, and steeling herself against it all, she quietly and quickly left by the hallway ambulatory toward her office.

She started past the sacristy, her surplice already folded over her left arm as she was unbuttoning her cassock and absently running her hand through her golden hair. Hearing a sudden noise, she glanced in the door, and was shocked to see Bishop Marks in the sacristy, almost doubled over as he gripped the counter. Startled, she instinctively called to him, and ran to him in time to catch him in her arms as he fell heavily. Although she almost crumpled from his weight, she, surprisingly strong, helped upright him. Immediately the rector appeared behind her, concern written on his face, but the Bishop tried to wave them both off, protesting shakily that he felt fine.

Amanda, still supporting Marks, who shrank from her touch, spoke gently to the vicar, a short and slightly plump balding man with pleasant face. "Father Anselm, the Bishop is ill. Please bring that chair from the hall and ask Dr. Howells sitting on the second pew left to step back here."

The vicar quickly nodded assent, the chair appeared on cue, and he disappeared. Amanda urged Marks to sit, as he regarded her with heavy-lidded eyes and clutched his chest, terror in his eyes. Seconds later, Dr. Howells appeared, a well-groomed man in his late sixties, white-haired and dapper, neatly dressed in a dark pin-striped suit and red bow tie. He was followed by Vicar Anselm and another priest, a small, thin man with red hair, pinched frowning features, dressed in an alb.

The doctor knelt in front of the bishop and took his wrist, quickly noting his weak pulse. Marks remarked, his trembling voice betraying what he had hoped would be his most acid tone, "Really, this is much ado about nothing." Then, drawing himself up with a greater touch of asperity, he continued with a grimace, "Do let's remove ourselves from the sacristy before we pose a spectacle."

Amanda said quietly, "Dr. Howells, there's the sofa in Father Anselm's study, if we can get him there."

The doctor looked dubious, but Marks stood up, tottering, and sputtered, "I am fine—let's go."

The doctor and organist flanked the arrogant ailing man and half-led, half-carried him down the hallway to the vicar's private office, the other priest trailing superfluously behind them. After helping the colorless clergyman to lean back on the couch, Dr. Howells proceeded to check his pulse again, stating business-like to Amanda, "We'll need some scissors to cut off his garb."

Marks immediately sat up, blustering, "I can undress myself without ruining a costly set of vestments." Addressing the priest behind them, he commanded, "Here, Adam, help me."

Amanda crossed to the vicar's desk and retrieved a pair of shears, handing them to the doctor. "Just in case," she quipped. Then she turned to the vicar who had just come in, and stated calmly and self-assuredly as she finished unbuttoning

THE WITHERSPOON LEGACY

her cassock, "Father, I will call an ambulance and stay in case the doctor needs something, if you will make sure the service concludes smoothly. Ken is playing the remainder of the service for me today."

Rev. Anselm started to protest, but she shook her head firmly. He pressed her hand and nodded, disappearing as the other priest came forward and helped the bishop remove his vestments. The doctor pulled off the priest's collar with some effort to loosen the fabric around the Bishop's throat and neck and felt for his pulse there, ordering Marks to recline back and prop up his feet. Amanda turned to Dr. Howells. "Is there anything else I can do, Doctor?"

Marks again stirred, a look of abject misery on his face as another pain hit. Doctor Howells turned to the priest and stated, "There's the phone—you call 911 and get an ambulance rolling stat. Amanda, please run to my car and get my bag. You might want to stop and get some cool water, and maybe filch a little of that sherry out of the parlor, in case we need it. But please hurry."

Amanda left quickly. As the clergyman was dialing, Dr. Howells flung the discarded vestments out of the way, muttering about trappings of office, and felt Marks' forehead with his left hand. Marks felt compelled to make some light conversation, so he asked, "Am I still ticking?"

"A little unsteady and weak, I would say," answered the doctor, "and you're cold as ice to the touch. However, wearing too much regalia and strutting around like a peacock probably aggravated the situation."

Marks, ignoring the doctor's barb, decided to pretend a bravado he did not feel and to steer the conversation toward his thoughts during the service. "It was a beautiful service. That woman—the organist—has she been here long?"

Howells, choosing not to comment on the Bishop's characterization, answered briskly, "Yes, although no thanks to you and your former appointee here, who tried to run her off. Don't pretend you don't know who she is."

"She's good; I never realized . . ." Marks stammered, a pained wariness reflecting in his face. "I guess she knew the decedent well?"

Howells quelled Marks with a look of disgust. "What—you've forgotten her name as well? Of course Amanda knew Marjorie Witherspoon very well."

Marks, embarrassed, stuttered, "I meant nothing by—"

Howells curtly cut him off as the doctor took his coat off and rolled up his shirt sleeves. "You are just plain old Steve Marks in this old man's eyes. I'm not that much older than you, and remember when you and 'the decedent', as you call her, were an item, and we all thought it might turn into something more, before you—you—" the old man's eyes flashed with a momentary rancor, "well, never mind that now."

Marks murmured an inaudible retort as Amanda returned to the room with the doctor's bag and a tray with water, sherry and glasses. She turned to the bishop's assistant. "Mr.–"

"It's Reverend Brownlee, Bishop Marks' curate," retorted the small red-haired man, half-sneeringly.

Amanda, ignoring his supercilious manner, continued authoritatively, "Whatever. Here, make yourself useful and take the doctor's bag from my fingers." Then turning to Dr. Howells, "Here is a cold cloth as well for the invalid. Will you need anything further from me?"

Marks interrupted with a weak smile. "You could at least pretend some concern for your Bishop."

Amanda made no reply, but flashed her golden green eyes on him briefly, her face reflecting something akin to malevolence. In that second he felt another jolt of recognition. She turned to Howells. "Doc, I will be in my office if you need me for anything—just pick up that phone and dial '25' and you got me."

Dr. Howells, having just pulled out his stethoscope and sphygmomanometer, looked up. "Thank you, Amanda Katharine," he said, as Marks' glittering eyes followed her out of the room. Checking the patient's blood pressure, Howells then turned to Marks, stating, "This sounds pretty serious, Stephen. I want you checked into the hospital."

Marks and the curate with one voice demanded, "Is that necessary?"

Howells stated matter-of-factly, "Yes. You," pointing at Brownlee, "go to the side door to let the paramedics in. We will try to get the good bishop out of here with a minimum of fuss."

Brownlee stammered, "But the auditor's meeting tomorrow—"

Howells cut him off. "Cancel it." Turning to look for Amanda, he remembered that she had already left the room. Turning back to Marks, Howells asked, "How long have you been having these spells?"

Marks looked at him for a moment, then at his assistant, who was still standing gaping at the two men. Howells turned to Brownlee, and in his coldest voice ordered, "What part did you not understand? Go let the EMTs in NOW!"

Marks imperiously urged his assistant, "Go on; do as he says."

The priest, scowling, bolted from the room. Howells pointed to his retreating back. "Where did you find that one? Never mind. Answer the first question—how long have you been having these spells?"

Marks hesitated, as if deciding whether to confide in the doctor, before answering slowly, "For a couple months, maybe longer."

"Symptoms?"

"Shooting pains, faintness, cold sweats, nausea, some numbness at times."

"Yes, I thought so. So you're not going to fight me about checking this out?"

Marks winced. "It's just stress," then seeing the doctor's scowl, added, "No, Malcolm, whatever you say. I guess you can now take your revenge on me."

"I take my oath seriously," Howells responded flatly, "and it's totally irrelevant that I think you a son of a bitch. But don't worry; I won't be the one treating you—I'm handing you off to the finest cardiologist I know."

Marks coughed weakly. "Can we keep it discreet? I would like as few people knowing about this as possible."

"Whatever." Howells poured a little sherry into a glass. "Was this brought on by Marjorie's letter? She told you, didn't she?"

Marks sucked in a breath, suppressing a shudder. "O my God . . . ." His voice trailed off, as he looked away from the doctor, biting his lip. "You knew? About the letter too? Is it . . . her?"

Howells, stone-faced, divined Marks' meaning and watched him several seconds without remark, before the doctor downed the sherry himself in one gulp.

"Yes to both, Stephen. But she doesn't know. Now is not the time to discuss it. I want you to get a grip and calm down. I don't want you to code on me right here in the church you seem to hate so much."

Howells broke off as the emergency medical crew came in bringing a gurney. He turned to them and rattled off instructions, then turned back to Marks. "I'll see you at the hospital."

Amanda remained in the dark at her desk until she felt reasonably sure that the Bishop and EMTs, the mourners and funeral entourage had cleared the hallway. Bereft and knowing that her reserve of composure was depleted, she could not bring herself to go to the graveside service and pay her last respects, and was overwhelmingly ashamed of her breach. *I'm so sorry, Marjorie*, she prayed.

Resolutely refusing to allow herself to give in to the feelings of desolation, she spent the time desultorily logging into her computer the summary of the church service and music used for the Sunday morning service and afternoon funeral, a chore that occupied her without demanding deep thought. Then, she sat, elbows propped on desk in the room lit only by the lamp on her credenza, staring at the computer screen, as the cold words of the program flooded her mind with images:

BURIAL OF THE DEAD: RITE ONE
HOLY EUCHARIST

Prelude:
L'isle joyeaux (piano)—Claude Debussy
Pavane for a dead princess (piano)—Maurice Ravel
Prelude No. 4, op. 23 (piano)—Sergei Rachmaninoff
Preface to Introit—*Cortege et Litanie* (organ)—Marcel Dupre

Introit Hymn—*Praise, my soul, the King of heaven* (tune *Lauda anima*)

I heard the voice of Jesus say (tune *Third Mode Melody*, Thomas Tallis, arr. for choir and organ A. Childs)

Opening Acclamation/Anthem 1, Collect and Prayer
The First Lesson—Isaiah 61: 1-3
Gradual Psalm 130—from John Rutter's *Requiem* (choir, cello, chamber/organ)
The Second Lesson—I John 3: 1-2
Sequence Hymn—*The strife is o'er, the battle done* (tune *Victory*)
THE HOLY GOSPEL—John 11: 21-27
Homily—The Rev. Colin Anselm, Rector

The Apostles' Creed
Prayers of the People
Confession of Sin and Absolution
The Peace

Offertory Anthem—*Pie Jesu* (boy soprano and organ) from Gabriel Faure's *Requiem*
Offertory Hymn—*Ye watchers and ye holy ones* (tune *Lasst uns erfreuen*)

Eucharistic Prayer—The Right Rev. Stephen A. Marks, Celebrant
Sanctus (choir and organ)—from Gabriel Faure's *Requiem*
The Prayer of Consecration
The Lord's Prayer
Agnus Dei (congregation; from Healey Willan's *Missa de Sancta Maria Magdalena*)
Communion:
Cantique de Jean Racine (choir and organ)—Gabriel Faure

Post-Communion Prayer
The blue bird (choir)—Charles V. Stanford
The Commendation
Recessional Hymn—*Ye holy angels bright* (tune *Darwall's 148th*)

Amanda's solitude was interrupted as the door to her office opened and a figure furtively slipped into the dim room, stopping in front of her color copy machine with his back to her. He pulled a document out of an envelope, placed it on the glass for copying and started hitting buttons. When nothing happened, he muttered a curse.

Amanda calmly interrupted, "The copier has an energy-saving feature. Just give it a minute."

The man jumped, startled, and turned toward her, throwing her a frightened, then baleful look. She recognized him as Adam Brownlee, the bishop's surly curate. Just then, the copier sprang to life, and two copies were made and exited the hopper. Without saying a word to her, he grabbed the papers and fled her office. Amanda looked at the closing door, then shrugged wearily.

She turned her attention to the corner of her desk, at a framed snapshot of her and Marjorie Witherspoon from a past Easter, both with preposterously frilly hats on, arm in arm laughing at the camera. Amanda closed her eyes and allowed herself to reflect.

It was Marjorie, her best friend's mother, who took Amanda under her wing when Amanda first returned home to Mainville after law school and a brief, successful but unsatisfying stint with a medium-sized law firm down in Orlando. Amanda had come home to help care for her terminally ill mother. Marjorie had approached Amanda, knowing of her musical prowess as a teenager, about taking on the organist job at St. Catherine's because of the dearth of available musicians. Amanda had demurred, because her musical training was in piano. However, Marjorie persuaded her to try the task while working as a government lawyer eight years ago, just as Marjorie had later urged her to take *pro bono* a succession of cases involving children Marjorie had chosen to champion, after Amanda left government work to open her own practice.

Amanda had been raised Baptist and had no experience playing Anglican service music or chant, having only attended a few services at St. Catherine's now and again with her childhood friend Monica, Marjorie's daughter. Therefore, Marjorie personally took on the role of teaching her, singing the lines with her clear mezzo-soprano voice to Amanda's accompaniment. And Amanda exceeded her organ instructor's expectations at lessons, spending one to two hours almost every night per week trying to master the organ after long days in court or at the office. Amanda was her own worst critic, never believing that she could perform classical music as well as her music degree-carrying colleagues. Amazingly, Amanda did well in whatever she undertook, showing herself to be an aggressive but scrupulously honest attorney, and exhibiting the same characteristics toward her music and business. She found that the two vocations somehow complemented each other in providing some sense of satisfaction and accomplishment.

Then four years ago Amanda's husband Andrew, an FBI agent, was killed under unexplained circumstances. Amanda, in shock, was reserved and stoic during the funeral, but collapsed afterward and shut out everyone, disappearing from work and church and withdrawing from the world. Again it was the older and wiser Marjorie Witherspoon, who had herself lost her husband and daughter in a tragic automobile accident approximately fourteen years before and understood Amanda's pain, who managed to break down the barriers, get Amanda to pick up the pieces and go on with living.

Marjorie persuaded Amanda to remain in private practice for herself, and helped her invest Andrew's life insurance proceeds in order to provide herself some security. Amanda drove herself to succeed, to fill the void Andrew's death had engendered. A year after Andrew's death, she took on an associate in the firm, an old high school classmate, Ralph Carmichael. Two years after that she was impressed enough with his abilities to do the unthinkable, after consultation with Marjorie and some hard thinking, and negotiated a partnership agreement with him. Business was booming and she determined that she could not handle the demand alone.

Marjorie, I'm all alone again, she thought. Who do I turn to now? Her hand rested on a musical score. Looking down, she noted that it was the finished manuscript of her latest composition, a choral arrangement to John Donne's Holy Sonnet *Batter my heart*. Her hand closed into a fist. She thought, God, you've battered it enough for now. I have nothing left in me.

Lost in her reverie, Amanda did not know how much time had passed, and did not hear the light tap on the door. She jumped as Father Anselm appeared in front of her desk. "Oh, dear, I'm sorry I startled you," he said sympathetically.

"That's OK, Father," she pushed the photograph back. "I was just finishing here."

Father Anselm nodded understandingly. "I'm sorry that you missed the graveside service in the uproar over the Bishop today."

Amanda closed her eyes a moment. "I wasn't up to it anyway, Father. One can keep the stiff upper lip for only so long." Her eyes misted.

Father Anselm took her hand and squeezed it. "There was only one Marjy, and we are the poorer for her passing into the heavenly delights. I knew what she meant to you. The service was beautiful, my dear."

"I wouldn't have let anyone else do it. I knew what she wanted. It was over the top, for sure, but the choir really wanted to do her most beloved music. I'm sorry I didn't finish out the service, but I know Ken did a great job."

Father Anselm smiled. "Yes, it is amazing what you have done with that kid, coaching him and paying for his organ lessons with your own instructor. He is very enthusiastic, and is already a fine musician. You were smart to advise him to pursue a double major in college, so that he will have two careers to fall back on."

Amanda blushed at his praise but smiled also, thankful to talk of something else. "Ken is the one to thank for his progress. We won't worry about him starving, and other musicians won't be looking down at him when he plays rings around them."

There was a pause, and suddenly Amanda blurted out, "Why did Marks show up? Why did he have a part in this service? Father, you know how Marjorie felt about him—"

Anselm walked around the desk and put his hand on her shoulder. "I'm so sorry, Amanda, but he insisted. I didn't have the time, or the heart, to tell you he was to be here." His face was suddenly very sad. "I could not say no to the Bishop, no matter how much I wanted to. You do believe me?"

Amanda stood and hugged him. "Of course I do. I just don't understand his burning need to grace us with his presence right now."

Father returned her embrace and released her. "Amanda, why don't you go on home and get some rest? I know you've been on the go ever since Marjorie was admitted to the hospital. You must be exhausted—it's been too much of a strain for you."

Amanda looked away. "There's still the wake, and I must make an appearance."

Father patted her shoulder. "Are you sure you're up to it? It's been a long day, with your playing both Sunday morning Eucharist and Marjy's funeral."

Amanda replied, "No, I need to be there—Marjorie always taught me to fulfil my duties. And I have already missed the graveside."

Father looked at her with fatherly concern. "I order you to take a few weeks off. If you need me, you know where to find me. Let Ken take the next few services for you, OK?"

Amanda placed her hand over his resting on her shoulder. "I'll consider it. Thanks, Pops. You're a good man."

Anselm murmured, "Thank you, my dear. See you next door," as he turned and left the room.

Amanda removed the diskette containing church bulletins from her computer and placed it into her purse. Then she shut down her computer and tidied her desk, finally cutting out the lamp and leaving the darkened room.

Chapter 3

The parish office suite was quiet as she made her way down the long dark hallway, which opened up to a well-lit lobby leading into the large furnished parlor, where she could hear the hum of mourners gathering. The ladies of the church had provided a post-funeral reception in memory of Marjorie, who had served for many years as beloved parishioner and patron to St. Catherine's.

Taking a deep breath, Amanda quietly entered, gracefully gliding across the polished wood floors covered with luxuriant rugs, speaking to each group of persons briefly as she made her rounds, thanking choir members and murmuring her appreciation to those expressing condolences. She felt as though her mind was on automatic pilot. Across the room she caught the eye of her law partner Ralph Carmichael, a handsome well-groomed black man dressed in smartly cut black suit, talking to a striking dark-haired man in tailored Armani gray who returned her gaze, a slight smile on his otherwise enigmatic face. Nodding to Ralph, she briefly regarded the stranger again as she hugged an older parishioner. Something about him seemed familiar.

As Father Anselm took her hand and introduced her to some visiting clergy, she noted in the corner of the room a familiar tall, broad-shouldered form in tailored black suit huddled deep in conversation with the bishop's curate. Flushed, frowning and tense, he turned, saw her and waved to her. She saw him talking excitedly and angrily to Brownlee, then he extricated himself as Brownlee exited the room, and made his way to her, engulfing her in embrace.

"Mandy-girl," boomed a familiar deep voice in her ear, "you look all in. Come sit on the settee here a minute." She felt his lips brush her cheek lightly, his grip on her not relaxing.

"Bill, I'm glad you made it back in time for the funeral," Amanda murmured.

The winsome sandy-haired man pulled her toward a small love seat and gently pushed her onto it. He said, "You're pale. I'm going to fix us a drink. I'll be right back."

As Bill left going to the bar, she watched his retreating form thoughtfully, until interrupted by parishioners. The lack of sleep seemed to be catching up with her; she had no energy. She sat quietly, dazedly, until a man in tweed blazer, a badge on his belt, came up to her, drink in hand. "Here," he said quietly. "Bill ordered it, and I figured you could use this."

"Thank you, Charlie," Amanda looked up at him thankfully. "You're a good friend." Their eyes met for a moment, before he turned away abruptly and threaded his way through the crowd.

In his wake Ralph arrived. "Are you OK?" he peered at her concernedly. "You weren't at the graveside, and I was worried about you."

"The Bishop collapsed, and I stayed behind and helped Dr. Howells with him. After that I just lost the nerve to go," Amanda half-whispered, her eyes downcast, as she sipped the liquid deeply.

"You missed Marjorie's graveside to assist Public Enemy No. 1? What a good Christian you are," he looked at her quizzically. Before she could ask the identity of the man to whom Ralph had been speaking, Ralph added, "There's Don Parker and Susan Gray."

Amanda was suddenly rueful. "I'm sorry I ran out on you Thursday. What did Parker say about our discovery?" She downed her drink agitatedly.

Ralph replied quietly. "Interestingly enough, he already knew, and he had gone straight to Susan about her son's indiscretion." At Amanda's questioning look, he added, "Not here—tell you more about it later. Did you get to talk to Susan?"

Amanda nodded wearily. "Yes. You and I need to confer before our employee little Arthur comes in to work tomorrow. Do you mind coming by the house for coffee on the way to the office in the morning? That way, we can plan strategy for dealing with this situation. Afterward, lunch is on me."

"Are you sure you want to come in tomorrow? You could use some time off," Ralph interjected solicitously.

"I'll be there," Amanda rejoined curtly, not looking at him.

"OK, OK," protested Ralph quickly, as Bill Barnes made his way back to them, a drink in each hand. "She doesn't listen to anyone. Bill, talk to her. She could use some time off," Ralph remarked to Bill. Ralph took her empty glass as Bill handed Amanda another and sat down beside her.

"So what else is new?" Bill retorted congenially. "And you think Mandy will listen to me?"

"I'll leave you in Bill's capable hands," Ralph excused himself, shaking his head at Amanda and blending back into the crowd.

Sitting beside Amanda, Bill took a sip from his own glass and slipped his arm around her possessively.

"Sorry I haven't been here. I didn't realize Marjy was that bad. I was in depositions all day Friday in Gainesville and stopped over for a Seminole Boosters' dinner Saturday in Tallahassee. I had to drive like hell this morning to get back in time for the end of the service. How are you holding up?"

"It's not been easy, Bill. I'm sorry you didn't get here in time to see Marjy, but she slipped into a coma Thursday night."

Looking at her intently as she sipped her drink, he hugged her as he said, "Did you get to talk to her?"

"When I got the call Thursday, I walked out on Ralph in a client conference and made it to the hospital as fast as I could. She was in and out. But she recognized me, and oddly, the last thing she did was mention your name."

Bill's eyes widened in disbelief as he swallowed quickly. "Me? What did she say?" he asked, amazedly.

Amanda's eyes misted as she recalled the event, her eyes dim to all the persons around them. "She looked directly at me, and said, 'Talk to—' and it sounded like 'Mack', and then 'Billy.' She was struggling at the time. But I promised her I would watch out for you, and she seemed to ease off. Not long after that, it was as though she drifted off to sleep."

Bill looked away and downed the rest of his drink in one gulp. "That's just like her," he mumbled roughly. Changing the subject, he observed, "Where were you after the funeral? I looked for you at the graveside."

Amanda briefly explained about the Bishop's collapse. Bill nodded, preoccupied as he stared across the room.

"I heard about it from Brownlee over there. Finish that up," he ordered, pointing to her drink, "while I get us another."

Bill relinquished his hold on her and disappeared in the crowd before she could protest. Amanda sat quietly, sipping her drink, knowing she needed to make rounds. Parishioners could be peculiar, and some were quick to take offense if they felt slighted. However, an overwhelming lethargy swept over her, and Amanda could not summon the energy to stand. Her limbs seemed wooden and stiff, and her head began to throb. *I don't need any more alcohol,* she thought.

Bill returned, another drink in hand. He took her half-full glass and placed the new one in her hand, urging Amanda to take a draught as he sat down beside her again, pulling her closer to him.

Amanda protested, "I've had enough."

Bill murmured against her ear, "There, there, it'll get your blood flowing. After all you've been through, you deserve it. Screw the gossiping old ladies. Everything is going to be all right—it'll all be over soon. You know, I'm here for you—everyone in this room is. You and I have been buddies all our lives, girl. What hell you have gone through, and I hate I wasn't here. I promise I'll be there for you from now on. I'll watch out for you, and you watch out for me, and we'll make old Marjy happy."

Amanda closed her eyes, feeling her defenses melt away and willing herself not to cry at his words. The warmth of the bourbon, strangely bitter to her lips, was stealing through her veins, and her head was feeling unusually heavy. Barnes, his voice seemingly far away, commented, "You're white as a sheet, Mandy," and held the glass to Amanda's lips as she demurred.

Amanda obediently took another sip and whispered her thanks. She sat passively, unconscious that she was leaning heavily against Bill for support as a cold nausea settled over her. Barnes kept his arm tightly around her, stroking her arm and rocking her gently as he rattled off inconsequential anecdotes about people in the room they had known all their lives. She nodded half-comprehendingly, lulled by his comforting chatter and finding herself increasingly unable to keep her attention on the people speaking to her and what they were saying.

Suddenly the nausea overwhelmed her, and she stirred confusedly. "Bill, I don't feel well," she heard her words as she felt herself slipping, the room whirling. She heard Bill calling urgently, "Mandy?"

She came to herself, and found herself lying on the same sofa in Father Anselm's office that had been occupied earlier by Bishop Marks. Ralph was standing over her, as Dr. Howells, sitting by her on the couch, was removing smelling salts and adjusting his stethoscope. Barnes was hovering nearby, looking anxiously at her. Her temples were pounding, and her heart was in her throat.

"What happened?" she managed to croak hoarsely, her throat and voice dry.

"Nothing that a little rest and food might not restore," scolded Howells briskly. "When was the last time you had something to eat? Bill, what do you mean, feeding her alcohol on an empty stomach?"

Amanda shook her head groggily, still trying to scatter the whirling wisps of fog and stop the drumming inside her head and churning in her stomach. Howells ordered everyone out of the room and for Ralph to get her a plate of food, then closed the door behind them. Returning to the sofa, he sat down beside her. Feeling the nausea rising, she leaned forward and he handed her a trash can as she vomited into it, then he mopped her face with a damp cloth.

He spoke softly, "Thank God I just got back from the hospital. I left our Bishop in the hands of Dr. Cardet, who is one of the best cardiologists in the country. Bill said you passed out at the wake. You know better than to drink on an empty stomach."

"I'm sorry, Doctor, but I wasn't thinking. I just started to feel really strange."

"How do you feel now?"

"Like I've been run over by a Mack truck, and it is backing over me to see what it hit."

"Nausea?"

"In waves."

"Are you taking any medication? Have you been drinking a lot with all this stress? Anything I should know about?"

Amanda shook her head cautiously, raising her hand to her head. "Doc, it's Amanda, remember? No, I'm not doing anything."

"Well, it may just be hypoglycemia. If you don't mind, I'm going to get a sample of blood and check. Let's rule out the blood sugar too. Your heart sounds erratic to me. Wouldn't you like to spend the night in our fine facility?"

Amanda grimaced weakly. "No, Doc, I'm all right, if my head and heart will just quit jumping around."

Ralph appeared with a plate of delicacies and a glass of punch. "Is she going to be OK, Doc?"

Howells looked up and smiled his thanks, taking the punch and giving it to the wan Amanda. "St. Catherine's ever-famous fruit punch—covers a multitude of sins. Take a sip of this, slowly. Ralph, she refuses my offer of hospitality—stubborn as a mule. Once she feels up to it, I'd appreciate it if you'd see the lady home. Make her eat something, will you?"

"Sure thing, Doctor. What do you want me to do with the people mingling outside?"

"Tell them she's fine, just suffering from starvation. No, they'll start a rumor that she's anorexic. Oh, what the hell? Let the old biddies talk. I'm going to draw some blood for testing and drop it off at the hospital as I check back on the Bishop. I'll let you know if anything shows up."

Amanda dutifully took a sip of the punch, but shook her head at the dainty sandwiches. Dr. Howells frowned at her, then followed Ralph to the door and murmured something inaudible. Ralph nodded and quickly exited, ostensibly to report on her condition. Dr. Howells pulled a vial from his bag and expertly extracted her blood quickly, then sat watching her.

"Feeling any better?" he asked, reaching over and munching a cucumber sandwich from the plate.

"A darker shade of pale," she answered, rubbing her temples. "But I think I can make it."

He again listened to her chest. "It's beating a little stronger. Amanda, I don't like this. I still think you should go in for overnight observation."

"No, Doc," insisted Amanda as firmly as she could muster. "I'm fine."

The door to the office opened, and Bill strode back in. "You gave us all a scare, girl," he said somberly. Turning to Doctor Howells, he asked sheepishly, "What's the verdict?"

Howells, shutting his medical bag and standing, asserted, "It is probably just the stress of the last few days and the fact that she probably hasn't had anything to eat. Ralph has promised to get her home. A day or two off wouldn't hurt, Amanda."

Amanda, slowly sitting up and finding her purse beside her, gingerly placed her feet on the floor and replied, "I'll consider it."

Ralph came in behind Bill. "Can you stand?" he asked. Ralph helped Amanda to her feet. She tottered, and Ralph caught her, swooping her up in his arms, purse and all. Amanda objected, but Ralph silenced her. "We'll just go out the service exit and try to avoid the masses, OK?"

Before Amanda could respond, he winked at Bill and carried her out, settling her in the passenger seat of his black Lexus sports car. As Bill protested, Ralph waved him off, getting in the car and starting the ignition.

Amanda leaned back wearily, mutely cradling her head in one hand while Ralph drove the short distance to her modest but neat framed cottage surrounded by tidy lawn and flower beds overlooking a picturesque public park.

She remembered nothing until suddenly the car stopped moving. Ralph was nudging her. "Amanda?" He said tersely, "Wait right there," and disembarked, quickly covering the distance to her passenger door. Opening it, he again effortlessly bundled her into his arms and carried her to the door. She handed him her key, and he expertly opened the door and entered, kicking it closed behind them.

He gently deposited her on the sofa in the austere but handsome living room, shedding his jacket and loosening his tie as he demanded, "Don't you have any groceries in this house?"

Amanda nodded dazedly. "I am feeling really queasy right now, and don't think I can eat anything."

"Well, I'm not leaving until you do. Then I'm putting you to bed, and will sack out here on the couch."

"You'll do no such thing," Amanda retorted, rising up slowly, holding her forehead. "I'm just fine, and will be good as new in the morning. We have work tomorrow."

"That's another thing—you need some rest. There's nothing at the office that won't wait. Damn it, Amanda, we just buried Marjorie."

Tears sprang to her eyes at the reminder. Amanda closed her eyes, willing herself not to cry. "You forget, I'm a partner in this firm, and we have to deal with Arthur in the morning. I'm going to take a shower to clear my head and then get some sleep."

"Well, I'm not leaving until I'm sure you're OK."

Amanda, her stubbornness and color returning as she argued, tried not to stagger as she rejoined in her lightest tone, "Well, stay as long as you like, but I'm not inviting you hot-tubbing with me."

Leaving him, she managed to walk steadily to the bathroom. Closing the door, she looked at the bathtub a moment before turning on the shower. Feeling the bile rising in her throat yet again, she made it to the toilet and vomited again. After a moment, she began feeling better. She removed her makeup and brushed her teeth, trying to rid herself of the bitter dryness in her mouth. As the water was warming, she made her way to the kitchen, where Ralph, sans jacket and tie, was critically reviewing the contents of the refrigerator and scowling. She reached past him, taking a pitcher out of the refrigerator and reaching for a glass and ice. Pouring herself a glass of tea, she held it up.

"The Southern elixir of life, a cure for most if not all ills," she explained simply, turning and retreating to her bathroom.

Stripping and stepping into the shower, she let the water surround and soothe her. Allowing herself to close her eyes and relax, she weakly placed her hands on the shower wall to support herself. She felt the tiny daggers of warm water on her face and shoulders loosen the tension and weakness as the steam spiraled upward. The shower became a womb, its warmth enfolding and cradling her, and she recalled William Wordsworth's theory of "the vision splendid" lost by the soul at birth.

Her thoughts momentarily unguarded, a vision of Andrew came to her unbidden and surrounded her, and she felt the tears streaming unchecked. Her body began involuntarily rocking as she remembered Andrew's voice reading the lines of his favorite Wordsworth to her, his baritone voice mellifluous.

Amanda wondered aloud, "How long does it take to get over you, Andrew Childs?" She thought how strange it was that the loss of one loved one seemed to reopen the wounds of loss for others gone before; one ends up grieving for all the past losses.

She whispered, "Damn it, Andy, I needed you today—I need you now." She let her mind wander down the stream of consciousness, to the fanciful young child she was, who would pray at night to God for someone to hold her hand. The metaphysical God seemed always so unsatisfactory in times of grief, when one longed for physical manifestations of comfort. Although God always provided relief eventually, it took longer to enfold the mind than the simple sense of touch, and she longed to have Andrew's physical presence with her once again. But he's not coming back, she reminded herself sharply, trying to rein in the choking despair.

"The mind is a terrible thing," suddenly floated in her head, something one of her former clients misquoted to her years ago, a phrase she and Andrew had laughingly used many times. My life is surrounded by a chorus of dead and forgotten poets, she thought melodramatically. As she turned off the water, she felt the first rush of cool air seeking by osmosis to rip her from her momentary cocoon and restore her to cold reality. This must be what it means to be reborn, she thought bitterly.

She quickly dried, feeling less woozy, and dressed in some dark cotton pants and shirt. Opening the bathroom door, she was greeted by the aroma of frying bacon and coffee. Surprised, she sauntered to the kitchen towel-drying her hair, to see Ralph busy at the stove. Not looking at her, he asked briskly, "How do you like your eggs?"

"This talent wasn't listed in your resume. Where did all this food come from?"

Ralph said smoothly, "I have nephews who owe me a favor or two and who ran to the store for supplies. Your answer is unresponsive and is stricken from the record. Please answer the question."

"Scrambled well-done, please, "Amanda capitulated. Although the thought of eggs seemed unappetizing, she reached for a piece of toast and began buttering it and stuffing it into her mouth, suddenly hungry.

Within minutes Ralph had completed breakfast with eggs, bacon, toast, coffee and orange juice. The table had already been set, and Amanda looked at him in admiration. "You will make Claire a good husband one day if you keep working at it."

Ralph smiled at her briefly. "Shut up and sit down, woman. I like to eat my cooking while it is hot."

Amanda seated herself while Ralph brought two cups of steaming coffee, then sat across from her. They ate in silence, Ralph sensing her exhaustion.

The phone rang, shattering the peace. Ralph picked up the cordless handset and handed it to Amanda wordlessly. Amanda spoke, then listened impassively.

"No, I'm fine, Bill.... No, I do not need you to come over. Ralph is here. The doctor told him to feed me. No, of course not—he is leaving soon, and I'm going to bed early. I don't need a babysitter."

A pause ensued. "Will? You don't have it? I don't know, probably so. Marjy was very particular in her business affairs, so I'm sure she left instructions."

Another pause. "I'll check her house tomorrow. Maybe...."

"Please, don't," Ralph heard her plead, and although he pretended to be engrossed in his plate he noted her eyes flashing fire. "I'm a grown girl, and can take care of myself.... Seriously, I'm really tired, Bill. Thanks very much.... talk to you tomorrow."

As she placed the phone on the table, Ralph rose with his plate. Amanda motioned him to sit back down. "There's no hurry," she said. "I just didn't want Bill over here tonight—I have no energy left to deal with him."

Ralph stated flatly, looking at her intently as he returned to his seat, "I thought I'd have to duel him over the honor of escorting you home. People in town still speculate about you two."

Amanda's eyes narrowed. "It's sad that the townspeople are so hard up for gossip that they have to make up stuff about me now.

"Ralph, you know without asking. Bill was my best friend's guy, for God's sake. I've known him all my life. He lost his wife last year, and he keeps dropping into my life from time to time. He's lonely when his schedule becomes open and he's without a female to adorn his arm. He's a shameless but harmless flirt. Don't worry about me and lost causes over men—I'm not in the market."

"Sorry, Mandy, just stating the scuttlebutt. You two certainly looked like a couple tonight. This is a small town, and people make up intrigue where they can. And Bill makes no secret that he considers you his property. Hell, you looked comfortable there."

"Yes, well, just remember I'm not Bill's or any one else's chattel. After tonight they've got material to make up stories about you and me as well. That doesn't do you and Claire any good."

"Don't worry about Claire and me," Ralph retorted, picking up dishes and carrying them in the kitchen. Rolling up his sleeves, he started filling the sink with soapy water. Amanda picked up her plate and glass, and brought them over, picking up a dishtowel.

"Why not? You are neglecting her, and should be with her instead of here with me."

"She's not here anyway—she's out of town."

Silently they finished the dishes, Amanda curious but not asking, and Ralph not volunteering information. Then Ralph looked at her and implored, "It's time you tried to get some rest. Don't you want me to stay? If not me, I can call my sister Louise."

Amanda smiled. "No, I'm feeling much better now. Thanks for dinner—er, breakfast."

"I won't try to talk you out of work tomorrow. I'll be here at 7:30 to talk about the game plan in dealing with Arthur. I'll let myself out."

Amanda remained in the kitchen until she heard the front door close, then began locking up. She suddenly thought of Bill's question about Marjy's will. *I cannot think about one more thing tonight,* she concluded, turning off the living room lights.

Chapter 4

The next morning, Amanda awakened groggily to the shrill insistence of her alarm clock. The previous night's shower and food had helped, and her headache was reduced to a dull annoyance after a deadened and dream-filled sleep. She lay still a few minutes, fighting the unusual feeling of lethargy, resolutely shutting out the memories of the past few days and willing herself to get up and face the day.

After making coffee and taking a quick shower, she readied herself for work. While applying makeup, she heard the phone ring. Finding the cordless handset in the living room, she carried it into the bathroom with her.

"Hello?"

"'Morning, gorgeous," Bill Barnes' voice greeted her.

"Oh, hi, Bill," she greeted him, shifting the receiver to the left hand to complete applying mascara. "What's up?"

"Just checking on you, as promised. How are you feeling?"

"Much better than yesterday, thanks," she replied.

"How about I take you away from all this? I was thinking a picnic on the beach, the wind whipping through our hair, you in a sexy bikini. What time shall I pick you up?"

"Whoa, Casanova, I'm a working girl. Ralph and I have a full schedule getting ready for trial next week. I'm not the high-priced attorney of the rich and famous like you."

"I heard Doc order you to take some time off and rest. I think he's right. We just lost Marjy. You can't just go on like nothing happened. I thought we might get away for the day—talk about old times. Don't say no."

"Bill, I—I just can't. Losing Marjy is still all too fresh in my head. Work actually keeps me going right now."

Bill rejoined vexedly, "You're just surrounding yourself with busy-ness to avoid the real issue, Mandy. You're all alone, and so am I. There's no reason for us not to be together. I can take care of you."

Amanda sighed. "Bill, I appreciate all that you do for me. But at some point we all have to work out some things for ourselves."

"If you'd just say yes I would make it all easier for you," Bill coaxed.

"But I just can't make that commitment right now," Amanda persisted softly.

"That's not the correct answer," Bill's disappointment was unmistakable. "But don't think you're going to chase me off. How about dinner one night this week? How about tonight?" he urged.

"For you, I'll see what I can do," she laughed lightly, defusing the seriousness of the conversation. "Now leave me alone and let me get ready for work so I can earn some money."

When Ralph appeared at her front door resplendent in dark blue suit and silk tie matching his medium blue shirt, Amanda was ready. She had decided on a black suit with long skirt, matching hose and heels.

She opened the door and Ralph walked in unceremoniously. He asked her, "How are you feeling?" as she led the way to the kitchen island and pulled out cups and saucers.

She replied briskly, "Better. Want anything to go with your coffee?"

Ralph shook his head. "I reviewed all Arthur's assignments and his desk drawers."

"Find anything?"

"*Nada*—in fact, the only major case he has been involved with is the Parker divorce, and perhaps our acting this morning will contain the damage. As I said yesterday, Dan Parker called Susan as soon as he heard. They're friends. He was laughing it off."

Amanda stated flatly, "I don't see how our client can think this is funny. Susan, though, was understanding when I divulged the dilemma—said Arthur had to grow up sometime and face the consequences of his actions."

Ralph interjected, "Art was a weaselly fellow, Mandy, and I didn't trust him with anything critical. He was a kid, damn it. I have reviewed everything—I think this is the extent of his indiscretion. However, I many times preached the gospel to him about keeping our business secret, so he cannot claim he didn't know better.

"Dan made several points in our meeting: (1) he confessed that he was a little free himself with the information of his extramarital affair to several at the club last weekend, and the news went straight to the Mrs. and her attorney; (2) he can't therefore be mad at Susan's little boy's subsequent indiscretion; and (3) this is a no-fault divorce state—if both parties are guilty of the scarlet "A", all other things being equal it's going to likely mitigate against issues of alimony and unequal distribution of assets. Don assured me that he does not hold us responsible and wants us to continue his representation.

"Tell you what—let me go in first and talk to Arthur. I think the good cop-bad cop routine works best for us, and I make a better good cop than you. Then you can come in after I've wheedled his confession out of him. You gonna fire him? If so, I'll pack his belongings, and it will all be over."

Amanda looked out the window at the birds feeding on the back lawn. "You mean I make a better bad cop, but that's OK. After the events of the last week, this is the last thing I want to deal with, but is firing him too drastic a reaction? I'm torn. I don't want to tarnish his reputation when he's just starting out, but we have clients' wellbeing at stake here. I told his mom that I could very well terminate his employment, and she understands my position on this. I'm sorry I didn't take your advice about not hiring him in the first place."

Ralph was silent, sipping his black coffee as Amanda added cream and sugar to hers. She realized he was being gracious in not saying 'I told you so'. They drank in a comfortable silence, both intent on their own thoughts.

Finally he broke the quiet. "I'm really sorry about Marjorie, Amanda."

"Me, too," Amanda replied shortly, standing up abruptly and turning away to hide her features. "Are you ready?"

Ralph shrugged, stood and led the way out, long used to Amanda's prickly avoidance of emotional display.

Moments later Ralph pulled out from her driveway in his sleek black Lexus hardtop convertible coupe, Amanda following him in a more sedate silver BMW sedan. Amanda, into more practical and inexpensive imports, had been bullied into buying what she called "the yuppie vehicle" by Marjorie, so even the vehicle was a painful reminder of her friend.

Soon they arrived at an older two-story Georgian brick building, the wrought-iron post holding a sign in front reading "Childs and Carmichael, Attorneys at Law." Pulling behind the building, Amanda viewed a good-looking but peevish man in his early twenties standing outside the back door, briefcase in hand.

As she down-shifted, her cell phone rang. She heard Ralph's voice. "I'll take him into my office. Give me twenty minutes with him, then you can stride in ready to roll. Don't take too long—we don't want to lose the momentum."

"Deal," Amanda acquiesced.

Ralph added, "And make sure you've powdered your nose and put on your lipstick—you should look your best when you're reaming someone."

He had hung up before Amanda could retort. She counted to ten before exiting, and slowly made her way to the building into which the two had just disappeared.

Arthur Gray was the son of an old high school friend who had asked Amanda to give him a job doing paralegal work while he tried to gain admission to law school. Amanda had given in and employed the young man, against her better judgment and the advice of Ralph and Sheila Turin, her assistant.

On the preceding Thursday, Amanda received a call from another attorney in town with the information that Arthur had been seen at the country club the preceding evening, apparently inebriated and bragging about his knowledge about certain confidential facts in an upcoming divorce case involving a well-known couple in town. She met with the informant, and after checking with the other witnesses whose names had been provided she was faced with irrefutable evidence that the young man had divulged information that her client Mr. Parker would rather have remained secret.

On Thursday afternoon, in the midst of discovering this information and consultation with Ralph and the client Dan Parker, she was called away to the hospital to witness the last hours of her best friend Marjorie Witherspoon as the latter succumbed in a valiant fight against cancer. On Friday, Amanda had gone to make sure Marjorie's home was secured and the alarm system on, met early with Father Anselm regarding planning the funeral, and was consumed in arrangements.

Amanda had decided the best course of action for the breach of confidentiality was prompt disclosure of Arthur's actions, to let the client decide whether he wanted the firm to continue representation, or to obtain another firm and seek recourse against Amanda's firm. During the meeting on Thursday, the plan had been formulated to determine whether any other cases had been compromised, and to deal with Arthur accordingly, the purpose of this morning's meeting.

As Amanda entered the office, her secretary Sheila looked up with relief. "Mrs. Childs, there is an attorney on the line from New York City, a Malachi Feinstein, who says he has Marjorie Witherspoon's will, is in town and urgently needs to see you a moment this morning."

"New York City?" echoed Amanda, her brow furrowing. "I'll take it in my office. Thanks, Sheila."

Entering the spacious room papered a light burgundy, she moved lithely across to her massive carved desk and picked up the telephone. After several minutes of brisk conversation, she replaced the receiver, deep in thought, before buzzing the secretary to inform her to note a 10:30 appointment with Malachi Feinstein.

Absently she looked at her desk and closed briefcase. Something doesn't seem quite right, she surmised. Opening her briefcase, she saw that her papers were askew. Alert, she looked at her inbox and noticed the contents were similarly in disarray.

Sheila peeked into the room. "Mrs. Childs? There's something I need to tell you before you meet with Arthur."

"That's where I was heading. What is it, Sheila? Come on in."

They both sat in the comfortable club chairs facing Amanda's desk as Sheila relayed her information to Amanda. Amanda's eyes narrowed as she questioned Sheila. "You're sure? This is really serious."

THE WITHERSPOON LEGACY

At Sheila's sober nod, Amanda stood. "Thanks, Sheila. You have just helped me make a difficult decision." Pausing, her eyes lighted again on the scattered papers in her inbox. "Sheila, have you noticed anything unusual this morning?"

"Yes," Sheila returned her sudden stare. "I left everything tidy Friday evening. But this morning items on my desk and yours seemed to be moved, documents not in order, things awry."

"Anything missing?"

"Not that I can tell so far," Sheila replied.

"But Arthur doesn't have a key," Amanda murmured. "No sign of a forced entry?"

"No," said Sheila slowly, "but I found the bathroom window unlatched."

"Does Ralph know this?"

"Not yet—he went straight to his office with Arthur, so I haven't had a chance to inform him."

"Thanks, Sheila," Amanda said absently, as she stood. Following Sheila out of her office, she made her way to Ralph's office, a sleek masculine office filled with mahogany and black leather, with dark-framed degrees, citations, awards and photographs lining the walls.

Entering, she saw Ralph leaning across his desk looking at an ashen-faced Arthur Gray. Without looking up at her, Ralph stated, "The young man swears that he had been drinking too much that evening and that this is his one and only transgression, and I tend to believe him, if it is possible to believe one in his circumstances. I think he knows already what you have to say."

The young man sitting in the client's leather chair facing the desk blanched at those words. Amanda, angry, asked Ralph, "But has he told you everything?"

Ralph looked at her quizzically. She turned to Arthur. "What business did you have removing the Witherspoon trust account ledgers and copying them on Friday?"

Ralph's jaw dropped as Arthur, terrified, stammered, "I—I—" but fell into an embarrassed silence.

"Arthur, I'm waiting for an answer," Amanda gazed at him steadily.

"I didn't mean any harm, Ms. Childs, and I've not given any copies out. They're in my notebook."

"And Sheila reports that someone has been in the office this weekend and papers were out of order and strewn around. Were you looking for something, Ralph?"

Ralph's jaw clenched. "No. Everything was in order when I was here Saturday."

"What were you looking for, Arthur?"

Arthur was white as a sheet. "Ms. Childs, I swear it wasn't me—I didn't take anything—"

"You either trespassed yourself or enabled someone else to do so. The bathroom window was unlatched. Ralph is anal about keeping this placed secured." Amanda's voice rose slightly, clasping her hands to keep from striking the young man before her. "Why? Who?"

The young man shrunk into his seat. "I promise you, Mrs. Childs, it wasn't me."

"I don't believe you, and I want to know why. Arthur," Amanda, trying to stifle her ire, "for the sake of your mother and my old friend, I stuck my neck out to give you a job when I really didn't need a paralegal. You've paid me back by making the granddaddy of all mistakes in this business. There are a lot of errors that the bar association and clients may forgive, but divulging secret information is the very worst. As much as I dearly love your mother and want to help you, I cannot pay good hard-earned money to some kid who then turns around and destroys this firm's reputation for integrity and ethics that I built with my own hands. And even if I did, there's Mr. Carmichael's livelihood at stake—he has put a lot into this firm too."

Amanda took a deep breath before continuing. "I'm not going to belabor the point, so you will get the short sermon. It is a basic fact of Ethics 101 that you preserve your client's confidences except in specific enumerated circumstances. Mr. Carmichael and I have preached to you about this, and you made the promise before we allowed you to see the client's files. You have stepped on your hardware big time violating ethical considerations by divulging confidential client information—do you think that when or if you apply for the bar the committee won't ask me as a former employer about your capabilities and ethical standards? Do you think I can or will lie for you? What do I tell them?"

Arthur stammered, "But, Mrs. Childs, I've apologized to Mr. Simpson, and I swear the trust ledgers were all I took," but she cut him off.

"I was debating this morning about giving you another chance. But Sheila caught you Friday in the act of copying the ledgers. Can you possibly share with me what you were doing? To whom were you going to give these copies? I have to assume it was you who left the bathroom window unlatched—it certainly wasn't one of us. For whom? Yourself? Someone else?"

Arthur, ashen now, stuttered, "Miss Amanda, I wouldn't do anything to hurt you at all. I didn't think—"

"No, you didn't think. Sheila didn't find anything else missing, but that doesn't mean a lot in light of what we know about your activities. Ralph, if you don't mind, I want any copies back, even if you have to personally escort him to the location. Furthermore, I expect a sworn statement from Arthur whether he shared that information with anyone else, and what else he may have done. If I find that you have divulged other confidences or do so after today, or if anything is found missing in the office, I may not be as lenient with you as I am today, although you may not think of my actions as such.

"You have branded yourself with a reputation that you will find hard to remove. Did you realize that a client's confidence is more important than gaining whatever it is you hoped to gain? Your actions may have cost more than possibly losing a client, or your job here today—the client can file grievances against Ralph and me, and could conceivably sue the firm. And the consequences to you aren't small—did you count those costs? Because your payday begins today! You are fired, and if you don't come clean on any other disclosures with Ralph, or if you disclose to anyone confidential information about our cases, I will be seeking all legal means at my disposal against you."

Sheila Turin, at her desk just outside Amanda's office, could hear the briskness in Amanda's voice if not the actual words said to the young man. She could tell from the tenor of the conversation that the young man was experiencing his exit interview, his desk would be emptied, and he would be escorted out the door. He would probably never work again in this area for the salary, benefits and prestige he currently enjoyed in this intern position. Poor silly bastard, she thought. What a way to start a Monday morning.

Sheila had worked as Amanda's assistant for the last seven years, the first two when Amanda was still in government service. In that time Sheila had heard many snippets and stories about her, but still found her hard to read. Thankfully she had never received any treatment from her employer other than professionalism and courtesy bordering on kindness. Sheila had on several occasions seen steel glints in the woman's eyes and had seen her curtly shred the opposition in deposition and in court. Therefore, she could only imagine the tongue-lashing young Arthur was getting, and knew he would remember it for many years to come.

Amanda came stalking out, crossed over to her office without a word, and shut herself in. About thirty minutes later, Ralph and Arthur emerged, the younger man carrying a box containing his personalty and hanging his hapless head. Escorting him out, Ralph returned momentarily, crossing the room in great strides and re-entering Amanda's office, documents in hand.

A few minutes later, Sheila paused before Amanda's door, wishing to genuflect before entering. Stifling the urge, she entered. Amanda was sitting rigid in her chair, her back to the door, papers in her hand, staring unseeingly out the window at the scenic fountain surrounded by summer coleus, with Ralph sitting at the conference table, his feet encased in polished tasseled loafers propped up on the table as he leaned back in his chair, his fingers interlocked and cradling his head. When he saw Sheila, he started softly whistling Chopin's Funeral March.

Amanda was conducting an oral post mortem on the event, thinking out loud. "Do you believe him, Ralph? Do you think the copies he gave you are the only ones? My heavens, the trust accounts. Sheila thinks only Marjorie's were copied—why? What did he say?"

"He said that upon her death he was asked by someone, whose identity he refused to disclose, to make copies of Marjorie's records to see what kind of work we had done for her. I threatened him with all sorts of repercussions, but he wouldn't tell me. He swears that the copies I recovered from him are the only ones, and that he did not have the opportunity to deliver copies to the person requesting them. He swears that's the extent of his indiscretions. I just don't know, Mandy."

"I am not sure exactly what to do, Ralph. We could seek an ethics opinion from the bar, and could talk to the police about a criminal investigation. Marjorie's records are not that important—we didn't do anything more than the occasional matter for her, and nothing consequential. However, we need to make sure we have contained the damage, because I will need to disclose to any other affected clients."

"What about the break-in?" she shook her head in frustration. "God, I didn't need this today. Should we call in Police Chief Petrino? I don't want to prosecute Arthur, but this problem is getting uglier by the minute." She was silent a moment. "Damn it, I'm sure there will be a new flurry of dilatory interrogatories in the Parker divorce case. And we have that last-minute deposition before the jury selection next Monday in the Garvin case."

Ralph remarked, "You're behind the times, what with dealing with Marjorie's sickness and death. Chances are after that Supreme Court opinion last week Garvin's erstwhile partner will be seeking settlement before Friday." Lapsing into his best ghetto impersonation, he continued, "You jus' chill, woman—I's the man on that case, and we gonna hump those honkies' butts."

Shaking her head, Amanda picked up a deposition transcript off her desk and threw it at him, and he caught it in mid-air. He looked at her smiling. She smiled back in relief. Ralph was a fine attorney, thorough, articulate and polished, having served four years as a prosecutor in the St. Petersburg area before deciding to return to his roots in Mainville. They had known each other since elementary school. He was good for Amanda, a funny and witty foil to her seriousness and compulsivity. She had never for a moment regretted his joining the firm; he had come with excellent references, and steadily lived up to her trust and confidence. And she admitted to herself that it was comforting to have a brilliant and competent colleague on whom she could depend.

Amanda groaned. "OK, thanks to both of you for forbearing to rub it in about my lapse in good judgment in hiring Arthur. I promise to put the white hat away and stick to being the bad cop."

At that moment, Sheila decided the time was ripe to broach the subject for her appearance. "If I might interject something totally off-subject here, there are some men of God here to see you on an urgent matter, some bishop's secretary and an accountant or something."

Amanda smirked, her eyes twinkling. "Which is it, a man of God or an accountant? Heaven knows he can't be both." Ralph hooted with laughter, and even Sheila smiled at Amanda's rare joke. "They either want a donation, or are here to deliver formal notice that the church is to sack me as organist and continue the good bishop's vendetta against me."

Ralph cried, "Three cheers—let us pray for Mandy's excommunication. Just think of the money we can make if she's freed from working for the church, and with that energy plowed into working for the grandaddy of all lawyers!"

Amanda shook her head. "With the Episcopal Church's share of agnostics and relativists, there's room for even the worst reprobates, so don't count on that. Sheila, it looks like we had a cancellation this morning and don't seem to be accomplishing a lot of billable hours anyway," she said, looking at Ralph pointedly in mock derision, "so why don't you usher our guests into the conference room and let them know I shan't be long. Let's get it over."

Ralph studied her. "Do you need me there for protection?"

"I'm not afraid of the big bad priests," Amanda retorted, hitting his head with a second transcript as she ducked to avoid reprisal. "Ralph, did you notice anything unusual this weekend when you checked on Arthur's work?"

"No, as I said, everything was in order Saturday," he looked at her quizzically.

"Did you look through my inbox or briefcase?"

"No," he answered slowly. "Why?"

"Because someone did," she was matter-of-fact. "We need to check to see if anything else has been rifled or taken—I'm thinking we might want to call Chief Petrino after all and make a report." She reached for the telephone receiver and waved them out of her office.

Chapter 5

Entering the firm's airy conference room which doubled as library, Amanda noted that the men had already seated themselves on the same side of the long table. She decided to sit across the table facing both of them. While crossing over to the table, she studied the men, and they both stood.

The taller one was dark-haired and handsome, bearing a briefcase but no clerical collar, in an expensive Italian cut dark gray suit, white shirt and black tie, gazing at her with compelling brown eyes and the hint of a smile. Beside him was a shorter, thin man with a shock of red hair, in a black suit and clerical collar advertising his calling. She recognized the latter as Adam Brownlee, the Bishop's curate, with whom she had the encounter the previous day. The first man she realized was the man talking to Ralph at the wake the previous day. Again she was struck by how familiar his face seemed to her.

The first man did not take his eyes off her as he shook her hand warmly. Mr. Brownlee, the shorter of the two, followed the other man's lead, uncomfortably stretching his neck to nod at her in acknowledgment, taking her hand briefly and coldly. Brownlee spoke first. "Good morning Mrs. Childs. I am here on diocesan business. This is Connor Thomson, who has been retained by the Presiding Bishop of the Episcopal Church USA to conduct an audit of the diocesan records."

Connor never took his eyes off Amanda, and she became warm under his examination. He spoke in a clear baritone voice, "I know we have no appointment, but if it is at all possible I wanted to elicit your help on a grave and urgent matter. Thank you for agreeing to see us."

She was forcibly struck by Connor's disarming smile and magnetic grace as he provided a business card from the inside pocket of his jacket. She stifled her old habit of mentally cutting the opposition down to size by imagining him in his underwear; after all, Sheila referred to these two as "men of God".

Impulsively Amanda asked, "Have we met before?"

Connor blinked in surprise, before recovering and murmuring provocatively, "No, I'd remember meeting you."

Amanda felt a blush creeping up her neck at his intense, amused scrutiny of her as he continued, "I did see you at Mrs. Witherspoon's wake yesterday. The music was riveting. It was you who planned the service, wasn't it?"

At her wordless nod, he continued, "I spoke to your partner Mr. Carmichael yesterday." As she tore herself away from his gaze to turn her attention to Brownlee, Connor asked, "Have you met Reverend Brownlee before?"

"Rev. Brownlee and I have never met until yesterday," Amanda replied smoothly. Connor seemed surprised by her answer. She noted that he was obviously not without means, with his tailored suit and masculine, professional and self-assured ease with which he waited for her to be seated before settling back into his own chair. Brownlee made a striking contrast, as he looked somewhat out of place and ill at ease being overshadowed by the other man.

Amanda tried to convey an ease she did not feel. "How may I help you, Reverends?"

Connor flashed another winning smile, which again confused her by reinforcing the feeling that she had met him before. Meanwhile he took the lead and was responding. "Well, to begin with, Ms. Childs, I am not a 'Reverend' as is Adam here. I am an attorney and CPA with the firm of Grayton and Shivers."

"Ah, the big international accounting firm," Amanda interrupted.

"Yes," Connor nodded. "I flew in yesterday for a meeting with Bishop Marks this morning on some diocesan fiscal matters. As you probably know, he has been hospitalized here, although for some reason he seems somewhat sensitive about that information's becoming public."

Amanda inquired politely, "How is the Bishop?" looking at Brownlee.

Brownlee shifted stiffly as he replied. "It appears that he had a heart attack; the doctors are not sure how serious it is. He is undergoing tests today to determine the extent of any blockages, and to decide the next course of treatment. However, he is asking to see you this evening."

Connor intervened. "I am here partly at his request. I wanted to meet you, and he suggested you can help me in my inquiry."

Amanda, feeling somewhat unbalanced under Connor's eyes on her, felt like a schoolgirl at the principal's office for some misdemeanor. She interposed impulsively, "If this is about any dissatisfaction he has with my conduct, he could easily have communicated notice to me of my termination by simply dictating a letter; there's no need for a meeting, particularly in view of the Bishop's current serious medical condition."

Connor's dark eyes pierced right through her as he pursed his lips amusedly. "Termination? I'm afraid you are mistaken. I was under the impression that he felt in your debt for your timely intervention on his behalf yesterday. He spoke nothing of terminating your services at St. Catherine's to me. Besides, is it his province to hire and fire the parish staff?"

Brownlee broke in, leaning forward as though anxious to take an active role in the conversation. "Any termination is, as you know, up to the governing body of St. Catherine's. And in light of the developments with Mrs. Witherspoon's will, I doubt you would be on anyone's termination list right now," he remarked, his small dark eyes boring into Amanda's unpleasantly.

Amanda turned her attention to Brownlee and repeated slowly, "Mrs. Witherspoon's will?"

"I am sure you were careful to avoid actually drafting her will," responded Brownlee smoothly. "Perfectly understandable in light of her bequests—I am sure you would have taken pains to avoid the obvious appearance of impropriety that would ensue if you had drafted the will."

Amanda, sensing the accusation in his remarks, stiffened and inhaled slowly to keep her temper from flaring. Her eyes smoldering with anger, she remarked, "Rev. Brownlee, I don't know what you are inferring . . ."

Connor interrupted quickly, with a sideways frown at Brownlee, "Rev. Brownlee is not here to infer anything, Ms. Childs. He only accompanied me here at the Bishop's request in order to make introduction."

"Whatever. I'm completely in the dark. I believe in the direct approach, so if you have something to say, spit it out," Amanda was cool, although inwardly she was bemused. What will? She remembered Bill's query the previous night. Why doesn't Bill have Marjy's will?

Brownlee countered brashly, "Surely, Mandy, we're not to think you don't know about Mrs. Witherspoon's latest alleged will and testament, so pretending innocence does not suit you."

Amanda looked at him coldly. "Only friends call me that, not persons I've just met, and certainly not those firing innuendo at me." Frowning, she took a deep breath to still her rising temper. "All I know is that Mrs. Witherspoon had no family, her husband and only child having predeceased her. She told me several years ago that she intended to leave a substantial bequest to St. Catherine's, because it had been such a source of solace to her and she intended that it continue to be so for others. We didn't discuss her other testamentary intentions."

Brownlee looked skeptical, as Jonathan's eyes narrowed. "So you are telling me you have no knowledge of the contents of this will?" the latter quietly asked, clicking open his briefcase, retrieving and handing her a copy of a document, opened to several marked passages.

Amanda took the document and thumbed through to the beginning of the document in true lawyer fashion, looking at it carefully. "Prepared last month by Malachi Feinstein. Wonder why didn't she use Bill or me to draw her will?" talking to herself. Then she began to read the initial pages, flipping through the pages of specific bequests, continuing to scan and read. When she reached the page initially indicated by Connor, her eyes opened wide. "My God!" she exclaimed incredulously, oblivious to the cleric sitting in front of her.

> 'I leave the sum of Two Million Dollars ($2,000,000.00) to Amanda Childs, as Trustee, pursuant to the terms of the trust created by separate document, for the construction, installation, and maintenance of a new pipe organ of her choosing and under her supervision for St. Catherine's Episcopal Church. Any remainder shall be deposited in the Organ Endowment Fund for the continued maintenance of the instrument as previously referred to in this instrument, as the designated Trustee shall see fit.
>
> 'I leave the sum of One Million Dollars ($1,000,000.00), for the creation of an Endowment for the maintenance of said instrument. The above-named Trustee shall be empowered and authorized to set up the terms for scheduling regular and needed upkeep for said instrument.
>
> 'I leave the sum of Three Million Dollars ($3,000,000.00), to create an Endowment to fund a salaried organist/choirmaster. The above-named Trustee shall be empowered to administer the endowment, to negotiate for salary, benefits and terms of employment, to interview, employ and terminate employment.
>
> 'All said funds shall be invested so as to accrue a moderate return in order to perpetuate said Trusts and Endowments, a committee to be appointed with the consent and approval by said Trustee to administer and oversee the investment.
>
> 'As and for the rest, residuary and remainder of my estate, both tangible and intangible, real and personal property, I will, devise, bequeath and give same to Amanda Childs, her heirs and assigns, to have and to hold.'

By this time Amanda was numb and barely comprehended the remaining paragraphs on the page:

> 'Should Amanda Childs predecease me, or should she die within the time period defined in this will as constituting simultaneous death, then the rest, residue and remainder of my estate devised to her shall be placed in trust for the specific benefit of St. Catherine's Church, the trustee to be designated as William Barnes, Jr.

'Should St. Catherine's Church cease operation and existence within any legal perpetuities period, then any funds remaining in trust shall be surrendered by the designated Trustee to the following list of charitable organizations then extant, in equal shares in fee simple:'

As Amanda turned the page and quickly scanned the remainder of the document, which also named her as the executrix of the estate, Brownlee rejoined smoothly, "That's a cool fifty million or more residuary after taxes. I would say you have done well." As Amanda's white face turned a rosy pink at his implied indictment, he continued, "Did you know that Mrs. Witherspoon had previously evinced her intention to leave the residue of her estate to the Diocese?"

Amanda suddenly understood where this conversation was leading, and her rising ire and her knowledge of Marjorie Witherspoon's feelings prompted her to respond. "That may be, Mr. Brownlee," she reverted to the 'Mr.', "but that has not been the state of her feelings for the last number of years. Number one, I'm told Bishop Marks has not darkened the doors of this parish since he became Bishop. Number two, I know that Mrs. Witherspoon voiced no desire or intention to me to leave any money to a diocese that had turned its back on St. Catherine's all these years. Number three, I had no idea that she would leave her fortune to me, but it is beginning to make sense because of her dream to keep St. Catherine's alive and thriving despite the diocese's not-so-secret agenda of closing its doors and selling off the property."

Now it was Brownlee's turn to flush. "You've got some cheek accusing the diocese of having an anti-St. Catherine's agenda, after all the financial support provided this decrepit parish all this time."

Connor, alarmed at the escalation of hostilities, quickly stepped in, "If we could all remain calm . . ."

Amanda, ignoring Connor, replied icily, "Mr. Brownlee," she again emphasized the 'Mr.', "I don't know what shell game you are playing, but I served on the vestry for two different terms, and St. Catherine's has received nothing from the diocese in the last fifteen years. In fact, the church was turned down flat every time it requested any consideration. I can set you straight in a New York minute about that. Marjy, Mrs. Witherspoon to you, was very specific about her feelings toward the diocese, because she has helped this church through financial woes and other troubles more than once.

"Now, you come into my office and interrupt my work schedule, accuse me of exercising undue influence over one of my dearest friends whom I have just lost, and spout some miserable drivel about the diocese supporting this parish. I don't know from where you hail, but that's about the rudest I've been treated in at least a couple weeks. In fact, most of my colleagues in the courtroom are nicer when they are about to gore me, and New York cab drivers treat each other with more respect."

Connor suddenly held up his hand. "Perhaps we have started off on the wrong foot. I am very sorry that we have come at such an obviously trying time for you. It was very wrong of us to accost you so soon after Mrs. Witherspoon's death." He paused briefly, as if allowing a moment for the dust to settle. "I sincerely apologize for Adam's outbursts—all of this was very inappropriate," he interceded, looking at the curate sternly.

Turning back to gaze kindly at Amanda, he continued, "I am very interested in your statements about St. Catherine's not receiving assistance from the diocese. I would very much like to sit down with you and the church records and compare ledgers. However, I don't have the diocesan records with me this morning. Please accept my apologies for our intrusion, and my condolences."

Brownlee started to say something, but Connor cut him off. Continuing, he asked, "Would it be possible for you to meet with me later today or this week? I would like to be able to review the church's records against my own."

Amanda replied coolly, "I am preparing for a trial commencing next week. I'm sure there is someone at the church office who can better accommodate your request. I no longer serve on the vestry, and I have confined my duties at St. Catherine's to assisting Father Anselm with planning the music and service, that is, until we find a real organist."

"Real organist?" echoed Connor. "I don't understand."

Amanda, looking at her hands, replied quietly, "We are seeking a trained, degreed, credentialed musician to take over the duties I have been attempting to fill. One of the stumbling-blocks has been providing suitable salary and benefits. I guess perhaps Marjy has provided the wherewithal whereby that can happen."

Connor frowned. "The church records are not in your possession?" he deduced.

"Of course not," disavowed Amanda, looking at him sharply. "In fact, Bill Barnes is the church treasurer, and can be contacted through the church or at his office. He is also an attorney in town."

Connor calmly explained his confusion. "It was my understanding that Mr. Barnes was the diocesan treasurer, and that you were in charge of the church's financial records. I was particularly interested in meeting with you over the church's records. As an independent auditor I can demand to see the books at any time. However, I would much prefer to do this with the church's assistance. I will contact Mr. Barnes. But at your convenience, I'd like to make an appointment to talk to you further, if you could spare the time. I realize that your legal expertise as well as your obvious interest in the well-being of St. Catherine's would be helpful to me in my examination of the records. I would like to schedule an appointment later today or tomorrow if that would be convenient for you."

"I'll have to review my schedule and get back with you. Now I really must cut this short. I have an important appointment." Amanda tried to sound curt and noncommittal, but found herself curious about the matter. Why an audit by the Presiding Bishop? And why does it involve little St. Catherine's? Puzzled as to why Connor would want to review the church's finances with her, but still inwardly seething, she stood, indicating the interview was at an end. The two men followed suit. Connor snapped closed his attaché and proffered his hand, which Amanda took somewhat reluctantly, as Brownlee turned away. As they were moving to the conference room door, Connor turned back.

"Oh, I forgot to inform you that when I met with Bishop Marks this morning, he was quite adamant that I tell you he expects you at the hospital tonight at 7:00. I apologize for the notice, but he is a pretty insistent man."

Amanda stared at the retreating backs of the two men. Sitting back down after the door closed behind them, she felt beheaded and gutted like a trout. Her eyes misted as she thought, Marjy, is this true? What have you done?

Amanda leaned back and stared at the ceiling, trying to sort matters out in her head. While she relished a good fight representing someone else, she did not enjoy being personally involved in controversy. And her deceased friend had just landed her in the middle of one.

Behind her, the telephone buzzed. Picking it up, she heard Sheila's voice. "Bill Barnes is on the phone, and says it is urgent."

Everything is urgent today, she thought, and hit the blinking button. "Amanda Childs; may I help you?" she said automatically, her mind still numb from the news she had just received.

"I cannot believe you. Damn it, Mandy," she heard Bill saying furiously. "All this time, you play the innocent doe, and now this."

"What?" asked Amanda curtly.

"Just got a copy of an 'alleged' new will by Marjorie, where you're the heir apparent. You have been busy, haven't you, getting your hands on her fortune?"

"I don't know what you are talking about. I've just seen a copy of this will myself, in the hand of the Presiding Bishop's auditor."

"Who?" Bill demanded hoarsely, as Ralph walked into the conference room and placed a canned soft drink in front of her. She murmured thanks while Bill's voice continued across the line, "How did he get it?"

"I don't know that, either, Bill, and I really don't appreciate the accusations. I didn't anticipate it this morning from strangers; I damn sure don't appreciate it from someone I consider a friend."

Bill sounded exasperated. "Mandy, don't you see? You've put me in an impossible position. The diocese has a copy of a previous will where Marjorie left her money to the diocese. The Bishop will not let go of that prior will without a fight. You will have to fight for every dime of that legacy, because they will try to make a case that you exerted undue influence over Marjorie to procure that will. And why shouldn't I wonder about this? This document is prepared by some schmuck in Manhattan. Why not me?"

Why not you, indeed? Amanda wondered. Aloud she replied, "I don't know, and I'm as clueless as you. I can understand Marjy's not leaving the money to the diocese, and you can too, after the way things have gone the last several years. But why me? This came out of left field."

"Well, you'd better be finding yourself a good lawyer."

Amanda, stung by the accusation in his voice, hung up the phone on him indignantly without replying. Ralph looked at her concernedly.

"Your 10:30 is here, some guy with a Brooklyn accent. What's up?"

"My headache is returning. What a morning—first firing Arthur, then being surrounded by hateful lawyers, including one I thought of as a friend, making lurid accusations," returned Amanda, staring at the ceiling. "Pinch me—this has to be some continuing nightmare.

"Do you mind taking this meeting with me, Ralph? This has to do with Marjy's will, and I'm really confused right now. I could use another head on this one. Just please give me a minute to gather my thoughts before bringing him in here, will you?"

"Gee, are you going to inherit anything?"

Amanda glared at him angrily. "That's not the half of it. Get out of here and let me have a quick nervous breakdown."

Chapter 6

Amanda, alone in the conference room, suddenly felt drained. The burden of the last weeks' events weighed heavily on her slim shoulders, and she realized that she was alone. Yes, there were many friends and acquaintances, plenty of social activities and the demanding business of her chosen profession, but Amanda was reticent about sharing her innermost thoughts, even to friends such as Ralph Carmichael or Bill Barnes. Amanda, ever wary since Andrew's death, kept the doors closed against developing a closeness to others.

The suddenness, violence and mystery of Andy's murder had wrenched from her the very fabric of her psyche by taking the one person with whom she felt whole, at one. She had learned to swallow and hide the hurt. Through the years with Marjorie Witherspoon she had weaved a close relationship, and she had found a true friend to whom she could pour out the secrets of her heart. Marjy's loss of family had been sudden, as had Amanda's own, and as deep. They shared much free time together, Marjorie filling that time with projects and tasks for her younger charge, and Amanda finally found that she could laugh again.

Marjorie had never re-married, although Amanda had tried hard but unsuccessfully to pair her with Dr. Malcolm Howells, a bachelor who had been Amanda's family doctor all her life. Amanda's scheming toward this goal in the end had created a great camaraderie between the three. Doctor Howells and Marjorie, who had themselves been lifelong friends, had become surrogate parents to Amanda, who had lost her father to sudden illness while she was in law school, and her mother to lingering cancer not long after her marriage to Andrew.

Now Marjorie too was gone. Amanda, still trying to make sense of the events of the last week, sat woodenly, helplessly awaiting some stranger in order to discover the meaning of this will now apparently making the rounds and creating even more havoc. *Where is this will, and why is everyone but me getting a copy?* she wondered. *This isn't like you, Marjy.*

She heard a light knock on the conference room door, and Ralph Carmichael entered with a medium-built man with balding white-gray hair in expensively-cut dark suit and carrying a large briefcase. Amanda stood and proffered her hand. "Mr. Feinstein?"

"Yes, and you must be Mrs. Childs," he greeted her, warmly shaking her hand. "I am happy to meet you at last, although I am very sorry for the circumstances under which we meet. Mrs. Witherspoon's description of you was so delightful, and I made a promise to come in person. I was at the service yesterday, but did not have the opportunity to meet you and to tell you how lovely and fitting it was."

"Thank you so much, and please sit down, Mr. Feinstein. Can we offer you something to drink? No? If you don't mind, I've asked my law partner Ralph Carmichael to sit in, because I trust him implicitly. I'm not functioning on all cylinders right now."

"I understand completely, and console you in your loss. Mrs. Witherspoon was an extraordinary woman."

"Yes, she was. Forgive me, Mr. Feinstein, for my inquisitiveness, but did you know her well?"

"Yes, her husband and I were actually business colleagues and friends for many years. I had done legal work for him in New York for many years, and had set up the trust fund for their daughter Monica when she left for college. The deaths of Jerrod and Monica were wrenching for me as well. After their deaths, Marjorie came to me about estate planning needs."

Amanda, her curiosity sharpening her lawyer's examination skills, pressed on. "I'm sorry for sounding impertinent, but Marjy never mentioned anything about her association with you or about her will to me. I am confused and have a great many questions, and I have been shown a copy of a document only this morning purporting to be her latest will."

Mr. Feinstein nodded unperturbedly, opening his briefcase and bringing forth a sheaf of papers. Handing her an envelope, he asked, "Did it look like this?"

Amanda, noting her name on the envelope in Marjorie's handwriting, opened the envelope, retrieving the document inside. Quickly she scanned the pages. "Looks like it, all right. This is also a copy. Who has the original?"

"Marjorie knew that you would have many questions. My firm possesses the original, and is prepared to file it once you have approved and executed the initial probate documents. Marjorie gave me strict instructions, in person and in writing, about who was to receive copies upon her death. Furthermore, she mandated that the probate proceedings be filed as quickly as possible. She was apprehensive about a challenge."

As Amanda handed the document over to Ralph to review, Feinstein continued. "You see, I did the preceding will right after the death of her husband and child which left all her monies in trust to the diocese for the benefit of St.

Catherine's. However, several years ago, she became unhappy with that will, and more importantly, with the diocesan governing body. We discussed a codicil. Then she became seriously ill. That was her first bout with the cancer. When it went into remission, we met again. It was then that after several drafts, mainly regarding the smaller specific bequests and recipients thereof, that she signed this last will."

"Why me?" Amanda asked simply.

Startled, the man showed his white teeth as he smiled at her. "Why on earth not? Marjorie loved you. As hard as it was losing Jerrod and Monica, she still had you. She told me that God had blessed her. She trusted you to ensure that her wishes were fulfilled, and to put the money to wise use. Most importantly, she loved you to distraction, my dear. She was so proud of you."

Noting the tears glistening from the young woman's eyes, he continued. "However, she knew that she was saddling you with a heavy responsibility, and was insistent that I provide you information and help you with as much of it as you would allow. She was also adamant that the petition be filed by our firm as soon as possible, and that you come to New York to be briefed regarding the estate, also immediately. She was very concerned that if the diocese filed a contest, which I tend to doubt but she certainly felt possible, that the estate be represented by a firm competent in the field. Our firm has offices in Tallahassee and Miami, and has handled much estate planning and litigation for our clients in Florida.

"If, once letters of administration are received, however, you should choose another firm, you are within your rights to do so. But we need to schedule a meeting this week to inform you of the various assets and how her accounts and funds are set up, and for you to inform me how you wish to proceed. Meanwhile, please review the draft of the petition for administration, the powers of attorney, and other documents we will have to file to initiate probate."

Rising, as Amanda and Ralph followed suit, he asked, "I would love to stay longer, but my plane leaves at noon, and sadly I must be on it. I know your schedule is hard to change on short notice. However it is imperative that we meet soon so that I can brief you, and I want you personally present in my office to sign the original probate documents. Are you able to give me a date, preferably this week, by which I could expect you at my office in Manhattan?"

Amanda's head was reeling. No, don't go, she mentally screamed. This is too much. Feinstein turned back and held out his hand to her across the table. She reached out and grasped it. "I know," he said simply, as if he read her mind. "And I want to answer as many questions as I can. That's why it is urgent that we meet very soon. I have much more to tell you than can be disclosed in the few minutes I have here."

She mentally reviewed her calendar. Ralph cut in smoothly. "I'm smelling settlement of the Garvin case—we are only arguing damages on the one remaining count now. I can handle it, Mandy."

Amanda still hesitated. "This is a lot to take in, Mr. Feinstein. Can I make a few calls and call you, perhaps tomorrow?"

"Please do," he said, releasing her hand and reaching into his bag, handing her another large envelope. "My business card is attached to the documents. My personal contact numbers are on the back; I want you to feel free to call me any time. There are also copies of the deeds and other transfers Marjorie executed; the originals will be provided to you when we meet. As you may well realize, some of Marjorie's investments are short-term and fluctuate. Also, some of the investments and properties were placed in your name by Marjorie prior to her death, and are at your immediate disposal without probate should you need them. I will await your call as to when to expect you, and am at your disposal should you have any questions."

Taking her hand and squeezing it warmly, Feinstein added gravely, "Amanda, if I may call you that, time is of the essence. Please do not delay."

He left, followed by Ralph. Amanda, spooked at his last words, stared at his retreating back, then quickly made her way to her office and shut herself in, deep in thought.

Picking up the telephone, she dialed a number. After several rings, a voice came on the line. "Ken, this is Amanda. How are you?

"I am calling because I am going to have to be out of town a few days on business. Would you mind terribly covering for me at church the next couple of weeks? No? You're a dear.

"Can you be at the planning meeting this afternoon? Do you think we could move it up to, say, 1:30? You can? That would be wonderful. Thanks for checking with him for me, and I'll see you then unless I hear from you otherwise."

As she hung up the receiver, Ralph entered her office, shutting the door behind him. Lightly, he asked, "What am I supposed to call you now? Ms. Heiress? Your Highness?"

Amanda silenced him with her eyes as she moved to her small conference table to lay out the papers provided by Feinstein. "Don't start," she warned. "You got lunch plans?"

"With you, remember? I'd think a rich woman like you would treat her law partner to the finest. I was thinking Chez Pierre and a bottle of Dom Perignon, but I'll bet you were thinking deli and working through lunch here at the office."

"Ralph, my ass is grass. I'm about to be sued by the diocese for exerting undue influence over my best friend. Bill was just saying vile things to me on the phone before the meeting."

"Is that why Jon Connor was here this morning?"

"Jon?" Amanda stopped in her tracks momentarily. 'Jon' rang some bell of familiarity in her brain. "Are you sure? He gave me his card—it says 'Connor Thomson'. Yes, at least I think it's related—something about the church's financial records and the will. By the way, I saw you talking to him yesterday."

"Yes, he came up and introduced himself to me after the graveside service. We met before in college. He seemed like a nice man, really sharp."

She briefly described the meeting with the two men and the telephone conversation with Bill Barnes. She concluded, "The whole world is mad at me. I can understand if you are mad at me too about all this mess, but I assure you I did not have anything to do with this. I'm at a loss here. I promise I won't drag the firm down with me if I'm sued."

Ralph hooted with laughter. "Mandy, I'm not mad at you—that is the most preposterous thing I have ever heard! It seems to me that you would be the most logical beneficiary under Marjorie Witherspoon's will, and what's more, there's no one in this town that does not know that fact. Bill knows better, and he's just killed too many brain cells with Crown and Coke if he even thinks that you are capable of stealing Marjy's estate."

"Well, I certainly hope our trial next week does settle. It's turning out to be a full week."

Sheila's voice buzzed over the intercom. "There's a call from attorney Quattlebaum on the Garvin case."

Ralph said, "I'll take it. The opposition is running scared. Maybe we won't have to try that case after all."

While Ralph took the call at Amanda's desk, Amanda sat at the conference table trying to review her calendar and prioritize the upcoming cases, methodically making a list of tasks she needed to do. She had trouble concentrating because her mind was still on the morning's events.

Ralph hung up, triumphant. "They want a meeting this afternoon. I love it when a plan comes together. I think I can knock down the amount they'll settle for to less than what we proposed at mediation."

Noting her preoccupation, he added, "I assume you're going to the church this afternoon, so I'll take the Garvin meeting without you. I'll bribe Sheila to go get us some food, and we'll review this paperwork from this hot-shot New York attorney over lunch, OK?"

As she nodded, the intercom buzzed again. "Mrs. Childs, it is Connor Thomson on line 1."

Amanda remonstrated, "What is it—'Kick Amanda Day'? Tell him to go to hell."

Ralph said, "Let me take it." He picked up the phone. "Ralph Carmichael here; may I help you? Hi, Connor, it's nice to talk to you too. No, I'm afraid Amanda had lunch plans and an all-afternoon appointment. Can I help you? Sure, I'll be glad to give her a message." Listening for a moment or two and writing on a pad, he recited back a number. "Yes, it has been an ordeal, but she's a very understanding person. I'll make sure she gets the message. Good day."

Ralph replaced the receiver, puzzled. "I stand corrected on the name. Mr. 'Thomson' sends his sincerest apologies for Mr. Brownlee's outbursts this morning, and would like to meet with you later today or this evening. He is here for the next couple of days, if you could find the time. He sounded quite sincere."

"Sincere, my ass," retorted Amanda, her eyes not leaving the documents she was perusing.

Ralph gave her a broad grin. "I love it when you talk dirty. I'll order lunch—be right back."

A few minutes later he returned, and Amanda was still at her spot at the table, reading documents. He sat down at her desk computer and punched up the internet. She asked absently, "What are you doing?"

"Checking out Feinstein, both on the net and with an investigator friend of mine. I don't want you signing anything until we're sure of him."

Amanda, finishing one sheaf of papers, picked them up to move them, and an envelope fell out. Picking it up, she saw that it was addressed to her in Marjorie Witherspoon's handwriting. Opening it, she found a letter addressed to her, and read:

'My Amanda, dearest daughter and friend,

'I know that if you reading this, then I am gone and have left you once again all alone. I am also aware that my will probably has caught you quite unawares. I thought many times about telling you, but I knew you'd try to talk me out of it. There was no one else I could trust, and no one else I loved more than you.

'You don't know what it meant to me when you were there for me after Jerrod's and Monica's deaths. My soul mate and my future hopes died with them. But I still had you, and it was God's gift back to me, something I didn't deserve and had no right to expect. And your simple child-like faith in God made me see through the tears and realize that there was something after death. I could not believe that someone as complicated and as intelligent as you could believe in a just and loving God, omniscient and omnipotent. You restored my faith.

'When you lost Andrew, that faith was sorely tested. You taught me that we all are here for God's purpose, and our job is to find and fulfill that purpose. But just as God planted you here to teach me, so did he put me here to return the favor to you. Your life has been on hold since Andrew's death. I want to see you happy as you have made me happy.

'There are things happening in this parish and diocese of which I cannot tell you. I no longer trust the diocese, but the reasons why I lost that trust are old and deep-rooted. My old and trusted advisor Malachi Feinstein and his firm are the best in the field, and he will not steer you wrong. He helped Jerrod multiply our wealth, and can be trusted completely. He is privy to my plans and wishes for you and the estate.

'I of course want to see "our little charges", as you and I have called them, taken care of, and know you will do so. But the bulk of the money is for you—do something for yourself, my child.

'There are those who will not be happy with this new will, and you need to be extremely careful. Stephen—I shudder when I write his name—has been a vindictive man, and has never forgiven me, although he is the one who desperately needs forgiveness. I feel he will try something, and the most obvious tactic will be to challenge this will.

'You must meet with my trusted advisors in New York without delay, who will relay information to you in person that I do not entrust to pen and paper. The cabin and its contents are at your disposal—I've already had title placed in your name, along with several other assets. Please think fondly of your times there with Andrew and with me.

'Amanda, there is something about my past that affects you, something that I could never bring myself to tell you, and still cannot write it down. Malachi, God bless him as the true friend he has been, has been entrusted with this burden. I only hope that once you have been told you may forgive me for withholding this news for so long. I only have your best interests at heart.

'Nevertheless, the time for tears is past. You must find love and laughter. All of us who have gone on want that for you. I plan to tell your mom and dad how wonderfully you turned out. There are so many things I would like to say to you, but mainly I want you to know that life does go on.

'May God's all-sufficient grace remain with you and sustain you, my child,

Marjorie'

Amanda stared, unseeing and unheeding, still clutching the letter written in her friend's familiar hand, tears streaming down her face unchecked. She felt as if her heart would burst. All the pent-up emotions of loss and grief welled up inside her. She closed her eyes and in her mind was back at Marjy's hospital bed, as Amanda clutched her hand and unknowingly rocked to and fro reciting the Nicene Creed to her while Marjy lay unresponsive. She was unable to pray, to join in Father Anselm's recitation of the litany at the time of death, burying her head impotently in her hands as she helplessly waited. She remembered only Dr. Howells gently raising her and enfolding her in his arms, telling her Marjy was gone, and how she could not summon tears. Now the tears rained, and she could not stop the tide.

"I'd give anything to have you back," she screamed, suddenly beside herself. "What am I to do? Everyone is gone: Monica, my parents, Andy, and now you. I'm so alone."

In her desolation she had forgotten that anyone was there. Ralph put his hand on her shoulder, then knelt beside her. She placed her head on his shoulder, and he held her and rocked her back and forth as she sobbed.

Sheila silently brought in food and placed it on the table, leaving them.

Chapter 7

They remained in that posture for some time. Amanda, lost in her rage and pain, wept uncontrollably, unable to stop. Finally spent, Amanda pushed herself away, flushed with embarrassment, and Ralph did not resist. She began apologizing profusely. Ralph cut her off.

"I do believe that's the first time I've ever seen you cry, counselor," he said gently. "Damn sure time, don't you think?"

Amanda mumbled through her tears. "Even as a kid I would lock myself in the bathroom to cry. I never wanted to let anyone see me vulnerable. Thank you, Ralph."

"Say no more; we'll keep it our little secret. But you really need to refresh your makeup before letting anyone else see you—you will scare the neighborhood children."

Amanda smiled wanly as she stood up and headed to the adjoining washroom.

As she washed her face, Ralph called to her, "Feinstein is on the up-and-up—quite an impressive reputation, and high marks with Martindale-Hubbell and the New York Bar. Malki is a bastion of the legal society."

Amanda stopped. "What did you just say?"

Ralph started to repeat himself, but Amanda stopped him. "Malki—Malachi," she thought out loud. "Marjorie was trying to tell me I needed to talk to Malachi Feinstein. It all makes sense now."

Amanda explained to Ralph Marjorie's last words to her. "And she said I was to take care of Bill, or watch over him, or something like that."

Ralph retorted, "Bill could certainly use a keeper. But I'd rather it wasn't you."

"Why not?" Amanda was direct as she walked out of the washroom and faced Ralph. "I mean, why don't you think Bill and I together is a good idea?"

Ralph looked away from her, fingering his lapel. "I just don't see him being who you deserve, and Marjorie had even higher standards. Bill's our friend; we grew up with him. But Bill's number one concern is Bill. Would he be faithful to one woman? It hasn't happened yet. And," he added meaningfully, "I don't really think Marjy wanted you to be Bill's caregiver. She always wanted the best for you." He paused, a thought flitting across his brow. "Amanda, you're not actually thinking seriously about Bill again? I mean, do you love him?"

It was Amanda's turn to look away. "I have no illusions about Bill," she said slowly. "Sometimes I get tired of fighting him. I'm all alone, and Andy and Marjy aren't there anymore. Wouldn't it make sense? But no, I am not in love with Bill."

"But you've always been independent, a fighter," Ralph protested. "You want to give all that up and become submissive little Mrs. Barnes, holding tea parties, being Bill's arm ornament, and sitting in the background cheering him on?"

"It wouldn't be that bad," Amanda laughed, but the laugh was hollow. She knew that Bill always sought the limelight, and Ralph was at least partially right. It would be nothing for Bill to expect her to play the part of a society wife, and her own life and career would take a back seat to his ambitions.

Amanda shook her head, irritated. "I don't want to waste time talking about Bill. The paperwork Feinstein left looked in order. I saw nothing amiss there. And you can read Marjy's letter. She recommended him highly, and I know her handwriting as well as my own."

Ralph turned away, hiding the smirk on his face. Amanda had skirted the issue again.

As she repaired her makeup, Ralph munched on a sandwich and read the letter, his brows furrowing in concern. "This sounds sinister to me, Amanda," he ruminated. "I cannot imagine a skeleton in Marjorie's closet. Wonder what that's about. But we need to get you to New York as soon as possible. What about today?"

Amanda objected, "Ralph, I'm not leaving until I've cleared this calendar and made arrangements at the church. I have an arraignment in the morning, and I promised to be there. We both have mediations in the afternoon. And I've got to see Bishop Marks this evening. I'm actually curious now about why he wants to see me. It's possible I can get out of here by Thursday morning or so."

Amanda reviewed the solicitor's instructions regarding the documents. Ralph joined her at the table, and started reviewing the papers as she completed her perusal.

"They look kosher to me," she looked sadly at the pile. "What do you think?"

"Yes, but I'd like to review them one more time. Do you mind?"

"No," Amanda replied, suddenly tired. "Keep them overnight." She picked up Marjorie's letter and Feinstein's card and placed them in her purse.

Ralph quizzed concernedly, "Aren't you going to eat something? You really should."

Amanda picked up one of his potato chips and crunched it, as Sheila entered the office with various pleadings and letters. Amanda carefully reviewed the documents provided her and signed them, providing succinct instructions about filing.

"I'm out of here. I'll be at the church if you need me. And," she smiled at Ralph, "thanks for everything."

Ralph walked her out. She stated, "Good luck with the meeting—tell them to accept your terms or deal with both of us on Monday at jury selection."

Ralph rejoined good-naturedly, "That threat should do the trick. Quattlebaum is intimidated by me, but he is 'pee-in-his-pants' scared of you." He laughed at her surprised look. "That's why you make the better 'bad cop' of the two of us. That natural aloofness, plus your out-preparing the opposition, does the trick every time."

She shook her head at him, smiling, and waved goodbye. Pulling out of the parking lot, Amanda noticed a brown older-model Mustang parked across the street, the driver hidden behind a newspaper. Odd to see someone parked on that side of the street, she thought, as she accelerated, her mind moving quickly over her list of things to do.

Arriving at the church a few minutes later for the meeting, Amanda met Ken outside her office. Opening the door, she invited him in. Over her shoulder, she thanked him again for taking the next Sundays, adding, "But I want to make sure you're not doing anything crazy like transcribing Wagner's entire 'Ring Cycle' for organ and performing it during services while I'm gone."

Ken, a fair-haired freckle-faced young man with pleasant face, laughed. "I wouldn't do that—well, maybe I would, but I won't. Father would beat me if I did. What did you think of Ravel's *Berceuse* segued into 'Fairest Lord Jesus' and 'Abide with me' a couple Sundays back?"

"I wouldn't have thought of it, and it turned out nicely. You know, we taped that service for Marjorie, and she specifically mentioned her delight in your improvisation. However, she hooted several Sundays back when you hid 'The Yellow Rose of Texas' in a postlude. That was a little wild."

"Yeah, she would have been one of the few to even recognize the music," Ken laughed. "But what about your playing Lemare's *Andantino* the Sunday after Valentine's Day?"

Amanda's eyes shone as she looked at the young man fondly. "You're supposed to do as I say, not as I do. I'm not a good role model for you. Of course," she said, her eyes twinkling, "if you'd like to come back from college and take this job off my hands full-time, I promise not to boss you too much."

Ken regarded her. "You know I'd jump at the chance to be full-time organist at St. Catherine's."

"I know, and there's no one I'd rather have. You have a fine sense of musicianship, and a feel for the liturgy and the worship style these people want.

That's something many degreed musicians have trouble developing, and you are a natural.

"However, Ken, I don't want you to embed yourself here in this small town, at least until you've had a taste of the options and can make an informed choice. You have your entire life ahead of you, and you don't want to one day wake up with a bag full of 'what-ifs'. Get your college education and your degrees, enjoy your time away from here and take the time to decide what you really want."

Ken refuted stubbornly, "But you came back to Mainville."

Amanda frowned in acknowledgment. "But I tried it elsewhere first. I learned valuable lessons away from here, and came back only through the necessity of my mother's illness. After Mom's death, particularly with Andrew gone so much with his work, if it had not been for Marjorie, I might have felt some claustrophobia and resentment. Who knows whether I would have stayed? But I would not trade a moment of those memories for anything.

"And Ken, if you should decide that Mainville is where you want to return, as long as I'm here there's a place on that bench for you. And if you go elsewhere, I'll be glad to provide a reference and assistance for you."

Ken replied feelingly, "Thank you," and they both smiled.

Father Anselm walked in. "Hi, you two. Are you ready? We can meet in here if you like."

Ken sobered as they took their seats at Amanda's small conference table. "I'm going to miss all of Miss Marjorie's encouragement and helpful hints."

"And her calls on Tuesdays to make suggestions of music for the following Sunday," added Amanda nostalgically. "I used to tell her to just come to the meetings and make herself at home, but she always said she was better as a committee of one. She always had great taste in classical repertoire, and good ideas. She taught me everything I know about the liturgy."

Father Anselm added with a twinkle in his eye, "She would sometimes even give me instructions on points to give in sermons."

"She was a lot of fun," interjected Ken. "And you could tell the worship service meant so much to her. She was always so appreciative of a job well done, whether you took her advice or not."

"I will certainly miss her," said Amanda somberly, trying not to tear up. "We're about to find out if we can plan a service without her, and it won't be the same. She kept me from being too serious about everything.

"Speaking of which, Ken here has taken a vow to cease and desist pranks while I'm gone," she stated to Father Anselm, as she tried to interject some humor into the tense situation and feigned a stern look at Ken.

"I just want to entertain the troops," Ken winked teasingly.

"Don't entertain them so much that they're spoiled when I return," rejoined Amanda, throwing a paper airplane in his direction.

"OK, kids, let's get to work," Father Anselm gently called them back into order.

Amanda went to her desk and turned on the computer. Within minutes they had draft bulletins in hand and were discussing the next three weeks of services, including the Feast of St. Michael and All Angels. Amanda went to her desk, pulling up appropriate service music and Anglican chants for the Gradual Psalm stored on her computer for them to review and choose, and the three discussed the hymns, themes and scriptures in order to mesh the service components into one.

Amanda enjoyed this aspect of her job at St. Catherine's. She had always believed that the Almighty deserved the finest service full of their best efforts and preparation. Years ago she had fallen in love with the liturgy and music of the Episcopal Church and its progenitors, and felt that what she did was part of her legacy from Marjorie Witherspoon, who had loved the Church and its splendor and had instilled that awe in Amanda. She knew that she was truly blessed, with a wonderful man of God as a vicar, a young enthusiastic and truly gifted assistant willing for any opportunity to play, a dedicated and talented choir to rival many larger churches, a pleasant, competent and accommodating church secretary, and a historic restored instrument, albeit somewhat small for the space, in a beautiful church. She also knew that many church musicians would love to have half the cooperation and camaraderie she enjoyed.

Before 3:00 they had hammered out the basic services and the rough drafts were provided to the church secretary. Father Anselm had noted the signs of recent crying, and had matched Amanda's businesslike tone during the meeting, avoiding further reference to Marjorie.

As they completed the meeting, Amanda looked around the room wistfully. "As kids Bill, Monica and I played hide-and-seek in here during vestry meetings. Marjorie once showed me a special hiding place, which they never found."

Coming out of her reverie, she thanked Father Anselm and Ken. "I'm going to swing through and spend a little time at the organ before leaving."

Entering the church, she made her way to the console. Retrieving a tote bag hidden from view, she pulled out her organ shoes and her volume of Franck. Soon she was lost within herself, alone with the instrument and her thoughts as sounds of the *Chorale No. 2 in b minor* washed through the building. Being at the console allowed her to escape the turmoil of her current existence.

As she left the main sanctuary, she stepped next door to the chapel. Standing in front of the columbarium, she placed her hand on a small brass marker over one of the receptacles which read simply 'Andrew Geoffrey Childs', and the years of his birth and death. She closed her eyes, swallowing convulsively as she tried to block out the flood of pain. "What happened to you, Andy? Will I ever know?" she whispered. She stood there expectantly, as if awaiting an answer, before turning dispiritedly to leave.

The sun was at its most aggravating level in the sky as she left the church and crossed Church Street to her car. Waving to a policeman sitting in his car down the block to her right while about to unlock the driver's door, she noticed a flash of sunlight glinting off a car as it came hurtling toward her at high speed. Galvanized into action, she instinctively leaped around her car, twisting and falling onto the sidewalk. She recoiled in horror when she heard the terrible crash of metal on metal as the racing car made contact with her own. Then, as quickly as it happened, the little car sped off, screeching tires and swerving down the road.

Dazed, she looked after the car as the policeman sprinted toward her, talking excitedly into the radio microphone attached to his shoulder. Running up to her, he cried, "Amanda, are you all right?" all the time furiously shouting directions for backup into his radio.

Amanda just sat on the sidewalk, stunned, trying to catch her breath. Although she could not see the driver's side of her car, she knew it was damaged. The heel of one shoe was broken, her hose was torn where a knee had scraped against the sidewalk, and both palms and the left elbow were lacerated. All she could say was, "He ruined my Ferragamos—my first and only pair."

Then, angrily she jumped up, barking excitedly to the policeman, "Charlie, don't just stand there—go find him and give him a ticket or arrest him or something—yeowch!" as she put weight on her left ankle and tumbled forward, the policeman reaching for her and preventing her fall.

Police Chief Charles Petrino, a good-looking dark-haired hulking former All-American linebacker, was excitedly and angrily giving descriptions and directions into a microphone perched on his shoulder. "Church and Third heading east; brown Mustang, about '76 or so. You tell them to get the bastard, OK? Lorene, dispatch an ambulance—patch through to me—I'm at the scene."

Addressing Amanda, he ordered, "Why don't you stay seated on the sidewalk until the ambulance gets here?"

Amanda petulantly replied, "Ambulance? I don't need no stinking ambulance. Let's go after him."

Petrino, listening to her while providing further instructions to the dispatcher, frowned and shook his head. "I'd like nothing better, but I've got officers hot-footing it after him—I'm not leaving you alone. Let's have you checked out first. Please sit down."

He gently pushed Amanda into a sitting position on the passenger side hood. Amanda reluctantly sat back, wincing at the throbbing in her ankle and knee. Charlie took her hands and looked at them, asking her to flex her fingers, wrists and elbows. When he gingerly took her injured ankle, she arched in pain, but bit her lip and demanded, "What about my car? Don't worry about me, check the damage there."

Charlie looked at her and stated flatly, "You don't want to know."

Amanda groaned. By that time a few others had gathered on the street, and the ambulance was whining its way to the scene. Soon the emergency medical crew arrived, complete with gurney, and gently deposited Amanda, still clutching her purse, in the ambulance and whisked her away to the hospital.

The examination by the EMTs and the ride in the ambulance to the hospital were largely uneventful but hardly painless. Amanda was ushered in the emergency room immediately, her eyes blazing, and Dr. Howells was there to greet her.

Amanda, wincing while being unceremoniously dumped onto the examining table, said, "I thought you gave up on-call and ER duty a long time ago, Doc."

Howells smiled. "I did, but you forget I have a very important patient here."

"Ah yes, the Right Reverend."

"You were the one to whom I was referring."

Touched by his answer, Amanda for once had no reply.

One of the paramedics, a burly blond-haired fellow with strong biceps and serious expression, stated, "I don't think anything's broken, but she twisted that ankle right smartly. She gave the Chief hell for even calling us. And watch out, Doc—she's a lawyer. There's no anti-venom for her bite," he added, with a sideways grin at Amanda before hastily exiting.

Howells thanked him, turned to Amanda, and scolded her, "Can't you behave, Amanda Katharine? Let the men do their job."

She hung her head like a chastened child, as he turned to the nurse and ordered X-rays. Now brisk and professional, he asked Amanda questions about pain, feeling and probing the knee. Amanda grabbed some isopropyl alcohol and gauze from the nearby examining table and began swabbing her palms and elbow, muttering, while Howells, looking at her and shaking his head, completed examination of her injured knee and ankle.

"I happen to agree with Matt—I don't really think anything is broken, but we'll do a battery of pictures anyway."

Amanda grimaced. "Didn't I give a donation to the hospital just last month? I know you got some blood last night."

Howells sternly reprimanded her. "You're a lawyer, aren't you? Enough said—we're going to check you out. Besides," his eyes twinkled, "if you raise any objection I will have to refer you to the Bishop for discipline."

Amanda scowled. "That wasn't even funny. Did you get any results from my blood last night? Am I diabetic or something?"

Howells, suddenly all seriousness, replied, "I have sent off the sample to the lab. Don't worry—I'll let you know. I want to keep you in perfect health."

Howells, being the chief of staff and senior physician, was used to getting his way, and within minutes Amanda was being wheeled into the X-ray lab, where she spent what seemed like an eternity being photographed.

Back in an ER room, she decided to try to make herself look presentable. While balancing on her good ankle, she washed her hands and looked at her image in the mirror. The curtain opened, and there stood Charlie.

She peered at him through the mirror. "Did you get him?"

Charlie's face darkened. "The perpetrator has eluded us so far, but I have a so-so description and a partial tag. Hey, you look awful."

Amanda sulked. "You are such a flatterer. I don't guess you're going to ask me to the dance."

"I don't think you'll be dancing for the next few days," Howells cut into the conversation, walking in behind Charlie. "Nothing is broken, and you're an extremely fortunate girl. You hit the knee hard, so let me know if you have any pain or discomfort from it. That ankle is swelling and needs bandaging, and you will be pretty stiff tomorrow. I don't know how you were so fortunate to avoid breaking anything, and the sprain appears mild, thanks be to God. However, you'd do well to stay off it and keep it elevated. Maybe you could take a few days off."

Amanda retorted facetiously, "Bill always said I was a linebacker for the Packers in a former life. It must be all that Taebo I watch on DVD in my spare time."

As the words were echoing Father Anselm walked into the room. As he walked up to Amanda, arms wide, Amanda could see a figure hovering in the corner of the ER. Strange, she thought, but that looks like the bishop's curate.

Father Anselm hugged her. "Oh my girl, I'm so very sorry. I was just coming by to visit Bishop Marks, and I met Rev. Brownlee in the hall, who told me that you had been brought in on a stretcher. That this could happen—what is the world coming to?"

Amanda, knowing that Anselm was excitable and had a heart condition, said quickly, "Oh, Father, it was just some freak accident. Don't you worry one minute. Dr. Howells has me as good as new, and everything will be fine."

Dr. Howells, following Amanda's lead, joined in. "Yes, Colin, she is in one piece, and you know I won't let anything happen to her," he confirmed matter-of-factly, carefully wrapping the ankle in an ace bandage.

Leaning back and critically examining his handiwork, he continued, "Perhaps a nice warm whirlpool bath, keep the ankle wrapped and elevated, an icepack for swelling, and let me know if you experience any other pain or discomfort." Handing her a bottle of pills, a prescription and tube of ointment, he continued, "This is for pain if you need and will use them, and some antibiotic cream for the abrasions."

Amanda gingerly hopped down from the examination table. She turned to Charlie. "My car?"

"Towed to the impound yard for pictures and your instructions. I will be happy to chauffeur you home."

Howells asked quickly, "Don't you want to sample one of our fine wheelchairs?"

Amanda scowled. "Not really."

Howells interposed. "I really do insist—it is, as you know, hospital policy."

Behind him appeared an orderly wheeling in a chair. Amanda was bustled into it before she could protest. "OK, OK. Good evening, Father and Doctor, and thank you for your help. Come on, Charlie, let's take a ride."

Charlie grabbed the handles of the wheelchair, saluting the two men and leaving the confines of the ER.

Chapter 8

Once tucked into Petrino's unmarked squad car, Amanda sat docilely until Charlie made it around the car and let himself in. As he cranked up and eased into the light traffic he casually asked, "You been pissing off anyone lately that might want to take you out?"

Amanda smiled wryly, then fell silent as she looked at his gruff expression. "Not that I know of. I haven't had time, with work and Marjy's being sick. Why?" she demanded, suddenly suspicious. "You saw it all—don't you think it was just some drunken fool who got scared and didn't stop?"

Petrino shrugged, although his jaw was clenched, as he continued to maneuver the car. "Maybe you're right. Tell me, what do you remember?"

Amanda thought for a minute. "I saw the car coming, and I knew for sure he was going to hit me. I just moved without thinking. When I heard that crash I thought I was gone, and shut my eyes."

"Can you tell me what you remember about the car or driver?"

"The car—an old ugly brown 70s Mustang, but with chrome enough to still shine. The driver—a big burly guy, black, with a bald head. It all happened too fast and with the sun partially in my eyes for me to tell you any more. But it's funny—I could swear that the same car and driver were parked in front of my house earlier today."

Petrino countered eagerly, "Really? And did you know him? Recognize him?"

"I can't really say." Amanda was noncommittal.

Petrino glanced at her inquiringly as he turned a corner. "If you come up with anything else, you're to call me."

"Sure, but tell me why you are on patrol duty. Aren't you the Chief of Police?" Amanda wanted to know.

"I was just filling in for Eddie so he could be off today."

Amanda absently smoothed her lap, and pill bottle, the prescription slip and ointment fell to the floorboard. She retrieved them, asking Petrino, "Will you do me a favor and throw this away for me?" holding the bottle and slip of paper.

"You might just need that," he admonished, but she shook her head, dropping them in the seat beside her. Finding her purse, she opened it to deposit the tube of antibiotic. She leaned back in the seat, realizing how exhausted she felt.

They were driving down the street toward the Witherspoon residence. As they came in sight of the large estate, Amanda noted that although it was only about 5:00 there were lights on inside the residence, which sat in stately fashion at the end of an azalea-lined driveway. And in front of the house was an older brown Mustang, dented down the passenger side.

"Charlie," Amanda cried excitedly, pointing at Marjorie's. "That's the car. And I didn't leave lights on at Marjorie's. The timers are set for dark."

Petrino grabbed his microphone excitedly, calling for backup. He stopped in the driveway, the car partially shielded from view from the house by a row of crape myrtle trees. As he cut off the ignition, they could hear the insistent alarm. "You stay here," he half-whispered, as he pulled his revolver and quietly left the car.

Amanda gazed trance-like as Petrino slithered up to the house, then disappeared behind it. Almost immediately, she saw another police car come into the neighborhood and pull up in behind the Mustang. Two officers got out, guns drawn, and glanced inside the Mustang before making their way to the house. She saw them go in through the front.

As she gingerly eased herself out of the car, a third law enforcement vehicle pulled up, and one of the two officers came out and gave an all-clear signal. Then she noted Charlie walking out to the car.

"Amanda, there's been a break-in. No one is in the house, but apparently Marjorie had a safe that has been disturbed. Could you come in and tell me if you notice anything amiss?"

He held his hand out, as Amanda hobbled toward the house, Petrino supporting her. Stopping at the door, she inputted the code into the little box beside the door, silencing the alarm. Inside the home looked undisturbed except papers were scattered on the desk and on the floor around it, a picture was off the wall and the safe had been hammered with a sledgehammer, still nearby.

Petrino examined the safe, as the third cop was taking pictures and trying to find fingerprints to lift. "It looks clean," the officer said, dusting the safe with a brush.

One of the other officers came in. "Place is secured, sir," he informed Petrino.

Petrino turned to Amanda. "Did you know what was in it?"

Amanda nodded. "I'm pretty sure."

"Can you tell me if you think anything is missing inside?" Petrino inquired.

Amanda stepped over to the safe, and inside saw nothing but a velvet jewelry case. Inside, she found a double strand pearl necklace.

Petrino asked. "Do you know of anything else that should be in here?"

Amanda shook her head. "Not really. I had told Bill last night I would check to see if her will was in here, but I was pretty sure it wasn't. The pearls were worn by Marjy at dinner the night before she left for New York. I don't know of anything else; this was all I remember being in there that night. She kept most valuables and documents in her safe deposit boxes."

Petrino turned to the officer. "Did anything else look disturbed?"

"No, sir," the officer replied.

"Amanda, I hate to ask, but do you mind checking the place to see if everything is here?"

Amanda hobbled from room to room in the huge cavernous house with Petrino, trying to determine if anything was missing. As she opened drawers and cabinets, the haunting and familiar smells of lavender and cedar assaulted her, triggering memories of her times with Marjorie, of the hours she, Monica and Bill played together in the now huge silent rooms. As she finally turned to Charlie to report that she could find nothing gone, as if her thoughts had summoned him, there stood Bill Barnes.

"Billy," she breathed involuntarily as she looked at him in surprise. "What are you doing here?"

He looked at her intently, his face enigmatic. "I was at the hospital to see the Bishop. Father Anselm told me that you had an accident. I was coming to your place to check on you, and saw the cop cars all over Marjy's. Are you OK?"

Amanda replied tiredly, "Yes, I am fine. Charlie, I don't see anything missing, but I can't be sure. Wait a minute—I just thought of something."

Bill stepped forward. "Damn it, Charlie, after what she's just been through, can't you just put an officer to secure the place and get her off her feet?"

During Bill's tirade Amanda made her way back to the library, to the desk in front of the safe. She opened the desk drawers one by one. "They're missing."

"What?" asked Petrino excitedly, coming up behind her.

"Marjorie's laptop and her diskettes. We bought each other matching notebook computers, and kept in correspondence. She loved the internet and doing e-mail. I almost never asked a question with her around, because she would immediately start a Google search for the answer. She was addicted. But it's gone, and so are her diskettes. She was meticulous about keeping her correspondence, inventories, and stuff like that on disk."

Petrino started asking questions about details, taking notes as Amanda tried to recall information for him. "Anything else that you can think of?" he demanded.

"Sorry, no," Amanda shook her head.

"Enough, Charlie," Bill interrupted. "I'm taking Amanda home," he commanded. "Look at her. She's dead on her feet."

Amanda, suddenly realizing how sore she was and grateful for Bill's intervention but uncomfortable about being alone with him after his accusations earlier in the day, murmured her thanks as the two men helped her to Bill's car.

Petrino told her, "We'll secure the home, and put a detail on the place. I also want this car impounded and inventoried—checked for prints, other evidence. Amanda, I'll talk to you later—get some rest."

Alone with Bill in his cream-colored Cadillac sedan, Amanda said nothing, but closed her eyes, still smarting over their phone exchange earlier that day.

In a few moments, Bill pulled into her driveway. "Honey, we're home," Bill quipped lightly as he scrambled out of the car. He ran around to her door and opened it. "Here, take my arm, or—just wait a minute . . ." and before she could protest he reached down and bodily picked her up, kicked the door shut, and strode purposefully with her to her front door. "If Ralph can do it, then so can I. Where's the key?"

"It's probably unlocked."

"Damn it, Mandy," he rebuked her angrily, trying the door and finding it unlocked.

Amanda laughed. "Don't be so melodramatic. There are no murderers lurking inside."

Bill warned, "Shush," then gingerly set her down on the bench just outside the door. He quietly and carefully opened the door a crack and peered in, and raised the fingers of his left hand to his lips dramatically to motion her to silence. "Stay here," he whispered as he disappeared down the hall.

In a few moments he was back, apparently relieved. "All appears clear, and I checked the closets, the windows and doors. All is locked securely."

Again picking her up, he carried her into the living room and gently lowered her to the sofa. His face was close to hers. "Are you OK? I can always stay with you."

Amanda laughed nervously. "No, I'm a big girl."

"So you told me last night, then look what happened? You scare me, Mandy."

"I promise to put on the deadbolt as soon as you're gone," Amanda whispered conspiratorially.

"Are you going to tell me what happened?" Bill demanded, straightening up.

"Just some drunk hit-and-run."

Bill stood over her a moment. "Want me to get you anything—pills, a drink?"

Amanda, suddenly remembering her reaction to the bourbon from the previous evening, replied quickly, "No, thanks."

Bill sat down on the sofa beside her. Amanda tried not to stiffen as he took her hand in his. "I'm sorry about what I said earlier today over the phone. I was out of line," Bill beseeched her, gently kissing the scratches on her palms, his fingers lightly running up her arm.

Amanda held his gaze with her own. "Your accusations hurt, Bill—that was below the belt. You know me better than that. I would never do what—what you accused me of today . . . ." her voice trailed off as the memory of his words returned.

"I know, I know. First you passed out last night. Then when I heard you were injured this afternoon, I went out of my mind. There's something about you that always drives me a little crazy," he coaxed, pulling her toward him. He held her to him, stroking her hair. Amanda momentarily relaxed against him, tired and drained. It felt good to be held by someone. She pulled away to thank him, but saw the look in his eyes. As she tried to resist, he cupped her face with his left hand and kissed her slowly on the lips.

Amanda whispered, "Don't, Billy, this isn't right."

"It's Bill, now, remember? We're adults now. And this is the rightest thing I've ever done," he murmured huskily against her lips as his arms held her in a vise and his kiss deepened. Leaving her mouth to nuzzle her neck and running his hand down her torso, he continued, "You know you've always been special to me. God, how I loved it all those years when you looked at me with those puppy-dog eyes. I loved it even more when I got you riled, and you spit fire at me. Then I went and married Celeste—that was all Dad's idea. There's not a day passes I'm not sorry that I let you get away. Fate has dealt us some strange hands, but we're meant for each other, Amanda."

Amanda, her mind whirling, trying to extricate herself, pushed at his shoulders gently and said softly, "I saw your dad at the funeral yesterday. How is he?"

As she had anticipated, Bill released her, muttering a curse. "That son of a bitch. He's kept us apart too long, meddling in our lives."

Amanda rejoined gently, "He had nothing to do with it, and you know it. You are I have never been destined to be more than friends. If it hadn't been for Monica, you and I would never have run in the same circles. I outgrew my schoolgirl crush for you a long time ago, Bill. You and I have gone our separate ways, you with Celeste, and me with Andrew. It all turned out for the best."

Bill took her arm, his voice pleading. "I miss you so much, Mandy. All those good times, all those memories—you can't just push them aside. We're both alone now, and it's time we moved to the next level. You need me to look out for you, particularly now with Andy and Marjorie gone, and I need you to keep me in line. You want me too, if you would just admit it. What are you waiting for? Andy's not coming back, Mandy. But I'm here."

Amanda turned her face away as he stroked her cheek. Bill's words stung, but she had to acknowledge that they were true. What was she waiting for? And why not Bill? She said slowly, "Sometimes I just don't know what to think about you,

Bill, and the stunts you pull. But you've plenty of responsibilities and interests other than me. They even say you're running for judge next year." She continued quickly. "I'm just not on the make, Bill, and have no intentions of being another notch on your bedpost."

"That is unjust," growled Bill, his face flushing, his hand tightening on her arm as she winced.

Amanda laughed nervously, trying to shake him off. "Is it? You're just poor and pitiful right now because you don't have a Miss Texas currently hanging on your arm. This is Amanda you're talking to, remember?"

Bill not so gently pushed her back against the cushions, his mouth finding hers again and claiming her possessively, crushing her and stifling her cries of protest as one hand explored her breast. "There was a time when you longed for this. Your body still does. Mandy, don't deny it. You're driving me mad."

Too weak to push him away, she remained passive. It's been so long; why don't I reciprocate, just say yes to him? she wondered. One small spark of encouragement from me, and the deed would be done. I do want him, she thought, wanting badly to stir against him. No, she argued with herself, remaining still.

Exasperated, he finally released her. "Damn it, Mandy, don't be a cold fish. You know I would never hurt you. You're not like any of the others. We could be good together, Mandy. And you can't deny there was a time when you'd welcome my advances. What gives?"

"Don't go there," Amanda warned, her eyes flashing. "I'm no longer a silly schoolgirl with her heart on her sleeve. I don't love you that way, and truth be told, you don't love me either. So quit hitting on me."

Bill held up his hands in mock surrender. "How long does it take to convince you that we're destined to be together, Mandy? And what has love got to do with it? You can't deny the bond we've shared all these years since childhood. You know you're still attracted to me. I would be a good addition to your new status, and a good lover," he added, his hand running up her thigh to squeeze her butt. "Mmmm," he mumbled.

Amanda was having the same conversation with herself, and was almost convinced until she heard the words "new status". She stiffened and tried to sit up to distance herself from Bill.

Suddenly his face darkened. "But maybe there's someone else you've set your sights on? Someone else that is part of your future plans? Maybe it's your good buddy Ralph?" His hands grabbed her wrists.

Amanda's eyes flashed. "How dare you even suggest there's something going on between Ralph and me?" Angrily she tried to pull away, but he was too strong for her, and she was wedged on the couch with him between her and freedom. He positioned himself on top of her as she struggled. As he let go of one arm to grab her hair and force her down again roughly, she pushed against him and begged, "Please, Bill, there's no one. You're hurting me. Quit manhandling me."

His eyes locked on hers, and they stared at each other, both breathing hard, but their anger spent. She censured him softly, "I just think there's better for both of us than settling for something less than love."

He kissed her again, a punishing kiss, then let her go. "There's no such thing as true love, knights in shining armor, and living happily ever after, Mandy. You of all people know that." He sat up, and noticed her holding her wrist. "I'm sorry, girl," he added, suddenly contrite, taking it, rubbing it gently and kissing it. "It's just the thought of you with someone else drives me mad. I really didn't mean to get physical. Here you are, already banged up, and I come on like gangbusters."

"It's okay," Amanda responded automatically. *Now why did I just say that?* she wondered. *Why give him hope? Why not?* she argued with herself. *I'm so confused. I am still attracted to him. Aren't Bill's advances better than a lifetime of loneliness, longing for what I have lost forever?* "I'm just so tired and sore, and can't deal with you as Casanova right now," she finished weakly.

Standing up, he stated resignedly, "I know. My timing sucks. But I do love you, Mandy, as much as I've ever loved anyone in my life, although you don't believe it."

Amanda, unable to stop herself, queried, "Isn't it my 'new status' you love, Bill?"

Bill surprised her. Rather than being angry, he sat down animatedly. "Mandy, I don't give a rat's ass about your status. I've always wanted you. But don't you see, we could get Dad to accept you now that you are an heiress. We won't have him to worry about any more. We can be free to do as we wish."

Amanda took his hand in her own two and berated him tenderly. "But Bill, you are already free. You don't need his acceptance. I don't need his acceptance. Besides, what will you do if the diocese should oppose the will?"

Bill stared at her uncomprehendingly. "You just don't understand," he said flatly. "There's so much at stake here."

Amanda, alarmed, asked, "What? What is at stake? Bill, is there something you aren't telling me?"

Bill massaged his forehead tiredly. "No. I'm just trying to figure it all out in my head, Mandy. I want for everyone to be happy, and I'm trying to come up with a plan that does that. Maybe it's wrong of me to still want to please Dad. Let's not fight—just drop it."

He stood again, as though to dismiss the subject. Irritably he questioned, "Here, let me get you some water. Didn't Howells give you anything for pain?" He headed to the kitchen.

Amanda called, "If you insist, there a pitcher of iced tea in the fridge."

After several minutes he returned, a glass of ice tea wrapped in a tea towel, which he placed on a coaster on the table in front of her, a questioning look in his eyes.

Amanda averted her eyes before asking casually, "You didn't answer my question. How is your dad?"

"Goddammit, Mandy, this is not about him. The issue is us."

Amanda sighed. "Bill, I am genuinely concerned about you. The man raised you, even though his every contact with you seems to bring out the worst in you. And yesterday he was back in town. You're obsessed again with making him happy. I know how he gets to you."

Bill looked at her, frustration written on his face. He spat, "The man is busy terrorizing the finest private nursing facility the state of Alabama boasts. He still thinks he is judge, and carries on like royalty. He's constantly demanding, never satisfied. Nothing changes."

His face softened and turned contrite. He echoed, "Enough of that. Let's not fight. You look really tired."

"You are right—I'm really tired. A little rest and I'll be good to go tomorrow."

"Won't you let me stay?" he pleaded, running his fingers through her hair hopefully.

"No," Amanda insisted, finally shrugging free of his touch. *I'm so close to saying yes to him,* she thought with self-loathing. *It's nothing but my fear of loneliness.* "Get out of here," she smiled weakly.

"OK, I'll leave you alone if you insist. Get some rest and I'll check on you tomorrow. But neither of us has to be alone—let me help you. And, Mandy-girl, please promise me you'll be more careful."

"I promise," Amanda breathed slowly, barely concealing her desire to ask him to stay as he reached down and brushed her lips with his, caught both her hands, kissed her scratched palms, then quickly relinquished them and strode out the door.

After he left, Amanda, nervous at being alone, ignored the glass of tea, stumbled around and rechecked the locks on the doors, before going to run a warm bath. As she carefully unwrapped the ankle and the gauze over her knee, she ruefully remarked to herself, "That's going to leave a mark."

Chapter 9

While running her bath, Amanda tried to take her mind off her throbbing ankle. She retrieved the glass of tea and sipped it, her mind in the past. She thought of Bill's overtures with mixed emotions, a fact which surprised her, given her past interest in him and her long abstinence from intimate relations with the opposite sex. It would be so nice to hand all my affairs to a man and let him take care of me, she thought. And Bill would do so, to the extent of shutting her out of the informational and decision-making loop. That's what she didn't like. Bill was raised to think that women should be sheltered and remain at the mercy of their men's beck and call, something inimical to Amanda's independence, long-honed from necessity.

"He's so insufferable and egotistical," she said aloud. However, she knew that there was a time years ago when she felt very differently about him. The event awakened memories of a night years ago she had hoped to forget, when she almost made the ultimate fool of herself. She tried to close off her mind to the memory, but because of Bill's recent advances it kept pressing upon her.

During their senior year in college, about a year after Monica's death, Bill had showed up at her apartment late one night, very drunk. He pounded on the door and awakened her from a sound sleep. Still disheveled and groggy but concerned about her friend, she had let him in, plying him with coffee and sandwiches as he tried to engage her in banter.

The next thing she knew he had her in his arms. Caught off guard, her passion kindled for the one who had seemed forbidden to her for so long. Before her was the object of her long obsession, wanting to make love to her.

He hauled her against the wall and smothered her in embrace with a force that left her breathless, kissing her roughly and passionately. Without thinking she responded hungrily to him, cradling his head in her hands as she kissed him back. He ran his right hand down the buttons of her nightgown, expertly unbuttoning them with lightning speed, and cupped her breast in his hand, stroking her seductively. Desire overwhelmed her as he continued undressing her. She felt her mind whirling out of control, wanting nothing but to be with him, trying to close her mind to the warning bells in her head.

He whispered to her, "You've always wanted me, Mandy. Say it. I want to hear you admit it."

Amanda, her reason slipping away, moaned, "Yes, but Bill, I can't go through with this."

He pinned her to the wall with his body and caressed her skin. Amanda gasped at the sensations caused by his bare chest pressed to hers, heightened by his thigh thrust between hers as he molded himself to her. Bill murmured huskily, "Monica's dead. There is no one but you and me, here and now. This is our moment. You want me, and I want you. It's simple—give in to it."

Amanda panted, "But I don't live in the here and now. I never have. And there's no future in this."

"You'd live longer and have more fun if you'd learn to take life as it comes," he mumbled provocatively, as his tongue ran down her neck before he imprisoned her breast in his mouth. Her senses whirred. As his body continued to surround her, one hand reached inside her panties as he reached down with his other and unzipped his pants. At the sound cold reality set in. In panic she frantically tore herself away, gasping an excuse, running to the bathroom and shutting herself in, panting as she leaned against the door.

Amanda spent a small forever staring at herself in the mirror with loathing, torn, her loyalty to her dead friend and her strict Christian upbringing, warring against her long hidden schoolgirl crush for Bill. Until this night she had always held her feelings in check, but after Monica's death whenever his path crossed hers she felt the mask slipping. She had managed to counter his relentless teasing with a carefully contrived facade of indifference, matching his flirtations with calculated barbs and put-downs.

She knew, staring in the mirror, that she wanted to know what it felt like to act on this long latent lust. However, she realized in that one cold moment of clarity that as much as she had longed for an opportunity to be with Bill, she couldn't go through with it. There was nothing casual about the sex act to her, and she knew there was nothing serious about Bill's coming on to her. She was well aware of his reputation around campus as a ladies' man, and of his father's disdain for her as a suitable companion for his son. Her parents' strict Baptist discipline had instilled a moral code into her nature which she was unable to breach, even in order to fulfil a fantasy. And Bill was ever obsessed with making his father proud of him, seeking his father's stamp of approval on everything he did. No, there was no future with Bill.

Her mind resolved to deny him, she had returned to the bedroom, where she had found Bill sprawled on her bed, fast asleep. Looking at him for a long time, she came to the realization that Bill was not what she really wanted. The epiphany grew that she was content with the unrequited banter of wills between them. She realized that Bill was nothing more than a flirt and playboy, and she was not emotionally equipped for a casual fling. Deep inside she still harbored a dream of giving herself to someone who would be hers alone, and knew that she would be unhappy settling for less.

Later Andrew had reappeared in her life, and she found the fulfillment she craved. But then Andrew had been suddenly and brutally torn from her. Now the familiar lion still periodically circled and teased his prey. The difference was that after that night she had not been tempted by Bill's flirtations, at least until now; in fact, although she kept telling herself she should be flattered by his attention, she kept fending him off. What am I waiting for? she wondered to herself irritably, suddenly unaccountably angry at herself.

Pondering over what Bill had said, Amanda was not blind to the fact that Bill saw in her a chance to merge her new fortune to his and bend his father to his will, making Barnes Sr. accept her as a suitable wife while Bill exerted his influence over her yet again. But had this somehow become a paramount goal for Bill? Why? She thought back to his words: "There's so much at stake here." Nothing made sense.

Amanda's thoughts suddenly focused on Marjorie's last words to her: "Watch out for Billy." It seemed that even Marjorie was trying to push her into Bill's waiting arms, which seemed incongruous given Marjorie's past remarks of disapproval at Bill's reckless perennial pursuit of Amanda. Maybe Marjorie had no faith that I could carry on alone, Amanda thought unhappily, and was trying to steer me toward another guardian. What a sad specimen I must be. Or, Amanda reflected soberly, maybe Marjorie was warning me to steer clear of him and his advances, that she was convinced he was not good for me.

Shaking her head to clear her mind from reminiscing, she took another sip of the tea. I really need to brew a new pitcher—this doesn't taste as good, she mulled irrelevantly. Her mind leaped to the day's accident and the driver of the brown Mustang. Grateful to think of anything else, she wondered who would want to run over her. There's probably a queue, she thought ruefully. Not all my appointed clients have been happy campers, and God knows there have been more than a few disgruntled persons on the opposing side.

Allowing herself to relive the accident, she speculated on the driver. She only glimpsed him for a second, but why did he seem familiar? Drinking her iced tea, she tried to recollect from where she might have met someone who looked like him. Was it the same car that was in front of her house? Of course it was; how many cars like that would be found in Mainville? And why was the car found at Marjorie's home? Why did he break in there, and what was he looking for? Why were the computer and diskettes taken, but not the pearls or silver?

Then thoughts of the interview with Arthur that morning surfaced. Why was he copying the ledgers? What was he looking for, and for whom? Was he being truthful that he didn't break in and go through the office? Who else would have broken in and why?

Returning to the bathroom, glass in hand, she regarded her mussed appearance in the mirror. She realized she had not checked in with her partner, and debated about calling Ralph, but decided he had probably gone home for the day. She drank a deep draught as she headed to the bathroom.

She soaked in the bathtub, trying to ease the soreness setting in from her rude contact with the sidewalk. She gingerly washed her lacerations and noted that the ankle was not as swollen as she had feared, only tender. She tried not to let her anger rise over the damage to her car or shoes. Get a grip, she told herself brusquely. Better them than you. She drank her tea, holding the cold glass against her cheek a moment.

Thoughts of Andrew came unbidden to her mind. Amanda closed her eyes and longed for his kiss, his touch, his voice. She thought brutally, Quit haunting my dreams, my days and nights. Nothing is going to change the fact that you're never coming back—can't we leave that door shut?

Her mind flowed in an unfettered stream of consciousness. She thought of Andrew's voice saying, "Be careful," just as he did every morning before they would leave for work. Marjorie's letter, Attorney Feinstein's words, and now Bill's warning her to be careful were enough to make anyone paranoid, she thought as she took another drink of her tea.

Completing her ablutions, she stumbled drunkenly getting out of the tub. She felt strangely lethargic as a headache asserted itself. She went to her closet and settled on a pale cream pant outfit. She sat down on the sofa, letting her hair air-dry and rewrapping her ankle, as she drank more tea. Funny how drowsy she felt.

The telephone rang, jarring her back into reality. "Hello," she said tentatively into the receiver.

"Ralph here. Where have you been?"

"Oh, I'm glad you called. I need a favor. You see, my car's in the hospital, and I need a lift to work in the morning," Amanda cut to the chase in order to avoid a long explanation.

"What happened?" he demanded.

"My car was hit, and I was tied up most of the afternoon with that," responded Amanda, grimacing at her gloss-over of the facts.

"Are you OK?" he asked solicitously.

"A little sore, but fine," she answered, wincing as she shifted her weight on her ankle.

"You sure?"

Amanda felt a stab of nausea. Trying to ignore it, she replied, "Yes, as long as you don't mind being my chauffeur tomorrow. I have that arraignment at 9:00 at the courthouse, and need to pick up the file at the office. Then Sheila can probably get me a rental car."

"OK—7:30 again?"

"Fine," she assented, as the doorbell rang. Thank God, she thought. I can avoid a long explanation to Ralph. "There's someone at the door—talk to you later."

Hobbling to the door, she peered out the security peephole, sighed then opened the door, her headache asserting itself more prominently.

"Mrs. Childs?" a faintly familiar sensuous baritone voice greeted her. "I've not been lucky in making contact with you about that appointment. I hope you are not one of those attorneys who never return phone calls."

Amanda started guiltily. "I'm sorry, Mr. 'Thomson', is it? Ralph did tell me you called the office, and I've just not had the opportunity to call back."

"Please call me Connor. May I come in?"

She paused awkwardly. "Certainly."

"Thank you," he said, as she reluctantly relented and stepped aside to allow him to enter. "I am sorry to hear of your accident today. Father Anselm told me when I visited the hospital this evening."

Amanda, suddenly remembering her appointment with the Bishop and looking at her watch confusedly, realized that it was 7:30. "Oh, no, I have compounded matters by missing the meeting with the Bishop."

"That's quite all right, Mrs. Childs," asserted Connor briskly as he glided past her into the room. "The Bishop is being transported to Pensacola tonight for more extensive treatment. Although Bishop Marks seems rather imperious, apparently his authority has been overruled by his cardiologist, and in any event you would have been unable to see him."

She noted that Connor's eyes quickly scanned the room, which was pleasantly but austerely decorated. The interior walls, like the outside, were painted a pale gray, and the trim was set off in white. The walls were bare except for one abstract print over the mantel. Likewise the furnishings were spartan and devoid of items expressing the owner's individual personality.

Connor patiently waited for Amanda to lead the way as she continued to look at him woodenly. "I know it is the ultimate breach of the Southern code of etiquette for a stranger to pursue you to your *sanctum sanctorum*, but hope that you will not mind my bothering you for a few minutes."

She pointed to the club chair by the sofa and indicated for him to sit, while she slowly and painfully regained her former position at the sofa. Lightheaded and queasy, she stumbled just before reaching the sofa, and he quickly reached out to steady her, his hand making contact with her waist.

"Are you sure you're all right?" he questioned anxiously.

Unnerved by his closeness and her sudden physical discomfort, she murmured an embarrassed thanks and sank to a sitting position. Although she felt strangely, she was able to note that he was again dressed impeccably, jacketless in tailored trousers, with white shirt and royal blue tie. He waited for her to be seated before settling himself in the chair, leaning forward slightly to face her.

Connor began the conversation. "Ah—I see you have not checked your answering machine yet."

Amanda colored as she followed his gaze to the end table, where the answering machine was impatiently blinking. He doesn't miss much, she mused. She smiled politely. "I must apologize—this has been far from a normal day. How may I help you?" God, she prayed, please make the headache stop and let him be quick and out of here.

Connor's return smile dazzled her. "You are certainly a paragon of the direct approach. I didn't want to take any more chances of missing you, and I'm not a man who likes to wait."

Amanda mentally sized him up, well believing that he was accustomed to having things his way.

Connor continued. "Let me begin by assuring you that I am sincerely sorry for the loss of your friend Mrs. Witherspoon. She was a wonderful woman. It was the height of rudeness for me to accost you so soon while you are still grieving and obviously in shock. Sometimes in the zeal of pursuing business and juggling schedules we lose sight of what is happening around us. But that does not excuse my conduct."

Amanda felt another pang of nausea, and swallowed quickly. "I was not expecting your news, much less accusations of improper conduct."

Connor, contrite, replied, "I assumed that the Bishop asked the Rev. Brownlee to accompany me only for the purpose of smoothing our introduction. I apologize for unwittingly being the vehicle to aggravate any animus that exists between you and Brownlee."

Amanda laughed shortly. "I only met Mr. Brownlee yesterday when the Bishop collapsed. I also was clueless to the alleged 'animus', as you put it, other than he obviously lacked the Southern graciousness to which we are accustomed in these parts."

Connor looked nonplussed. "Oh. I seem to keep making matters worse with my assumptions. If you please, let's start over." Leaning forward and proffering his hand to her, he continued, "How do you do? I am Connor. It is nice to meet you."

Amanda, mollified, took his hand solemnly, feeling the warmth and pressure of his grip. "Likewise, Connor. Please call me Amanda."

"I know you are tired and probably sore from your ordeal, Amanda, and I won't keep you. But in the spirit of our newfound acquaintance and to show your acceptance of my apologies, I wonder if you would do me the honor of joining me for dinner while I am here. I realize that you are still in mourning, and it is presumptuous of me to impose. However, as a stranger in town, I am unfamiliar with the local color, and it would be so much more pleasant to explain my *raison d'etat*, loosely speaking, in surroundings more congenial than the church or your office."

Amanda looked into his compelling eyes and took a breath, trying to maintain her composure although her stomach was inexplicably churning and her head spinning. "I do not wish to seem ch—churlish, but neither do I want to waste your time. I'm afraid that you really are chasing the wrong squirrel, inasmuch as I am not serving as treasurer or on the vestry. I fail—to see how I can be of use." She was having trouble expressing her thoughts. *What's wrong with me?*

Connor paused. "You see, the Presiding Bishop's records listed you as the church treasurer. I have been corrected on that point."

It was Amanda's turn to pause as she took in what Connor said. It seemed that her mind was working in slow motion. "Bill Barnes has been the treasurer for quite some years now," she replied slowly, her voice sounding far away. "While I served as junior warden and vestry member for a couple terms, I have never served, nor aspired to serve, as treasurer." She paused a moment. "Maintaining the office trust accounts, the church recital series fund, and my checking account is more than enough accounting for me, thank you very much. But what you are saying makes sense, because from time to time mail would come addressed to me as church treasurer, and I always just turned it around unopened to Bill, attributing it to clerical error."

"But Mr. Barnes is the diocesan treasurer, is he not?" Connor asked innocently.

"Yes, he serves both the diocese and St. Catherine's. Not too long after Bishop Marks was ordained, the diocesan treasurer resigned, and Bill, whose father and the Bishop were old friends and distant kin, just offered to do the diocesan affairs without charge." She paused, swallowing hard to fight a wave of nausea. "I just assumed (there I go, but I was not serving on the vestry then) that the vestry received official sanction for Bill to perform both functions. Is that a problem?" questioned Amanda, trying to anticipate where Connor was going with this line of questioning.

"I don't know that he has broken any accounting procedures in this state, but like attorneys, accountants must in business avoid all appearance of impropriety. Mr. Barnes has agreed to cooperate in providing all the information we request.

"However, my request for dinner with you serves a double purpose. Because of your close involvement with the church and its mission, you could be of immense help in filling me in on some history. But more importantly, a mutual friend of ours told me that if I was in the area, I should look you up."

Amanda, trying to focus as she casually sipped some tea, queried, "And who might that be?"

"A former colleague of yours—an attorney named Alex Roberts."

"Alex! And just how do you know Alex?"

"We were roommates in college. I ran into him last week, and over a few drinks he had some stories to tell about the days you both served as public defenders."

Amanda colored slightly. "We did work closely together several years ago, and he and his wife Mary remain dear friends of mine. I haven't seen them in a while."

"Yes, he mentioned that you haven't seen a lot of your friends in the last few years."

A shuttered look came over Amanda. Just then, the telephone rang. "Excuse me, please," murmured Amanda, reaching for the receiver as another pang of nausea hit her.

"Amanda," the male voice greeted her. "I just wanted to check on you and make sure you made it home all right."

"Yes, Charlie, thank you. I am OK, just a little shook up."

"Is there anything you need? Would you like a unit placed outside your house to keep an eye on you?"

Amanda thought a minute, her thoughts cloudy and wandering.

"Amanda, are you there?"

Coming to herself, she realized that she didn't want to become a prisoner in her own home. "That's very nice of you, but I'm sure it was some fluke. I realize the car's being at Marjorie's seems highly coincidental, but there could be any number of explanations. The driver could have happened to ditch the car there. Any number of people knew about Marjorie's death, and the burglary may not even be related." Her voice seemed to fade away at the end.

"Well, I wanted you to know we are checking all the angles. I will let you know when we find anything. I have someone watching the Witherspoon residence, and a locksmith coming to check the safe and doors. He'll be contacting you for instructions tomorrow. An officer will be patrolling your area. If you think of something or need anything, please contact me. Are you sure you're OK?"

"Yes. Thanks, Charlie," Amanda said shakily as she replaced the receiver.

Connor regarded her. "So the car was found? Where?" he asked flatly.

"At Marjorie Witherspoon's home," Amanda replied confusedly, surprised at his question, but concluding that he was only listening to her conversation with Petrino. "We found the place burglarized this afternoon. But they have no leads yet."

He gazed at her for a full minute, and Amanda felt herself getting warm. She reached again for the glass of tea, her hand shaking convulsively, and took another deep drink as Connor continued, frowning as he regarded her intently. "It is my understanding that you have been the church musician for approximately ten years, and have had close relationships with several of the members, including Mrs. Witherspoon."

"That is correct," replied Amanda simply, then suddenly stood as a wave of nausea hit. "Excuse me," she gulped, knocking over the glass and bolting from the room.

Closing the bathroom door, she barely made it to the toilet before repeating her performance of the previous evening. After several moments of retching she shakily stood, bathed in a cold sweat, and washed her face in cold water at the lavatory as the room reeled. What is wrong with me? she thought irritably, gripping the vanity in desperation.

She heard Connor's voice outside the door. "Amanda, are you all right?"

She stood at the lavatory for a moment and dried her face. She opened the door, trying to act nonchalant, but fell into Connor's arms as her knees gave way under her and the room spun. He caught her, picked her up and strode into the bedroom with her.

She was barely aware of her surroundings as he gently placed her on her bed and knelt over her. "Amanda? Can you hear me? Are you ill?"

"A bug of some sort. I was out of it last night too. I'll be OK," she muttered, her voice slurred. "I feel better already."

Connor lifted her eyelids and looked into her dilated eyes, and felt her wrist for her fluttering pulse. "I'm calling Dr. Howells. I think I should get you to the emergency room."

"No need," whispered Amanda, trembling. "I tell you, it must be some kind of flu. It's just that I'm almost never sick, and it comes on so fast." She smiled, trying to convince Connor that she was feeling better than she was, although she was chilled to the bone and his face was out of focus.

Connor flipped open his cell phone, dialing a number. "Dr. Howells, this is Connor Thomson. I'm at Amanda Childs' home, and she has just had another episode like last night. She refuses to let me take her to the emergency room, saying it is the flu. Would you mind terribly coming over?"

Amanda protested faintly as he turned his back to her. "Thank you very much, Doc. I'll let you in."

Connor gazed at her anxiously as she lay shivering. In one fluid motion he whipped off the quilt neatly folded at the foot of the bed, and sitting next to her, wrapped her in it and held her to him. "My God, you're cold as ice. Do you have extra blankets?"

She looked at him uncomprehendingly. Suddenly his face changed, and she reached out to him. "Andy," she whispered, clutching at him.

He gently propped her back against the pillows. "Lie still." He reached for a decorative wool throw draped over a chair and wrapped it around her. "I'm going to let the doctor in. I'll be right back."

Before she could demur, he had left the room. Rising shakily to follow him, she felt an overwhelming fatigue take over, and the room whirled and grew dark.

The next thing she remembered, Dr. Howells was sitting beside her. She felt a fog surrounding her as he pulled a thermometer out of her mouth and spoke to her, asking her what she had eaten, what had she done during the day. Connor appeared, a cup in his hand. Dr. Howells took it from him and held it to Amanda's lips, urging her to sip. It was hot coffee, and Amanda looked questioningly at Connor.

"Fresh from a deli down the street," he replied shortly.

After several minutes, Amanda felt more alert. As she tried to focus on answering questions posed by Howells, Connor strode back into the room, dropping two unlabeled medicine bottles on the bed in front of her and Howells.

"What's this?" Howells asked sharply.

"Perhaps Ms. Childs can tell us," Connor asserted coolly. "One was open on her kitchen counter, another in the bar alongside a half-empty bottle of Wild Turkey."

Howells emptied the bottles' contents into his hand and looked at the pills curiously, then at Amanda. Amanda stared transfixed at his outstretched hand.

"Looks like alprazolam," Connor answered the unspoken question.

"And I found these under the cushion of the sofa," Connor continued, his eyes piercing Amanda coldly as he handed another bottle to Howells, who examined the contents.

"Hydrocodone? Oh dear God, Amanda." Howells' voice was tense. "That's not what I gave you for pain. Where did you get these, Amanda?" he inquired, his face drawn and solemn. He visibly aged before her.

"I've never seen these before," Amanda whispered tremulously.

"Amanda, I need to know the truth from you if I am going to help you. This stuff is nothing but bad news. Are you experiencing pain? Why would you be taking these? Are you taking alcohol with them as well?" Howells interrogated her sternly.

Amanda gazed at the doctor, her eyes brilliant. "I swear, Doc, I don't know where they came from. No, I haven't been drinking."

Connor looked at her dubiously, but Howells returned the pills to the bottle and took her hand in his. "I'll need some more blood, Mandy. How do you feel?"

Amanda squeezed his hand weakly. "I'm better. Maybe throwing up helped."

Connor disappeared again while Doctor Howells expertly drew more blood. When he started discussing removing her to the hospital, Amanda rallied and objected. Feeling her strength and alertness return as it did the previous evening, she sat up shakily and argued him into submission, refusing offers of assistance.

Shaking his head with frustration, Howells, took her hand. "You do trust me, Amanda? You would tell me if something is going on?"

Amanda squeezed his hand. "I trust you with my life. I would not lie to you, Doc, and I would not take anything without consulting you."

Connor returned with a bowl of soup and some crackers on a tray. Placing the tray on Amanda's lap, he looked sternly at her. "Eat it—let's see if we can counteract the damage."

Continuing to look at her, Connor asked flatly, "Amanda Childs, what are you doing in possession of drugs like that without a prescription? You got some death wish? Self-medicating for depression or something?"

Amanda looked at him bewildered. "I'm not a druggie, if that's what you are asking. All I've had today was a couple of chips and—and a glass of iced tea," she finished lamely.

Howells quelled Connor to silence with a look, waving him into the next room as Amanda picked up a spoon and tentatively tasted the soup. She listened intently.

Once outside the bedroom door, she heard Connor demanding, "You are going to admit her to the hospital, aren't you? Doesn't she need her stomach pumped? She's a danger to herself, if nothing else. This explains last night."

She could hear Howells reply tiredly, "I can't believe that. She refuses to go." His voice lowered, and Amanda could not hear him. "I'll get lab results quickly. I'll make the decision then. In any event I'm not leaving her alone tonight. We'll go from there."

Howells returned to the bedroom. Amanda still sipped the soup, and color was returning to her face. Howells sat quietly watching as she ate the soup, then sat and held her hand as Connor took the tray away.

After a while, Howells listened to her heart again and asked, "How are you now?"

"Better," she nodded. "I don't understand it. Two nights in a row."

"Nausea?"

"It seems to have subsided—just a headache," she replied, rubbing her temple.

The doctor patted her hand, resignation in his voice. "You win, Amanda. I am running the blood to the hospital, and will return. Mr. Thomson will stay here until I return. And you need to stay in tomorrow if possible."

Amanda smiled tightly, and Howells knew she intended to defy his last words of advice. Sighing, he placed the pill bottles in his bag. Connor, standing in the bedroom doorway, escorted him out, then returned.

Connor sat down in the chair beside the bed as Amanda propped against pillows. She could feel his eyes scrutinizing her. Amanda, drawn and pale, could think of nothing to say as he continued to regard her silently for several minutes, then looked around the room. The bedroom was also bare of personalty except for one picture on the dresser. Walking over to it, he picked it up and examined it. The picture was of Malcolm Howells and Marjorie Witherspoon dancing at a formal affair.

Amanda watched him. "That was at my wedding reception. Doc gave me away, and Marjorie planned the whole thing."

Connor nodded silently, replacing the picture and coming back to sit beside her. "I notice you're not keen on folderols."

"Folderols?" Amanda echoed uncomprehendingly.

"My grandmother's term for decorative items, pictures, knick-knacks," Connor's hand swept the room.

"The place is functional, which is all that matters," Amanda replied defensively, looking away.

"You got any other drugs stashed away in here?" Connor asked bluntly, his jaw set.

Amanda's cold eyes whipped around and met his. "Why don't you search for yourself?" she challenged tremulously.

"Don't mind if I do," Connor sprang up, opening the closet and running his hands through her clothes. He began opening drawers and feeling inside as Amanda caught her breath sharply at his audacity, her mouth open in surprise. As he finished, the doorbell rang.

Connor left the room, and momentarily Dr. Howells returned with him. Howells was firm. "I'm going to stay with her. I'll sack out on the couch. If she is no better by the time of my 6:00 rounds, I'll bundle her off to the hospital."

Amanda sighed resignedly. "I'm much better, Doc."

"I'll be glad to stay as well," Connor stated emphatically. Amanda shook her head. What a strange man.

Howells shook his head as well. "I've got her from here."

Connor turned to her, his look softening as he shrugged. "You've had a traumatic day. But if you are better tomorrow, the dinner invitation still holds. I would be happy to pick you up here about 7:00. If you are not up to going out, I'll bring dinner to you."

Amanda surprised herself by accepting, as Howells looked on, his brow furrowed. Connor took her hand briefly, a questioning look in his eyes, then strode toward the door.

Amanda called weakly, "You have my permission to search the entire house and confiscate any drugs you find, if you don't believe me."

"I've already taken the liberty of doing so," he said tightly, not looking back as he exited.

Howells murmured, "Nice man, isn't he?"

Amanda laughed shortly. "There's a patient for you. Got a case of bipolar disorder, if you ask me. One minute he's charming; the next he comes on like a cop about to make an arrest. Go figure."

Chapter 10

Amanda woke to find Howells sitting beside her bed. She stretched and groaned as her sore limbs rebelled and her head screamed obscenities. "What time is it? Have you been watching me all night?"

"A little after five o'clock," he advised softly. "And I've gotten some rest. You've been dead to the world, girl. I've kept checking your vitals, but you never stirred. How do you feel?"

"A little bleary, and my head hurts," she replied. Suddenly remembering, she asked, "What about the labs? What caused this, Doc?"

Howells answered with another question. "What did you do after you left the ER yesterday?"

Amanda tried to think. "Charlie was taking me home, and we went by Marjy's. There was a break-in. Then Bill showed up and brought me home. Then Connor Thomson was here. That's it." She paused. "The door was unlocked, but why would someone leave drugs in my home? Why?"

"You don't know where the pills came from?"

Amanda's eyes glistened from tears. "I swear, Doc, I've never seen them before. I do not know."

"Did you have anything to drink?"

She shook her head vigorously under his scrutiny.

Howells remarked gravely, "I took a grave risk not admitting you to the hospital last night. There was a high probability of overdose in your system, two nights in a row. You could have died." He paused for emphasis. "At the hospital I would have had more resources to counteract the damage." He paused, his eyes softening. "Thankfully, I think your reaction to drugs and regurgitation actually saved you. Thank God—from what I read sometimes the drugs inhibit the gag reflex. Based on the lab results I gambled on the drug's quick elimination rate." He paused, his eyes brilliant with unshed tears. "I love you too much to take that risk again, Amanda." His meaning was unmistakable. "Next time I won't take 'no' for an answer. I'll commit you involuntarily if that is the way to protect you."

Amanda closed her eyes, the tears close. Doc doesn't believe me, she thought. She stirred, realizing that she was still fully dressed. "I've got to get ready for court this morning."

Howells was firm. "You need to stay where you are."

"And would you stay in bed if you had patients who needed you? I know you better than that. And Shanna needs me this morning," Amanda was equally firm. "Get out of here—I've wasted enough of your time, and you're much too expensive to make these overnight house calls."

Howells shrugged and kissed her cheek as he stood. "I expect to hear from you by noon as to your status, or I'll send cops and paramedics."

"Deal," she whispered, noting his shining eyes as he took his leave.

When Ralph Carmichael appeared in dark suit, blue shirt and yellow tie at her front door, Amanda was waiting. She broke with her self-imposed moratorium on taking medicine, swallowed two aspirin tablets for the residual headache, and wore extra makeup to cover her pallor. She decided on a black pant suit and flat heels to minimize the appearance of her injuries. However, as she met Ralph at the door, as best she tried she could not conceal the limp.

Ralph looked at her suspiciously. "Horseback riding?" he asked sardonically.

"Skiing accident," she retorted with the best smile she could muster. "Ready?" she continued, trying to change the subject.

Ralph escorted her to his car. They were quiet several minutes as Ralph drove, his jaw clenched. Amanda knew that look and decided to wait him out.

"Are you going to tell me about the accident?" he finally growled.

"Just some hit-and-run outside the church. Ruined a fine pair of shoes, scratched me up, and crashed my car."

"Police catch him?" Ralph wanted to know.

"Not yet," Amanda informed him.

"Incompetent bastards," Ralph swore under his breath, pulling into the parking lot behind the office. "I thought we had made a major improvement by electing Charlie Petrino as chief. Do you need to come into the office? If you will tell me what you need, I'll get it for you."

"Just the file—there's not much in it. The clerk has copies of the probable cause affidavits at the courthouse for me, and my client is being brought by the juvenile authorities at 8:30 so that we can talk before the case is called. I filed a motion for adversarial probable cause hearing—hope I'm right."

Ralph looked her over closely as he parked in front of the office. "A little heavy on the makeup this morning—are you sure you're OK?" he commented, his eagle eyes missing nothing. At Amanda's stony silence, he sighed, exiting the vehicle without waiting for an answer.

Amanda waited quietly as Ralph went in the office to retrieve the file. She tried to concentrate on the morning's agenda, having promised to represent one of the minors Marjorie had previously befriended who had recently been arrested.

Ralph, re-entering the car, handed her a red file folder. "Sheila is worth her weight in gold," he said. "She has already picked up the clerk's documents, and wheedled investigation reports out of the police department for you."

Amanda scanned the file as Ralph drove to the courthouse. He inquired, "Who's the client?"

"It's Shanna Arguelles, from the church youth group. Remember Pedro, the guy that did yard work for Marjorie and is starting his own business? She's his niece. He used to have her work some with him, to keep her out of trouble. She's fourteen and charged with principal to armed burglary and grand theft along with some other kids, bad kids. Marjorie was encouraging her to get out of that neighborhood. Her grandmother and aunt in the neighboring county were willing to take her, but the school district and high school athletic association have been fighting over whether Shanna could change schools and continue to play volleyball. Volleyball and violin are all she's interested in, other than hanging with these kids that keep getting her into trouble."

"Well, once in a gang, it's hard to get out," Ralph interjected.

"Well, according to Pedro, word on the street was that this incident was to be her initiation into the gang. But for a screwup at the detention center, she'd have been right in the middle of it. I'm going to try to get her out of this town and with her aunt. It's the only chance she has, or the juvenile delinquency folks will have her locked down with the really bad criminals and she won't be able to play sports. You know, she is a good kid, and has a talent with the violin."

"And she's a mean volleyball player, too," Ralph chimed in. "She almost knocked my head off at the church social a couple months back."

Pulling in front of the courthouse, he let Amanda out, who gingerly made her way in the courthouse, greeting the security officers. Heading up in the elevator with one of them, they chatted amicably until the elevator opened on the fourth floor. Amanda hobbled to a group of people standing outside a courtroom, and found her client, a tall, muscular girl, in shackles and dressed in detention garb.

Making arrangements to talk privately with the girl in an interview room, Amanda reviewed paperwork with her and discussed her case, until a bailiff came to the room to inform them that court was being called into session. The case was announced as Amanda and her client entered the courtroom, and they quickly moved to the front and took their place at the podium before a thin gray-haired severe-looking man in black robe.

"Shanna Arguelles appearing, represented by Amanda Childs," Amanda stated rapidly, the court reporter taking down her words. "Your Honor, my client has been arrested on a violation of conditions of supervised release, and an underlying charge of principal to burglary of an occupied dwelling. We plead not guilty, and I have filed a motion to dismiss the information, and in the alternative request release on recognizance or immediate adversarial probable cause hearing."

"On what grounds?" asked the judge, reviewing the pleadings handed him and not looking up.

"While it is true that Ms. Livingston was accused of being an accomplice in the charging document, you will note that none of the affidavits signed by witnesses describe or name her as one of the perpetrators. Furthermore, the defendant was still in the custody of the juvenile authorities on the night of the burglary."

The judge turned to the clerk of court and requested the file. Reviewing a document, he remarked severely, "Counselor, the notice to appear signed by your client shows that the defendant was released last Tuesday."

Amanda countered, "But, Your Honor, please note that the release sheet reflects that the juvenile authorities actually held Ms. Livingston in secure detention until the next day."

The judge looked at the file again, angry spots appearing on his cheeks. "How does the State respond?"

The prosecutor, a young lanky guy loosely garbed in a brown suit, nervously stood. "Your Honor, the State has not had time to interview the witnesses to determine the reason for the discrepancies. However, we are standing by the charges until I've had a chance to review the case."

Amanda protested icily, "I'm sure that once the prosecutor finds time in his busy schedule to prepare his case, he will still be without probable cause to pursue this matter. I am taking the liberty of providing the Court and the State with copies of the police investigation reports, and the victim witnesses stated to law enforcement that my client, known to them, was not seen in the group that broke in. I am unaware of any other evidence linking my client to the charge, other than she was with the wrong people when the arrest warrants were served."

The judge turned back to Amanda. "Counselor, your point is well taken. I can and will dismiss the information based on the face of the record. You realize that means that the State can refile the charges if or when it figures out what it is doing," he continued, throwing a baleful glance at the prosecutor.

The prosecutor jumped up, "Your Honor, we object, and do intend to pursue prosecution."

The judge replied, "I knew you'd say that—objection overruled. Ms. Childs, what is the status of your client's living arrangements upon release?"

Amanda responded, "Your Honor, she has a grandmother and aunt residing in the next county, which is part of this Court's jurisdiction. The home has been tentatively approved for placement by the child services agency. Inasmuch as she was previously adjudicated a dependent child, I am asking that the Court release her to her relatives and order that she be allowed to transfer to that school district.

I have here her mother's written consent and executed power of attorney in favor of the aunt. I believe that the child services agency representative, her caseworker and their attorney are present this morning and on notice that we intend to make this request. And her aunt is here and willing to answer any questions."

After further discussion and confirmation by the parties, the Court ruled in Amanda's favor and released the girl to her aunt. Amanda quickly and quietly spoke to her client, admonishing her to keep clean and giving the girl her card. As they moved toward the courtroom doors, Shanna, her shackles released by the authorities, threw her arms around Amanda's neck.

"I'm so sorry about Miss Marjorie," she cried. "I promise I won't let her down."

Amanda put her finger to her lips to remind the girl to be silent as she hugged Shanna back. In a low voice Amanda told her, "And now you know where bad decisions might land you. Call me, and please don't give your aunt any trouble. That's what Miss Marjorie would have wanted. I'll figure out how you can play volleyball at the new school, if I have to beat up the high school athletic association myself. Keep practicing, and do your best in school."

Amanda added quietly as they moved down the aisle of the courtroom, "I may be out of town on some business the next few days. If you need me, you can call Mr. Carmichael. He'll help you in any way, and knows how to reach me."

Watching the ecstatic girl leave with her relative and caseworker, Amanda started to follow her out of the courtroom. The bailiff interrupted her. "Ms. Childs, the judge is calling for you."

Amanda, surprised, turned back. The judge acknowledged her and waved her forward. "Mrs. Childs, will you approach the bench?"

Amanda came forward to stand before the bench and face the judge. He regarded her solemnly, his voice low. "Mrs. Childs, you know if there's anything I can do . . . ," he paused awkwardly, as if unused to kindness. "I know you and Marjorie Witherspoon were close. She thought a great deal of you."

Amanda said feelingly, "Thank you, Judge Kilmer; that means a lot to me."

The clerk called the next case, and Amanda briefly shook the sullen prosecutor's hand before exiting the courtroom.

Once out in the hallway, she looked around for Ralph, when she felt a hand on her arm and was wheeled around. Too surprised to say anything, she looked into the eyes of Bill Barnes.

"What are you doing here?" he hissed quietly. Dressed in a dark suit, he looked handsome and exuded confidence.

"Hi, Bill," Amanda found her voice. "What a lovely greeting. I'm happy to see you too. Where did you expect me to be?"

He backed her up against the wall, placing one hand on the cool marble behind her head. "The question is how are you? You don't take care of yourself. Are you ever going to learn to take your doctor's advice?"

"How do you know I'm not doing so?" her voice was even and betrayed no emotion.

"You're pale," he murmured. "And I talked to Dr. Howells last night about you."

"You did what?" Amanda was astounded. "You have no business prying," she added hotly.

"I'm not prying; I'm looking out after you," Bill's tone was gentle. "I called your home this morning; you did not answer. I went by your office this morning to see you. Found out you were here, and also found out you're free the rest of the day. Your mediation cancelled." He smiled at her discomfiture. "I think today's a good day to elope."

"Yeah, right," Amanda rejoined, but Bill did not return the smile. "You're not serious?"

"Why not? Why not today? It's going to happen sooner or later," Bill tucked a stray tendril of her hair behind her ear. "We could take a short trip across the state line and tie the knot."

"Whoa," was all she could muster. "Bill, there's too much going on right now," she managed, too surprised to come up with anything else.

"Or maybe now that you're the big heiress, you're holding out for a prenup," he suddenly mocked, his face moving closer to hers.

"Actually, I never thought about that," she said simply. "As an attorney, don't you think, though, that's a good idea?" her eyebrows arched up, baiting him.

"Amanda!" she heard Ralph calling her name, and turned to see him and Connor walking toward them. Barnes followed her gaze, and laughed as he took her wrist, leaned forward and brushed her lips with his own possessively.

Amanda turned away quickly, a flush appearing on her cheeks. "Please don't, Bill. I gotta go."

He smiled sardonically as he stood watching her walk as gracefully as she could toward Ralph and Connor, before waving to the men and following her.

"Good morning, counselor and counselor," Bill addressed the men, ignoring Amanda's tenseness as she blushed under Ralph's stare. Barnes made small talk as Amanda took a deep breath. She noted Connor's eyes on her, and seethed inwardly.

Bill put his arm around Amanda's waist. "Yep, court against Mandy is like facing the hurricane. I'm sure she won." Pulling her to him and roughly kissing her again, as if staking his claim, he murmured, "I'll see you later, darling." He whispered in her ear, "I'm serious about today; call me. I'm waiting." Winking at Connor, he added, "If I can be of any service to you, just let me know. Good day, gentlemen."

Amanda made no response, glaring at him as he strode confidently away. She could feel Ralph's eyes boring into her as she finally found her voice. "Connor, I hear you've already met my law partner, Ralph Carmichael. Ralph, Connor is an attorney for one of those high-faluting law firms that get the nice big contracts with the Presiding Bishop and Fortune 500 firms."

Ralph looked at her unsmilingly. "Yes. Actually, we've been discussing you." At Amanda's questioning look, he turned to Connor and continued, "Connor, I don't know what Amanda did to the Bishop, but whatever it is, as her lawyer, we plead guilty. In mitigation, I must point out that she does not discriminate, meting her harsh treatment to all men, including Bishops, equally. I've noticed no appreciable difference in her treatment of women, for that matter. I will argue that excommunication is a fair sentence for her, so that she will be free to make more money for our firm."

Connor smiled, but the smile didn't reach his eyes. He joined in Ralph's half-hearted attempt at revelry. "Oh, I'm afraid that the defendant's punishment will be much more severe. I'm sure I can obtain a life sentence of hard labor at St. Catherine's for Ms. Childs."

He turned back to Amanda, staring at her closely. "Are you feeling better?"

As Amanda felt his eyes on her and nodded wordlessly, Ralph looked at her suspiciously.

Connor held up a sheaf of papers. "I just happened to be here to obtain some public records. Pretty tough on that prosecutor, weren't you?"

Amanda looked at him innocently. "Why, I was Southern charm itself. Actually, I cannot take credit for any of that. Sheila and her contacts in the police department handed me my case on a silver platter."

Connor shook his head. "You made a comment last night about recital series funds. Do you keep records for that fund?"

Amanda looked puzzled. "Of course. I keep a set at the office and at the church. I make quarterly reports to the vestry and treasurer, so those should be in the minutes."

"Would you mind terribly providing me a copy of your records? I could drop by the office later and pick them up."

"I don't see why not. I'll ask Sheila to make you a set of copies as soon as I get back to the office, if you wish."

Connor smiled tightly. "Great—I'll go by there now. I will claim you at 7:00 this evening at your house. Good day. Later, Ralph."

As they watched his retreating form, Ralph asked sarcastically, "A date?"

Amanda said nothing, reading Ralph's dark mood as they made their way out of the courthouse, and speaking briefly to people they met on the way. Ralph and Amanda got into his car.

"What's wrong?" Amanda asked, sensing his coldness and tight features as they pulled out of the parking lot.

"Why didn't you tell me the truth about your accident?" Ralph exclaimed angrily.

"I did tell you the truth. Why?"

"Charlie called me this morning to check on you. Seems there was a little more to it than you chose to share."

"Ralph, it was a hit-and-run, and I was banged up. What else is there to tell?"

Ralph, his countenance stormy, raged. "The car was found in front of Marjy's house, and the place had been broken into. You told Charlie you thought you saw the car in front of your house earlier. That makes it a wee bit more suspicious, doesn't it? Do you have any idea who would want to kill or maim you? Why would someone steal Marjorie's laptop?"

Amanda sighed and ran her fingers through her hair. "I don't have a clue," she admitted ruefully.

"Were you going to tell me you passed out again last night, or had that slipped your mind too? I had to hear about that from Connor. He found drugs in your house, Amanda. What's that all about? Don't you think you might confide in me, that you might need someone to protect you?"

"Since when?" Amanda demanded, goaded into furious retort. "I can take care of myself."

"And you're doing such a fine job," Ralph hissed angrily, his eyes not leaving the road. "And aren't we real chummy with Bill? Since when do you make a public spectacle of yourself kissing men at the public courthouse?"

Amanda did not respond for a moment, struggling to control her frustration and to find the right words to say. Then she reached over and touched Ralph's arm. "You know Bill as well as I do, Ralph. You also know that was one of his staged scenes. I'm really sorry, Ralph, if I didn't fill you in on the accident. There's really nothing else to tell."

She sighed. "My life has become more convoluted than a soap opera, and I'm just reeling from it all. Don't be mad at me—I really need you. You're my anchor, my friend. I am counting on you. I apologize for not telling you all, but I knew you'd worry."

Ralph said nothing, but his face softened as he pulled up to the office.

Chapter 11

Ralph turned to Amanda as he put the car into parking gear at the law office. "Why don't you take the rest of the day off?" he pleaded. "Sheila stated that your mediation for today cancelled, you're limping pretty badly, you look all in, and you need to be making arrangements to go to New York. I bet you haven't even called Feinstein."

Amanda frowned. "I forgot in all the excitement. Ralph, I need for you to do me a favor, even after as much as you've already done. I need all the locks changed at Marjorie's place, and two sets of keys, one for you and one for me."

"Partially done. Locksmith changed locks last night, and called awaiting your instructions. Charlie's still providing surveillance. I'll take care of it."

Amanda exited the car with him. "I need to pick up my calendar and phone book and check the messages."

She noted a gray Mercedes in the parking lot. As they were walking up the steps to the back door, Ralph demanded gruffly, "What was that little scene with Bill at the courthouse all about?"

Amanda frowned as she opened the door. "Hell if I know, Ralph. One minute he's threatening to sue me; the next he is coming on to me in public. He wanted to elope." As she walked in, she came face to face with Connor.

"Oh, you beat us here," she exclaimed breathlessly, embarrassed that he must have overheard her.

"I try not to let any grass grow under my feet," he replied, his face a mask.

Uncomfortable, Amanda looked past him. Her eyes narrowed and her face froze as she spied a huge arrangement of flowers on the counter with card attached. The grouping of exotic white lilies like those used at Marjorie's funeral were mixed with crimson roses.

"They just came," Sheila remarked, seeing her response. "There's a card attached."

The scent of the flowers conjured up memories of Marjie's funeral, and Amanda snatched the card self-consciously. Opening it she read the hand-written message:

> You think we are as different as red and white, but we are the same, Amanda. We belong together. Let's merge and finish what we started so long ago. Bill

"Damn," she muttered under her breath in disgust, throwing the card in the garbage can. Ralph, standing behind her, reached for the card and read it.

"Billy's on the warpath again," he said softly. He tossed the card back into the rubbish.

Amanda, suddenly all-business, addressed Sheila. "Mr. Thomson here wants copies of the recital series financial records. The file is in my right desk drawer. Please make him copies."

Avoiding the flowers, she turned to Ralph. "I'm taking your advice. Please take me home. And Sheila, please get rid of those flowers—take them home, give them away, anything."

"Do you need anything else from the office?"

"I will later, but not right now; only my calendar, phone book and Feinstein's card in my purse. Good day, Mr. Thomson."

She stalked out of the office, Ralph looking at the flowers and shrugging. "What a persistent cuss—he sure knows how to push her buttons. Later, Connor," he remarked as he followed in Amanda's wake.

Soon they were on their way. Ralph spoke. "I've got a meeting with a new client at 1:00, but can bring you anything you need after that. Let me run into the deli and get you a bite of something to eat. You look pretty wan, and at least you can hold out until your big date tonight."

Amanda purposefully did not rise to the bait in his last words, and the remainder of the trip was in silence until Ralph dropped her off in front of her home.

Amanda felt the rest of her strength leave her as she hobbled inside, and she sat down heavily on the couch, leaving her purse on the floor beside her and the covered styrofoam plate on the coffee table.

After several minutes she stumbled into her bedroom and chose some all-cotton pants and red top for comfort. Sitting down and propping her ankle up on the sofa, she decided to finally check her messages from the previous day, and noticed that the number had grown.

The first was a short one from Ralph. "What's up?" The second was a slightly familiar baritone voice. "Mrs. Childs, this is Connor Thomson. Again I wish to apologize for the Rev. Brownlee's impertinence this morning, and to see if we might meet this week. I find that my plans have changed, and I would be available anytime the next two days at your convenience. I will be staying at the Villas Resort. My number is . . . ," as she surprised herself by scrambling for a pen to write down the number. "Thanks for any assistance you can give me."

The third and fourth messages were from Bill Barnes and Charles Petrino, asking after her condition. The last message was from Malachi Feinstein. "Mrs. Childs, I have not heard from you. Please call me as soon as you receive this message to allay my concerns."

Picking up her receiver, she dialed the New York number, and was soon put through to the senior partner himself. The older man's voice relayed his anxiety as he said, "Mrs. Childs, I have been so worried. I hope that we can prevent further delay."

Amanda replied, "Everything is fine. I'm trying to wrap up affairs here so that I can fly out no later than Thursday, if you would like to schedule a meeting." Reviewing her calendar, she continued, "I'm sorry that I cannot make it sooner. Will that be convenient?"

Malachi responded, "I want you here as soon as possible. There's much to inform you. I will set up the meeting for Friday morning. If you can get away sooner, please notify me, and I will have someone meet you at the airport. And Mrs. Childs, I want to stress that you must be careful. In case you haven't noticed from the provisions of the will, you must survive Mrs. Witherspoon for thirty days, or the funds will pass on to a contingent pour-over trust."

Amanda nervously laughed. "Please call me Amanda. I did notice that provision, Mr. Feinstein, but have little control over the date and time of my demise."

"Just promise me to take every precaution, Amanda. Our Marjorie would not have wanted anything to happen to you."

Amanda announced solemnly, "I promise. I'll see you Friday."

Amanda spent the next hour making several telephone calls, trying to retrieve messages from Sheila and dictate responses, and making a plane reservation for Thursday morning to New York LaGuardia. She notified the Feinstein firm of her arrival time, and made calls to make sure the housekeeping staff was notified that she would be visiting Marjy's "cabin". The term was what she and Marjorie had nicknamed a penthouse apartment on Park Avenue owned by Marjorie. Marjorie and Amanda had spent many hours at the "cabin" when they wanted to get away from work and the pressures they faced. Marjorie loved the city, with shopping, the opera, the music and churches, and had enticed Amanda away whenever possible. They had only shared the secret of the cabin's existence with Ralph and Dr. Howells for the purpose of emergency contact.

Next she put in a call to Alex Roberts, chatting with him a few minutes and gaining some basic information about Connor Thomson. Then she pulled the styrofoam container toward her and took a few bites of the chicken salad desultorily.

Amanda suddenly realized that she had not checked her mailbox in the last few days. Jumping up, she winced as her injured foot made sudden contact with the floor. Stumbling to the front door to retrieve the mail, she noticed an older model dark blue Malibu parked across the street. Pulling the mail out of the box beside the front door, she looked again, then froze momentarily. Swinging around quickly, she stepped inside and bolted the door, dropping the mail on the floor.

Amanda stood behind the curtain, peeking out at the car and driver. Although she could not see him clearly, she was certain that the man was the same man who had attempted to run over her the previous day. The face was even more familiar, and she was more and more convinced that it resembled Claude Brown. But how can that be? she thought. One convicted as a habitual felon must serve eighty-five per cent of his sentence, and that was only six years ago. Maybe I'm not good at math, but eighty-five per cent of sixty years is more than six, right?

As she continued to watch, she saw the man talking, and noticed he was holding something that appeared to be a cellular telephone. He nodded in the direction of her house, then quickly pulled out, leaving the scene. She strained to pick out a license number, but realized there was no tag.

Now what do I do? she thought. I'm going mad.

Feeling her panic rising and frantically dialing the number of the local police department, Amanda asked to speak to Chief Petrino immediately. After explaining that it was urgent and she needed no ambulance or fire truck, and after waiting a moment, she heard a familiar voice on the line.

"Petrino speaking; may I help you?"

Amanda cut in quickly, "Charlie, it's Amanda. I'm sorry to bother you."

Amanda had a sudden thought. What if she was wrong? She couldn't go off accusing a man of stalking her who was ostensibly rotting in prison. She needed to get a grip; the man in front of her house might have been acting purely innocently—she couldn't swear that it was same man who hit her, and certainly not that it was Claude Brown. She was letting the unremitting stress of the last few days get the better of her.

"Amanda, what's wrong? Where are you?"

"It's nothing, Charlie," Amanda interrupted. "I apologize—I guess I'm just stir crazy. I'm doing some work at home. Have you any more leads?"

"We have a BOLO out on the driver. There were no fingerprints in the house or car, but my man was able to locate a shoeprint where he kicked in the front door. Bold bastard, wasn't he? Don't worry—we'll find him."

"Well, I just thought I would check."

"Are you sure? The receptionist said it was urgent. You OK?" Charles' voice was anxious.

"Yeah, I'm just frazzled, and so sorry I bothered you."

"My offer of a unit to watch you is still open."

Amanda thought a minute. It was tempting, but she rejected that course, at least until she had more evidence upon which to base her speculations. "No, thank you."

"OK, but I'll be happy to do it. And I'll check in with you in a little while to make sure you're all right. You're not alone, are you?"

"Yes, but I've got plenty of work to do, and am about to order Ralph to bring me some more."

"I don't like the thought of you being there alone."

"Really, I'm just fine," she persisted. "You're making me nervous."

"If you're sure. Amanda, take it easy, OK?"

"Later." Amanda rang off, then on a hunch dialed her office number.

"Sheila, is Ralph still in with his new client?"

"Yes, but he said to interrupt if you called. Just a minute," and Sheila put her on hold before she could protest. She didn't like interruptions when meeting with clients, because she wanted her clients to feel that they were getting her undivided attention.

When Ralph answered, Amanda plunged in, "You got a little free time to do something for me?"

"And it's good to hear from you too. How much money you got?" he laughed. "You always say to get the money up front."

"Very funny," retorted Amanda good-naturedly. "That's not a great line to use in front of a new client."

"Well, I excused myself, saying it was an emergency, and am talking to you from your office. By the way, we amended the originally proposed Garvin settlement agreement, adding the new terms, and my mediation also cancelled, so yes, I do have some time for you this afternoon. What's up?"

"I'm sorry to bother you, but when you're finished, I could really use your help. I need you to do two things for me, if you don't mind."

Amanda quickly reeled off what she needed. Ralph asked, "That's three things, not two."

"I know—attorneys can't count."

"You gonna tell me what this is all about?"

"As soon as you get the information. Just bring it over ASAP instead of calling me with it, and I'll explain all. And Ralph," trying to keep the urgency out of her voice, "just humor me and please hurry."

She rang off before he could ask more questions.

Making sure she had locked all the doors and peering out the windows again to make sure no one was lurking, she went to her bedroom closet. She still felt her heart racing. *I'm trapped here with no vehicle. But I'm overreacting,* she kept telling herself; *it wasn't him. If he was out of prison, Charlie would have told* me. Nevertheless, opening the closet door and reaching for an overhead box, she gingerly deposited the box onto the bed. Gazing at it, she hesitated a minute, taking a deep breath, then rummaged inside and pulled out a .357-caliber Smith and Wesson revolver, 4-inch barrel. She gazed at the pistol for a full minute. Then cocking open the cylinder, she examined the gun a moment, before snapping it closed and replacing the weapon in the box.

Retrieving a second gun, a Beretta 9mm 92-F semiautomatic, the one worn by Andrew the night he was killed and subsequently returned to her by the faceless FBI upon her repeated formal request, she reached in the box for a soft cloth. Sitting on the bed next to the box, she methodically wiped down the gun, inspecting it, particularly the chamber, carefully. Next she pulled out two clips, checked to see if they were full of ammunition and loaded properly, and placed both on the bed beside the gun before returning the box to the closet. Sitting on the bed, she carefully examined the gun once again, snapped one clip into the handle, and ensured that the safety was on. She then held the gun up and looked down the sight. Andrew Childs, she thought, all that target practice you put me through may not have been in vain. It's been so long. Thought I'd never pick this up again, but you never know. Maybe I won't shoot myself in the process. She held the pistol next to her chest a moment, her eyes closed, as if to conjure some connection to Andy through the cold metal.

She made rounds throughout the house, checking doors, peering through curtains. Returning, weapon in hand, to the living room, she noticed the mail still littering the floor, picked it up and again peered through the curtains to assure herself no one was lurking outside, then sat on the couch, sifting through the mail while tucking the gun under the sofa cushion within easy reach.

After reviewing the mail and sorting sympathy cards, bills and junk mail, she propped up her throbbing ankle against cushions on the sofa, leaned back and closed her eyes. She felt the tension smothering her. She tried breathing deeply, trying to slow the thudding of her heart. She remained motionless.

The doorbell rang, jarring her back into reality. She didn't know how long she had been sitting there, and instinctively reached for the weapon, her right hand tensing around the butt of the Beretta. Then she heard Ralph's voice.

"Amanda, are you decent in there?"

Relieved, she called out, "Yes, come on in," and heard the key in the lock.

After the door closed, Amanda turned eagerly toward Ralph, her arms already reaching for the stack of papers in Ralph's hand. She purposely evaded his questioning look as he demanded, "And since when are you, a Southern lady, entertaining strange men in your home without permission?"

"What on earth are you talking about?"

"Connor happened to let me in on the fact that he had been to see you last night, when you had your swooning episode."

Amanda blushed under his scrutiny, leafing through the papers to cover her embarrassment. "Firstly, I am not, nor have I ever been or hope to be, a lady. I resent the very accusation. And secondly, he came seeking me out for information. I could not well refuse the Presiding Bishop's man. And thirdly, I didn't even offer him a drink of water."

"Speaking of which, what kind of branch water do you have to drink around here?"

Amanda waved her hand toward a door located under the stairwell leading to the tiny attic loft. "I haven't even opened the door to the bar in over a year. Enter at your own risk."

While he searched until finding a bottle of single-malt Scotch and a Waterford tumbler, she leafed through the file. Ralph interrupted, "You want anything? I know you don't drink this stuff. What happened with Connor last night?"

She shook her head no—Glenlivet was Andrew's choice, and she kept some around out of habit. Turning back to the stack of papers, she sifted through them. Finding what she was looking for in the file, she pulled out another sheaf of papers stapled together, rummaging through until she found the page she wanted. "And what did you find when you called the prison?" she inquired, suddenly all-business.

"I'll be damned," Ralph exclaimed, and she didn't know if he was referring to her successful dismissal of Connor from the conversation or to his next revelation. "That SOB escaped from prison six years ago, and is still at large."

Amanda sucked in her breath, stung. "Six years ago? So Claude Brown is at large. That makes comparing the judgment of conviction to my notes moot, except . . ." her voice trailed off as she scrutinized the pages before her. "Shit—excuse me, that just confirms my unladylike status. Look at my notes of the sentence on my file."

Ralph read aloud the file notes written in her handwriting. "11/26—call to PDO, talked to Deborah. File reflects Sentence = 30 years Counts 1 through 3, concurrent with each other, but consecutive to sentence of 30 years Counts 4 through 6, also concurrent with each other; total 60 years. Sentenced as habitual felony offender. Confirmed with clerk of court. Requested memo attached to file to attorney—file NOA and check down commitment when received."

Amanda explained, "I filed the sentencing memorandum on his behalf before leaving the public defender's office. I had already left employment by the time he was sentenced, so my successor represented him in court that day. But I called to check on the sentence. He was given 60 years' prison; as a habitual offender he was required to serve 85% of that sentence. Now read the uniform commitment."

She handed the papers to Ralph, who scanned them. After a moment, he gave a low whistle. "What a mistake! Thirty years' concurrent all counts, and no habitual felony status checked. That means, with gain time and provisional credits he would have only served about a fifth, or less, of thirty years. Who let this happen?"

Amanda replied, "The clerk's name I recognize. She retired and left this area about a year later. But it is the responsibility of both the attorney handling the hearing and the appellate attorney to check down the judgment, because the notice of appeal would have to be filed before a copy of the commitment is generally received. Of course, the prosecutor's office should be scrutinizing these and has primary responsibility. Although the defense counsel has a duty not to take action detrimental to his client, he is also under an ethical obligation to prevent fraud on the court."

Lost in her thoughts, she continued. "But a sentence that is incorrect on its face can be corrected at any time, and the record on appeal would reflect the pronouncement of the sentencing court. I wonder what happened to the appeal, because it would have been complete before Brown apparently escaped, and someone would have caught the mistake."

Ralph interrupted. "I can tell you. I called the clerk's office to check the status of his case since the escape. The last reference in the file was an appellate opinion—the appeal was dismissed."

"But why? Of course, it doesn't really matter—Claude is on the streets anyway."

Ralph sat in the chair facing her. "So you are telling me this was a client of yours, and he escaped? Why are we pursuing this? Unless . . ."

"I can't swear it, but the man who tried to run me over yesterday looked an awful lot like Claude Brown. And what's more, I thought I saw the same person parked in front of my house earlier this afternoon."

Ralph gave a low whistle. "So a disgruntled client is after you? Did you call the police?"

Amanda grimaced. "I wasn't sure if it was him."

She continued absently, "He was the most obstreperous client I ever had, and the last case I tried before leaving the public defender's office. I knew his brother and sister for years—they are great people—but Claude was the black sheep of the family. He was facing 180 years for six counts sale and distribution of cocaine, habitual. That's justice for you—sure, he was a scumbag, but at the time the state wouldn't prosecute the child molesters and rapists, and they wanted that kind of time for a small-time doper and drug dealer.

"Anyway, the state refused to deal because it was part of a huge sting and round-up of a gang of these thugs. The state was seeking the maximum sentence in order to avoid the hassle of filing federal racketeering charges on all these guys' arrests, and we had to try them all—nothing to lose, in other words. I managed to get the line-up identification and the taped transactions suppressed, but we still had the eye-witness undercover cop on the stand IDing my guy. You know how hard that is to combat, and I lost the motion to sever the counts for trial—the court ruled they were all part of a continuing course of action."

Ralph said quietly, "Been there, done that. Of course, I was on the other side."

"This cop was squeaky clean—I knew him, knew his record, checked it twice. All I had left to argue was that he could be mistaken, but that law enforcement and the media pressure to convict were so great that the cop couldn't back down on the positive ID."

"And?"

"Moral victory—jury was out two hours. But we lost the war, and Claude was convicted on all six counts. But the bad part was that he was his own worst enemy. I had to fight him throughout the whole trial. He told me he wasn't going to help me with his defense. He told me that no matter what I did, he was going to sue me and file a grievance with the bar. He decided he wanted the tapes and his mug shot, itself proof positive that he was a previously convicted felon, into evidence after I got them suppressed. He said the picture didn't resemble him. I almost went for his throat in the holding cell when he said that—it was the spitting image of him!" Amanda exclaimed, her eyes flashing at the memory. "Then he wanted to testify—the state had all his court files and certified copies of his numerous prior convictions.

"The judge asked the jury to retire several times so that he could admonish Claude and prevent mistrial, and I even had to put my own objections to those of my client's actions I could ethically voice on the record outside the presence of the jury. After the verdict, he went crazy—the bailiffs pulled him off me, and he screamed he wanted an appeal, that he would kill me first chance he got, and that he'd be my roommate in hell, only in more lurid language, of course."

"But he's been at large for over five years—why would he show up now? I didn't even know he was not in prison, so he's had a clear shot all this time if he wanted to come after me. And why hasn't anyone notified me that Claude escaped? What does it mean?

"And Andy was still alive when he escaped," she added, more to herself, as though she had forgotten Ralph was there.

Chapter 12

Ralph, noticing her preoccupation, tried to bring her back to the present. "We need to call the police with this information. What say I call Charlie, order in some Chinese or something, and we spill what we know? I'm not leaving you here alone."

Amanda snapped out of her reverie. "I've got dinner with Connor at 7:00. What time is it?"

Ralph, exasperated, remonstrated. "Didn't you hear me? You don't need to go ANYWHERE, Amanda Childs. Your life is in danger. We need to get some cops here to protect your ass. Are you listening to me?"

Amanda shook her head. "Ralph, you listen to me. There are still some questions we need answered. There's more going on here than we know. Besides, you want me held prisoner here while Claude roams free, knowing exactly where I am?

"And this Connor fellow keeps showing up, sniffing around. I'm really intrigued—there's something going on there too. The Presiding Bishop doesn't order audits for the heck of it, particularly at little St. Catherine's. Maybe Mr. Thomson is working for the Bishop or for someone else. I think it's worth the dinner to troll for information."

"I know you're tired, but you're also over the edge if you think I'm leaving you alone with anyone right now—"

"I won't be; I'll have this," whispered Amanda, pulling the Beretta out from under the sofa cushion.

"Damn it! Where did that come from?" Ralph cried, startled.

"Andy taught me how to use it, so no one will take me without a fight," Amanda remarked coolly.

Downing the remainder of his drink in one gulp, Ralph walked around the sofa, placed the empty glass on the end table and knelt in front of Amanda. "It didn't save Andy," he reminded her soberly, watching the color drain from her face. "Please put the gun away and let me call Charlie," he pleaded.

Amanda looked at him dully. "I know I'm not making sense. Just hear me out. Claude has been running loose all this time. No one notified me. Read my lips—it's in the statute. They wanted to charge him with aggravated assault on me after the attack in the courtroom. I said no—I did my best to win that case despite him. In my mind he was my client, and I was leaving the public defender's office—it would do neither of us any good to add another charge to his rap sheet. For God's sake, he was facing the rest of his life in prison.

"But I was listed to receive statutory notice of any change in his prison status. Andy insisted on that. In fact, our worst fights were over Claude Brown."

Amanda remembered back to the night after Claude had attacked her in court. Andrew had made it home earlier than usual, and she could tell that something was not right. When he asked about her day, she replied that everything was fine. When he pressed her, she was noncommittal, until he finally blew up when she was undressing and he saw the bruises on her neck and shoulder.

"When the hell were you going to get around to telling me you were attacked by your client in open court today?" he had shouted, throwing a book across the room and hitting the wall with a thud.

Amanda had stared at him, aghast. That was a side of Andrew she had never seen.

"How did you know?" she sputtered.

"Charlie called me," he replied shortly. But as quickly as he had erupted, he had enfolded her in his arms, contrite and concerned. "Does it hurt?"

Although she was sore, she was not about to admit it, still sensing his ire beneath the surface.

Andy kissed her gently, as he examined the injuries and his fingers traced the marks on her neck tenderly. She tried not to wince. "Amanda, something in me died when I heard about it. I know you love your work. I would never interfere with your career choice, but I cannot handle this. I know none of us has any promise of tomorrow. But you are juggling fire with the Claude Browns you currently represent, and I can't always be there to protect you from events like what happened today. I want to march to the jail and castrate the son of a bitch.

"Do anything else you want, but I'm begging you to leave the public defender's office, now. For me. For your own safety."

"But Andy, you're in more danger in your job than I am," she argued, but he gently placed his finger over her lips, his favorite way of silencing her.

"Amanda, I carry a gun and can defend myself. You are not afforded the same amenities in your job."

She had seen his fear for her, had heard it in his voice. After arguing about it until the early hours of the morning, she had finally and reluctantly agreed, giving her notice the next day and setting out in private practice.

"Amanda?"

Ralph interrupted her thoughts, bringing her back into the present. Amanda rushed on. "Charlie Petrino helped pull Claude off me in the courtroom, Ralph. He was there that day. I see Charlie almost daily, and all this time it has slipped his mind? No, he receives an internet prompt from the state at least once per month on outstanding warrants, which is printed out and passed around. This would be newsworthy, but it wasn't in the papers. Besides, isn't Charlie supposed to be my friend?

"Now, if I'm right, Claude tried to run me down yesterday. Charlie was there—he saw it happen. Granted, he may not have seen the driver, but had the means to apprehend him without too much trouble—couldn't someone have caught him? I know, I know. Everyone makes mistakes; criminals elude police. Just call me paranoid—don't look at me like that—but this does not add up."

Ralph responded slowly, "You are talking about Charlie Petrino—remember? We all grew up together. I mean, the guys in blue historically haven't won many awards for their competency around here, but, God, what you're saying—"

Amanda, equally somber, whispered, "I know. It's crazy. I am paranoid. But can you come up with any other explanation? Just give me a minute to think."

Ralph stood up, picked up his glass and made his way back to the bar, pouring a generous measure of spirits into the glass and sipping slowly. Amanda remained silent, her mind whirring, staring unseeingly at the gun still in her right hand.

Ralph spoke up behind her, his voice low. "Sorry to break in on your thoughts, but we have got to get you out of here and lying low, at the very least. If you don't trust Charlie, that's cool. But let's get you a few things in a bag and make you disappear or something."

Amanda derided him. "What's this 'we'? You need to be worrying about Claire." Claire was Ralph's longtime girlfriend who Amanda had urged him many times to marry.

Ralph again gulped the contents of the glass. "Remember I told you she's out of town? She's not teaching this semester, and has gone to Cincinnati to see her parents for two weeks, maybe longer. She didn't want me along, because she had a class reunion and wanted time to 'reevaluate' our relationship."

"Ralph, this is serious. Why didn't you tell me? You don't need to lose her. You should be with her, not in the middle of a mess with me."

"Amanda, don't change the subject. Besides, Claire and I agreed to this separation—neither of us is sure, and if after this time we aren't, doesn't that say something? Meanwhile, you're in some big trouble, and we need to DO something, and soon. Dark will be falling before long."

Ralph suddenly had an idea. He sat down on the coffee table facing her, took her hands in his. He whispered, "The farm. You haven't been there in forever—everyone knows you have avoided the place since Andy died."

"I don't know...." she began doubtfully, her voice barely audible. She repressed a shudder.

Ralph replied quietly, "It's the safest place around here I know, with Fred around."

Amanda hesitated uncomfortably, then mused slowly, "There is still power to the place. It'll buy me time enough to make arrangements to get out of here and to New York. I'll go out tomorrow."

"How about right now?" Ralph demanded.

"No, I've got unfinished business with Connor Thomson tonight. Sheila can rent me a car, and I'll have time to warn Fred I'm coming out."

"I don't like this," Ralph began, but Amanda cut him off.

"'You can't always get what you want,' like the Rolling Stones' song. But I'll pack a few things and let you put the bag in the trunk of your car, if that would make you feel better. I'll even let you be my bodyguard for the evening."

She jumped up, wincing at the forgotten injured ankle. She carefully laid the Beretta on the sofa, then walked into the bedroom. Calling out from the bedroom, she asked, "Was there any bourbon left in the bar? I could sure use a stiff one now—I'm desperate enough to drink blended whiskey."

Ralph shrugged at losing his argument with Amanda, something to which he had become accustomed. He searched through the bar. Finding an unopened bottle, he unsealed it and poured two fingers in it, replacing the top. Striding to the kitchen, he soon returned, the glass clinking with ice cubes the way he knew Amanda liked it. He knocked on the partially closed door of the bedroom and struck the glass through the opening.

"Thanks," he heard her say as she took the glass.

Returning after several minutes, Amanda had changed into a navy silk pantsuit, pulled her medium length hair back into a chignon, and applied lipstick. She carried an airport carryon bag, which she unceremoniously dumped on the sofa. She unzipped the cover. She began packing a few items of clothing, her mind working in random fashion. She went to a storage closet and pulled out a black computer attaché, into which she placed her laptop and charger and a cellular telephone charger, and into which she carefully emptied and sorted the contents of the injured briefcase. Next she changed purses with a speed at which Ralph could only marvel. She returned her discarded items to the storage closest.

She walked back to the sofa. "Oh, yes, I need this," and picked up the gun from the table. She hesitated a minute, then carefully placed the gun inside the attache, along with a box of ammunition and the additional clip from her pants pockets. Adding her cellular telephone and another ammunition clip to her purse, and as a last thought the slip of paper with Connor's telephone number, she zipped up the carryon and velcroed the computer attaché closed.

Turning to Ralph, Amanda said matter-of-factly, "If you don't mind, I'll leave my computer and attaché in your car, just in case. OK?"

Ralph grabbed the cases and carefully opened the door, looking to determine if anyone lurked outside. Soon returning, he closed the door behind him, looking at Amanda's stubborn chin.

Amanda noted his eyes on her, and turned her back on him as she said lightly, "Mr. Feinstein kindly pointed out to me that I must survive Marjorie for thirty days to inherit."

Ralph put his hands in his pockets as he regarded her silhouette. "I also noticed that. I thought that was a somewhat archaic convention not much in vogue by estate practitioners nowadays."

Amanda agreed. "Me, too. There could be several explanations, of course."

"Of course. Like what?" Ralph was dubious.

"Oh, I don't know. Malachi Feinstein struck me as old-school, a man who enjoyed his conditions precedent and simultaneous death clauses. Why, I still ask my clients about the option. It doesn't matter much most of the time, except with larger estates, and in avoiding unintended double tax consequences to the loved one's families."

The telephone rang, causing Amanda to jump. Ralph picked it up. "Hi. No, you're not interrupting anything. I just brought her some work she requested. Just a minute."

He covered the receiver. "It's Bill. He called the office earlier for you. I forgot to tell you."

Amanda took the receiver. "Hi, Bill . . . . I'm OK, just a little stiff. How about you?"

"Did you get my flowers?"

"Yes, thank you," Amanda frowned at the mouthpiece.

"I'm worried about you," she heard him reply throatily. "I really want to see you. I planned on coming by there tonight, but have some last-minute business I need to do in Milford. If I get back late, I could stop by," he added hopefully.

"No, don't bother. I have plenty of work on this end to occupy me," responded Amanda briskly. "Don't worry about me."

"But I do," his voice was edgy. "Mandy, all you have to do is say the word. We'd make a good team. You know I'm not one to take 'no' for an answer."

"Slow down. Don't shirk your obligations for me." Amanda was firm. "Let's not rush into this, Bill."

"Mandy, stop turning me away. This has been in the works for a while, and you are just stalling. Quit playing games with me." His frustration was obvious. "I'll call you later."

Amanda rang off, and turned to see Ralph peering out the window through the curtains, his lips tight. "Your date is here," he observed. Turning earnestly to face her, he importuned, "I'm not telling you your business. I know you want to meet with this guy, and three's a crowd. However, I don't want to leave you alone right now."

Amanda responded slowly, "I'm always happy for your company, and I agree that I'm a little nervous with someone out there gunning for me. But I believe Connor was trying to make amends last night. Besides, he is a friend of a friend of mine, and I don't believe Alex would have a jerk look me up."

"How about I go to dinner with this guy and see what it is he wants? Join us if you want—I leave it entirely to you. Besides," she added with a twinkle in her eye, "I think I can take him. If he tries anything, I'll just kill and eat him—I AM pretty hungry."

Heading to the door as the doorbell rang, she stopped as Ralph asked stiffly, "What does Bill want now?"

Her hand on the doorknob, she scoffed lightly, "The usual."

She opened the door to Connor, dressed impeccably in dark gray summer-weight suit of herringbone design, white shirt and royal blue tie. He looked at the two of them and asked, "Amanda, are we still on for dinner? Ralph, please join us."

Ralph related hesitantly, "I've got some business to take care of. I'll take a raincheck," his eyes not leaving Amanda.

Connor rejoined smoothly. "I have my car right here, and will be glad to see the lady home. I promise I won't keep her out too late."

Ralph looked at Amanda, still hesitating, but nodded. "Great. I'll see you later—call me about the game plan."

Amanda stated, "My computer is still in your car. Will you keep an eye out for it?"

Meaningfully, Ralph looked at her and queried, "Are you sure?"

Amanda nodded, turning to Connor. "I'll call you later, Ralph. Let's go. If you don't mind, I made reservations at Jack's for us." She gave directions as they walked out, Ralph watching the street and neighborhood as they drove away, checking to make sure the car was not being followed.

Chapter 13

Connor led Amanda to the gray Mercedes sedan she had noted earlier, opening the passenger door for her. She slid in, taking note of the immaculate leather interior and the computer attaché, not unlike her own, on the back seat. Closing her door, he glided around to the driver side, settling in and turning the ignition. The engine sprang to life.

Expertly steering, he quickly and smoothly maneuvered them out into the street as she navigated, and within minutes they were in front of a dark, carefully tailored brick building with green awnings over the door and windows.

Again he was out in a flash and at her door offering her his hand as she stepped out. Again she felt a spark at the firmness of his grip, as he released her hand, taking her elbow, striding beside her and opening the door for her.

A young woman was at the door, and upon seeing Amanda and the handsome man beside her, spoke politely and briskly. "Good evening, Mrs. Childs. We have your table ready. If you will come this way, please."

Leading the way to a secluded table near a gurgling and picturesque water fountain, she seated them, handed them menus, and asked, "Would you like an aperitif while you are reviewing the menu?"

Connor answered, "Glenlivet straight for me, please. Anything for you, Mrs. Childs?"

Amanda, hearing Connor order the same drink Andrew favored, hesitated before answering, "Nothing but water with lemon for now."

As the waiter left, Connor inquired, "I hope I didn't offend you by ordering a drink. I notice you did not. You're not trying to convince me you're a teetotaler?"

Amanda smiled. "If you have talked to Alex, you will know that I am not. We spent a lot of time doing our best brainstorming in local watering holes. However, I seldom drink these days. I've always associated drinking with celebration, and I've had little to celebrate recently. Besides, I feel I need to keep my wits about me during this meeting."

THE WITHERSPOON LEGACY

Connor smiled. "Surely I'm not that intimidating? I noticed that you had a drink at the wake."

"Yes. I must be out of practice. It made me extremely sick, so my tolerance must not be what it used to be."

"Alex told me to ask you about, how did he put it, 'the asshole defense to DUI', and how to win violation of probation hearings using the concept 'corpus delicti'. I am prepared for some very good lessons in criminal defense tonight."

Amanda laughed. "There are not enough hours tonight to tell those war stories, and Alex tells them so much better than I do. I can't believe he would defer to me, as fond as he is of a good story."

Connor, watching her amusedly, stated flatly, "He didn't. He couldn't resist. I never laughed so hard. Did the term refer to the defendant or the police officer?"

"Initially my client wore the sobriquet, but the LEO ended up fitting the bill as the testimony presented itself," Amanda replied modestly. "Alex hated my client, and refused to help me with the investigation or court prep. He told me he wanted to be invited to the man's autopsy. So I started out with a so-so case and an obnoxious and insistent client. The trial was entertaining, and we won, even though my client got stroked with the hefty speeding ticket. The judge hated him too by the end of the trial.

"But," she diverted attention from herself, "I find myself somewhat at loss, inasmuch as it seems you know more about me than I do you. But I did want to ask you one question—weren't you the infamous lawyer that once represented the defendant in the 'courthouse cake fraud caper'?

Connor laughed out loud, a pleasing sound to Amanda. "You don't disappoint, Esquire. You've done your homework."

"I had a few minutes today to confirm with Alex by phone that you were who you said you were."

An unfathomable look flitted across Connor's face momentarily. "I fell into that case—I was doing a brief stint with a law firm just after passing the bar, and was at the courthouse obtaining some certified copies of convictions in a case. I heard the chief of police asking the clerks to sign some affidavits of complaint. The more I overheard, the more improbable the whole case sounded. I started laughing at them. I ended up becoming enamored with the whole thing and took the case for free. It seems that this guy was riding a bicycle all over town and selling cakes to people, ostensibly for charity. The clerks at the courthouse not only bought cakes, but typed him up a sign-up sheet to help him keep up with his customers."

"And he didn't deliver on the cakes?"

"That's just it," laughed Connor. "Everyone got a cake. Some complained the cakes weren't very good. The story came out that supposedly the individual to whom the 'charity' proceeds were to go didn't get any money, and that the cakes were probably discards from a grocery store bakery. So the chief of police walked into my client's house, hauled him downtown, forced a confession out of him and confiscated evidence, namely the sign-up sheet, from his home, all without a warrant. When I jumped up and down that they had no case of theft or fraud, then they trumped up some charge of his soliciting without a license."

"The clerks in that office were all good-hearted girls, and I threatened to expose them as accomplices. They weren't sure if I was serious or not, but the motion to suppress hearing was a hoot. And I never let them forget that case."

Amanda laughed, visibly relaxing. "A lawyer has to find his fun where he can. Our subject matter is generally so serious. So tell me—you and Alex were college roommates?"

"Yes. It made for an extremely diverting education."

"Who taught whom the extreme etiquette techniques—the charm, the 'get the door for her', 'kiss her hand' stuff?"

"Oh, I don't know," Connor laughed shortly, watching her intently. "We both had moms who were anal about old-school gentlemanly conduct, chivalry, and putting women on a pedestal. I guess when we got together we just compared notes. It seemed to work well."

"I'm hoping that's not how you obtained the 'summa cum laude' label next to your degree," Amanda countered lightly.

Connor's eyes narrowed shrewdly. "No, I had my share of fun, but didn't party as much as Alex. I studied hard. Actually, school was never that hard for me. Alex had a harder time with academics, and I had to coach him through calculus so he would graduate. Speaking of which, Alex informed me you sported a record number of honor cords around your neck at graduation."

Amanda looked at the fountain. "I grew up sort of nerdy. My parents were fundamentalist Baptist, very sheltering and strict. Knowledge was a journey to exotic sites for me—I craved more and more, and books were my outlet. I loved to read and learn. And I was shy one-on-one, although I enjoyed being with people. For some reason I always wanted to be a lawyer, and everyone thought I was crazy, ill-suited for that type work. I just never seemed to fit in any one group at school, and was more comfortable with books, except when I was with Monica and Bill. So I was very different from you."

"Maybe, maybe not," he replied, as the waiter served their drinks. They broke off conversation to order dinner, Amanda selecting a glass of sauvignon blanc with her grilled salmon with steamed vegetables, Connor merlot with his steak and declining another Scotch.

After the waiter left, they sipped their drinks in silence, until Amanda broke the ice. "I am assuming this meeting is really for business, not pleasure, *nyet*? Please feel free to jump in and ask me what you need to know."

Connor's expression was enigmatic. "I didn't bring all my records to pore over with you. Your free time is limited, so yes, it is helpful to obtain some information from you. However, based on Alex' description of you, I was intrigued and wanted to meet you. There must be a good story behind a lawyer with your reputation and ability immersing herself in church musician and *pro bono* work in this tiny hamlet. What would make you come back here and throw away all your free time?"

Amanda tore her gaze away from the bubbling fountain. "Don't know, really."

"Tell me about Bishop Marks."

Amanda avoided looking at Connor, sipping her water. "I really don't know that much about him. I'm sure there are better sources of information."

"Oh, come now, he was originally from this area. I know already that there is some history between him and Marjorie Witherspoon. I was hoping you could enlighten me. Father Anselm has already informed me that you and Mrs. Witherspoon were extremely close, so I don't believe you are ignorant."

Amanda pursed her lips, finally turning her eyes on Connor. "What exactly are you looking for?"

"You were here when Marks was consecrated, weren't you?"

"I came on board as church musician somewhere in that time period after Marks' consecration, yes."

"What do you know about Bishop Marks?"

"I know that he left this area, made his mark elsewhere, and suddenly he was elected as bishop of the diocese. I knew that Marjorie, who was serving on the vestry at the time, was not that keen on him, and I asked why. I don't remember her answer at the time—I just knew that there was something she didn't want to talk about then.

"He was on board, and not longer afterward began making life difficult for the semi-retired priest we had at the time. The guy was a crusty individual, but very Anglo-Catholic. He sang a fabulous Eucharist, and that's what the congregation wanted—they really liked him, and he them. Within a year Father Campbell was forced into permanent retirement."

"Then what?"

Amanda looked at Connor, a hint of anger in her voice. "What have you been told?"

Connor studied her quietly. "I'm just curious, that's all. Father Anselm had alluded to his predecessor and your resignation from the vestry."

Amanda's eyes flashed fire. "I fail to see where any of this is relevant to your audit."

Connor looked at her over the rim of his glass and murmured, "Forget the audit, Amanda. Let's not spar with each other. Indulge me, please."

Amanda took a deep breath at his disarming smile, trying to relax her defensive posture. Again he seemed familiar. She did not understand it. "It was a year from hell, in every way. Marjorie was senior warden, and I had somehow lost my mind and accepted the junior warden position, mainly because I knew Marjorie was ill. Cancer had been found, and she was undergoing a series of radiation and chemotherapy. I agreed to be junior warden to take as much off her during her treatment as I could, because the church was in trouble and she refused to let the treatments interfere with her bounden duty to St. Catherine's. My husband Andy was off on assignment somewhere out West—he couldn't even tell me where he was. I was frustrated not knowing his whereabouts and when I would see him.

"What I didn't know was that Marks had forced a new priest down the throats of the previous vestry. When the man arrived, he swept through like a hurricane. He took control, which was fine, but things went from bad to worse, particularly financially. We had a rash of deaths in the parish, the old guard going one by one. While they were leaving memorials for specific purposes, nothing was replacing their tithes and pledges. Other members were leaving in disgust because of the radical change in the service, liturgy and the sermons. I was generally given my marching orders as to service music on Saturday before the service, if not Sunday morning just before prelude—lots of praise choruses. The hymns, the chant, were disappearing.

"In the meantime the diocese denied the previous vestry's request for intervention and emergency funds. I was receiving all these strange invoices and bills, and when I asked, the priest was spinning stories to suit the situation, attempting to divide and conquer the vestry and congregation. I caught him in several lies, but couldn't understand why. Because Marjorie was gone so much, and all but a couple of the vestry took an almost instant dislike in him, I was left hanging in the middle, attempting mediation between opposing forces.

"One day he called an emergency vestry meeting and issued an ultimatum—triple his stipend or else. Billy Barnes, I mean Bill—he doesn't like being called 'Billy' any more—backed him. I looked at the financial figures and asked Bill what was I missing—where was the money to pay him? I was willing to compromise for the sake of peace in the parish, but the rest of the vestry said not only no, but hell, no.

"That Sunday in his sermon he said that he couldn't stay at the church under the present governing body, and that the wardens of the church were against God and church growth. It was Marjorie's first Sunday back after several weeks of treatment, and she was very weak. I was so angry, and she looked like she was going to collapse.

"I called and made an appointment with Bishop Marks that week. Marjorie insisted on accompanying me, as sick as she was. I was so afraid for her. But instead of meeting with the Bishop, we ended up seeing some underling, who informed us summarily that the Bishop sided with the priest.

"The phone was ringing as Marjorie and I arrived home. It was the priest, who began cursing and screaming at me. I was not used to that, particularly from a priest, and might have responded in kind. But because Marjorie was there when I took the call, I tried to remain calm and keep as much of it from her as I could.

"Then he said that, let me see if I can quote him exactly, 'someone needs to get off their ass and talk about stewardship on Sunday as part of the annual pledge campaign.'"

She paused, taking a drink. Connor waited, then prompted her, "And?"

The corners of her mouth hid the beginnings of a smile. "That was the straw that broke the camel's back. I lost it. I told him that I really didn't think he wanted the spawn of Satan speaking to the congregation."

"What?" Connor asked in amazement.

Amanda sipped her water, as the waiter appeared with the salad course and their wine. After he left, Connor demanded, "And?"

"Marjorie was listening to my side of the conversation, and thought I had lost my mind. The priest asked me to repeat what I said. I explained that he had told the congregation on Sunday last that Marjorie and I were against him and God, and intimated we were the spawn of Satan, so I didn't think I was worthy to stand up and speak to the congregation under those circumstances. He hung up on me."

Connor shook his head, choking with laughter. "You're making this up, aren't you?"

"No," affirmed Amanda with a slight grin. "The next Sunday I tendered my resignation from the vestry. It was the Sunday before the annual church meeting and new elections, and Marjorie's term as senior warden was ending. I felt the church could handle him without me."

"And what happened?"

"I'm not sure, but I think he tried to have me excommunicated. Never heard of that in the Episcopal Church. Bishop Marks was demanding my termination. However, before he could succeed, the new vestry had a taste of what this priest was like, unanimously asked him to step down, and notified the Bishop of their decision, like it or not."

"Then what?"

"Marjorie intervened, along with a committee of church members. I don't know the details, but they demanded that the Bishop leave me alone.

"The church began the selection process for a new priest, and after some time and wrangling, Father Anselm was selected. I was asked to stay on as church musician; I was doing it *gratis*. They really couldn't afford to find another organist anyway. The bishop denied another request for emergency funds—seems the previous priest had depleted his discretionary funds and then some, leaving unpaid bills all over town, and Marjorie infused more cash into the church."

She paused, then continued, more as if talking to herself. "You know, Marjorie could have owned St. Catherine's and run it any way she wanted to. She kept the church running in the black, but other than her tongue-in-cheek suggestions and requests, she remained in the background except when responsibility was foisted on her. She always encouraged others to take leadership roles, and was always generous with her money and time."

Connor interrupted. "The church made requests to the diocese for financial assistance?"

"Yes, several times," Amanda affirmed solemnly. "I did not during my time on the vestry, but the previous vestries had on several occasions, and an emergency request was made after I resigned."

"How much money did the diocese pay out to your knowledge?"

Amanda regarded him, her brow furrowed. "I thought you knew this. Nothing. Bishop Marks was very clear. St. Catherine's was on her own. 'Don't call him—he'll call us' was his motto."

"Never?" Connor was direct, staring at her.

"Never," she echoed emphatically. "If not for Marjorie, the church would have folded a long time ago. She was St. Catherine's equivalent of a Rockefeller or Vanderbilt."

They were silent as the waiter brought their meal course.

"What about before Marjorie?" Connor wanted to know as soon as he was out of earshot.

Amanda smiled. "This is all part of the history of St. Catherine's and the tradition handed down to me from parishioners now dead. Many years ago, the church had entered into a business plan to become a full parish with full-time priest. This is an old parish which began when the area was settled over a century ago. It consisted of a handful of Northern immigrants and a circuit-riding bishop with a dream. The church struggled for many years with supply priests and laity just trying to keep the doors open, particularly during the depression and war years. Many of the older parishioners had invested monies into a trust or endowment to ensure the survival of St. Catherine's. Marjorie's family was committed to the cause. She was a third-generation communicant of St. Catherine's.

"A few years after Stephen Marks became bishop, the church had a major crisis, when it was discovered that the church treasurer before Billy had allegedly invested trust funds in some very shaky stocks, which took a nosedive. Billy," she unconsciously reverted to calling him 'Billy', "stepped in as treasurer, but was not able to avoid the catastrophe. Marjorie intervened, saving the church from abandoning some critical capital improvements, new roof, preserving the windows. She also infused more money into the trust fund, but for some reason

Billy could only keep the fund afloat, and was not able to invest and restore it to its former status."

"So Barnes was the church treasurer by then?"

"He was both church treasurer and diocesan treasurer by then. The church treasurer was killed in a freak automobile accident, if I recall the story correctly. Billy stepped in as treasurer right out of law school when he first came home."

Connor inquired, "Where did Barnes stand on the priest situation after you resigned from the vestry?"

Amanda smiled tightly. "Billy always had an amazing talent as liaison—I never knew from moment to moment which horse he was backing. He was sympathetic to me, but he understood the priest's position, and the Bishop—Marks is a cousin to Billy's dad—was really pushing him to make this situation work, et cetera. Marjorie and he often clashed. Marjy always tried to force him to take a position during vestry meetings, and he always wiggled free. Marjy always said Billy was a born politician."

"And you have not taken a leadership position in the church since then?"

"You got it," finished Amanda simply.

"What about the Bishop and Mrs. Witherspoon? What is the story there? I'm sure you know, and neither the Bishop nor Mrs. Witherspoon is available to tell the story."

Amanda, looking suddenly tired, replied, "Little of my information came from Marjorie. Every now and then she would drop hints or divulge snippets. It was from other parishioners that I know what I know.

"Apparently Stephen Marks and Marjorie dated in high school, and it was an accepted assumption that they would wed one day. It did not come to pass. Marjorie went off to college, and it was my understanding that she broke it off with Marks, who did not take it well. I do not know all the facts, but he did leave the area.

"I had it on good authority, from a former vestry member who has gone on to his great reward, that Marks swore vengeance upon her and St. Catherine's. What happened that would occasion such enmity I do not know, although I would have liked to know. Most of those who might know are dead; maybe Doc knows, but he's not telling.

"I remember the day Marjy and I left the bishop's office after our unsuccessful meeting, she gripped my hand in the car and said, 'And to think I almost married that sod. Thank God he showed his true colors. But then I never would have had . . .'"

Amanda paused. Connor prompted her, "What?"

"I don't know," Amanda confessed. "I prompted her, but she was crying and I was afraid she might collapse. She did end up in the hospital that evening. So I never knew. I do know that Marjy disliked Marks so much that it was a great sacrifice for her to confront him on my behalf, something I would never have asked of her, but I have always been grateful to her."

"How did you come to know Mrs. Witherspoon? Start at the beginning—I have time."

Amanda looked at him warily. "You are insufferable," she remarked plaintively.

"And you are being very diverting."

"I have nothing to hide," she said, sipping her water, "although this is painful right now." Her eyes were brilliant as the thought of Marjy momentarily overcame her.

"I am sorry, Amanda," he said, covering her hand with his own.

Amanda looked down at his hand, her face impassive as her mask slipped back into place. "Well, my history with Marjorie is a long one, but I'll try to make it digestible if possible." She quickly removed her hand.

"Marjorie, who apparently had enough wealth to do whatever she wished, loved children and became an elementary school teacher. She taught me in second grade. Her only daughter Monica and I became best friends all through school until Monica's death.

"Mrs. Witherspoon was so encouraging to me in class, and made a little shy girl from a working-class family believe she could do anything. She even made a secret deal with the school librarian so that I could check out three books instead of one per week, and could read the third—and fourth-grade library books. I truly loved her, and she in turn kept an interest in me throughout my school years."

"And you were classmates with Bill Barnes?" Connor questioned.

Amanda nodded. "Yes. Bill, Monica, and I were buddies. Monica was one grade behind us in school. Monica should have been a spoiled child, but was sweet and loved by all. Billy was always quite infatuated with her. Billy," she caught herself, "Bill was all-American in sports and class president. Monica was homecoming queen, cheerleader and class favorite. Bill's dad was a lawyer who expected Bill to follow in his footsteps and to climb the social ladder. Bill's mom died when he was ten, and his dad ruled Bill with an iron fist.

"Everyone expected Bill and Monica to marry. But for some reason they generally invited me to tag along with them on outings. We did practically everything together, the 'Three Musketeers'. We'd double-date—Bill would ask one of his friends to go with us. Bill always seemed to consider everything a game and loved to compete in everything, academics, sports, whatever, but I wasn't terribly competitive."

Amanda's eyes dropped to her plate, suddenly self-conscious.

"Upon graduation from high school I received a full scholarship to Florida State. Bill was expected to go to Alabama like his father, but he wanted to play football at Florida State—go figure. The team was expected to become national champions, and several of his high school teammates had signed on there, including Charlie Petrino. So Bill made a pact with his father that if daddy would let him go undergraduate to FSU, he would go to Alabama's College of Law. Monica finished high school, and then was accepted at Yale. She wanted me to transfer and go with her, but my family and I couldn't afford that, and were too proud to accept the assistance offered by the Witherspoons."

"And?" Connor demanded when she paused.

"Surely this is quite boring to you," Amanda protested, her demeanor suddenly cloudy.

"On the contrary, please continue."

Amanda paused, blinking back sudden tears. "It was my junior year. Monica was coming in for Christmas break, and she and Bill were going to a big fraternity holiday dance. Bill was all set to propose to Monica, and had even bought the ring and showed it to me. However, her final exam schedule interfered, and she wasn't going to make it home in time for the dance. Bill, generally never at a loss for a date, at the last minute couldn't swing one, so he called me. I stood in for Monica, and that was the night I met Andrew.

"Anyway, Mr. Witherspoon had business in New York, and picked up Monica from school so they could drive home together. Somewhere in New Jersey a drunk driver crossed several lanes and hit them head-on." Amanda paused, taking a sip, pain flooding her face. "Monica was thrown through the windshield and killed instantly, and Mr. Witherspoon hit the steering wheel and was pronounced dead on arrival at the hospital."

Amanda's eyes misted. "All our lives came to a crashing halt. Mr. Witherspoon was an only child, Mrs. Witherspoon was an only child, and Monica was their life. Marjorie lost her entire family in one night. Bill's ordered little dream of the good life happily ever after with Monica was crushed. My best friend was gone."

Connor was instantly sympathetic. "What a terrible ordeal for all of you."

Amanda continued relentlessly, as though afraid to stop, "When I got the word, I of course immediately came home and went to Mrs. Witherspoon. She told me that I was her family, and that she was counting on me to make good.

"I went back to school and plunged myself into work. I made it into law school there, and Bill went on to Alabama. Marjorie and I kept up correspondence, and she threw herself into children's causes and church work."

They were interrupted by the waiter's asking if they needed anything else. Amanda, looking at Connor who indicated in the negative, shook her head.

"But how did you and Mrs. Witherspoon become so close?" he resumed the conversation.

"Marjorie kept in touch with me, and checked on my progress. I would spend time with her every break. I knew how much she missed her husband and Monica, and she was good to me. She insisted on planning my wedding reception. When my mother became terminally ill, Andrew knew I wanted to move home to be there for her. I took a job with the Public Defender's Office locally, and he decided at that time to try to transfer to the Florida Department of Law Enforcement.

"The Bureau had other ideas, and kept him on the payroll while throwing him a local assignment here every now and then. Mostly he was still away. At that time, Marjorie cornered me about taking on the musician post at St. Catherine's. They had no one, and she had a plan to install an organ. I told her my training was in piano, not organ. But she insisted.

"Well, the next thing I knew, I was immersed in learning organ and researching consultants for the church, as well as practicing criminal law. And Andy was gone a lot with his work. Marjorie hired a consultant, and we found a beautiful little historic Hook & Hastings organ in excellent condition through the organ clearing house and had it installed in the church. I was working with building up the choir, something I had not done before. And Marjorie kept me busy."

"And your husband?" Connor asked, watching her intently.

Amanda avoided looking at him as she swallowed convulsively. "Andrew was killed four years ago," Amanda said, only the tremor in her voice betraying any emotion.

Chapter 14

"I'm very sorry," said Connor, his eyes meeting hers momentarily before she looked away. "How did it happen?"

"I was never able to find out any details from the Bureau, just told he died in the service of his country. Closed casket, highly confidential investigation—that's all I knew. There was a sea of law enforcement at the funeral. Andy was well known and liked by his colleagues. The feds denied me information, and kept putting me off when I asked."

Continuing quickly, lest she break down, she continued. "And Marjorie pulled me up by my bootstraps and put me to work. She kept me from wallowing in self-pity, and volunteered me for all sorts of community service. She saved my life. We were good friends to each other. And that's that," Amanda finished lamely.

Connor asked, "And Bill?"

"Bill got his degrees, found and married his debutante and took over his father's practice," Amanda quipped lightly.

"He must have taken Monica's death hard."

Amanda looked away. "We avoided the subject." She fell silent, feeling Connor's eyes boring through her. The silence became palpable.

Finally Connor broke the silence, steering her back to the subject. "And you and Bill, what exactly is the nature of your relationship, if you don't mind my asking?"

Amanda fingered her glass, studying it intently. "We are still friends. We have each gone our separate ways, but we still have cases against each other, we throw business to each other, we have lunch from time to time, we do church together. Bill's wife drowned in a freak accident last year, so we're both widowed. Sometimes Bill drops back into my life—we have dinner, he flirts, he calls—mainly when he's lonely and has nothing better to do."

"You looked like more than friends at the wake and again this morning at the courthouse. And those flowers seem to indicate otherwise."

Amanda, her eyes glittering, looked at the fountain. "What has my relationship with Bill got to do with anything?" Her tone was defensive.

The subject was dropped as the waiter approached and removed their plates, asking them if they wanted dessert. They declined and both ordered coffee. They were silent until the coffee was served, the chef following the waiter to the table.

"My dear Amanda," he took her hand and kissed it, his accent matching his Latin appearance, "I am so very sorry about Mrs. Witherspoon." He paused, looking around the restaurant. "If not for her and you," he waved his hand to include the premises, "I would never have been able to realize all this."

"Thank you, Jack, but you made this happen," Amanda squeezed his hand affectionately. "Jack, this is Connor Thomson," Amanda introduced the two men.

"Nice to meet you," he shook Connor's hand warily. "*Son novios?*" he addressed her, lapsing into Spanish, his eyes raking Connor as he frowned inquiringly.

"No," laughed Amanda, flushing. "*La cena es muy bueno,*" she diverted his attention to the meal. "As always, superb."

"*Gracias,*" he beamed. "I do my best. *No gusta los pasteles?*"

"No dessert for me, thanks," Amanda replied, and Connor shook his head.

After they were again left alone, Connor again engaged her in conversation. "Talk to me about the church recital series," Connor eyed her over his coffee cup.

Amanda, grateful for the change in topic, was happy to oblige. "Let's see—where to start? When we got the Hook and Hastings, Marjorie wanted a dedication recital. She knew this great organist from New York City, and she retained him to perform. The church was packed, and it was a hit. We had no venue for truly classical music in the town, and she decided that she and I would fill that need at St. Catherine's. As if our plates were not full enough, she initiated a fund and a drive for a recital series. She seeded the fund with $10,000, and we were off.

"She had me join the American Guild of Organists with her, and I started hobnobbing with all sorts of musicians in churches and at colleges. We were going to recitals everywhere, listening to good music, organ, piano, chamber music, selecting potential performers, negotiating prices. We put them up at her place, which was nicer than any hotel. I would cook for them, or we'd take them out to four-star restaurants and show them the countryside or beach. Marjorie kept me hopping—the whole weekend of the recital was like a party, even though it was a lot of work."

"I notice that your records show an average of $25,000 annually in revenues. What was the maximum in the fund that you can recall?" Connor asked casually.

"Oh, never more than $30,000—it was a tiny series, and we never had more than 4-6 events per year," Amanda replied.

"Oh?" queried Connor, his brows furrowing. "Where did the rest of the monies go?"

"'Rest of the monies'? Excuse me?" Amanda's brows creasing in a frown.

"Are the records you gave me complete?"

"Pretty close. I can't swear to it, because I never actually handled the money, except if a check came in the mail to my attention by mistake. Someone else counted the proceeds at the recitals and gave me a tally. The church secretary or Billy would generally notify me if a donation came in. I gave my quarterly report based on the information provided to me."

"Did you ever disburse monies?"

"I have some blank checks in the desk drawer at the church office, but I have never written one to my recollection. I always paid for necessaries out of my pocket, and did not seek reimbursement, for I considered it part of my contribution to the series."

"Did you ever receive reimbursement from the series?"

Amanda thought a minute. "I don't think so. I played a recital or two *pro se*, and don't remember ever receiving anything in reimbursement for my expenditures."

"And you're sure that the fund never grossed more than $30K? What if I told you that I've seen records that the fund was grossing between two and three million per year?"

Amanda laughed heartily. "Of course, I would want some of what you've been smoking." Then she noticed that Connor was regarding her without smiling. She stared back, aghast. "You can't be serious?"

"Very serious. And even larger sums are making it through the bank accounts of St. Catherine's, most of it being channeled directly through your fund. Would you have any explanation for that? Or for transfers made in your name from that fund?"

Amanda looked at him dumbfounded. "What are you talking about? That can't be so, not even in my wildest dreams."

Connor continued. "I'm afraid it is true. Have you any knowledge about a corporation named WWAC, Inc.?"

"No," Amanda said slowly, then snapped her fingers. "But I did see it on a church financial statement once. I was told it was a typographical error. What is it?"

"Ostensibly a multi-national corporation, providing business expertise, consulting, services to St. Catherine's and the diocese. What kind of services—contracting?"

"I have no idea," Amanda shook her head dumbfounded.

"Why not?" Connor was direct. "You are listed as president and CEO, as well as treasurer. Are you telling me you are not affiliated at all with this company?"

Amanda gasped. "Why would I be? I've never heard of it except that one time."

"Do you currently have any off-shore or international bank accounts? Any large savings accounts recently created?"

Amanda felt her throat go dry, as she realized that behind Connor's questions and sudden formality was a veiled accusation. "No, Mr. Thomson," she replied icily, "I have no such accounts, only my very modest personal deferred compensation and investment accounts. Would you like to see those statements as well?"

"That might be helpful, maybe later," he rejoined politely. "Ever visit the Caymans?"

A cold chill came over Amanda. Trying rapidly to make sense of his questions, she wanted time to think about the implications of what he was saying. She questioned anxiously, "I'm afraid not. Am I being accused of something?"

"Amanda, a lot of money has passed through the coffers of St. Catherine's, sometimes as much as $10 million in a year. Some of it is earmarked as capital improvement grants from the diocese, and some of it as related to your fund, ostensibly very large charitable donations for the organ and the recital series, only to disappear. I have letters of solicitation purportedly signed by you, and 'thank you' letters to these contributors, over the last seven years. I have one of the latest ones, dated only last week."

He pulled out some papers from his inside jacket pocket and handed some to her. She looked through some. "Yes, this is from me—I routinely send personal 'thank you' letters to all contributors." She looked at another one. "I have never seen this," she replied slowly. "I don't send direct solicitation to anyone. I only send notifications of upcoming events, and in the notification will give the information in case someone wants to contribute."

"But that is your signature?"

"I admit it looks like mine, but I swear I've never sent this. I'm at a loss." Amanda's face paled.

"How do you know the identity of the contributors?"

"After recitals I will request copies of any checks. Sometimes I get them, other times I am sent only the names and addresses. I immediately send out the letters. As contributions come in, I'm given the contact information to put the contributor on the mailing list, send out letters and flyers of upcoming events."

"How do you know the amounts of the contributions?" Connor wanted to know.

"I don't always," Amanda admitted. "But if the amount of the contribution is not provided with the contact information, around the end of the month I call and ask, for my report."

"Who do you contact?" Connor was curious.

"Bill," she said simply.

"In writing? E-mail? How?

"Telephone always," Amanda responded. "Bill thinks it beneath him to type; he is old-school lawyer with some pretty female around to take dictation, type and answer phones. So I call him."

"Are you telling me you don't actively receive and disburse the funds?" Connor asked dubiously.

"Generally not, unless someone personally hands me a contribution," Amanda asserted. "Where did this solicitation for funds come from? This is against our policy."

"Policy?" he demanded.

"Yes. Marjorie and I decided when we initiated the organ fund and recital series that we would never beg for funds," Amanda related.

Connor pointed to the letter in her hand with her acknowledged signature. "How much was this contribution?" he questioned.

"I would have to check the records, but I think it was five-hundred dollars," Amanda recalled.

"How about $50,000?" Connor refuted.

"Not even close," Amanda breathed. "There's no way—"

"And do you know this contributor?" Connor asked.

"No. But there are contributors from everywhere, people who have been to a recital or have visited St. Catherine's while on vacation. Sometimes Bill will tell me about some businessman who said he came through once and saw the church and organ, and wanted to contribute."

"What if I told you this person does not exist? That many of these people don't exist?"

"That can't be," Amanda stuttered. "From where did the money come? Nonexistent persons are giving gobs of money to my church and series, and I know nothing about it?"

"Precisely," Connor's answer was quiet but chilling. "And I have also been provided photographs and documentation of you visiting Grand Cayman banks on several occasions," he added, proffering a photograph. She took it reluctantly, as if it was a snake, and looked at it, a look of fear crossing her forehead.

Amanda was shocked. "No. I admit it looks like me, but—" she stammered.

"And I also have a list of dates when you have been in the Caymans, with documents showing you making several large transactions," Connor persisted, his eyes boring through her.

"I've never been to the Caymans," she denied, reviewing the list he presented to her. "I'm not sure about all of them, but I know that on these dates," she pointed out several, "I was with Marjorie in New York City."

"And do you have anyone who could verify that you were where you say you were?"

"Well, Marjorie, and, well—Ralph and Dr. Howells knew where we were," Amanda faltered. She realized that while Ralph had contact information when she and Marjorie were on their trips, he did not know where they stayed. While Dr. Howells knew about the penthouse and had visited there, many times, he would not necessarily be able to verify her story. And Marjorie was gone.

Amanda felt light-headed, a trickle of fear running down her spine. Connor continued, "I would like an opportunity to meet with you tomorrow and show you some more of what I've discovered thus far. I do obviously have more questions regarding your involvement with the series and the fund. And I would appreciate it if our conversations remained unshared with others for now. Amanda, this is serious."

Amanda, the trickle turning into a flood of terror as she realized that he was speaking of matters that could be criminal in nature, rose to her feet awkwardly. As she did Connor rose also. She stated coolly, "I'm sorry, but I'm clueless here. I don't know what to say. I have no idea what you are talking about."

There was an uncomfortable pause as they stared at each other, before Amanda looked away. "I do, however, wish to thank you for a lovely evening."

Connor, sensing Amanda's sudden aloofness, responded, "I'm very sorry—I did not mean to offend you. I'm not here to accuse you, Amanda. But you do agree this looks very bad. I'm just trying to get to the bottom of this."

Amanda remained silent. Connor regarded her, his face impassive. "Alex warned me that you were riveting, and he is right. You should consider writing as a side line. I will be obtaining more records from various sources tomorrow to review, and hope to call on you."

Amanda replied coolly. "Well, with our trial settling, I am leaving for a couple days on urgent business Thursday. Please feel free, however, to leave a message at my office with any questions relating to your business."

"Oh—going out of town?"

She did not respond. Connor finally replied, his voice full of reluctance, "Thank you for your time. Shall I get the check?"

Amanda, still standing, remained cool. "No need—it's taken care of. Shall we go?"

They walked out to the car, and again Connor opened her door for her. Unsmilingly she slid in, shrinking from him and preoccupied with his news. He steered the car in the direction of her home, and they remained silent. However, as they neared her home, she peered ahead, then tensed visibly at the sight of the dark blue Malibu parked in clear sight of the driveway. Before Connor could slow to turn in, she laid her hand on his arm and ordered tersely, "Please don't slow down. Keep going."

Obviously surprised at her request, he accelerated, glancing around at her. "What is it?"

Bending down out of sight as they passed the car, she reached for her purse and cell phone. Speaking in as calm a tone as she could muster, she replied, "Oh, I forgot my computer is still in Ralph's car. If you don't mind dropping me off at his house, I would much appreciate it. Just down this road, and turn right at the next light."

Quickly dialing Ralph's cell number, she waited, hardly daring to breathe. She felt Connor silently regarding her as he turned the corner. Finally Ralph's voice came on the line.

"Ralph, are you home?"

"Yes. What is it?"

"I'm sorry to bother you," Amanda began almost breathlessly, "but I left my computer in your car and think I may need it tonight after all."

"Amanda, what's wrong? Is it Connor?"

"Yes and no," she said, looking at Connor, "I'm afraid it's that Brown business again. Mr. Thomson is being kind enough to drop me off at your house, so that I can pick it up. Perhaps you and I can discuss the case a few minutes tonight, and then you can take me home."

"I'll be waiting for you."

"Good. We'll be there momentarily."

Connor's eyes narrowed speculatively. Amanda gave him directions for the short trip to Ralph's home. She knew he was watching her closely, as she surreptitiously and chronically gazed out the rearview mirror on the way to Ralph's home. As he pulled up in front of the multi-leveled ranch house, Ralph opened the front door, striding toward the car.

Amanda quickly turned to Connor, hurriedly finding the handle of her purse. "Thank you for a lovely evening."

Connor gripped her wrist and roughly turned her to face him. "What is it, Amanda? I thought you weren't leaving until Thursday."

Amanda said smoothly, her face impassive, although the pressure of his touch on her wrist had an unusual effect on her already rapid pulse, "It's just that I have some business to accomplish before my trip, and it is imperative to discuss some matters with Ralph and pick up my computer."

He gripped her tighter. "Don't run away. Please tell me what is going on, Amanda Childs. Perhaps . . . your substantial assistance could go a long way to mitigate . . . ." He did not finish the sentence.

Amanda's eyes dilated in horror at those words. *He's talking prosecution*, she thought, suddenly faint. Then disengaging herself and slipping out of the car before he could say anything else, she walked quickly toward Ralph, who took her by the arm and steered her into the house as Connor slowly drove off.

Once in the house Ralph locked the door. He turned to Amanda. "What now?"

"I'm in trouble, Ralph. Big trouble. But I can't go home. The blue car was in front of my house again tonight. I asked Connor to bring me here."

"Were you followed?"

"I don't think he saw me. I hate to impose on you any further, Ralph, but I cannot go back home," she repeated, more to herself than to him.

"I agree. We need to call the cops, and get you the hell out of Dodge tonight."

"No cops," Amanda protested forcefully. "I need a plan."

She paced the floor a few minutes, too anxious to notice the pain in her ankle. Ralph knew when she was in this frame of mind to keep silent and let her think. He sat down in a chair in the foyer and watched her.

After a few minutes, he broke into her thoughts, too anxious to wait. "What if I call Charlie and tell him that I just rode by your house and saw a dark blue car, no tag, with a man matching the description of the man who hit you?"

"OK," agreed Amanda meekly. "But let's go see if he's still there first."

She grabbed her purse as Ralph reached for his car keys. Together they stepped out into the garage and got into Ralph's Lexus. Amanda reached for the bag in the back seat, pulled it across to rest in the floorboard before her and rummaged through it.

"Just in case," she explained quietly.

Ralph backed the car out, and sped off in the direction of Amanda's house. "How did the date go?"

"As I said, I'm in trouble," muttered Amanda, not taking her eyes off the road. Quickly she relayed a short summary of the interrogation by Connor. Ralph listened, his face scowling. "I'm not guilty, Ralph," she finished. "But the signatures look like mine, and the pictures—"

Ralph let out a low whistle. "Amanda, these are dangerous allegations. There's no way in hell they can be true. What are we going to do about them?"

Amanda did not answer. A block prior to her house, he took a right and slowed down, circling the block. From a block away they could pick out the car. He pulled up behind a car parked at the curbside.

"Call now," Amanda urged, never taking her eyes off the car. "And Ralph, don't tell him where I am."

Ralph picked up his cell phone and dialed the police department. Reaching a dispatcher, he asked if he could leave an urgent message for Petrino to call him, leaving his number.

Moments later, the phone rang. "Carmichael here.... Listen, I just rode by Amanda's house, and there was a dark blue car with no license out front. What worried me is that there was a guy in it that matched the description of the guy Amanda said tried to run her over. Can you get someone to check it out?"

A pause occurred. "I don't think so," he said. "She was having dinner out tonight." Amanda gave him a questioning look. "Thanks a lot—you can reach me at this number. I'll see if I can locate her, OK?"

He hung up, looking at her. "Let's sit here a minute and see what happens."

Within less than a minute, the blue car pulled out from in front of Amanda's house. Ralph and Amanda looked at each other in alarm. Ralph slowly eased out into the road and followed some distance behind the car, in order to avoid detection. Looking out his rear-view mirror, he noted softly, "Damn."

"What is it?" Amanda asked anxiously.

"We're being followed," Ralph spoke tensely.

The blue car turned and made its way directly to the law office. Ralph told Amanda, "Get down," and pushed her down in the seat as he sped up and passed the blue car parked across from the entrance of the building.

Ralph accelerated, turning onto the highway. "That does it," he stated. "Stay down until I can get to a quiet place."

He drove several minutes before pulling off on a quiet stretch of road and rounding an abandoned block. Stopping, he cut off the lights and watched silently as the gray Mercedes swept past. That was the car Connor was driving, he thought, but decided not to tell Amanda his suspicions. Turning to Amanda, he ordered, "You can get up now."

As she straightened up, he continued, "We're getting you out of here."

"Where?"

"The farm. It's perfect. No one will think of looking there, because they know how you are about the place."

Amanda's eyes filled with tears. "Ralph, what am I going to do? I don't think I can go on."

"Yes, you can," Ralph cut in brusquely. "Don't go soft on me now. It's all going to be OK. I'll get you to the farm in one piece, and we'll take it from there one step at a time."

Amanda murmured her assent, as Ralph squeezed her hand and took off, accelerating rapidly and watching his mirror.

"What about Connor's accusations?"

Amanda replied, "I haven't the foggiest what he might be talking about, Ralph. All of the events of the last few days get more and more surreal. I am beginning to think I'm going mad. I know that series—I made it my business to know what we raised and what we had to spend, what worked with the audience, and what didn't. I'm confused."

Ralph said nothing, but his hands tightened on the wheel. Exhausted, Amanda fell silent, studying the road ahead.

Alone with her thoughts, she began to assess the unreality of her situation, trying to fight the fear that assaulted her. She tried to assure herself that the events of the last few weeks were just an enormous nightmare, from which she would momentarily awaken.

She tried not to think about how much she missed Andrew. She had always thought of herself as independent and self-sufficient, and had always maintained a tough exterior to the world, never revealing any weakness or emotion. Andrew had introduced her to a feeling of security and enfolded her in love. She had reciprocated, letting him rage about life's injustices, and together they managed to achieve a catharsis from the frustrations of daily life and the extreme vocations they had chosen.

When Andrew was killed, Amanda exploded with rage against his unknown killer. She had lost something most precious, and wanted someone to pay dearly for that transgression. As the questions surrounding his senseless and mysterious death remained unresolved, she felt that small iota of solace slowly suffocating, and the anger expanded to include the known habitable world. She felt that the only way to survive was to shut down and not feel.

A few weeks after Andy's funeral, she dropped out of sight, no longer able to face any more sympathetic eyes, and wrathful and impotent at not knowing the reason behind his death. It was Marjorie who finally located the missing Amanda several days later, alone at the farm, the telephone off the hook. The girl was rigid, sitting in the driving rain in fetal position in a chair on the dock overseeing the lake. Beside her were several empty bottles of alcohol; Amanda was incoherent, shivering from exposure.

Marjorie called in Doctor Howells, and together they managed to get her dry and warm and to fight the high fever and pneumonia which developed. Once the initial danger was past, Marjorie moved Amanda to her own home, nursed her back to health, held her and rocked her until Amanda began crying, let her cry, then called the finest clinical psychologist in the area and bade him make a house call, followed by several more, until Amanda began to come out of her self-imposed cocoon.

Once Amanda had physically recovered, Marjorie had involved Amanda in project after project to keep her busy and thinking of others, and Amanda had been quiescent, partly because of her love for Marjorie, partly because of the causes themselves, and partly because the immersion prevented her dealing with life without Andrew. Amanda began avoiding the farm because it was filled with memories, and bought the antiseptic little cottage in town close to the office, the church and Marjorie. Now Marjorie was gone, and in the ensuing events Amanda again felt lost, her life spiraling out of control, and again she was returning to the farm.

Amanda's journey into the past was cut short by the sound of a cell phone ringing. Ralph answered it. "Carmichael here . . . No, I'm not sure where she is. I checked the office, but didn't get an answer. She may still be at dinner—I don't know where. Did you find the car? . . . . No . . . . Well, yes, I could be mistaken, but I'm just really concerned . . . . OK, let me know. I'll stay in touch."

Ralph announced, "That was Charlie. He said he couldn't find the blue car, but they are looking for you now."

"Damn," muttered Amanda. A new thought occurred to her. "What if I'm being charged? Connor's questions weren't coming out of thin air. What is going on?"

Ralph's jaw unclenched. "Let them look. We'll soon be there. Just lean back and relax."

Amanda closed her eyes, moving her lips in silent prayer. She felt as though she was sinking into the depths of a dark pool, the troubles and memories surrounding and engulfing her.

Chapter 15

Amanda could smell the faint scent of his aftershave on her pillow, and felt his fingers running through her hair and caressing the nape of her neck before cupping her chin in his hands, something she had always enjoyed his doing, and he knew it. She felt him kissing her hair and whispering in her ear, "I want you, Mrs. Childs."

"I've waited so long," she mumbled, reaching for him, "where have you been? I'm so lost—I can't live without you. Kiss me . . ." hungrily awaiting for his mouth to descend onto hers as she felt him pull her to him.

He was suddenly gone. Not finding him and feeling the pillow beside her, Amanda opened her eyes. She was alone in the bed, the bed Andrew and she had shared. The early rays of sunlight filtered through the lace sheers, casting fantastic patterns on the soft ivory of the wall. "Andy?" she called softly.

Turning, she was brought up short, yanked rudely back into the present. Ralph sat slumped in the wicker chair a few feet from the bed, sans jacket and tie, a shotgun across his knees and a box of shells on the table at his right. Beside him were her computer attaché, carryon bag and purse.

Under the covers she was still fully clothed. As she gazed over at Ralph, he raised his head and looked at her. A flood of consciousness assaulted her, the events of the last days rushing back to fill her memory as Amanda muttered dully, "How long have I been out?"

Ralph related, "You didn't stir when I brought you in last night. I stopped at Fred's to let him know you were dropping in for a few days, so he would know we weren't intruders and shoot us. He provided the artillery in case we had to fight wild varmints. He's already come by to check on the place and bring groceries before dawn. For all I know he's on stake-out somewhere out there."

Fred Vaughan was the nearest neighbor to the farm, their lands adjoining. In fact, Andrew had bought the land from Vaughan, and arranged it so that the only road providing egress and ingress to their home went through a gated pasture next to Vaughan's house. Fred was a retired military officer who Amanda suspected had ties to the CIA or some covert military group, because he carried himself ramrod straight with a military bearing, he was proficient with any number of firearms and other weapons, and he would periodically go missing for short periods of time without explanation. Otherwise, he raised cattle, tended his land and kept largely to himself.

After Andrew's death Vaughan had quietly assumed the duties of mowing and maintaining the property. When Amanda realized that their home was still fraught with Andrew's memory that kept threatening to overwhelm her, she bought the small cottage in town and negotiated with Vaughan to manage the farm in her absence. Vaughan proved an excellent caretaker, and soon assumed responsibility for all the utilities and maintenance, Amanda giving him the run of the place and writing out a check monthly to reimburse the expenses and to pay him for his services. It was a mutually satisfactory arrangement.

Raising herself up in the bed, Amanda realized how stiff and sore she was. The tension of the last weeks, combined with the aftereffects of the accident, had left their results. Rubbing her neck and shoulder, she reprimanded Ralph. "You know, there is an excellent guestroom next door. You don't have to stand guard over me, although it's awfully gallant of you to do so. Between Fred and Bozo and myself, I'll be fine. And people will talk if we both turn up missing."

Ralph laughed then. "Amanda, being involved in scandal with you could only enhance my reputation. And if it were true," his eyes met hers for an instant, "I think we might both enjoy it."

Amanda thought she had given up blushing, but felt the color creeping up her neck. Rising, Ralph turned his back to her as he carefully leaned the shotgun against the wall, continuing in as light a tone as he could muster, "But it would never work. You and I both know that you'd be unfaithful—you're still sleeping with ghosts," as he walked out of the room.

Mortified at the thought he had witnessed her dream, she kicked off the covers and stood up. Padding into the kitchen area, she found that Ralph was already brewing coffee. She leaned against the counter and expounded, "Really, now that I'm here, it's unlikely that anyone, especially Claude Brown, would look for me here. I doubt he knows about this place, and anyone who does know about it also knows it is the last place I'd be."

"OK, OK, I get the message. You need protection, Amanda. However, if you don't need a knight in shining armor here, I'll go back to town and be one there. We need to set up a schedule for you to call in, or I'm coming back with guns blazing. Deal?"

"Deal," conceded Amanda as she looked at herself in a hallway mirror and realized how disheveled she looked.

Returning to the bedroom and adjoining bathroom, she groomed her hair, washed her face and brushed her teeth. She mechanically made the bed, unlocked the briefcase and started unpacking the contents, laying them out on the bed. She set up the charger and placed her telephone in it. Carrying the laptop and its charger into the living room to set up on the desk, she saw Ralph carefully knotting his tie and putting on his jacket.

Checking in the refrigerator, she noted that Fred had provided the larder with staples. "You want some breakfast?" she asked, trying to keep the conversation light.

"No, thanks," he said, trying to smooth his close-cropped hair.

Going up to him, she reached up and straightened his tie as she half-whispered, "Ralph, you really are my best friend. I don't know how I could ever repay you for all that you've done for me. I—"

Ralph put his finger on her lips, silencing her, took her by her shoulders and kissed her on the forehead, then turned her loose.

With his back to her, he examined his tie in the mirror and asserted, "You know not to take me too seriously, but I mean what I say now. If or when we get you out of this mess, you need a man, no strings, no commitments, just some good clean sex. It hurts to see you waiting for a man who's not coming back."

Amanda, stung, lashed out defensively, "And you need to commit, Ralph. You've got a gem of a girl, but you're a playboy afraid of settling down. It's time you became a real man."

"A real man?" Ralph smiled, but the smile didn't reach his eyes. "What's that? I thought I was doing quite well."

"You know—trading in the sports car for a SUV, coaching little league, having kids, mowing grass, loving one woman completely. Don't let Claire go. There are no soul mates out there, and life doesn't wait. Lasting love is commitment and hard work, and you get out of it what you put in."

"What about you and Andy?"

Amanda, mute, just shook her head.

"Oh, am I going to finally win an argument with you?"

Amanda, finding her voice, breathed, her voice trembling, "God would not be that cruel." Afraid of breaking down, she took a deep breath and tried to make light of the subject. "Growing up, all I wanted was two things—a bicycle and a soul mate. My parents were too afraid that I would get hurt to let me have a bicycle, and Andy's gone."

Ralph was immediately embarrassed and contrite. "Oh God, Mandy, forget I said that. I'm sorry. You're my best friend, too, and I was way out of line. It's just that you are so sad, and I'd do anything to change that. You know, when I saw you this morning, I suddenly wanted what the two of you had."

Amanda confided, her voice unsteady, "No, you don't. Our marriage was like an extra-marital affair. We were both married to our work, Andy even more so than I. It took a lot of work and effort to make time for us, to find a balance between the isolation and togetherness, and to keep from smothering each other when we were together. And then I was forced to be self-sufficient the rest of the time while he was gone God knows where."

Ralph looked down at his shoes. "I'm sorry, Mandy. I never meant to create more pain this morning by bringing all this up. Just forget I said anything. I'm out of here. You know where I am."

Turning away, he patted his pockets for his keys, suddenly brisk and business-like. "I called Sheila at home this morning and asked her to cancel all our appointments for today. Told her you were doing some shopping and getting ready for a trip to Marjy's cabin for a few days. Told her I would be back later today. That'll be our story, and maybe we'll throw everyone off the scent."

"Fred checked out Andrew's truck, and everything seems to be in working order there in case you need wheels. Anything else?"

Amanda thought a minute. "What about Charlie? Connor Thomson?" She looked at him, the air heavy with the unsaid anxieties from the previous night.

"I can't explain last night. I still think Charlie is friend, not foe. However, even if he is a good guy, he may be forced to come after you. If he calls, I'll tell him the same story, and we'll take each day as it comes. Same with Connor. You and I need to do a little investigating of our own."

"Sounds like a plan to me. Get out of here, or I'll fall in love with you just for being so smart."

"Hey, I'm really sorry about this morning," he implored earnestly, his hand on the door handle. "I expect you to check in with me no later than lunchtime."

Hearing his car pull away, Amanda had a sudden idea. Calling Sheila, she requested the phone number for Claire from Ralph's rolodex, then swore Sheila to secrecy. Calling, Amanda spent several minutes on the phone talking to Claire. Replacing the phone, she felt better for having attempted to intervene and mediate on Ralph's behalf with his girl.

Amanda looked at her watch. It was 8:32. All the present troubles came rushing back. Her mind was in turmoil, and she did not even know where to begin. What do I do next? she asked herself. She sat down at the table with a cup of coffee and tried to organize the chaotic jumble of thoughts, but try as she might she could not seem to calm down. I can't just sit here, she thought, but my brain is not functioning normally. I do not understand why I'm so tired. I need to be coming up with some way to attack these allegations against me.

She suddenly noted the mounted trout on the wall over the kitchen counter, and wanted more than anything to walk to the stream for a few minutes fly-fishing.

Disgusted at her failure to concentrate, she went into the bedroom and began rummaging through the chest of drawers.

A few minutes later, she was shod in oversized long-sleeved shirt, old khakis and waders, and had found her basket, rod and a hat with a few flies. She let herself out, but a large brown Labrador retriever was lying on the porch and jumped up as she turned.

"Bozo," she cried, and the dog ran up to her, smelled her clothes, and wagged his tail. She knelt down and rubbed his head while he tried to lick her face. "I missed you, boy," she murmured, straightening up. As she did so, she noticed the figure sitting in the rocking chair on the porch. Without a second look she knew who it was.

"Hi there, Fred. Thanks so much for letting me come up on short notice, and for the groceries."

Fred Vaughan, in garb similar to what Amanda was wearing, tipped his hat as he stood facing her. "Miss Amanda, you've been gone too long. Every time I mow this yard I hope to see you on this porch. You belong here."

Amanda dropped her fishing gear, took his hand, then threw her arms around him. "You have no idea what you have meant to me. The place looks just wonderful," she added, looking around in admiration.

"Mr. Carmichael tells me you're trying to get away for a few days without anyone finding you." Vaughan paused. "He says you are in trouble. I'm very sorry to hear about Mrs. Witherspoon—she was a fine woman. Trouble just keeps lighting on your doorstep."

Amanda acceded, looking away, "Yes, it does, Fred."

"You going to try your hand at those trout? If it was Montana, it would be a little early in the day, but these trout here don't know that. It's plenty warm in the morning time for them to eat."

"I thought I would just play around and see how rusty I really am. I don't care if I catch any, just want to give them some entertainment. Why don't you join me? You could easily show me up, maybe give me some pointers."

"I figured you'd want to be on your own. I just wanted to see if there was anything you needed."

"No, you've seen to everything for now. I'd enjoy someone to fish with. Let's go."

Together they walked out to Fred's truck, where Fred kept his fly fishing gear stored, then took off walking down to the lake. Veering off onto a path running parallel to the lakefront, they walked silently side by side, Bozo following, sometimes running ahead of them.

Andrew, an avid fly fisherman, had known Vaughan from work connections, and for many years the two were perennial fly fishing companions. When he and Amanda became seriously involved Andrew had approached Vaughan and contracted to buy a twenty-acre corner of his huge tract. Vaughan had received fishing, hunting, and grazing rights to all the property he sold Andrew, and when Andrew and Amanda became engaged, they drew up plans and began construction of the house, a two-story open farmhouse with dormers and porches.

After Amanda and Andrew were married, he had taken her fly fishing. Amanda had grown up fresh-water fishing with her father. She had seen others fly fishing on occasion, but had never tried it herself. She became fascinated with it, particularly after Andrew had given her and she had read Norman Maclean's *A River Runs Through It* and learned of fly fishermen's disdain for other types of fishing. Andrew for her birthday one year had taken her to Callaway Gardens for a fly-fishing school, and they had planned a trip to Montana to try out her skills in the Big Blackfoot once she achieved some proficiency. The trip never came to pass.

Below the lake lay a breathtaking stream, the sunlight's brilliance dappled by the old-growth trees and tall saplings irregularly lining the banks, past which the fish lay, bred with centuries of cunning and good eyesight. Amanda had never caught a fish in this stream, but Andrew had assured her that because of the clearness of the water it was an extreme challenge to fool the fish.

Wading to a spot where Andrew had planted her during one of his lessons, she tied the fly to the line, fumbling due to her long abstinence from such activity. Soon she was counting to herself, trying to lose herself in the rhythm.

Vaughan walked on downstream to a bend just in sight, and soon there was nothing but the sound of flowing water and the chattering birds overhead. Amanda knew that fly fishing, like organ playing, was part art, part skill, and she kept the practice up and prayed the art might reveal itself to her.

After an unsuccessful hour or so, she went to sit on the bank with Bozo, petting him and watching the master at work. The sheer beauty of the tiny line with the fly attached and its gavotte upon the waters was like a shot of some elixir, psychically smoothing the tangled tresses of Amanda's mind. She could feel the panic and unreality of the past days loosen their hold, and her chest began to relax its grip on the rest of her body. Laying aside her basket, hat and rod, she lay back on the grass in the shade of the tall trees, studying the green patterns of the leaves spread out above her, Although the oaks were still green and not yet turning, the poplars were sporting yellow leaves, some already browning, and the maples' green was paling. The leaves on the pear tree Andrew had planted on the bank were already fading and falling, and she could hear the lazy buzz of bees tempted by the overripe fruit already sampled by the birds. She marveled at the greens in nature, how the green of May differs from the green of July and again from the green of September. She felt she could always look at the leaves and tell the season in this place.

For the first time since before Marjy's death her mind cleared, and she could hear the organ music of Maurice Durufle in her head again. She drowsed to the sound of frogs and bees. The next thing she knew Vaughan was standing over her, stroking Bozo. She stretched and thought, Seems I'm getting very good at embarrassing myself. She apologized, "I guess I didn't realize just how tired I was."

He noted wryly, "The Good Book says something about those not working not getting to eat. You've been asleep on the job. In the meantime, I have had to fill these baskets."

Sitting up, she noticed that he had indeed filled both baskets with trout. "I'm so sorry," she said shamefacedly.

"No bother," the corners of his mouth turned up slightly. "The rule Andrew and I had was that the loser had to clean the fish, but I know how tenderhearted you are. We used to laugh about the fact that you, cold-blooded lawyer that you were, couldn't look a fish in the eye and cut its head off or eat it with the head on.

"Tell you what—I'll clean and filet them if you will cook them. Call Ralph and invite him to dinner. Make a list of whatever else you need from town. I'll bring you some fresh asparagus, and you'll have a nice meal."

"Only if you will join us," Amanda countered.

"All right—I can handle that."

Walking back up the path to the house, Amanda suddenly had an idea. "Fred, where is the nearest place I could plug into internet and e-mail? I need to do a little research."

Vaughan looked at her in surprise. "Your powers of observation are slipping. See that little dish on the back of the roof? I installed satellite internet out here." Smiling, he continued, "I decided I needed to keep up with the times, so I had a dish installed at my place. So while they were here, I thought, 'Why not do it out here as well? Maybe one day you'd come back.'"

Amanda shook her head in amazement at him, thanking him.

Arriving back at the farm with their catch, Amanda realized that it was time she called Ralph as promised. While Fred was busy cleaning fish, she went inside and retrieved the cell phone, dialing the office while looking at the satellite hookup discreetly set up under the desk.

Sheila's voice came on. After identifying herself, Amanda asked for messages. Before Sheila could respond, Ralph's voice broke in.

"There's a plethora of messages here, but I'm dealing with it, OK? How do you feel?"

"Actually, I feel better," Amanda admitted. "Fred wants you to come up for dinner tonight—I'm cooking fish."

"It's good to hear you're cooking again—how long has that been? You bet I'll be there."

"What's up?" Amanda asked in her best interrogator's voice.

"Well, Charlie called—no sign of blue Malibu or culprit. He wanted to know where you were, and I told him that you're up at Marjy's cabin for a few days. He wanted to know where that is, and how to reach you. I told him that I didn't know the exact address, and that as soon as you reached there and called in I'd get you in touch with him. But he didn't seem rabid to find you, like he had a warrant for you, surprisingly."

"Good," replied Amanda. "What else?"

"Connor wants to meet with you again."

"He has lots of documents I might like to see, but that can wait," interjected Amanda, more calmly than she felt. "I think he also has an invitation for me to a jail cell, which is more reason to stay away."

"Another item. Bill had called Sheila yesterday afternoon and obtained Connor's phone number from Sheila. He left a message that you were not to worry about the church and the audit—he would handle it."

Amanda laughed mirthlessly. "He's a little late, but that's OK. God, if only he could. If he can get me out of this trouble I need to marry him. Anything else?"

Ralph paused, and she knew he was not happy with her comment, even in jest. "Settlement paperwork is on my desk. I told them you were out of town, and they had to deal with me. If you trust me, everything looks in order, and I can get Garvin in to sign off."

"Fine," she agreed, surprising herself. She was never one to shirk reviewing everything that left the office, but realized that Ralph could be trusted to handle the matter without her. I've got bigger fish to fry, she concluded to herself.

"Oh, and something else. Bill called again this morning. Sheila says he sounded testy and was looking for you. I'm about to call him back and let him know you are out of pocket for a few days."

"Thanks. By the way, Fred has the internet installed up here, so I thought I would do a little checking on the information Connor Thomson was leaking last night in his interrogation. I'll call you if I come up with something."

"Dinner's at sevenish—bring some dessert from Marciano's. I'm not feeling THAT industrious. And Ralph, be very careful. If there's someone after me, he may be watching you as well. This has to be bigger than just Claude Brown, but I can't figure it out." Amanda rang off, questions still nagging her.

Amanda quickly planned the rest of the menu and checked for what items she needed, then made a quick grocery list for Fred.

She decided to sit on the front porch for a few minutes while Fred was gone. She sat in a rocking chair, Bozo lying nearby, watching the panorama of the sky. In the east the sky was pockmarked with a few fluffy clouds. But the west was covered with dark menacing clouds and thunder. As her eyes lighted on the old rosebushes laden with the last blooms of the season, she heard the noise of rain on the metal roof of the barn behind her. She listened to the rain as it encroached to the east and overtook the horizon. She watched the large drops of rain as they bounced off the blades of grass like smooth stones skipping on the surface of a pond.

Then, as quickly as it came, the rain was gone. The smell of the rain coupled with the old-fashioned roses and fresh-mown grass filled Amanda with the melancholy of days gone by, of moments on the porch swing with Andy, sharing the paper, or in their bed, listening to the rain pelt the metal roof with a staccato energy, as they made love. She felt the stirrings of the old longing, the familiar stab that had sent her fleeing this lovely place. Funny how the farm with all its poignant memories from which she once ran was now her refuge.

The cell phone rang. At first she could not place the sound, then realized the source of the shrill insistence. Going inside, she retrieved the phone. "Hello?"

"Where the hell are you?" Bill's voice cut through her thoughts. "I've been beside myself with worry about you."

"Why, Bill, that's sweet of you," stalled Amanda, wondering if Ralph had talked to Bill. "Didn't Ralph call you?"

"Yes, but he's mighty tight-lipped about where you are."

"I'm on my way to Marjy's cabin," Amanda decided to go with a half-truth. "I needed to get away for a day or so, and thought I could think clearer away from town."

"You tell me where you are right now. I'm coming to you," said Bill testily.

"Why, Bill? What's up?" demurred Amanda, suddenly nervous.

"You're in no condition to be off by yourself, and with some maniac out there loose after you. What was Ralph thinking?"

"Maniac? Where did you get that idea? I'm fine, Bill, really. Please don't worry about me."

But Bill persisted. "But where are you? Mandy, don't be so God-damned mysterious. You're all alone out there, God knows where, with only that damned Negro of yours knowing where you are."

Amanda, shocked, breathed, "How dare you—"

"The whole town is talking about you and him. It's disgraceful."

"For your information, he has a girlfriend, and I've never been so incensed in my life—"

Changing his tack, Bill's voice suddenly softened. "Mandy, please don't shut me out. Let me come to you. You need my protection."

Mandy suddenly had a revelation. She understood exactly what Bill was doing. He was pushing the buttons to make her react to him, to get her to feed him the information he sought, just as he had done for most of their lives. She silently cursed herself, angry for not recognizing the tactic after all these years.

Bill was saying, "You're my number one concern. Let me know where you are," he crooned. "Let me be with you, Mandy."

Amanda suddenly thought about asking him about Connor's revelations about the recital series and the funds. He's the logical one to explain all this, she surmised. Of course he has to know what is going on. But something held her back. She knew it would mean a longer, more entangled conversation with him, with his demanding to see her and hear everything. Bill can help me, she argued with herself. He can get to the bottom of it, resolve the mess, protect me. I really do need his help. It all makes sense to ask. But she was just not yet ready to pay the price, even in her current predicament. I need to think, she chastised herself. I need to work out what questions to ask, how to approach him, she thought, but knew she was stalling.

Amanda sighed. "I'm sorry, Bill, but I just have some things to work out. I'll call you back later, I promise."

As she hung up she noticed that Fred had returned, a couple sacks of groceries on the counter. She smiled, but then saw the stern look on his face. She realized that he must have heard some if not all of the conversation.

Her face flamed as she met his accusatory stare. "It's not what you think, Fred."

"It damn sure better not be," he swore, surprising her with his ferocity. "Don't let Bill Barnes screw with your head any more. Do you love him?"

Amanda laughed. "Heavens, no. I realized a long time ago I never loved him. I was once crazy about an idealized version of him. I've only lost my heart to one man in my life."

Fred started removing items from the bags. "I always wondered why you let him make a fool of you."

"Many women would be flattered—would it be so bad if I let him catch me?"

At Vaughan's stony silence, Amanda closed her eyes. "It's not like there's a queue of knights in shining armor waiting for me."

"How would you know? You're still waiting for someone who's not coming back."

Amanda flared. "I'm trying, Fred. It's hard. That's why I left this place—everything reminds me of Andy."

"Running away isn't the answer—you have got to face the facts."

"Well, then, maybe I need to 'merge', as he puts it, with Bill. I'm so tired of fighting, of waiting," Amanda baited him.

Fred's eyes narrowed. "Mandy, there's better out there for you."

Amanda quickly deflated. "Bill's just an old friend, Fred. When he shows back up in my life there is an agenda, something he wants. I just wonder what it is now."

"Isn't it obvious? The papers say you're a gold mine right now," Fred countered flatly.

"The papers? Oh my God, I didn't think about the media. But surely the Barnes' fortunes are not that depleted," Amanda laughed.

"You never know. Just watch your back," warned Fred gruffly.

Amanda thought to herself, Yet another 'be careful' has landed at my feet.

"I will," she promised yet again. "I'm sorry, Fred. I'm going to get a shower, then I'll be ready to start dinner. Thanks for the groceries and the advice."

Chapter 16

Amanda decided to try out the internet. She quickly hooked up her laptop computer, and soon had it on and was trying to follow the laborious instructions left on the desk by the installer.

Finally arriving at the world wide web, she quickly did a Google search for Grayton and Shivers. Checking personnel, she found the name 'Connor Thomson' and clicked on the link. No photograph appeared, only an e-mail address. So much for that.

Next she logged on to the site of the Secretary of State, Division of Corporations. Running a search for WWAC, Inc., she discovered that it was multi-national, registered in Delaware, with an ancillary address for the corporation in Milford, a town about 45 miles away from Mainville. That's interesting, she thought, jotting down the address.

The next screen netted her the name of the registered agent, "W. Witherspoon", at the Milford address. I know of no Witherspoons left in this area, and Marjorie and Jerrod never spoke of other living kin, she thought to herself. Who is W. Witherspoon?

Conducting a search for officer or board of directors, she suddenly received a jolt. Listed as CEO and president was "Amanda Childs" with the same Milford address given, and the treasurer and vice-president was also listed as "Amanda Childs".

Amanda sat back and stared at the screen. That seemed a huge coincidence. Apparently Connor had found this information and determined that she was one and the same with this person. And why not, with documents bearing her signature and photographs of someone who was her double. But how to prove otherwise to him? She printed the page of information to show Ralph.

Remembering that she had not checked her e-mail since Marjorie's death, she did so desultorily, not expecting much. Marjorie was her main e-mail correspondent other than an organist e-mail list to which she contributed periodically. Downloading and sorting through the mail, mechanically deleting junk mail and unimportant list posts, she suddenly came upon two posts, one from "Marjorie", dated yesterday, and a second from "W. Witherspoon", dated this date.

Her heart in her throat, she opened the mail from "Marjorie": "It's beautiful here, and I miss you so much. Hope you will join me soon. Marjy."

Her blood turned to ice, as she struggled for breath. Whoever has stolen Marjorie's computer is playing a nasty joke, she told herself, but she could not tear her eyes from the message on the screen.

Angry at whoever would play such a cruel prank, she opened the next e-mail. It read simply: "We need to meet ASAP to discuss our mutual business interests. W. Witherspoon."

Frightened now, she was transfixed, immobile, unable to think. In a burning rage, she hit the reply button: "I don't know who the hell you are or what game you are playing, but yes, I'll be happy to meet with you. I have some friends in the law enforcement community I'd like you to meet."

She sent the message, then wondered at whether she had been prudent in doing so. She wished that she could confide in Petrino. But it looked like Petrino was in league with Claude Brown. And there might be warrants any time now for her arrest. Dealing with Connor's allegations without anyone to turn to for assistance made her feel even more isolated than ever. Turning her attention back to the e-mails, she thought anxiously, I'm being framed. Someone is messing with my head, but why? Is it Claude Brown? What is the purpose? What do I do?

Looking up at the old pendulum clock on the wall, she realized that she needed to shower and get ready to prepare the evening meal. She quickly printed out the two e-mails also, leaving them on the desk.

Later, Amanda, out of the shower, looked in the closet at the items she had left behind, clothes that had reminded her of Andy. Finding a flowing gauzy cotton dress of yellow with tiny blue rosebuds, she remembered an anniversary picnic down by the stream with Andrew, and how they had spent the afternoon lying on the bank examining clouds and leaves, talking of their future together. She remembered the flash of sunlight framing his head above hers on the blanket beside the flowing water.

Abruptly, she cut off the memory, slamming the closet door and throwing the dress on the bed. "Stop it," she said aloud to herself. God, why don't I just have sex with Bill? That will get him off my back and get my mind off Andrew. She laughed to herself for such a ludicrous thought. My parents would have made Jewish mothers look tame. Everything seems so hard, so fraught with guilt and dire consequence. Life just seems so much harder than it has to be. Maybe I need to subscribe to Bill's philosophy.

Applying makeup and towel-drying her hair, leaving it curling in tendrils framing her face, she slipped on some casual clothes for cooking and walked out of the bedroom. There on the desk was a note from Fred: 'Ralph called, and said he's bringing a friend, so look sharp.' She shook her head at Ralph's perpetual joking, troubled wondering who he was trusting with the secret of her whereabouts.

Going into the kitchen and finding an apron, she was soon busy concocting her secret lemon dill sauce for the fish. Because Fred had caught enough fish, she was lightly pan frying half and broiling the other, using different seasonings for the two recipes. She prepared the asparagus and salad, and found some luscious German rolls contributed by Fred from a local bakery. Opening the refrigerator, she found three bottles of chardonnay chilling. She made a pitcher of her omnipresent Southern iced tea, and looked at her watch, carefully determining the time to start each dish.

Fred appeared in the doorway, in pressed khaki trousers and duck shirt. Amanda looked at him admiringly. "Wow, you're a sight to see."

"Not as lovely as you," he returned the compliment. "Can I help?"

"I've already got the fish broiling in the oven, and am about to put on the filets for pan-frying. After that I want to go slip on my dress, if you will watch the fish for me one moment."

She busied herself accomplishing the tasks, then handing him the spatula, said, "I'll be right back."

Moments later, she returned, her golden locks curling around her face, decked in her yellow dress and smelling faintly of perfume. Vaughan looked at her and said, "Wow!"

Amanda blushed slightly. "There's nothing much to do. Ralph should be here any minute. Everything else is ready. Would you like some of the lovely wine you've brought?"

"No, I think I'll wait. Do we have spirits on hand for our guests?"

Amanda remarked ruefully, "I haven't checked. Everything should be as I left it. Andy kept a few extra bottles down in the cellar with his special wines."

Fred crossed over to the bar and checked. "Looks like you have everything but Scotch."

"What, no Scotch?" a voice boomed from the doorway. Ralph came in, a confectioner's box in hand, followed by Connor.

Amanda, caught off guard, her face registering shock, breathed, "Oh, shit," before catching herself and murmuring, "Hello, Connor; how are you?" as Ralph handed the box to Fred, kissed Amanda on the cheek and looked around the bar himself.

"What shall we do?"

Amanda glared at Ralph, and attempted a tight smile. "There's probably a bottle or two in the cellar. One of Andy's colleagues at the Bureau sent him a case of Glenlivet from Scotland for an anniversary gift some time ago, and I'm sure there must be some left."

Fred offered, "I'll go check," but Connor interrupted, "Allow me—your hands are full."

Amanda intervened. "Guys, you'll never find it. Fred, please watch the fish in the pan while I run down there."

She opened the cellar door. "Darn, the light bulb must be burned out," she remarked. Reaching to her right, she retrieved a flashlight and turned it on, proceeding down the stairs.

She heard Ralph urging, "Go after her, man. Don't let her be breaking any fine bottles of Scotch."

She heard steps following her down the stairs gingerly, as she flashed the light before her. Reaching the cellar floor, she rummaged behind a box or two in the tiny space, almost losing her balance. Connor reached out and steadied her, and she let out a small nervous laugh, anxious at his proximity. Damn Ralph, she fumed to herself. Why is Connor here?

He made some compliment, but she was so faint with fright she could barely remain focused. He then spoke lowly, "Amanda, I'm sorry for the way I broke the news last night. I want you to know I believe you."

Amanda's heart skipped a beat. But is it enough that he believes her? she thought. Maybe he's just saying that to gain my trust. "There it is," Amanda indicated, shining the light at a box at Connor's right.

Connor reached for the box and retrieved two bottles of Glenlivet. He turned. At that moment, startled by his closeness, she dropped her flashlight.

"Darn," she exclaimed, as the crashing of the flashlight on the hard floor was heard.

Connor, Scotch bottle tucked under each arm, took her arm and provided his own flashlight to her. "Here—lead the way," he said huskily. "I can't maneuver with both Scotch bottles and a flashlight, anyway."

She could feel his eyes on her as he followed her back up the dark stairwell to the light of the kitchen. Amanda resumed her place at the stove, a light flush of pink, her heart fluttering wildly. As she started serving up the food, she ordered Fred to serve as bartender and Ralph to open the wine for dinner. She quickly finished preparing the table, and placed the dessert in the refrigerator for later.

Ralph handed her a bourbon, and held his own glass in the air. "To the miraculous resurrection of Chef Amanda—may this repast be up to her glorious standards, and be one of many delightful evening meals to come."

All raised their glasses and drank, before Amanda encouraged them to take a place at the table.

As the salad was passed along with Amanda's homemade dressing, Ralph commented, "You look exceptionally pretty tonight."

Amanda beamed briefly, before inquiring, "What's the latest on our case next week?"

Ralph looked at Connor in mock disgust. "See what a slave driver she is—only interested in work. Work is fine; all is well—the papers are signed on the settlement, and I will cancel the trial tomorrow."

There was a lull in the conversation as platters of food were passed. Ralph spoke quietly to Amanda, "I guess Bill made good on his threat and got in touch with you?"

"Yes, he did," Amanda affirmed, her voice even.

Fred turned to Ralph and winked. "I've heard that in some states it is a defense to murder if the victim needed killing. Is that true, Ralph?"

Connor laughed, answering for him. "It depends on whether it is a Democrat or a Republican and how much the campaign contribution was."

They all laughed good-naturedly, as Ralph poured more wine in their glasses. Ralph avoided Amanda's accusatory stare. Vaughan looked over questioningly at Amanda, who returned his gaze with a tight smile. The rest of dinner was low-key mixture of anecdotes and jokes, with no mention of the events of the past few days. Amanda wondered to herself why Connor was invited, and was still confounded over his remarks the previous night, but found herself noting his puns and witticisms. He tried to meet her eyes several times, but she tried to keep hers averted.

Ralph voiced suddenly, "What we need is some dinner music," as he stood up and headed toward the living room.

Amanda quickly rose. "Let me show you where the stereo and albums are."

Following him into the living room, she stopped him at the desk. "Why did you bring Connor?" she hissed quietly, her hand gripping his arm tightly.

"Oh, I'm almost forgot—he drove the rental car," Ralph replied casually, handing her a set of keys. "I got you 4-wheel drive."

"I don't understand why you would push me to come out here, then disclose my location to the enemy," Amanda contended, her voice low and angry.

"I have excellent reasons, but the explanation can wait until after dinner," Ralph rejoined quietly. "I promise all will be revealed."

"Wait a minute; I want to show you something," she suddenly recalled. Pulling out printed copies of the Secretary of State web pages, she showed them to him. Then she pulled out printed copies of the e-mails received. Ralph whistled softly.

"What is this?" his face creased in a frown.

Amanda shrugged her shoulders. "This is a cruel joke, or someone is involving me in a diabolical game, Ralph. I don't know anything about this corporation. But if we can find out whoever stole Marjy's computer, I think that will solve at least some of the riddles. Connor must know this information regarding the corporation, which was why he was asking me those questions. But we have to find out who this is, and who is behind this mess."

There was a noise behind them, and Connor stood in the doorway, regarding them, his face inscrutable. "Are we having dessert or what?" he demanded lightly.

Amanda returned to the kitchen and began providing coffee and dessert dishes, while Vaughan helped serve up cheesecake tartlets with fresh fruit and cream on top. Ralph rejoined them in the kitchen. A few minutes later, the music of George Benson was wafting through the room. Ralph looked at Amanda and asked anxiously, "That's not too painful?"

"It's nice," she stammered, trying to shut out the flood of memories the song recalled.

They had their dessert largely in silence. As they were finishing, a slow seductive selection began. Ralph came up to Amanda.

"Could I have this dance?"

Amanda protested as Ralph took her hand and forced her to her feet. They danced together, drifting into the living area as the turntable crooned 'This Masquerade". Amanda's heart constricted.

Amanda finally begged off dancing, and sat down in a chair, as the others finished their coffee. She excused herself to the kitchen after asking everyone regarding more coffee. When she returned Connor was standing next to the grand piano, covered with a white matelasse blanket.

"What's this?" he mused aloud, laying his hand on the coverlet.

"Amanda's piano," Ralph answered for her. "When she was in high school, everyone thought she would go on to major in piano performance. But she showed them."

Connor turned to Amanda. "Would you play?"

Amanda demurred. "It hasn't been tuned in a while, and I'm rusty."

Connor in one move swept the coverlet off the instrument, then opened up the keyboard cover. He walked over and took Amanda's hand and guided her to the bench.

Amanda looked at the instrument a moment with fondness, then started playing Claude Debussy's "Clair de lune" softly and sensuously. The room was silent as she finished. Then she launched into a sweet minimalist piece.

When she completed it, Connor was standing at the other end of the piano. He stated in a low voice, "Debussy and Sibelius—like a spring breeze."

Amanda breathed in sharply, staring at him intently. She stood up, intending to leave the room, then sat back down and began to play. Completing the piece, she noticed that Connor had disappeared. Ralph and Fred, noticing her melancholy preoccupation, began light-heartedly discussing the morning's fishing and laughing at Amanda's falling asleep.

Fred and Ralph clamored for the job of doing the dishes, so Amanda sat alone on the back screened porch, enjoying the view of the full moon casting its light over the pond. Lost in her thoughts, she hardly noticed that Connor had joined her, sitting in the other rocking chair. She finally felt his eyes on her, and turned to look at him.

Sitting in the dark, Conner broke the silence. "You talked of meeting your husband the night of the fraternity party. Would you mind telling me about it?"

Amanda, still uncomfortable with him and not trusting Ralph's confidence in him, but more relaxed from the effects of the wine, decided to throw a curve of her own. "You first—why don't you tell me about your marriage?"

Connor was silent a moment. Amanda felt a tiny sense of satisfaction that perhaps she had silenced him for good, before he replied, "That's fair, I guess. I assume Alex told you about that. The divorce has been final for several years. There's not much to tell. We met at a friend's wedding. It was infatuation for her, but I mistook it for something more. It was a whirlwind romance, courtship and wedding.

"Then I came home early one day, and found her with one of her co-workers. We were together a year. I really thought maybe it was my long hours and that I was neglecting her, and suggested counseling for us. Then one day a couple months later I came home and the place was empty—she had gone and taken everything.

"I was served papers, hired a lawyer, and finally settled. I was bitter for a while. But life goes on.

"I was pretty cynical about women, but a friend of mine showed me how good marriage could be. I'm holding out for that. That's the short version. Your turn."

Amanda looked at him, but he leaned forward and spoke. "I know that you are upset with me. This is a part of my job I don't like. But, Amanda, I believe what you told me last night. I want you to believe me. Please tell me about Andrew—I'd really like to hear."

Amanda, disarmed by his words, sighed. "Andy and I met the night of the frat dance. Andy was a former member of the same fraternity, but at Duke. He had graduated from the FBI academy, and was actually on campus at FSU as a recruiter for the week. He received an invitation to the bash.

"I had noticed him at the party, but so did all the other girls there—he certainly turned heads. Bill was off doing his thing, flirting with the debs, drinking too much and doing that bizarre male bonding thing. I was not fond of these parties—I talked to some of the people there, but mainly tried to remain invisible. I had agreed to go with Bill once or twice before when he didn't have a date, partly in promise to Monica to keep an eye on him, because he did like to drink too much.

"I had wandered into the small library of this huge house, where they had pushed a grand piano to make room in the big room for the kegs and dancing. I sat down in there and started playing quietly, bored waiting for Bill. Andrew had grown tired of the party, but had found a quiet place to await his buddy until he was ready to leave. Andy came up to me and we started talking.

"He asked me to dance—the DJ was booming some hokey slow music throughout the whole neighborhood. I think it was "Colour My World". I told him I wasn't a very good dancer. He pulled me off the piano bench and started teaching me. We began laughing because I was stepping all over his feet. I was flattered at all his attention.

"Billy had disappeared. I started to just walk back to my dorm, and Andy offered to walk me home. I said yes. We sat on the steps and had a Coke and laughed. Then he left."

"No romantic kiss under the arbor?" Connor quizzed lightly.

"Afraid not," Amanda smiled. "But he showed up at Monica's funeral a few days later, just out of the blue. I was surprised to see him. After the wake, we went out for coffee, and he asked for my phone number. I thought, sure, why not? I figured he was too good to be true."

"Then what happened?" persisted Connor.

"Near the end of first year of law school, almost two years later, he showed up out of nowhere and asked me for a date. I was shocked—had given up on hearing from him. I almost said no. But I didn't." Amanda laughed softly. "You'll never guess where he took me."

"Where?"

"A colleague's wife was a Fred Astaire dance instructor, and Andy set up dance lessons for us. He was a great dancer, and we had a ball. We had several dates and a few more dance lessons."

"What was he doing all this time?" Connor asked.

"He was a special agent with the FBI, serving in Maryland for a while. He had connections with the Presidential administration in office at the time. Then he was working some case out West, which made it difficult for us to see each other. Then when I graduated from law school, we both were able to get jobs in Central Florida, and he asked me to marry him."

"Marjorie was ecstatic—I think she saw little babies to coddle. When I announced our engagement, she talked me into getting married at St. Catherine's, and planned the wedding. I really didn't want her to go to all that expense, but knew she was doing for me what she was denied doing for her own daughter, and I didn't have the heart to refuse her.

"Andy and I went to New York City on our honeymoon. The second night we were there he took me to the Blue Note. He had gotten me interested in jazz. He surprised me with the autographed album. It was a perfect evening."

"His death must have been very hard for you."

Amanda replied, as though Connor was no longer there, "I went to some obligatory function in D.C. once with Andy. He was called away to confer with some brass, and I ended up in a group with several NASA scientists disputing the dimensions and shape of the universe. As their arguments got more and more esoteric, people would drift away. But it was fun to watch them in action, and I didn't want to appear uninterested in what they were saying.

"They finally excused themselves to look for paper and pen to write out formulas to each other. I was left standing there alone, gazing at this large Kandinsky towering over the mantel. I was thinking that the mantel was probably not the ideal place to put it, but if you got it, flaunt it. Besides, I liked Kandinsky.

"I knew that the universe was larger than a plane of several light-years wide, because I seemed to spend my life sticking somewhat out of place with the rest of the universe. There were moments when I was reminded that all human experience was pretty much universal, but I remained a committee of one, angry and ready to hit the world.

"Andy grounded me. He pulled me back into orbit, and gave me perspective. He made the overwhelming manageable, and the mediocre and common something extraordinary. I miss that most of all."

As though coming to herself and realizing that Connor was there, she grew warm with embarrassment and apologized. "Please excuse me. I don't know why I ran on like that."

Connor replied quietly, "That's OK. I was just wondering how the men at the party could notice anything else but you. You apparently weren't wearing this dress."

Amanda laughed, her face suffused in pink. "That's the sort of response I would expect from Alex."

"I knew I could make you laugh," Connor remarked. His tone suddenly serious, he added, "I know exactly what you are talking about, Amanda. I didn't mean to make light of it. I'm sorry about Andy. I know it must have been devastating."

Suddenly inflamed by his sympathy, Amanda stared ahead. "Yes," Amanda sneered. "I'm here, and he's not. I live with that every day. I don't know what happened to him—no one will tell me. He haunts me, and everyone feels sorry for me. I don't need your pity, Mr. Thomson. And you now know much more about me than you wanted or needed to know."

Her anger rising, she railed, "I don't know who you are, but I know that I'm the prime suspect in your probe. And to answer your questions, no, I don't know why my name is listed as CEO of WWAC, Inc., on the Secretary of State's records. I don't know what the hell is going on. I don't know why you have signatures that look like mine, or photographs that look like me. I don't know why I'm getting e-mail from dead people and unknown registered agents. My life is a shambles, and I feel like I'm the continuing butt of someone's cruel joke. I'm not stupid; I know this spells big trouble. I'm scared I can't convince you, much less anyone else, that it's not me."

Standing up, she stared at him, her eyes large, mirroring her fear. "And 'substantial assistance' is not an accountant's term; it's a cop's. I know where this is heading."

Amanda stalked off, walking down to the dock bathed in moonlight. Avoiding the chair where Marjorie had found her after Andrew's death, she stood at the end of the dock, listening to the sounds of the night, trembling with fear and hot at the same time, ashamed of her outburst and sorry for her angry disclosures. I'm screwed, she thought despairingly.

She was there for what seemed a long time, when suddenly she heard a voice behind her. "Amanda, who do you think is sending these e-mails? Please confide in me."

She lashed out at him, "You know a lot you are not telling me. The Glenlivet, your description about the Sibelius—Andy used those words. These aren't coincidences, are they? How do you know this stuff? Is someone setting me up? Is it you? Who are you? I don't have to tell you anything—if you got evidence against me, just have me arrested and be done with it, but quit these games."

"Amanda, why was a deposit of $400,000 made to your checking account from the recital series fund last Friday, the date Mrs. Witherspoon died, then to a Cayman's account?"

"My God!" she cried. "I swear it cannot be true. Stop it!"

Amanda turned and stumbled, falling headlong toward the edge of the dock and the pond. Connor grabbed her by the waist and bodily pulled her back against him. Amanda pushed at him, muttering, "Leave me alone," but he silenced her, crushing her in an embrace and kiss that left her stunned and dizzy. She was unable to resist, and he imprisoned her mouth again, a long, lingering kiss that seemed to burn her like a hot brand. She savored the moment, before coming to herself and pulling away.

"No. How dare you?" she asked tremulously. He silenced her again, enfolding her to him.

Suddenly unable to stop herself, she found herself responding to him, wrapping her arms around his neck as he continued to hold her and devour her. She found herself unable to breathe, drowning as she molded herself to him and felt the warmth of his body flow through her, until he finally released her mouth.

Connor whispered, still holding her, "I can't help myself. I look at you and want you more than anyone I've ever known. And I feel so damned guilty feeling this way. But I do know one thing. Andy would not want you to keep up a shrine to him. He died saving you, Amanda. He loved life, but he loved you even more, and would want you to exorcise your demons and go on with life. You deserve to live, to love again."

She stared at him as the color drained from her face. He continued. "Amanda, there are so many things I need to tell you, but now is not the time. You're in great danger. I made a promise that I would protect you. Let me."

Amanda, past all reason, slapped him hard and full in the face. "How dare you—what do you know—"she began, but he refused to let her go. Enraged, she pushed him away violently. "Don't!"

She ran toward the house, as his cell phone erupted. "Connor here," she heard him say as she made good her escape.

She was ashamed at her wanton behavior and tried to calm her racing pulse, truly frightened. She heard him call to her, "How far to the airport?"

She gave no answer, running to the house, intent only on reaching her destination.

"I'll call you right back in one minute," she heard him reply.

She had no idea if he was behind her, but only had one goal of getting away from him. She gained the house and flitted through the house, slamming the bedroom door behind her. She heard Ralph call to her, "Amanda, what's wrong?"

She heard Connor's voice asking Ralph how far it was to the nearest airport. What did he mean that Andy died saving her? How did he know Andy? What did he know? She only knew it was time she found out. Striding over to her computer attache, she retrieved the Beretta and the clip and slipped back to the door, listening.

Connor was speaking rapidly. "I'll be there as soon as I can. Have a plane waiting—I can be there in thirty. Yes, can you get some back-up surveillance here?"

Then apparently he was talking to the men in the room. "I need Amanda in New York—she needs to be on that plane in the morning."

How did he know I was flying out tomorrow? she thought angrily. He was still talking. "And you must keep all this to yourself—no one knows yet but my men and Chief Petrino. It's imperative that we not blow the cover until the operation is complete."

Suddenly realizing that Connor could answer her questions about Andy's death and that he was leaving, she yanked open the bedroom door and marched out, pointing the Beretta at him. "Who the hell are you? What do you know about Andy? You don't think I'm going to just let you walk out of here without an answer? This is my life, and I deserve to know. Why are you here? What happened to Andrew? What's happening to me? I want answers, and I want them now," she demanded, her eyes glittering and her voice quavering, but her hand steady as she pointed the gun at Connor.

As he turned to her, her heart went to her throat. He slowly took the gift card out of his breast pocket, and walked toward her. The safety audibly clicked off as she whispered hoarsely, "No further, please—answer my questions."

Ralph, alarmed, advanced slowly toward her and said softly, "Mandy, for God's sake, put the gun down. Jon is on our side. He's a federal agent."

Connor continued toward her, and slowly handed the yellowed card to her as she continued to point the gun at him. He quietly declared, "The Glenlivet was from me."

Chapter 17

She took the card with her free hand and glanced at it. The card bore the inscription: "For you and your dream girl—may you have an eternity of happiness together. JMC."

Amanda faltered, but still holding the gun on Connor, walked the few steps to the mantel. Pulling a photograph down of two men on a boat laughing and holding a large mackerel, she looked at it, then at Connor.

"You? You're Andy's 'JM'?" she cried incredulously.

"Yes, Amanda. My real name is Jon Connor. I'm a senior agent for the Bureau. Andy and I were working together when he was killed. It's a long story, Amanda, and I want to tell you everything, but we've no time, and you ARE in danger."

He crossed over to Amanda and gently took the gun from her, placing it on the mantel. Taking both her hands in his, he turned to the two men, saying, "I need your help, both of you.

"Ralph, I need you to get me post haste to that airstrip. I'll explain on the way what is going on." Then he turned to Vaughan and asked him to help protect Amanda until reinforcements could arrive.

"Suffice it to say that under no circumstances can Amanda go back to town or have contact with anyone until she gets on that plane tomorrow morning. I'd take her with me tonight, but I've been vetoed on that. We don't know yet who all the collaterals are, and until the net drops it's been determined we cannot do anything that might warn them. I have a team on the way, but until they arrive, I'm counting on the two of you."

Amanda asked, "Who? Claude Brown?"

Turning to Amanda, Connor released her hands, saying, "I can't tell you yet. I'm convinced you're innocent, but I have still to convince others in the Bureau. I'm sorry to leave you right now. I'm sorry I can't answer the questions yet. Rest assured I'll be back, and I'll tell you everything." Touching her cheek, he paused and gazed at the stricken look in her eyes, then dropped his hand and abruptly walked out. Ralph squeezed her hand, whispering, "I'll be right back," as he walked by her to follow in Connor's wake.

Vaughan turned to Amanda as she stared impotently at the door from which the two men had exited. "I'm going to the truck to get some artillery. You might want to change into some trekking clothes."

"I'll only be a moment." Amanda crossed over to the bedroom, her mind churning, full of more questions and emotions. Five minutes later, she returned, in black twills and dark T-shirt, her hair tied back, Andy's Beretta in her hand. Vaughan, having returned, wore a holstered gun on his hip and had a shotgun in hand. He looked at her with satisfaction. "Good girl."

Amanda sat on the sofa, drained. A person who enjoyed control and liked having all the answers, she felt out of her element. "What do we do now?" she asked simply.

Vaughan replied, "Well, we are at a distinct disadvantage. We know not who the enemy is. However, we are probably fairly safe in this general area, we know our terrain, and we can need to plan our options carefully."

"Who is the enemy?" Amanda echoed. "Who is who?"

Vaughan looked at her sympathetically, but continued, his voice business-like, authoritative. "First, we need to douse some of these lights. Can you make up the bed to look like you're in it? We'll leave a bathroom light on. Let's cut off the rest."

Amanda sprang into action, glad for some activity that would prevent her from going mad with her thoughts, going into the bedroom while Vaughan went around cutting off all the lights. Amanda returned. "What now?"

"Do you have a thermos and canteen? We should have some coffee and water with us, as well as some dark jackets and blankets. We don't know but what we might have to take immediate flight."

Amanda walked through the room, lit only by the ghostly moonlight, to the kitchen. From an overhead cupboard, she pulled out two thermos bottles in a small carry bag. Vaughan took one from her and went to the refrigerator, placing some ice cubes in it before filling it with water, while she took what was left of the coffee and filled the other thermos. Then she went to a closet and pulled out two dark windbreakers and two Navy blankets. That task done, Vaughan spoke again.

"The moon is our enemy tonight, so we have to make her our friend. However, if anyone finally makes the connection between you and this place, they'll come looking. The problem here is that we have only one way out by vehicle, so I suggest we take what we think we'll need and head back in my truck toward my place, where we will have more flight options."

Amanda said, "Maybe we should take both vehicles. I think we need to take the phone and laptop for emergency communication." She picked up her attaché, unplugged the laptop and packed it, her phone, her gun, and the thermos bottles in it. She picked up her purse, attaché and blankets.

"Is that all?" Vaughan asked.

"Yes, sir," Amanda responded, her voice quavering as she realized it was not some drill.

Vaughan grabbed her arm. "Steady," he said. Both of them stepped out on the porch. Vaughan spoke quietly but sharply to the dog on the porch. "Bozo! In the truck, now."

The dog immediately obeyed. Vaughan nodded to her. "Let's go. You follow me—if we meet anyone, throw it in park and run like hell to the woods. Keep your Beretta by your side at all times."

Amanda slid into the 4-Runner and he climbed into the truck, and they took off down the trail, Vaughan leading. After several minutes of riding the bumpy road, they arrived. Vaughan motioned to Amanda to pull up beside him, and confided, "I'm pulling the truck into the barn, and we'll leave the faster and more maneuverable vehicle out front for a quick getaway. Here's a flashlight; go on in. Leave the lights off inside the house for now. Then we'll set up camp."

Amanda briefly wondered what "setting up camp" meant, but nodded and walked up to the house, letting herself in. Normally she would be smiling at what seemed to her Vaughan's sense of melodrama, but too much had happened too quickly for her not to take him seriously. She realized he was keeping her occupied with tasks, and she was grateful for the chance to escape the questions in her head.

The house's interior was simply but comfortably furnished, everything rugged and functional, a man's haven. The rustic paneled walls sported few photographs, but a full-bodied bobcat and an elk head were stuffed and mounted on the wall. At the end of the room was a huge armoire, open and sporting a television, several short-wave and ham radios, and a computer. Vaughan was a neat housekeeper—there was no clutter, in fact very little to give additional clues as to the nature of the man who lived there.

Momentarily Vaughan returned. He beckoned to Amanda, "Come with me," and led the way to his bedroom. Unlocking and opening a closet door, he flicked on a light, and Amanda saw that he had a varied arsenal neatly organized on the wall.

He looked at her surprised features. "What of this can you handle?"

Amanda coughed. "I've shot a .357, a 9 millimeter, and a shotgun once or twice."

"OK," he nodded, grabbing a couple of weapons and ammunition and handing to her, taking some for himself. "What I want to do in case they should come looking for us is to plant a weapon or two around for access."

They walked around the house, barn and yard and he carefully loaded and hid a weapon in various strategic spots. Then they returned to the house.

"Miss Amanda," Vaughan addressed her, "I think you need some rest. Nothing may happen, but it will be a long night. I'll keep a lookout on the grounds. I'm best doing guerilla warfare, but I won't be far away. Bozo will be on the porch, and will bark if anything moves. If you need me, just whistle.

"My guess is that we are safe here, but that whoever it is will try to contact you. Keep your gun close by, and wear your phone with the vibrate on, ringer off. If someone does show up here, I want you to quietly and quickly high-tail it to that shed beside the barn where we left that revolver, and hide in the shadows of that shed. If anyone comes within 50 feet of that shed, crawl behind that 55-gallon drum and make small and quiet. Shoot to kill."

Amanda swallowed and nodded. "Yes, sir."

"It's going to turn out all right."

At Vaughan's suggestion, Amanda quickly set up her laptop on the desk that slid out from the armoire, to check e-mail and have available for communication. She set up the program to notify her by a little alarm if e-mail was received. Then she sat down in a chair near a window overlooking the front yard and road, placing the gun with safety on beside her.

She sat there, and became lost in thought. She had never met Jonathan Connor when Andy was alive, and the name did not register when they did meet. Andy had only referred to his friend and colleague as 'JM', and once or twice as 'Jon'. That's why the name was familiar. She should have known his face from the photograph, but she avoided looking at photographs that reminded her of Andy.

She tried to make sense of his words earlier in the evening. So the FBI was investigating something that involved St. Catherine's? Why would he be posing as an auditor? In piecing fragments together, obviously there were some major discrepancies in the church financial records, more specifically the recital fund, which implicated her in embezzlement of major amounts of monies. This WWAC, Inc., was apparently a vehicle for transferring the money somehow. Someone was using her identity, but who and why? And why was the FBI involved?

Who was W. Witherspoon? If he was a relative, why had Marjorie never spoken of him? What business did he think they had to discuss? Because of the message, she assumed, maybe wrongly, that he must have Marjy's laptop. How else would he have her e-mail address? Why would he have stolen Marjorie's laptop and diskettes? Was there any connection to Claude Brown?

She was still mulling over these questions when Vaughan appeared. He said gently to her, "Amanda, you probably ought to sack out there on the sofa for awhile. It's been a while since Ralph left, and I thought he might be back by now. But he may be involved in dealing with a backup team and be delayed."

Obediently Amanda walked over to the sofa and lay down, her gun nestled under a cushion. Vaughan pulled one of the Navy blankets over her, before disappearing into the night.

She lay there fully awake for what seemed like hours, trying to recreate the last days in her mind, skimming for clues. Suddenly she heard the tiny alarm go off indicating that she was receiving e-mail. Getting up, she went to the computer and clicked "send/receive" with the built-in mouse. Instantly, a message, the sender entitled "Marjorie", appeared:

"I'm waiting for you. Ralph is with me. We'll be together soon. Marjy"

Amanda sat, transfixed at the message, her chest pounding, when the cell telephone suddenly vibrated. Startled, she grabbed the phone and activated it.

"Hello?" she asked breathlessly.

"Well, if it isn't Amanda Childs," mocked a slightly familiar voice. "I'm so glad to have a chance for us to catch up on old times."

"Who is this?" Amanda demanded.

"You don't remember your old friend, the one you took such great pains putting in prison?"

Amanda's memory focused, and she knew that the voice on the line belonged to Claude Brown. Playing dumb, she replied, "No, I'm afraid not. How did you get this number?"

The voice laughed mirthlessly. "I think you have figured out who I am. I have ways. I felt it was time we got reacquainted. You see, I have something you want."

"Are you W. Witherspoon? Do you have Marjorie's laptop?" Amanda asked, trying to keep the panic out of her voice.

"No, but Mr. Witherspoon is anxious to see you. No, I have here something larger than a laptop. Perhaps you are missing a law partner?"

Amanda's thoughts flew to Ralph. "What have you done with Ralph? Where is he? I want to talk to him," she sputtered in panic.

"Your Ralph is, shall we say, tied up at the moment and cannot speak. But I would just want to bet you'd like to have him back. Do you have pen and paper? I'm about to give you some directions. You better get them right the first time if you want to see Ralph again."

Amanda reached over, scrambling until she found pen and paper in her attaché. "Is he hurt? What have you done?"

"Just come to Milford, to 355 Industrial Park Drive, and walk in the east door of the warehouse in back. You got one hour. And, Ms. Childs, you'd better come alone, or—" The next sound was an ear-splitting gun shot, then the line went dead.

Amanda stared at the phone, her panic rising. Galvanized into action, she ran over, phone still in hand, and grabbed her gun and purse.

She rushed out the door, past the dog who began barking excitedly, and frantically flung herself into the SUV. As she tried shakily to place the key into the ignition, suddenly Vaughan was standing beside the truck. He jerked the driver door open and pulled her out.

"Amanda, for God's sake, what is going on?"

Amanda was crying. "I gotta go, Fred. He's got Ralph. He said I had to come alone."

Vaughan grabbed her by both arms and shook her roughly. "Get a grip. Start over—tell me what's happening. Who has Ralph?"

Amanda, unable to stop crying, stammered, "Claude Brown has my cell phone number. He just called. He has Ralph, and I have to come alone if I'm going to see him again. There's no time."

Vaughan pushed her back into the SUV, and ordered, "Move over, I'm driving."

She shook her head wildly. "No, Fred. Ralph is involved only because of me. I can't allow someone else to be endangered because of me, and I cannot jeopardize Ralph by letting anyone come with me."

Vaughan growled sternly, "Do you even know if he has Ralph? Do you know if Ralph is alive? I'm not letting you go alone. Where are we going? We'll come up with a plan on the way."

Amanda reluctantly slid over to the passenger seat as Vaughan quickly commanded the dog to the porch and to stay before climbing in beside her. "He said I only have an hour to get to Milford."

Vaughan cranked the SUV and put it in gear, spinning tires as he turned onto the road leading to town. "OK, who is Claude Brown?"

"Claude Brown is a guy I represented several years ago. He was sent to prison, and escaped."

"What's this address?"

"I don't know—some warehouse in Milford, 355 Industrial Drive. Do you know where that is?"

"Yes, that's a fairly isolated spot. I can get us there," muttered Vaughan grimly, an enigmatic look on his face. "What else did he say?"

"Nothing much that I can recall, other than I have an hour to get there," responded Amanda. "What is this place, Fred? You know something you're not telling me."

Vaughan glanced at her, his expression unreadable. "Amanda, look behind the seats in that duffle. I'm going to ask you to load some weapons there for us. We don't know if Ralph is there or if he's alive, but we do know it's a trap."

"Why a trap? What do you know, Fred? I can't take the chance that he will kill Ralph."

"Amanda, you're the quarry," Fred responded slowly. "We've got to come up with a plan of our own. I want you to hang on to Andy's gun. You'll need it, so try to keep anyone from taking it from you."

She gripped his arm. "What is this place?" she whispered. "I can see it in your eyes, Fred. Tell me."

"It's where they found Andy's body," Vaughan did not look at her, as he gripped the wheel tightly.

They rode in anxious silence, Amanda in shell shock, hardly conscious of their surroundings. Vaughan covered the miles quickly, although it seemed an eternity to Amanda. Finally arriving at Milford, Vaughan took a road that encircled the city, and turned onto an unkempt piece of pavement.

"Where are we?" Amanda queried.

"We're going into the industrial park by the back way," spoke Vaughan grimly. "I don't want to take a chance that this person has a lookout on the main entrance."

Driving slowly down the road, he suddenly extinguished the car's headlights, and turned in behind a building that appeared to be abandoned and crumbling.

Amanda asked, "Is this the place?" She shivered in dread, biting her lip, her breath coming out in short gasps.

Vaughan shook his head. "No, it's two doors down. I want to stake out the place. I need to see if I can sneak up and find out how many we have in there, what exits there are. Our best defense is a good offense, but we have to know the lie of the land.

"Amanda, listen to me and don't argue. I really need for you to stay here and crouch down. It's not likely that someone is going to come by here—this place doesn't look like it would be patrolled by security. However, just in case, I want you out of sight. I'll be back." He paused, his face grim. "Amanda, please trust me."

Amanda looked after him in anguish as he stepped out of the SUV and disappeared around the back of the building. Now that they were so close, she felt intense apprehension. Fred's remark about the place and its connection to Andy' death had shattered her. But so much had happened, she was numb from the unreality of the situation.

She looked at her watch. It was 2:30 a.m. *And I've got a 10:30 plane to catch*, she thought irrelevantly. She tried not to think of Ralph, because her mind conjured up images of him dead, and she could not accept that possibility. Her thoughts unwillingly turned to Connor. How well did he know Andy? What did he know about Andy's death? Why was the FBI investigating her? Did the agency really think she was guilty of criminal activity? Why had Jon kissed her? She still felt the pressure of his lips on hers, and realized with shame that she had enjoyed it. *Maybe Ralph was right—maybe I need some good clean sex. I don't know what is wrong with me.*

Then the thought of Ralph in danger assailed her again. She tried to banish it by wondering why someone would be trying to implicate her in wrongdoing.

Who would stand to gain? If she died within the thirty-day period, Marjorie's money would pour over into a trust for the benefit of St. Catherine's anyway. She could not solve the riddle. She wondered why Claude Brown would be stalking her and trying to kill her now, after all this time. None of it made sense. What is the connection?

Suddenly she could hear a car coming in her direction. She realized that she made a sitting target, and quickly jumped out of the car, her gun in her purse beside her. She ran around to the side of the abandoned building and flattened herself against the door, trying it. It was locked, but the double door next to it gave way. She quickly pulled herself inside, closing the door and leaning against it, breathing heavily.

The sound of the car receded, and she breathed a sigh of relief. Looking at the lighted dial of her watch, she realized it was almost 3:00. Where was Vaughan?

She panicked, then took deep breaths, trying to calm herself. She felt as if she could wait no longer. She had to determine for herself whether Ralph was at the warehouse. What if something had happened to Vaughan too?

Carefully cracking the door, she surveyed the landscape carefully, then let herself out. She followed the path Vaughan had taken around the back of the building, peeking around the building before taking the corner. She could see lights burning through the high windows inside a building just past the one beside the abandoned warehouse behind which she stood. Looking both ways to determine whether there was movement, she lightly ran to the next building and flattened herself in the shadows. Carefully picking her way around the back of the second building, she finally made her way in sight of the dimly lit exterior of the warehouse, much larger than the other two. Over the concrete loading dock was painted in large numbers "355".

She froze. Beside the loading dock was the blue Malibu in front of a 2-car garage. Trying to look in the garage windows, she could see nothing, but she found steps leading up the loading dock. She noticed drops of what looked like blood leading to the door. She silently followed the trail, and tried the door leading into the warehouse. Finding it unlocked, she slowly and quietly opened it.

She looked carefully before slipping through the door. The room was dimly lit, and she paused behind some high metal shelves. She stifled all thoughts of Andy in this place. Trying to get a sense of the room, she suddenly noted a rumpled and bloody figure slumped on the floor at the other end. A figure in a dark sweater was standing between her and the man on the floor. A voice she recognized as Claude Brown's was asking, "Come on, Ralph, tell me where she is hiding. Haven't you've had enough punishment?" He kicked Ralph viciously. Amanda watched in horror as Ralph moaned then did not move.

Not able to see anyone else in the room, she removed the gun from her purse, removing the safety and inching forward silently. When she was only about ten feet from the figure, she said quietly and authoritatively, "Don't move. I have a gun and I'll be only too happy to use it."

As the figure slowly turned, Ralph looked up at her through bleary eyes, and hoarsely yelled, "Amanda, look out!"

She was grabbed from behind, and the gun in her hand was suddenly and violently wrenched from her grasp, clattering to the floor. She was wheeled around into the arms of her assailant. Dazed and feeling something stick her arm, she started in horror. "Why are you—" she began.

Her knees disappeared from under her, as her attacker gently caught her and laid her down on the floor. "You were just the person I wanted to see," a familiar voice said, as the figure leaned over her.

She found she couldn't make any noise, as her throat muscles began to tighten and she couldn't breathe. The room began swimming and went dark.

PART TWO

Chapter 18

It was Sunday morning as Jonathan Connor eased his Mercedes sedan off the interstate onto the Mainville exit and looked at his watch. The principal Sunday mass was already in full swing at St. Catherine's, but he had time to introduce himself to Father Anselm before the Witherspoon funeral that afternoon.

Having asked directions of the friendly attendant at the convenience store where he stopped for gas, he was soon cruising along downtown Mainville. As he neared the church, he was surprised at the press of cars parked along the avenues bordering the church. Good attendance today, he noted as he passed the church and parked down the block near the Baptist Church parking area.

He walked back up the street, entering as the recessional party was making it to the narthex during the concluding hymn. Spying the man from his picture, he quietly walked to the rector as the acolytes and choir members were milling around chatting, heading out the door.

"Father Anselm?" he asked quietly. The man smiled and nodded. Using his pseudonym, Connor continued. "I am Connor Thomson—we spoke on the phone. If you have a moment to speak to me, I'll be happy to wait upstairs in the gallery until you are finished."

"That would be good," Father smilingly assented. "I will need to greet people as they leave, then will meet you upstairs."

Jonathan turned and took the stairwell two steps at a time. He restlessly roamed the empty balcony, and turned his eyes to the organist performing at the console located near the altar. Upon concluding the final hymn and waiting quietly for the dismissal, she launched into the postlude, which he recognized as a Bach fugue. He observed the woman at the console, an attractive woman with golden blonde hair, in deep concentration and oblivious to her surroundings as she weaved the voices of the fugue back and forth in a musical tapestry. He also noticed that several of the parishioners were sitting or standing near the front of the church intently listening. She has a fan club, he thought.

All too soon the music crescendoed to a thundering close, and those listening responded with enthusiastic applause. He noted that the woman, blushingly acknowledging their accolades, nodded to them slightly as she left the bench. He continued watching as she was mobbed by parishioners and took the time to speak to each one, drifting slowly out the room.

So that is Amanda Childs, he thought. She matches Andy's description. Wonder if she is really all he said she was, or if she's hiding something. I guess that's what I'm here to find out.

A few minutes later, Father Anselm appeared, holding his chasuble and stole. Walking up to Jonathan, he held out his hand, shaking it warmly. "Mr. Thomson, it is nice to meet you. The Presiding Bishop had nothing but good things to say about you. I don't have long, because I must get ready for the funeral—Mrs. Witherspoon was one of our most faithful parishioners. Bishop Marks will be celebrating, but I'm preaching, and will be called on to wait attendance upon him."

Connor returned his handshake with equal warmth. "Thank you so much for taking a few minutes, Father. As you were informed, I am conducting an audit of the diocesan and church records. I know I come at a bad time, and apologize for the intrusion.

"I have limited time in town, and was wondering if there was time today or tomorrow to meet with you. I'd like to discuss the audit with you and perhaps obtain some copies of documents."

"Mrs. Witherspoon said I should provide you all assistance possible. Today may be hard, young man, because after the funeral is a wake for Mrs. Witherspoon here at the church. You are welcome to stay for the funeral and wake. My duties require that I be there. And I promised Miss Marjorie to keep an eye on Amanda during and after the service."

"Amanda?" Connor repeated, trying to sound casual.

"The organist, Mrs. Childs. I'm concerned that her taking the service may prove too much for her. But she insisted."

"I see," said Connor. "She and Mrs. Witherspoon were close?"

"They were best friends," confided Anselm, turning his full gaze upon the questioner. "They had been a great help to each other in their respective losses."

"Losses?" echoed Connor.

"Mrs. Witherspoon lost her husband and daughter several years ago, and then Amanda lost her husband a few years back. They helped each other survive. They have both been self-appointed guardians to St. Catherine's, giving of their time, talents and monies to keep the doors open, sometimes when that very danger seemed to threaten. And not just St. Catherine's, but they have championed all sorts of children's causes in the community."

"Really?" Connor murmured. "I find this interesting. I'd love to hear more."

"Alas, I will only have time for a quick sandwich before Bishop Marks arrives, and then he will demand all my attention. I cannot provide all the church records until tomorrow, but we keep the income and expense statements on the bulletin board outside my office.

"Why don't I let you have a copy of them today, and then perhaps tomorrow we could meet with a little more leisure to provide you what you need and talk?"

Connor answered gratefully, "That would be very helpful, Father. Will the gallery be in use for the funeral?"

"It will most likely be used if there is an overflow of attendees—Marjorie was well known. If you are coming to the funeral, you should be here early, because Amanda and Ken have prepared a fine music program to honor Marjorie, and there will be about fifteen minutes or more of prelude music. Don't miss it."

Connor resolved to be there, as he thanked the rector, and they descended the stairs together.

Soon he had in his hand a copy of the statements posted for the last year in his possession. As he was leaving, he noticed a dull brown Mustang sitting outside the church front, with a black male sitting inside. Curious, he idly memorized the tag number as he walked to his car, passing the car.

Deciding it was too early to check into the hotel, he found a shop and ordered a sandwich, then found a quiet place to review the documents he had just received. Having accomplished both, he was sitting at a picnic table in a nearby city park overlooking a lake, poring over the papers when the cell phone on his belt vibrated. Picking it up, he said tersely, "Connor here."

"Has the eagle landed?" a voice questioned.

"Very funny," retorted Connor, taking a sip of his soft drink. "You got your equipment set up?"

"Roger, affirmative, and yes, as Bubba would say. We're ready to roll, and I've made contact with the local law enforcement. The sheriff is apparently terminally ill, and his chief is running the show while the sheriff is getting chemotherapy. That poor sod is up to his neck in a double homicide investigation, but has pledged support and assigned a couple of plainclothes to provide help.

"He seconded your suggestion of involving the police chief here, the Petrino fellow. I was surprised; generally there's turf war between local agencies, but apparently there's lots of cooperation between the sheriff and police here. But when I met with Petrino, therein lay a wrinkle or two. He's not too happy about handing over jurisdiction—he specifically said to tell you that he doesn't want any screw-ups on his watch. Get this—he's been to FBI Academy and worked for FDLE. He's third generation law enforcement, and knows everyone and every nook and cranny in the county. My guess is he's a font of knowledge about all your players."

"I know him well. He was a friend of Andy's. He has been extremely helpful already. It wouldn't hurt to run some of your findings by him. He's sharp, and he keeps his finger on the pulse of this town. When I talked to Charlie on the phone last week, he seemed pretty defensive of our female alpha. So is the Holy Father. How many men do we have?"

"We're short-handed," Zeke responded. "Bubba, Kimball, and I are here. Bubba has contacts in Pensacola and Panama City, and we've asked those offices for assistance as needed. Simpson is still tied up elsewhere, but he's no help even when he's here. We've drafted Petrino and his men, particularly his chief investigator, some guy named Manning, plus the sheriff's guys. Bubba has a meeting tomorrow with the Sheriff in Milford as well. Bubba has briefed them. What do you need me to do here?"

"Get on-line with the clerk of court's records, if they're on-line in this county and the next. Run updated property and corporation checks on our subjects. I want subpoenas ready to serve on the local banks tomorrow morning, so make sure the Pensacola office has a ready magistrate. We'll need to review those records against the church records I will get tomorrow. I am thinking I may meet with the Barnes fellow, who is also on the board at the bank and their attorney. If he's not cooperative I want the men ready to move in immediately, before he has time to warn anyone. Once we get those account records, we'll need to follow up with all the trails.

"See if there's anything more current dug up on Claude Brown. And while you are at it, run a tag for me." He quickly provided the number of the brown Mustang.

"What's that?"

"Oh, I'm just curious—I thought I saw a guy who looked like his picture this morning, which may not be anything. Maybe we could solve two cases at one time," Connor responded. "There's a brown Mustang in front of the church. If it's still there, get one of your friends to keep an eye on it for me. I'll check back in with you this evening. Remember, Zeke, Mrs. Witherspoon's death has suddenly made the stakes much higher. We gotta move fast and keep it tight. I want surveillance on Mrs. Childs."

"Done. We got a tap on her home phone, but no wires yet. The judge wouldn't budge on bugs in the law office, but did give us phone tolls. We can see who she's talking to, but not what they're saying. Attorney-client privilege and all that."

"OK," Jon's mind was already elsewhere. "There's more, but I'll call you as soon as I can make a list. Now I've got to attend a funeral."

Walking to his car, he was soon on his way back to the church. Again he found the avenues and parking lot lined with cars, and parked again near the Baptist church, walking back up the block. Entering the church about twenty minutes before the service, he noticed with some surprise that the entire nave of the church was full, and people were already ascending the stairs to the gallery. He joined them, and found a seat on the front row at the right end, same side as the organ console.

As he took his seat, the music began. Expecting the organ, he was surprised to find Amanda Childs across from the organ console at a grand piano in an alcove, playing Debussy and Ravel. He was entranced, then noticed as a young man took her place and she disappeared during the beginning strains of a Rachmaninoff prelude. Looking below him, he noticed an elderly man in a wheelchair being positioned by a nurse near the front, close to the pulpit.

Upon the conclusion of the three pieces, the organ pealed forth, and looking down over the railing he noted that Amanda was at the console. He sat in stupefaction and admiration as the Dupre rolled through the church.

Upon a brief silence after the organ solo, the organ boomed forth again with the introduction to the introit hymn. Connor stood with the rest of the congregation, and watched the procession of priests, acolytes and choir stream forth down the main aisle to the chancel. All those around him sang, "Praise, my soul, the King of heaven" as the organ beckoned them to worship.

Immediately upon the cessation of the hymn, the choir broke forth in anthem: "I heard the voice of Jesus say, 'Come unto me and rest; lay down, thou weary one, lay down thy head upon my breast.' I came to Jesus as I was, weary, and worn, and sad: I found in him a resting-place, and he has made me glad."

Looking at the bulletin in his hand, he noticed the arranger to be "A. Childs". He wondered, Could it be she wrote this? The choir was very good, and he wondered if they were professional or volunteer. As the anthem concluded, he noticed a tall blonde broad-shouldered good-looking man enter the gallery and take a seat on the other side of the gallery, looking around him. As their eyes briefly met, he nodded at the man, surmising from surveillance photos that it must be Bill Barnes, before turning his gaze back to the panorama before him.

The service, far from being dirgelike, was a glorious celebration of Marjorie Witherspoon's life in worship and music. The choir and congregation readily responded to the service, and Connor found himself drinking it in, spellbound. For the first time since the untimely death of his colleague Andrew Childs, Jon found himself missing the Sunday services at St. Thomas, Park Avenue, from which he had absented himself now for four years. He had utilized the age-old niche of eschewing the church and using the excuse of lamenting why God allowed the righteous to be destroyed.

As the *Agnus Dei* was sung, he noticed that the Bishop seemed shaky and quickly exited the altar area. Momentarily, he noticed that the organist relinquished her post to her assistant, quickly took the Eucharist at the rail and disappeared. His curiosity aroused, he quietly exited the gallery.

He walked out the front door of the church, and took a hard right and another, following the outline of the building around. He walked until he found an entrance into the adjoining building, and let himself in. He could hear voices, and decided to saunter in the hallway to determine where the Bishop and organist had gone.

He could hear a female voice saying, "Dr. Howells, there's the sofa down the hall in Father Anselm's study, if we can get him there."

Then he heard a thin imperious voice, but could not make out the words. Hearing people approaching, he quickly darted into the men's room, waiting several moments.

Carefully looking out, he could hear that the organ music in the church had stopped. He carefully followed the path he thought the voices had taken. As he walked down the quiet halls, he could faintly hear the choir singing. As he was about the round a corner, a door flew open, and Amanda Childs came out, hurriedly going out a side exit without seeing him. Continuing down the hall, he casually looked through a window by the door, and saw the Bishop, pale and shaken, reclining on a sofa, with a man in clerical garb and another man assisting him in removing his chasuble and stole. As he heard movement behind him and kept going, he heard the click of a woman's shoes and heard the door open.

Connor continued down the hall, hearing the faint sounds of an organ postlude and realizing that others would be flowing down the halls from the church proper. He walked the hall aimlessly, hoping to appear as a stranger who had lost his way.

He walked beside open double doors, and met an elderly woman. She asked, "Is the service over?"

He replied, "Yes. I was just waiting around for Father Anselm and admiring your church."

She beamed and began chattering about the historic parts of the church versus the recent additions. Connor pretended great interest, but was wondering what was happening down the hall. Momentarily, he saw EMTs appear with a gurney going into the room. Excusing himself, he slowly walked back toward the office. As he approached the office, he met Father Anselm.

"What did you think of the service?" Anselm asked him absently.

"That was one of the most uplifting funerals I've ever attended," Connor conceded.

"I told you. Hang around. The wake will be in the hall down there, and I need to stop here just a minute."

Anselm let himself into the room where Connor had seen the Bishop. Momentarily, the paramedics came out with the Bishop on a gurney. As they left, accompanied by a suited man Connor discerned was a doctor, Anselm returned.

"I have to go to the graveside. Would you care to join me?"

Connor assented, and they left together. Getting into Anselm's vintage black Mercedes, Connor admired the condition of the interior. Anselm, noting his interest, remarked, "One of my biggest vices. I love this car, and treat it like a member of my family."

Connor laughed. "I understand the feeling. It is a gorgeous vehicle. I couldn't help but notice, but wasn't that the Bishop being carried out just now?"

"Yes," declared Anselm soberly. "It is thought he may have suffered a heart attack. Amanda happened to find him on her way out to get to the graveside. Her quick intervention may have saved his life."

Connor persisted, "I guess that will be a great shock to the community here, having their Bishop brush with death."

Anselm was grave. "I would love to say so, but I'm afraid that most people of the parish do not know the Bishop, and those who do don't hold him in high regard."

Connor was surprised. "Why?"

Anselm said, "I'm the shepherd of this flock, and I do not want to speak ill of anyone, particularly my Bishop and one who is so ill."

Connor murmured, "I understand. But the Presiding Bishop asked me to determine not only the finances, but the politics and dynamics of what is going on. As I told you, the Presiding Bishop is worried on several fronts."

Anselm asserted, turning the corner, "There is bad blood between the Bishop and this congregation. He has not made visitation here since he first became Bishop; he has always sent a visiting bishop for the annual visitation. And the older members of this church maintain that the Bishop forced one predecessor into early retirement, and foisted another on to this church until he almost ruined the church and ran off Amanda, and the vestry demanded that he leave."

Connor interjected eagerly, "Father Anselm, what can you tell me about a past connection between the Bishop and Marjorie Witherspoon?"

Anselm regarded him severely. "I am not going to stir up old gossip, even for you. Suffice it to say that they were not on friendly terms."

"May I ask another question?" Connor tried to mollify the vicar's ruffled feathers. "You keep referring to a wake. Isn't that normally before a service?"

The priest smiled. "Here at St. Catherine's we've formed a tradition of hosting a reception for the friends and family after the service. For some reason we have always called it a 'wake' as well. I'm not sure if this is a practice confined to just St. Catherine's, or maybe shared by Episcopal churches in the South. Nevertheless, the ladies of the church revered Marjorie, and have pulled out all the stops." He pulled into the cemetery and expertly found a spot to park. "Here we are—I must go and complete the service, so please excuse me."

Connor exited the car after Anselm, and followed at a discreet distance, remaining in the background as the graveside service was concluded.

As mourners were leaving, he saw a muscled, well-dressed black man approach him and proffer his hand. "Aren't you Jon Connor?"

"Yes," Connor answered without thinking, then inwardly cursed himself, wincing that he was recognized and wondering if his cover was blown.

"Hi, I'm sure you don't remember me. I'm Ralph Carmichael, and you were a few years ahead of me at Duke. I remembered you from my first year orientation."

"Yes, I remember you; you're the NCAA basketball wonder. You were phenomenal. What are you doing here now?"

Ralph, beaming, replied, "I'm an attorney in town. This is my home town, and I decided after a while to return to my roots, so to speak. What about you?"

"I'm an attorney and a CPA, and had some business in town. I just met Father Anselm at the church and rode out with him."

"Did you know Mrs. Witherspoon?"

"Yes, we had met. She was a most intriguing lady."

"Yes, she was," Ralph agreed. "She had a heart of gold. This town and church will miss her greatly. Do you need a ride back? Feel free to join me."

Connor thanked him, and caught Father Anselm's eye, pointing to Ralph and indicating he was leaving with Ralph. Connor followed Ralph to a sharp black Lexus sports coupe. "Wow, you must have done well," Connor whistled, as they slipped into the car.

"I do all right. I'm still single, much to my mother's dismay. One has to keep the ladies impressed," Ralph smirked briefly.

They were silent a moment while Ralph maneuvered his way out of the cemetery. "That was a lovely service," Connor stated. "Fabulous music. I wanted to tell the organist what a great job she did, but didn't see her here."

"Amanda? No, I don't know why she's not here. She and Marjorie were peas in a pod. I'm concerned about her—she's been living on straight adrenalin the last few days."

"What do you mean?" Connor was alert.

"Well, there's been so much going on, and Marjorie's illness and death hit her hard. Amanda insisted on planning and playing the service. She's really exhausted."

"Are you friends?"

"Well, sort of. We're law partners. She always said that friendship and business don't mix, but underneath that prickly exterior beats a heart of gold. She's a damned fine attorney, and just damned fine." Ralph grinned.

Connor laughed. "Sounds like some endorsement to me. I'd like to meet her sometime. There's not any romance between you two?"

Ralph frowned and shook his head. "No, although she would make quite a catch for some lucky guy. Marjorie's death has dealt her a body blow—she's really torn up. She thinks she can hide these things, but sometimes she is transparent."

They pulled up to the church, Ralph expertly parallel parking the car near the side door where Connor had entered earlier. As they walked down the hall, Connor glanced in a window of an office two doors from the one in which the Bishop had been, and saw Amanda Childs sitting slumped at a desk in the dark, holding her head in her hands. He hesitated briefly before continuing to follow Ralph.

Ralph led the way to the parish hall, to a sideboard where various spirits and mixers were located. He and Connor prepared themselves a drink, and adjourned to a corner to talk and watch others arrive. The room began filling up, but still Amanda did not appear. The man Connor had observed during the funeral service made an appearance. Barnes, after speaking boisterously to several persons, ended up in a corner quietly talking with a man who Connor recognized as the Bishop's curate Adam Brownlee.

There was a small stir at the doorway, and he saw Amanda make her way into the room. Hardly hearing what Ralph was saying, he noticed her gliding gracefully around the room, speaking to people. Their eyes met and locked, and she gazed at him momentarily as if trying to place him. For the second time that day he wondered if his cover was blown.

Connor noticed Barnes take her by the arm and sit down beside her on a settee momentarily, then walk over to the bar. A man he recognized as Police Chief Charlie Petrino spoke briefly with Bill at the bar. The latter handed him a drink and pointed to Amanda. Petrino took the drink to her, exchanging a few words before melting back into the crowd. Ralph excused himself and walked over to her, engaging her in conversation. Connor thought about following him and introducing himself to her, but something about her arrested him, made him reticent to make that move.

Barnes then returned to Amanda, two drinks in hand. Ralph returned to Connor's side as the man handed a drink to Amanda and began talking earnestly to her, slipping an arm around her possessively.

"Who's the linebacker?" Connor nodded in Amanda's direction.

"You should recognize him," Ralph quipped. "That's Bill Barnes. You remember, he was once the All-American quarterback from Florida State when they won the national championship."

"Yes, he does look familiar. What—is he from here too?"

"Yes, this is the land where all the children are above average," Ralph joked. "We are all overachievers here in this tiny town. Bill's an attorney, and focuses on probate and tax work. He was married to some serious Old South lineage, and they did carry on. She was killed in a drowning accident last year."

"What about him and Amanda? I notice they seem close. What is their relationship?"

Ralph looked at Connor solemnly. "Oh, they're just friends from school days. The old biddies around here, and Bill himself, would like to make it out to be more than that, but don't listen to them. Amanda has had only one love in her life, and there's no room for anyone else."

"Her husband?"

"Yeah. What have you heard?" Ralph was suddenly suspicious.

Connor casually sipped his drink. "One didn't meet Marjorie Witherspoon and not hear about Amanda Childs. I take it they were good friends. Ms. Witherspoon didn't go into detail, saying only that he was a cop and was killed on duty. But that was some time ago, wasn't it?"

"Four years, but Amanda hasn't really moved on. Marjorie helped keep her from drowning in her own sorrow, but she's kind of stuck in neutral. No men in her life, nothing much except Marjorie, the church, her work, and Bill hovering around periodically."

"What's it like to be in practice with her?" Connor mused.

"Shit, man, she can run rings around me in her sleep. She's the bad cop of our team—always prepared, always ready to kick ass and take names. I have no complaints—she's the meanest white woman in a courtroom I ever met. I don't ever want to meet her in a dark alley. I want her on my side."

Ralph was engrossed in the conversation, but Connor noticed Amanda standing and wavering. "Ralph," he urged, grabbing the other man's arm and pointing, as he watched Amanda fall to the floor.

Chapter 19

A bustle of pandemonium broke out as people scurried to the fallen woman. Ralph bounded over to where Amanda lay, as Bill Barnes knelt over her, his hand clutching hers.

Ralph ordered authoritatively, "Move aside and give her a little air," as he checked her pulse. Following and standing behind Ralph and smelling the reek of bourbon, Connor noticed that her drink had spilled all over her black dress, and that there were several white flecks. He saw Bill pick up the glass which had fallen out of her hand.

As Connor moved closer, some elderly woman nearby was heard saying, "Poor dear, it's been too much for her," Another peevish looking woman at her side retorted quietly, with a hint of sarcasm, "I've heard Amanda is a closet lush—but apparently not good at holding her liquor in public."

Dr. Howells appeared, and immediately pushed his way forward. After an initial check, he ordered that Amanda be moved to Father Anselm's office. Ralph summarily picked up the unconscious Amanda, her purse handle still wrapped around her wrist, and bodily carried her out of the room, followed by Barnes.

Connor discreetly followed Dr. Howells, Ralph and Barnes out, and hovered in the doorway of the office as Ralph gently placed Amanda on the sofa. The doctor gently shook the girl and slapped her, speaking to her and trying to rouse her, but she was unresponsive. The doctor's bag appeared, and Dr. Howells reached in and found smelling salts, which he applied.

The woman's eyes fluttered open, and an audible sigh of relief escaped the three men. Howells asked Ralph to bring her something to eat. He ushered them out of the room and closed the door.

Connor stood in the hallway, looking in the window at the doctor and Amanda, as Ralph disappeared down the hall. It did seem as though collapsing at St. Catherine's was becoming a habit. As he looked around him, he noticed Bill Barnes eying him. Barnes walked over, his hand out.

"Hi, there. I'm Bill Barnes. I don't think we've met."

"Hello. I'm Connor Thomson. It's nice to meet you."

Barnes stiffened slightly as they shook hands. "You're the auditor from the Presiding Bishop's Office, aren't you?"

"Yes, and you're the diocesan treasurer?"

At Bill's nod, Connor continued. "I drove in for a meeting with the Bishop tomorrow morning. Looks as if that won't happen, with the Bishop's hospitalization. But maybe you might have a few minutes tomorrow morning for us to talk. I'd like to obtain some church records while I am here, at least."

Bill nodded, glancing in the window at the fallen girl. "Sure thing—happy to cooperate. I'm sort of a lazy bastard, so why don't you call around to my office about 10:00 in the morning? I'll try to make some time for you."

Then casually, he asked, "You know Amanda?"

Connor replied, equally casually, "No, I was just concerned when I saw her collapse. I had been talking to Ralph at the wake. He was kind enough to entertain a stranger, but then we found we had met back in college days, so it's a small world."

Bill, his eyes continuing to follow Amanda and the doctor, remarked, "I saw you at the funeral. Did you know Mrs. Witherspoon?"

"Actually, I met her at some functions in New York City. She was a delightful lady."

"Yes, but only if you didn't cross her," Bill smiled enigmatically.

Ralph walked past them bearing a plate of sandwiches and a glass of punch. Bill opened the door for him, then watched intently from the door. Momentarily Ralph returned.

A small group of people had collected outside. Ralph announced, "She's OK. She just hadn't bothered to have anything to eat in God knows how long, and fainted. I'll get her home."

Bill, relieved, asked, "She doesn't need to go to the hospital?"

Ralph looked at him with mock disdain. "Amanda agreeing to go to the hospital? Get a grip, Billy."

Without answering Bill opened the door and sidled into the room. Ralph turned to Connor and spoke, "I'm sorry we didn't finish our chat, and that you didn't get to meet Amanda."

Connor looked back at the woman on the sofa. "I understand. Is she really going to be OK?"

"Think so," Ralph frowned. "The doc is more concerned than he is letting on."

"Anything I can do to help?"

"No. I can handle her," Ralph laughed. "She's wiry and mean, but I'll at least get her home before she kicks my butt and throws me out."

"Perhaps there'll be time for us to get together and talk some more while I'm here," Connor suggested.

"Sure thing," Ralph agreed as he returned to the room.

Connor watched as he picked up Amanda again and carried her like a child out to his car, settling her in. Barnes followed them outside and appeared to object, but Ralph stopped him with a word and jumped in, driving off. Bill, his jaw set angrily, glared at the disappearing car.

As Connor wondered about the interconnected relationships he had observed, he felt a presence beside him, and found Dr. Howells watching the retreating car as well. Dr. Howells stuck out his hand and introduced himself.

"My Marjorie mentioned you to me, and placed great faith in you," the Doctor said very quietly. "She said you could be trusted, and that I was to make myself available to answer any questions you had."

Connor replied, "Mrs. Witherspoon said you would be of great help."

"I'm at your disposal. I need to check on Bishop Marks at the hospital. Care to meet me there? Then I'll be glad to give you a few minutes at my office."

Connor assented, and was soon in his car following the doctor to the regional hospital. On the way, he wondered about Amanda Childs. She seemed to be highly esteemed by those who were close to her. Was she capable of defrauding the church? Embezzlement? Laundering drug monies? If so, he had found no accusers yet. But there were still large amounts of monies disappearing from the diocese, as well as from the church's recital series, without an accounting, most traveling through a corporation named WWAC, Inc., on which the Secretary of State's records listed Amanda Childs as CEO and president. And Bureau men were on the trail of several transactions ending up in the Caymans, where it was believed that some of that was making its way into the hands of international drug dealers. However, no one, not even Amanda Childs, would be brazen enough to be openly named as officer of a corporation so obviously suspected of being involved in criminal activities, so that was too convenient and therefore highly suspicious to him.

He thought briefly about Andrew Childs. Andrew had been working on a case involving a cartel of black market pharmaceutical distributors that had allegedly branched into the illegal drug market and the internet gray market for drugs. Because of the internet connection and the reported incidents of sale of fraudulent drugs, or those that were placebo instead of the real thing, the FBI had become involved in the case. And that trail had led to Claude Brown, one of Amanda Child's former clients. But then Brown had escaped from prison and disappeared, the last rumors being he was hiding out in Mexico.

But Connor knew that Brown had resurfaced at least four years ago, before making another disappearance, and felt sure that the man he saw earlier that day met Brown's description. He hoped that one of his men had been able to locate and tail the vehicle. A positive identification could provide the means for arresting him, but Connor's superiors were more interested in tracking down who was behind Brown. Connor remembered he needed to call in after his meeting with the doctor.

Pulling into the hospital parking lot, Connor parked and followed the doctor inside. As they passed by the nurses' station on the first floor, Howells stopped and addressed a doctor writing in a chart.

"Bob, how are things going?"

"It's been a long afternoon, Malcolm," said the doctor, flipping the chart closed and turning to Howells. "May I speak to you just a second?"

"Of course," nodded Dr. Howells. Turning to Connor, he said, "My office is the second door there on the left. Please make yourself at home, and I'll be in momentarily." He addressed the nurse. "Stella, who's the blood tech on duty? Mike? Please buzz him and ask him if he could come to my office one moment stat."

Connor, curious about the Bishop's condition but knowing he must appear casual, did as the doctor ordered. The sign on the door read, "Malcolm Howells, M.D.—Chief of Staff". Walking into the small but comfortable office, he noted the walls littered with degrees, commendations and pictures. Walking over to his desk, Connor noticed a framed photograph of a younger Howells, Marjorie Witherspoon, Andrew and Amanda Childs in evening clothes, arm in arm, the Chagall mural of the Metropolitan Opera House behind them.

As he studied the picture and face of Amanda, he noticed her slim form, but was arrested by the eyes. Andrew had once remarked about how he lost all consciousness of what he was doing or saying when Amanda turned her full gaze on him. Connor had guffawed in derision at such seeming sentimentality, but now he saw how strikingly beautiful her eyes were gazing full into the camera, and how her features lit up when she smiled. Observing Marjorie Witherspoon's likeness, he noticed the affection in her face as she gazed at Amanda, and saw a similarity in their features he had not noticed before.

Dr. Howells entered and found Connor with the picture in hand. "Those were happier days," Howells remarked. "That was several years ago, before Amanda's husband was killed. Amanda had taken over the music at St. Catherine's. We had all met up at the Met to see *Turandot*. It was a big Zeffirelli production, very large and ornate, with Domingo and Marton. I paid some photographer there to take the picture. A wonderful night; they were so young, so much in love, so full of life and hope."

Replacing the frame, Connor queried, "If I may ask, how is the Bishop's condition?"

"Guarded," replied Howells, as there was a knock on the door, and a young man stuck his head. "You rang, Doc?" he asked.

"Yes, Mike," Doctor Howells motioned for him to enter. "Please come in just a minute. I have something for you." Rummaging in his bag, he brought forth a vial in a plastic bag and handed it to Mike. "Can you run some diagnostics for me—the works?"

"Sure, Doc, whose is it?"

Glancing at Connor, Howells replied, "Just put "Katharine" on the paperwork, and put the results for my eyes only."

As the tech left, Connor recalled that "Katharine" was Amanda's middle name, and surmised that the blood must have come from Amanda Childs. "What do you suspect caused Mrs. Child's collapse, Doctor?" he asked, surprising Howells.

"I'm not at liberty to discuss my patients with you, Mr. Connor," Howells' response was short.

"But there was something not right tonight? You suspected something amiss, didn't you?" Connor persisted.

"Mr. Thomson—" Howells began, but Connors interrupted. "Please call me Connor, sir. And if Marjorie told you about me, then your information could be very helpful, although I am not at liberty to explain to you right now."

Howells looked at him hard. "No, I didn't suspect Amanda Childs of knowingly taking any drugs, or of being drunk, if that's what you mean. I knew she was under a great deal of stress the last few days, and was probably not taking care of herself. But I cannot get her to take medicine when she is sick; she most certainly does not imbibe drugs otherwise, for good reason. She has a sensitivity to many medications. I've known her all her life, and have never seen or heard of her being under the influence. So if that is what you are asking, that is my answer."

"But you suspect something else," stated Connor flatly.

"I don't intend to speculate. I will know soon enough." Howells smoothly changed the subject. "To get back to your question about the Bishop's condition, Dr. Cardet says that he thinks Bishop Marks is stabilizing. They've not had the staff available, it being Sunday, to complete all the testing Cardet wants in order to determine whether there are blockages. He discussed with the Bishop having him life-flighted to Pensacola, but the Bishop insisted he had a meeting tomorrow and would not consent."

"I fear the meeting he's talking about is with me. I would not like to be the cause of his delaying."

"Well, perhaps we can speak to him, if Cardet thinks that will put the Bishop at ease." Howells stood.

They left the doctor's office together, walking down the hall to the entrance of the CCU. The nurse waved them through, and Howells led Connor into a private room where Marks lay, attached to monitors and IVs. Dr. Cardet joined them as they came close, and Marks opened his eyes.

"Malcolm, thanks for coming by," he said tiredly, his eyes moving to Connor.

Dr. Howells addressed him. "Stephen, this is Connor Thomson, the auditor. He did not want to be the reason why you delayed getting help elsewhere if Dr. Cardet here felt you needed it."

Marks' gaze lingered on Connor. "I'm glad to meet you. I want to extend our every cooperation to you. It is my understanding that you will want to interview Mrs. Childs, and I have given my curate, the Rev. Adam Brownlee, instructions to accompany you to her office in the morning, in order to make introduction and assist you in any way."

Connor murmured his thanks to the sick man, although he was inwardly fuming. From where did the Bishop get the idea that he wanted to interview Amanda Childs? How would Marks know that Amanda is a suspect? And although Connor did plan to talk to her, he did not want the complication of the Bishop's curate being underfoot. Connor suspected from what he had learned thus far that Marks was long used to manipulating people, and was trying to steer the investigation.

Marks continued weakly, "I have informed Dr. Cardet here that I do not wish to be moved until and unless I have been able to ensure that Mr. Thomson receives our every assistance. This audit is a grave matter, and I have personally assured the Presiding Bishop of my cooperation until all issues have been resolved."

Connor stated, "Really, Bishop Marks, we cannot take any chances with your health."

Dr. Cardet intervened. "At this point, I think it best we keep the Bishop here, and run more tests tomorrow. At that point we can ascertain the damage, if any, and determine whether it is prudent and in his best interest to stay here or to be moved to another facility."

Stephen Marks held out his hand to Connor. "Please come to see me tomorrow. I will worry until I know you have received everything you need. And when you see Mrs. Childs," he paused as if unsure what to say, "please convey my gratitude to her and let her know I expect her to visit me tomorrow evening at 7:00 so that I can thank her personally."

Connor, inwardly reluctant, agreed to visit the bishop the next afternoon. He suppressed a smile at the man's commanding tone to all those around him. Leaving the CCU, he walked with Howells back to the doctor's office. Expecting the doctor to summarily dismiss him, he was surprised when Howells opened his office door and motioned for Connor to return.

Howells said as he returned to his chair, "I did not ask if you had any other questions."

"Well, I do, but it may be something you may not wish to answer. Can you tell me about the Bishop and Mrs. Witherspoon?"

Howells looked sad. "Now that's some ancient history."

"But I'd really like to hear it from you, if you wouldn't mind. I had a meeting scheduled with Mrs. Witherspoon. Marjorie did not have the opportunity to relay this information to me before her hospitalization and death—it apparently all happened quickly."

Howells sat down, looking at the photograph on his desk. For a while he did not speak. Then, reluctantly he began. "I was a few years older than Stephen and Marjorie. They grew up and were in school together. We were all confirmed at St. Catherine's. It was pretty much everyone's guess that they would marry.

"During one spring break, they were both home from college. One evening, she showed up at my house, bruised and scratched up and out of breath. I had known her and her family all our lives, and we were in church choir together.

"She informed me that Stephen had forced his attentions upon her, and she refused him, wanting to wait until their wedding night. According to her he became violent, hit her once, and called her a 'Frigidaire' and other terms. I think she landed him a good one in the eye, because for a few weeks after he sported a black eye and tried to cover it up with dark glasses.

"I was off doing my final residency, but had come home that weekend for the confirmation of one of my nephews. She was highly embarrassed, and didn't want to go to the police or tell her parents. I did what I could for her, cleaned her scrapes and scratches, and urged her to press charges. She refused to do that, but the two of them were through.

"She sat with me at church Sunday for the confirmation, and Stephen came up. At first he tried to act as if nothing had happened, but she basically turned her back on him. He kept on, until she told him in a low voice that if he did not leave her alone she would press charges. He then made some vile remarks about her, angry she was sitting with me, and calling her a 'slut'. He remarked how dare she malign him, and threatened revenge on her and her family, the Stuarts."

"What happened?" Connor was immersed in the story.

"I'll be danged if he didn't go off to seminary and become a priest. I made it a personal crusade that he didn't make it back to St. Catherine's, even though he and old William Barnes, Sr., were buddies and kinfolks."

"How did you keep Marks away?" Connor wanted to know.

"The direct approach," Howells said simply. "I threatened him with exposure. Enough said."

"Then what happened?"

"Marjorie met this wonderful and equally wealthy Jerrod Witherspoon, and the next thing I knew they were engaged. There was a huge wedding, and they built a fine home and settled here and had the one daughter, Monica."

"You were in love with her, weren't you?" Jon asked softly as the revelation hit him.

"Young man, that dog is too old to hunt—let's leave him lay," Howells quelled him. "But to bring it to the present, Marks made Bishop, and he had not forgotten his promise. He took out his anger on St. Catherine's, in small and large ways. He felt he had been cheated out of marrying into the Stuart family line, with all the trappings and status. So he set out to obtain it however he could, and to bring down those he considered the cause of his aborted glory.

"Now I've answered your question. You answer mine—why is the Presiding Bishop wanting an audit? Why is this little church involved? Is this part of Marjorie's crusade? I have served on the vestry on and off for the last thirty years. I love St. Catherine's and don't want to see anything happen to her."

Connor, gazing at him, decided to share some facts. "Some major discrepancies have been discovered in the amounts of disbursements between the diocesan records and the records of St. Catherine's," he said slowly, adding, "and it appears that monies are disappearing through the recital series fund."

"What do you mean? What types of disbursements and in what amounts?"

"Monies are being paid out from the diocese to St. Catherine's, but not showing up in St. Catherine's coffers. And monies are being received and disbursed from the recital series fund, but aren't showing up. We are talking about two to three million per year, sometimes more, for at least the last six years, maybe longer. This last year it's been over $10 million."

"That just cannot be," Howells was firm. "Marks turned down all requests for diocesan assistance to St. Catherine's, and Amanda was faithful in her reporting of the recital series monies. Her reports were always approved as received."

"But the diocesan records are showing heavy assistance to St. Catherine's, and records provided to the Presiding Bishop are showing major contributions to the recital series. And for years no one has noted it or challenged it. Furthermore, the bank records are showing even larger amounts passing through the church accounts."

"Have you talked to Bill Barnes, our treasurer?"

"I'm supposed to catch him tomorrow. And I wanted to talk to Mrs. Childs in the morning if I can catch her."

"Well, I can tell you Amanda will be at work tomorrow. She's stubborn, and will not take leave even if sick. So unless she has a full schedule, you should find her at the office," Howells replied. "And I'd stake my money on whatever she tells you."

Connor stood up and shook the doctor's hand. "Thank you so much for your time, and I hope to see you again."

Howells, nodding distractedly, responded, "Connor, please, for your sake and hers, be gentle with Amanda."

Jon's amused look died as his eyes met Howell's somber one. "I promise."

Leaving the office, Jon was just in time to see the outline of Bill Barnes going in the door of the CCU. Wouldn't I like to know what he and the Bishop are talking about, Jon thought, as he left the hospital. He only hoped their man in the hospital happened to be close enough to overhear.

On the way to his hotel to finally check in, he called in. The familiar voice answered. "Are those subpoenas done, Zeke?" Connor asked.

"Yep, and ready for your instructions. But I got something even better. Apparently there was a bank audit just a couple months ago. I'm trying as we speak to cut the red tape to get my hands on it."

"Do you have a mole inside the bank yet?"

"I will in the morning. And guess what? The bank in town is a sister to the bank in Milford, not far from here. Same owners, same board of directors. How convenient. What about you—get anything good?"

"Lots of possible witnesses, but we need the records. Do what you can—the bank audit may obviate the need for the subpoenas, and may make for interesting comparisons anyway. If one bank is a branch of the other, we may get both records at the same time."

"What's for tomorrow?"

Connor replied, "I have to see alpha female tomorrow morning with unwanted company. Then I gotta see treasurer Barnes and Marks again. In the meantime we need to marshal all the information we can. What did you find out about that tag number?"

"It was a stolen tag not assigned to any brown Mustang, so a dead end. I passed the info on to Petrino and our boys to BOLO. Why?"

"You know why," Jon's voice was tense. "That guy looked like Claude Brown. We're going to get Andy's killer. I know he's not far away. I have a feeling about it. It's time to wrap that case up, and not let him get away again. And he's involved in this."

"We don't know that," Zeke replied. "But if it pans out, I'm with you. And Jon?"

"Yes."

"You know when Simpson gets down here he's going to want a warrant ready and marshals to arrest Amanda Childs."

"Doesn't give us much time if I'm right," Jon was weary.

"Get some rest, Jon. You're going to need it."

Chapter 20

It was Monday morning as Connor was leaving Amanda Child's office with Brownlee, cursing to himself and wanting to smack the little man beside him. He could not bring himself to speak to the silly smirking self-satisfied priest after the badly-aborted interview, and quickly drove him to the hospital. As he pulled up to the curb, Brownlee simpered, "Aren't you going to come up and report to the Bishop?"

Connor looked at him icily. "I don't report to your Bishop, sir, and even if I did, I would have nothing to report this morning, thanks to you. The next time I need your assistance, I'll hesitate to ask."

The man, shocked at Connor's anger, closed the car door quickly, and Connor sped off. He wanted badly to run the man down under his wheels. As he took the road and sped up, he started cooling off, and hit the speed dial on his phone.

"Connor's Laundry Service. May I help you?" a voice answered. "How was the *femme* Amanda this morning?"

"Good morning, Bubba," Connor smiled. "Where's Zeke?"

"He's here. Just a minute."

The familiar voice came on. "And?"

"She was cold as ice. That was a waste of good breath," informed Connor, "thanks to that ass Brownlee. I think the whole plan was to discredit her in my eyes."

"How did she react to the news of the will?"

"Feinstein obviously has not contacted her yet. She was in total shock. I'm sure it wasn't an act. She had no idea she was listed to inherit. Marjorie did not make good her threat to tell Amanda. I felt sorry for her."

"Then why was she cold as ice?"

"Brownlee started right away accusing her of exerting undue influence on Mrs. Witherspoon, and if she had possessed a rapier, there would have been sliced human steak on the table."

"She is still our main suspect, Andy or no Andy," Zeke reminded him.

"But I believe Mrs. Witherspoon's assistance will end up helping us flush out the real bad guys. The woman's not stupid, Zeke. She would not leave such an obvious trail. Other than this reference to WWAC, Inc., and the money disappearing from the recital series, we don't have much to link her, and the circumstantial does not negate the hypothesis of innocence."

"We're looking for 'probable cause', not 'beyond a reasonable doubt', man. But you must also think of this angle. Maybe she was running the scam, alone or with help, not knowing she was looking at inheriting a bundle from Witherspoon. Did you think of that?"

"The thought already crossed my mind. You know, I want her to be innocent, for Andy's sake."

"So do I. Maybe she is, and maybe she isn't. We got a job to do, don't forget."

"Well, I'm at the church, and from there I'm on my way to chat with Bill Barnes. I'll check back."

Pulling the Mercedes up to the side door nearest the church office, he alighted. He walked in briskly, and greeted the church secretary.

"Good morning. I am Connor Thomson, and I wondered if Father Anselm is in."

"Hello, Mr. Thomson. No, Father is not back from the morning hospital rounds, but he left a message for me early this morning, and I have something for you."

Approaching him, she held aloft six huge manila envelopes. "These are copies of the minutes and statements from the vestry meetings for the last six years. He said if there was anything else you needed, all you had to do is ask."

At his wondering gaze, she added, "Father Anselm and the Presiding Bishop go back a long way, longer than before he was a bishop. The Presiding Bishop called ahead, and Father Anselm doesn't stand on ceremony when the PB asks for something. I started making these copies last week.

"Oh, and I almost forgot. He asked me to make copies of the journals and ledgers for you. He was sure Mr. Barnes would not mind, and did not even call him before ordering the copies."

Connor suppressed a smile as she handed him yet another sheaf encased in a fan folder. "If you wish to verify that I have provided copies of all, or to review the originals, I will be only too happy to provide them for you."

"Thank you so much. This is indeed cooperation above and beyond my expectations, and I do very much appreciate your help. Please thank Father Anselm for me, and tell him I shall probably see him again before I leave."

Connor left, his arms full of the documents. He dropped them into the trunk of the car, then sat in the car musing. It was funny watching the Presiding Bishop make people jump, but he wondered if Barnes would be so happy if he knew that Connor received copies so quickly and without Barnes' consent.

Calling his contact, he quickly informed him that copies had been provided of the church records, and that those subpoenas could be held in abeyance for the moment. He also ordered that their men be on alert at the bank for service of the investigative subpoenas in case his meeting with Barnes was unsuccessful, to prevent document destruction.

"Oh, by the way," the voice informed him, "Feinstein is delivering the package to alpha and the others."

"I'm sorry Marjorie isn't here for this part of the plan. We need to be careful but move fast."

He was soon at the front door of a garishly Palladian building, possibly once an antebellum home. Walking inside, he noticed that it was lushly decorated, unlike Amanda's understatedly elegant suite of offices.

Stopping at a receptionist's desk, he gave his name and informed the woman that he had met Mr. Barnes the previous evening, and was hoping to see Mr. Barnes this morning briefly. She asked him to take a seat and disappeared behind a set of double doors.

He sat in an overstuffed chair and took in the surroundings. But his mind went back to the meeting with Amanda Childs. Try as he might, he could not shake the picture of her with her eyes flashing in rage at Brownlee's insinuations. God, she is beautiful when she's angry, he thought. But in mulling over her remarks during that meeting, he realized again that she stated that Bill Barnes was both church treasurer and diocesan treasurer. And if Barnes was pulling all the financial strings, he would be the logical choice to interview, as well as a possible suspect.

As if summoned by Connor's thoughts, the door opened and Barnes appeared, striding over to him. Connor rose, and they shook hands, Barnes clapping him on the shoulder and saying, "Come on in. Call me Bill. May I call you Connor?"

Connor, amused by his easy familiarity, replied, "Please do. And thank you for agreeing to meet with me on such short notice."

Bill ushered him into his office. "That's Southern hospitality for you; we aim to please. Tell me, what exactly may I help you with?

"Well, it has come to my attention that perhaps you serve as both diocesan and St. Catherine's treasurer, which may actually be a double blessing to me," Connor stated, surprising himself with the smoothness of his tone, as Barnes showed him to a seat and seated himself opposite him in an overstuffed burgundy wing chair. "Of course, as auditor it is imperative for me to compare ledgers. I hope that if I can obtain what I need I can be of as small inconvenience to you as possible."

Bill stared at him intently. "Let's get down to brass tacks, Connor. Why are you here? The Presiding Bishop didn't just decide to bring in an independent firm to do audits to stimulate the economy. You'll find that I'm very territorial, and want to protect what's mine." He paused. "What I mean is that this church and these people are my family. Roots go deep here, and if there's trouble, I need to know."

Connor's eyes met his unblinkingly. "It's quite simple, Bill. The audits for this diocese's accounts for the last three years are missing. It's not just this diocese—there are several sets of records that have come up missing."

Bill interjected briskly, "That can't be. I know Carroll Coughlin, the national treasurer, and he has been good about keeping up the accounts. My dad went to school with him, and we talk regularly. He's getting ready to retire, he told me. I wouldn't mind that job," Bill added with a laugh.

"But Carroll Coughlin's records seem to be in a bit of a mess since he took two months off in March, and no one, not even he, can lay hands on the audit reports. So while the national treasurer is busy trying to get his affairs in order, Bishop Cameron decided to import an outside firm for the limited purpose of helping pull together the records. If the records are discovered or can be easily reconstructed, that will shorten my involvement considerably and save face for the Church. So, you see, it's not what you think."

Bill relaxed noticeably. "I may even have copies of some of those reports around here," he declared. "And I intend to cooperate fully. It's just that, well, you know, auditors tend to make everyone nervous."

"Sorry to be the cause for concern," Jon interjected smoothly. "The Bishop of course doesn't want this to look like some sort of cover-up; therefore, the dirty word 'audit' popped out. However, he is not looking to borrow trouble, either. He doesn't want to start any scandals so soon into his tenure. Hopefully I'll be out of your hair with a minimum of fuss. But I do appreciate your help."

"No problem," Bill nodded.

"Have you been the treasurer for both diocese and church long?"

Again Bill nodded his head. "Yes, I took over diocesan work right after getting out of law school and getting my LL.M. It started out as an emergency, but I just stayed on. Steve—Bishop Marks, I mean—and my father were cousins and grew up together, and Dad and I had done some private work for him, so when the diocesan office lost its treasurer Dad volunteered me to take it on without compensation. They from time to time reimburse extraordinary expenses.

"And I have pretty much taken care of St. Catherine's business too. My mother's family was cradle Episcopal, and I grew up there. It just seemed to fall my lot. Amanda Childs is pretty much over the recital series. She and Marjorie approached the vestry for a line item on the budget, with the stipulation that the series would be self-supporting, and it has been."

Connor said slowly, "That's the organist who fainted last night at the wake, with whom Brownlee and I met this morning?"

"Yes. You've met her, then? I imagine she'll be a pretty busy woman from here on out."

"You mean about her being the major beneficiary under Marjorie Witherspoon's will."

"Yes, you heard about that? But of course, I guess Steve got a copy of the will this morning too," Barnes inserted smoothly. "You know, I've known Amanda all my life. I'm really bowled over by this new will and her inheriting Marjorie's money. I knew they were close, but Marjorie had provided a will long ago leaving the money to the diocese in trust for the church. It's hard when people are gossiping that your life-long friend might have cheated an older woman into leaving her fortune elsewhere. I just don't believe it. But I shouldn't be telling you all this."

Connor looked around the room as he said, "She seemed surprised when she saw a copy of the will this morning."

"She did? But that will was prepared just last month—I'm supposed to believe Mandy didn't know anything about it? And why didn't Marjorie come to me? She went to some Jew in New York. What am I supposed to think?

"I tried to get Mandy to come into practice with me here several years back, but instead she pulled that Carmichael punk in. I mean, sure he was a great athlete and all that, but damn it, she and I were close, or so I thought. Hey, I'm sorry, but I'm just bouncing off the walls after seeing that will. By the way, how did she appear this morning? I mean, after last night? Is she OK?"

Connor nodded, trying to appear sympathetic. "She seemed OK."

Barnes nodded. "Yeah, if I'd known she was already high, I'd never have gotten her that drink."

Connor's eyes widened. "High? Do you mean—"

Barnes said, "I shouldn't be talking about Mandy this way. But she hasn't been the same since her husband died. And Marjorie was extremely sick the last few weeks. Amanda was beside herself taking care of Marjorie, who was really her closest link with reality. And I do what I can to protect her. But I suspect Amanda has always had a source for drugs from her clients—she represented a lot of scum when she was a public defender."

Connor, his senses alert, asked, "What? Cocaine, methamphetamine?"

"I think it's more bootleg prescription stuff—Xanax, hydrocodone, pain meds. It's possible she played around with some Ecstasy too. She knows she can't get it from Howells. Listen, I really don't need to be telling you this. Mandy is very special to me. Damn it, she's really put me in a bad position."

"Why?" Connor asked.

"Well, I don't know but what Steve, when he is able, will want to challenge this new will. Of course, there may be a problem with whether the diocese has standing. But if undue influence is proven, then there's always a chance of arguing for reinstating the previous will. Else the estate may drift for want of relatives or escheat to the state.

"But I just don't want to go against Mandy, you know? Despite it all, we had some good times together growing up and in college. She was kind of an ice maiden in bed, but well, she eventually thawed out and made up for it in other ways."

Connor almost choked, but managed to appear unperturbed as he asked, "You're saying you were lovers at one time?"

"Well, let me just say that we comforted each other when my fiancée and her best friend was killed. That was Marjorie's daughter Monica. I guess you heard about that story."

"Marjorie mentioned her daughter, yes."

"Well, Amanda and I have always remained close, even though we went our separate ways and married others. We're both widowed now, and I'm trying to get her to see the light—you know, tie the knot. That way I could take care of her, get her some help. There's just sort of a special bond there that doesn't go away. We still see each other from time to time, pick up where we left off. You probably get my drift," Bill smiled meaningfully at Connor.

He continued. "However, this new will has thrown me for a loop—maybe I should have seen it coming. This is Amanda at her most cunning, my dad insists. And believe you me, she is hell on wheels. She's sharp. There's nothing slouchy about her in court—she's made me look like a fool more than once," he added, a touch of bitterness in his voice.

"What about her partner Ralph Carmichael?"

"Well, the scuttlebutt around town is that Amanda and he have had a fling. She was raised on the other side of the tracks—her family was awfully lower middle class. So she's not considered a lady of breeding in these parts, I guess. So it could be true. She's very loyal to him and he to her, so go figure. It's really touching. But I don't really believe it—I wouldn't be pushing her to marry me if I really thought she was doing the nasty with a black guy, now would I?"

Connor had to suppress a grimace at the pompous bigotry in Barnes' voice, particularly the references to 'breeding'. Jon had obtained his undergraduate and law degrees at Duke. What he had observed about Southern blue-bloods was not necessarily something to be proud of, but he realized that most small towns in the South possessed their own caste system—it was easier for a stranger to move into a Southern town and be accepted at a particular social stratum than for one born in the town to move up the class ladder. He was not unaware of the latent racism still alive, in the 'old lineage' families as well as the 'red-neck' enclaves found in all small towns, and not just confined to the South. He had also seen instances where persons' reputations were painted over with a broad brush by gossips and scandalmongers. He considered himself lucky being raised in

Colorado, where the western mystique of the rugged individualist self-made man seemed to overshadow the small pockets of the older families and communities that attempted to keep the blue-blood caste myth resuscitated. And his parents had energetically crushed that myth, instructing their children by word and example in the inherent equality of persons and the ability of individuals to aspire to be what they want despite adversity in circumstances.

Changing the subject, Connor asked, "What about Bishop Marks?"

"Oh, Steve is a pompous ass, but we get along fine. You have to realize, I was raised around and married into the pompous asses, and I've always prided myself on being able to figure out what makes them tick. Most of these old-money families live way beyond their means nowadays. They need financial planners like me to keep them fiscally afloat. And I'm pretty good at it.

"By the way, I heard this morning that the Bishop had a set-back last night. They think he's had another heart attack. It doesn't look particularly good. The people of St. Catherine's aren't fond of him, but that's more of the loyal militia rallying around the Witherspoon/Stuart clan. With Marjorie's death and the cessation of that line, things might actually look brighter for him, if he survives."

Connor hadn't really considered this point. "Well, thanks for all your help. I wondered if you might assist me in obtaining any financial records of the parish and diocese you might have. And I have a letter from the Presiding Bishop requesting copies of bank statements."

Barnes smiled confidently. "No problem. In fact, I have my little intern in there working on making the copies right now—figured you'd ask for them. My records are up to date, and I keep the latest church and diocesan records on computer here for convenience.

"In fact, if you come back by in about a couple of hours or so, I'll ask my girl to get the copies done post-haste for you. She has nothing else to do but stand at the copier. And what a great little ass and perky breasts—a joy to watch. You know what I mean?"

Connor smiled tightly as Barnes laughed, but by now was thoroughly disgusted. Barnes asked him casually, "You gonna talk to Amanda again?"

Connor replied, equally casually, "I want to ask her a couple questions if the opportunity arises."

Barnes nodded. "She's a busy lady, and impossible to track down during the day. And in the evenings—well, she's not always herself. When she marries me, maybe I'll save her from herself." He took a deep breath, his voice confiding. "I'd rather you came to me, though. Amanda's been through a tough time lately, and I don't think she's up to anything more right now. She's pretty low, and I'm trying to keep as much stress off her as possible, to keep her from doing something rash."

"I'll keep that in mind," Connor replied, as he gazed at a picture of Barnes on the wall. Barnes was decked in scuba gear and smiling, his arm around a curved blonde in a bikini, her face encased in snorkeling mask and gear, the background coral reef just visible in the clear water behind the boat.

Bill stopped behind him. Connor queried casually, "Caymans?"

Bill nodded. "Yeah, have you been there? I try to get down there a couple or three times a year, get a few underwater hours in. Taught Mandy how to snorkel there, as well as a few other more exotic moves."

Bill's meaning was not lost on Connor, as he smilingly thanked Barnes, promising to come back by later to pick up the copies.

Stepping outside into the sunlight, he was soon in his car again. He decided that he was most anxious to interview Amanda Childs, and called her office number. After asking the receptionist to speak to her, soon Ralph Carmichael's voice came on the line.

After learning that Amanda was not available and leaving a message with a profuse apology for the morning's fiasco, he explained that he would be staying a few days and would like to meet with her. Ringing off, he called in to his contact.

"How did the meeting go?" Zeke asked.

"Well, I wondered why alpha female had no enemies, but just found out that with friends like this guy, she doesn't need them."

"Productive meeting?"

"It was important on several levels. He made a lot of allegations for such a good friend of Amanda Child's. I'll have records shortly. Bill Barnes likes to frequent the Caymans as well, and he had a picture of a woman looking remarkably like Amanda Childs with him on a boat there. Let's not ignore him—broaden the net."

"Bubba is ahead of you there. But I have some bad news. We've also gotten pictures from the Caymans bank security cameras of someone transacting business that looks remarkably like Amanda Childs."

Jon was silent. The voice continued, "Sorry, Jon."

"I know." He hesitated, disappointed in the news.

"Our friend at the hospital is reporting that Marks' condition has changed for the worse. You got a message by the way from your 'service', a la Bubba. A Dr. Howells called and wanted to speak to you."

"I heard about Marks' setback from Barnes. I'm going to the hospital now. I really want to approach him, and don't want him to die on us. He could be an asset to the case."

The voice said, "Wait a minute." There was a pause, then Bubba's voice was heard. "Great news—the federal reserve guys are going to cooperate with us. Do you know how many country clubs I had to page to find one of them this weekend?

Anyway, I think I can pull all bank records without any subpoenas, and this bank is a branch of the Milford bank. We won't have to tip our hand."

"You made it look like a routine Federal Reserve query?"

"Yep. We're covered."

Jon smiled. "And Barnes is having his stuff copied for me to pick up in an hour. Anselm had financial records and minutes ready for me this morning. They're almost overly cooperative."

"The trap is springing."

"Yes, but who is setting it? Later," Connor was terse as he hung up.

He decided to try Amanda Childs' home, and called information. He was surprised that the number was listed, and dialed it, getting her answering machine. He left a message there too—the mystery of Amanda Childs was even more intriguing.

Arriving at the hospital, he was soon knocking on Howells' door. Hearing a gruff "Come in", he entered and found the doctor eating a sandwich.

"Hello, Connor, please come in. If I had known, I'd have ordered you one of these healthy turkey things," Howell said, sipping some hot tea. "Can I get you something?"

"No, sir. I just got the message that you had called, and wanted to drop by and see what I could do."

"Well, apparently last night, the Bishop's vitals went all out of kilter. I really think he ought to be moved if Cardet thinks he is stable enough, but now he insists that he cannot leave without talking to you. He was quite erratic last night, but the nitro seems to be settling him down a bit, and his vitals are much better today."

"Would you mind coming with me to see him? Cardet didn't want any more excitement, but he has a stubborn patient. So I agreed to hunt you down."

"Sure, I would be glad to talk to him."

"Well, let's go. That sandwich can't get any worse for the waiting."

They walked down to CCU and were admitted by the nurse. Going into the Bishop's private room, they found Dr. Cardet with the patient. Spying them, Bishop Marks imperiously beckoned Connor forward. Connor stepped up to the bed, and the Bishop stated simply, "I'm afraid I'm about to die and I need to confess my sins."

Connor, taken aback, interjected, "I'm not a priest, sir—" but the Bishop waved him to silence.

"You don't understand. I have information that you need, and I will not leave this hospital without telling you. I'm afraid I won't make it, one way or the other."

Connor stared at him. "What do you mean, Bishop?"

The Bishop met his eyes. "I'll tell you, but don't you need a tape recorder or court reporter to take this down, in case I don't make it?"

Connor turned his gaze to Dr. Cardet. "Is he up to our taking a taped sworn statement from him now?"

Cardet said, "His signs are improved from last night. I want to get him to Pensacola, but we have much of the same equipment here, and he refuses to go until he does this. The sooner we can satisfy him, the better for his sake."

Connor said quickly to both of them, with Howells listening on, "I need to make a quick call, and I can have the equipment and reporter here shortly. We'll proceed now, if you both agree."

Surprised, they agreed, and Howells escorted Connor back to his office and left him in privacy to make his calls.

Connor called his contact. "You'll never believe this. The Big B wants to make a sworn statement. I need a recording device and stenographer here on the double. Then we need to probably provide some surveillance to get him moved out of here to a hospital in Pensacola. Seems he changed for the worse last night. I don't know what he is going to say, but let's get a move on. First floor—come to Dr. Howells' office two doors down from the nurses' station and ask for me. And make it discreet."

"I'll have someone there ASAP."

Connor paced the floor, trying to organize his thoughts. What was so pressing that the Bishop had to say? Was it going to implicate Amanda Childs? Was anyone else in on this operation? Was there a connection between Childs and Claude Brown's being in town?

Connor knew the story from Andrew about Amanda's representation of Claude Brown. Although Amanda had remained tight-lipped about her clients and would never divulge any information regarding her cases, even to Andy, Andy had shared with Connor what he learned from Charles Petrino about Brown's attack on Amanda and threat against her life. It was a subsequent threat against Amanda by Brown that led to Andy's murder.

His thoughts were interrupted as Dr. Howells knocked and entered, with a lab report in his hand. Connor stared at him intently. "Are you sure that Amanda Childs would not be strung out on drugs, even obtained on the black market?"

Dr. Howells looked at him, surprised, laying the report on his desk. "Amanda Childs has always had a distaste for all drugs of any kind. As a child she would refuse to take medicine. More than once she would get so sick I'd have to inject her with medicine, and she hated shots too. Then we discovered her hypersensitivity to certain drugs.

"While she was in college her dad died when his liver ceased functioning. The specialists had not discovered what was causing his problem, but in the meantime they were poisoning him with all sorts of drugs to treat the symptoms. No one apparently thought to run a simple liver function test. I was not his treating physician at the time, because one of his symptoms was an extreme paranoia, and he discharged me in favor of other doctors. Amanda tried to reason with him, and argued with the doctors. Then he died. She always saw that as further justification for keeping drugs out of her system."

"So if someone alleges she is getting drugs illegally from her clients, you . . ."

"Would not believe a word of it," Howells finished for him. "I cannot explain the toxicity levels in her blood for GHB, gamma-hydroxybutyrate, from the blood test I took. I just broke all sorts of privacy laws telling you this, but I know she was stone sober during church and the funeral. You heard her play—she was superb."

"But she was alone in her office between the graveside service and the wake," said Connor.

"But Father Anselm went in to talk to her before the wake, and other than her being weary and sad he detected nothing amiss."

"You're not saying someone—"

"I'm not saying anything right now," Howells interrupted testily. "I have my own suspicions. I've sent the sample to an independent lab, and it will take a couple days for them to tell me, but I'll know exactly what it was when they are through. GHB is a date-rape drug, not in high demand by voluntary drug users nowadays, except perhaps in the clubbing scene."

"Doctor Howells, let's keep this between ourselves for now, OK?" Connor said.

Howells gazed at him as if unsure to speak. Finally, he said, "I know who you are, Jonathan Connor."

Jon started. "Did Marjorie tell you?"

"Yes. She said you gave your word to her. You've got to protect Amanda Katharine. I don't know what's happening, but she's the daughter I never had. I trust Amanda—I know her." His voice faltered. "Someone is out for her."

"Who?" inquired Connor.

"If I knew, he wouldn't be alive long," warned Howells, his features grim.

Chapter 21

"Dr. Howells, I'd like you or Dr. Cardet in there with me. I would like to prevent any adverse medical consequences to the patient during the interview, if possible. I intend to talk to the Bishop first and see what he has to say. It may not be anything worth recording, but I'm not taking any chances. If it is, I'm going to have to divulge who I am and Mirandize him for a taped, sworn statement. We'll have the recording and stenographic people ready. If you don't mind, I'd like to stash the crew in here until we see."

"No problem—I'll leave word with staff to expect them," Howells replied, and Cardet nodded solemnly.

Soon the court reporter appeared, along with an analyst, both of them decked in white doctor's coats and carrying their equipment discreetly in a wheeled carryon bag. Howells had arranged to have Stephen Marks placed in a private suite adjoining the CCU, and as the orderlies and nurses were busy trying to check all the monitors and equipment, Connor met with the analyst and reporter in Dr. Howells' office. Momentarily, both Drs. Howells and Cardet entered, and a briefing was held regarding the protocol for the interview.

When they were ready to begin the interview, Connor entered the Bishop's room with Dr. Howell, while Cardet watched the Bishop's monitors from the nurses' station.

"Bishop Marks, are you feeling all right? Are you feeling up to talking to me?"

"Yes, I feel better," the Bishop insisted imperiously.

"Before we go to tape, I'd like you to feel free to talk to me with only Dr. Howells present."

The Bishop looked at both faces. "I'm afraid for my life."

Howells asked, "Are you feeling discomfort or pain? If so, please let me know."

"No, no, it's not that. I'm afraid I won't leave this hospital alive, whether by act of God or man."

Connor frowned. "Tell us why. Has someone threatened you?"
The Bishop hesitated, fear in his eyes. "Yes," he finally said. "Last night."
"Who?"
"Billy Barnes. You see, I was all set to go through with the plan. But when I saw Marjorie in that coffin, and I gazed upon Amanda Childs at the funeral, I knew she could see right through me. I feared Marjorie must have told her all about me. I know I have failed God and carried my grudge to extreme limits, but to frame that lovely girl, Marjorie's and my child, the child I never knew—"

Connor, worried that the frail man was overly excited, put his hand gently on the Bishop's shoulder, and said, "I'm not following you. Slow down, please. Are you saying Bill Barnes threatened you last night?"

"Billy was here to 'give me a message' that I wasn't much use lying in a hospital bed, and might as well be dead. He told me to stick to the plan, or the only way I'd leave this hospital was in a body bag."

"Why? What was 'the plan', as you call it?"

"He knew the story about my threatened revenge against the Stuarts from his dad. We came up several years ago with this 'fool-proof' scheme, when I became Bishop, about granting the requests for assistance for St. Catherine's and disbursing monies. It actually began before Billy was treasurer. Bill came up with the idea of St. Catherine's trust fund and a way to invade it. That netted us a tidy sum. Then the treasurer retired, and was killed in a freak accident. So we installed Billy as treasurer.

The plan was that St. Catherine's requests would be granted in the diocesan records, the money would be disbursed but would never reach St. Catherine's. Billy told them the requests were denied, and we split the proceeds, the monies being deposited in off-shore accounts. I think the operation expanded to charitable donations to the organ and recital series funds, and monies from there were diverted too. And Billy apparently had some business on the side; he was using the fund for funneling monies, creating fictitious donors."

The Bishop took a deep breath, and Connor and Dr. Howells, both alarmed, asked, "Are you OK?"

The Bishop nodded emphatically. "I want to tell you all, and get it on tape. But please hurry. I want to make it right. I'll go to prison, I'll do whatever. But I'm afraid Billy will walk in at any minute and stop me."

Connor gazed at him. "Are you sure you know what you are saying, Bishop?"

The Bishop glowered back at him. "As sure as anything in my life."

Connor held up his hand. "I need to level with you. I am not who you think I am. I am Jonathan Mark Connor, Senior Special Agent, Federal Bureau of Investigation."

The Bishop looked at him in surprise, but showed no fear, only relief. "I felt that in time the feds would catch up with me. I felt my days were numbered anyway when the Presiding Bishop announced the audit, although Billy assured me the transfers, if found, could not be traced back to us."

Connor stated, "I can provide you with protective custody, but only in exchange for your cooperation and truthful testimony. I don't have authority to offer you immunity at this time, but your cooperation will go a long way in the U.S. Attorney's decision."

"Bring your people in here and let's get started," urged the Bishop firmly. "And don't forget to read me my rights—we want this legal."

Connor, though surprised at his willingness, could not but smile at his manner of issuing orders, and quickly left to summon the analyst and reporter. Once they were set up, and the doctors checked Marks' vital signs and gave the go-ahead, Connor read his rights to the Bishop, and they rehashed the information that the Bishop had already given to Connor.

Connor then asked, "Can you provide specifics about this 'plan'?"

Bishop Marks imperiously specified times when requests were made and disbursements occurred. Then he added, "Marjorie and Amanda Childs played right into it."

"How is that?" Connor wanted to know.

"They created the recital series fund as a line item on the church's budget. The money was deposited in St. Catherine's general fund, and Amanda was the one who mainly authorized disbursements from it, although Billy was the one signing her name. Several wealthy patrons of the series gave some very generous donations, which didn't make it to light. And Bill came up with the idea of soliciting large contributions from wealthy patrons. Furthermore, Billy was creating fictitious donors, and channeling monies from his operations through the account. Billy was pretty busy keeping two sets of books, but he is brilliant, just like his dad. And Billy and his dad were both part owners of the bank and on the board of directors. It made the transactions a piece of cake. Who would suspect a church?

"Bill felt pretty confident he could keep a lid on everything, and was frat buddies in college with the national treasurer. Because of that, no audits were ever done. In fact, I'm not so sure but whether the national treasurer wasn't involved in some of the same shady business, or getting kickbacks. I believe there were other conspiracies in which he was personally involved in the thefts."

"We are aware of that possibility," Connor stated quietly.

"Billy claimed to be able to wield great influence over Amanda and Marjy, and to hear him talk the vestry was putty in his hands. But we didn't count on the past Presiding Bishop's retirement a couple years ago, and this new one's sharp business sense.

"And I never dreamed Marjorie would die—I knew she was sick, but I always dreamed that one day we'd reconcile. Shows you what a foolish old man I have become. I had no right to her after what I had done, I let her slip away, and she dealt me the ultimate blow."

"I'm very sorry," Connor murmured.

The Bishop continued excitedly. "I had a child out there, and never knew it. I should have been prosecuted for sexual battery, but nothing happened. And the ultimate consequence was not only losing her, but never knowing my child. And she was right in the path of the plan to destroy her."

"Child?" Connor echoed confusedly.

"Marjy wrote me a letter, which I received from Father Anselm upon my arrival here on Sunday, on Marjorie's orders before she died. She said that she had to forgive me for the past, and therefore she had to let me know that a child had been born and adopted out to a good home and parents. She wanted me to know that the child had been well provided for, and did not know her true parentage. She hoped that I would be Christian enough to honor that secret for the girl's sake, because she had wonderful parents for whom she cared deeply. And Marjy charged me with protecting her from harm. Somehow Marjy knew or suspected our scheme."

Connor started. So Marjorie had acted on her own in an attempt to protect Amanda. "This letter," interjected Connor, "do you still have it?"

Marks looked distressed. "No; after my heart attack, I lost it. I had hoped that it was still in my clothing, or that Adam found it. I've asked him to locate it, but so far it's not been discovered."

Connor asked, "Do you know the provisions of Marjorie's will?"

Marks closed his eyes. "Yes. The previous will was all part of the plan—not only was Marjorie keeping the church alive by infusing funds while we drew off the contributions, we were also counting on the previous will because it left the monies to the diocese in trust. With such a rich fund, we planned to siphon it off slowly until we could all retire to some nonextraditing country. But then Marjorie threw in the curve ball, and left this new will. A copy was in a second envelope delivered with the letter.

"But Bill said on the phone last night that it couldn't be better if he had drafted it himself. What with Amanda Childs as the primary beneficiary, all suspicion pointed at her, the simultaneous death clause and resulting trust, he felt confident that the situation was going to take care of itself."

"How did Barnes know about the will?"

"Billy had a copy in hand, probably from Adam, my curate."

"Is Brownlee in on this scheme?"

"No, but Bill is so chummy with him that Adam confides everything to Bill. Adam's a silly man, although useful in his own way."

"Are you sure Barnes has not implicated Brownlee?"

"To the best of my knowledge. I've kept him out of this business—the fewer people who knew, the better. And Adam has a good heart; he's just easily swayed."

"Who else is in on this?"

"Bill has someone on his secret payroll, a man he calls only 'Brown'. He's acted as courier once or twice. Billy and this Brown manage the side business, which Billy maintains multiplies the wealth from what we get with this scheme. I believe some monies passed hands with the national treasurer."

Connor's eyes narrowed at the news about Brown. "Do you know how Bill planned to take care of the situation with the new will?"

The Bishop replied slowly, "No, Billy did not confide in me last night. I am worried."

"Is Amanda Childs one of the conspirators?"

"No, no—she is the one evidence was planted on to take the fall."

"How do you know this?"

"I've seen Billy forge her signature on checks and other documents. I know he has a business set up in her name through which the monies are being funneled."

"Do you know the name of this business?"

"It's WWAC, Inc., or something like that." Marks suddenly clutched Connor's arm. "You've got to do something. You see, I think Amanda Childs is my daughter, and I don't know what Bill might do to her. But she's in danger."

Connor, surprised, asked, "Why do you think that?"

"Because she's the right age, Marjorie would never abandon her child, Marjorie has made her the primary beneficiary in the new will, and," finished the Bishop, his eyes glistening with unshed tears, "she has my eyes." He sniffed. "And I never knew until the letter."

Connor asked, "If you think that, why then did you set up for Brownlee and me to go to Amanda Childs' office?"

"Two-fold: When Bill found out about the new will, he pumped Adam full of the idea that she was guilty of exercising undue influence over Marjorie—that whole idea's funny now, I guess. Bill was insistent that I push you in Amanda's direction, and I was sure if I didn't he'd find out from Adam that I didn't. And I surmised that if I did that and you met her you'd be suspicious of my motives."

"You were right," Connor nodded quietly. "Anything else you wish to tell us?"

"I guess that's it," said Marks, suddenly appearing very old.

"That concludes the interview for now," Connor addressed the stenographer and analyst recording the interview. They turned off their equipment, and quickly unplugged it and left the room. Connor turned to Marks.

"We're having you flown out of here this evening, if Dr. Cardet approves it. I have a team that will accompany you. You'll be under our protection, and I most sincerely hope that you recover completely and soon. But Bishop Marks, chances are great that you will be charged."

The Bishop took his hand. "I'll do anything necessary, testify or answer more questions, but you really do have to protect my daughter. And promise not to tell her—she's lost her parents and Marjorie, and her husband too, I've been told. I don't want to destroy her life by saddling her with my shameful past. She's too fine for that. And I've done nothing but cause her pain already."

Connor shook his hand gravely, then turned to leave the room. Dr. Howells started to follow him, and Marks called, his voice hoarse with emotion, "Malcolm? I'm so sorry. I know you loved Marjorie. I ruined things for the two of you. I am ashamed and sorry. I know I can never make it right now."

Howells looked at him somberly. "I know," was all he said as they left the room.

Connor stopped and spoke to the analyst outside the door, thanked the stenographer and ordered a transcript. He left with Howells, who checked with Cardet about the advisability of moving the patient.

Once in Howells' office, Howells' telephone rang. Howells picked it up. "Howells here." He listened intently. "I'll take it myself. I'm on my way."

Turning to Connor, he said, "I'll be back—they need me down at the emergency room. Some automobile accident trauma is coming in, and the staff is short-handed."

Connor nodded as he pulled out his cell phone and called his contact. "We have a taped sworn statement. The team needs to be in place stat—I want him protected out of here and to avoid all contact with Barnes. We have to proceed cautiously—we still don't know for sure what contacts Barnes may have here in the hospital or elsewhere. Plus we need to examine this statement and nail down some corroboration to his story. Talk to you later." Thankful he had left his briefcase in Howells' office earlier, he pulled out his Beretta 9-millimeter and slipped it in his back belt.

He went back to the CCU and met with Cardet. After discussion, they decided to forestall contact between Barnes and Marks by giving out that he was doing worse and could not have any visitors. After posting the analyst downstairs to guide the team up, he went in and sat with Marks while waiting for the chopper.

Marks smiled weakly. "I'm glad you came back. I know you and Howells must be pretty disgusted with me. You know, I was such an arrogant, grasping fool all these years. I only lived for myself. I went through the motions of religion, but I guess it didn't mean much to me, violating someone as sweet and pure as Marjorie.

"For the first time in my life, I have been brought face to face with my own mortality, and with another life for which I am responsible, and to whom I need to make amends. I never acknowledged what I did to Marjorie, and that self-centeredness, that violation and my unrepentance have made me, a Bishop in the Episcopal Church, a reprobate in the worst way. I could have stopped this a long time ago; I could have faced the music and Marjorie and asked forgiveness and tried to make amends. But I never even imagined the news she gave me. A daughter!"

Connor looked at him soberly. "I can't change your past. But what you've done today is a good start."

Marks asked, "Will you do me a favor? Will you go and check on Amanda when you leave here? Don't let anything happen to her. In fact, if you recall, I had you ask her to meet me tonight at 7:00. I really wanted to just talk to her, ask her about herself. But that would not be wise, and she's in enough danger without Bill's finding out I wanted to see her."

Connor promised. "I'll probably still be around here in case she shows up to see you tonight," as the analyst brought in two other men in white coats and Dr. Cardet.

Cardet informed them, "The helicopter is on its way and should be landing in about ten minutes."

Connor introduced the doctor to the team members. He gave instructions to them quietly outside the room as Cardet supervised the medical staff in preparing Marks for transport.

Once the helicopter came into view, the team moved quickly, transporting Marks to the roof. Connor followed as backup and lookout, and watched the helicopter out of sight. Then he went to Howells' office and called in to his contact, requesting backup for surveillance of Amanda Childs.

The voice stated, "I've asked for backup, but don't have authorization yet. I figured you might know by now—alpha was almost run over in front of the church this afternoon. She's at the ER."

"What?" shouted Connor. "Damn it all, we need to be protecting her."

"We had Petrino on the watch, and he's with her now. He cussed like a sailor at us for letting the perpetrator get away. He says he can't trust us to do the job right. He's a loose cannon."

"What do you know?"

"I'm pretty sure Claudius is back in town—looked like him. We found him and are tailing him rather than picking him up—Simpson's orders. I hope he'll lead us to something interesting."

"Simpson wants us to just follow him? He got away last time. Damn," Connor swore. "Just don't let him get away this time—we've got trouble enough." Connor briefed him on the basics of the statement and Marks' allegations against Barnes, along with Brown's probable involvement. Concluding, he said, "I'm going downstairs to check on our alpha."

Turning, he saw Dr. Howells entering the room. Standing, he asked, "How is Amanda?"

Howells, surprised that he already knew, replied, "She has some minor lacerations and a sprained ankle, but it is not severe. Charlie is taking her home—she of course wouldn't stay at the hospital." Howells turned angry. "She needs your protection. You cannot let anything happen to her, or I'll be hunting for you myself."

He looked at Howells. "Petrino's with her—she's safe. But you didn't tell me everything, did you?" he accused. "What was this about a letter to Marks? What letter?"

Howells glared at him, silent. Connor pressed, "Who delivered it? You?"

"I'm sure Colin Anselm was entrusted with that task," Howells answered quietly.

"Why didn't Marjorie tell me? Why didn't you tell me?" Connor demanded icily.

"Marjy had her own affairs to attend to, which were none of your business," Howells' reply was equally cold. "And Marjorie planned to defy you and tell Amanda immediately, only she didn't get the opportunity. When she came home from New York, I met her at the airport. She told me about the will, and that the FBI was involved. I could tell she was sick; she was failing fast. I knew it was near the end. I took her immediately to the hospital and called Amanda. But by the time Amanda got there, Marjorie was slipping away."

Jon was silent, his loyalties torn. Howells turned on him angrily. "I'd have already told her, but there hasn't been time, and Amanda wasn't in any condition to be told last night. Hasn't the FBI ruined Amanda's life enough? Her husband's gone, and thanks so much for keeping her in the dark about how he died. They both sacrificed so much for the 'cause'. Now she's a prime suspect in some scheme, and you strong-armed Marjy into cooperating in order to save Amanda again. But Marjy has her own resources, and although I didn't approve, she took the chance of notifying Marks and appealing to him to save his only daughter."

"So Marks raped Marjorie Witherspoon, and Amanda is the child of that union?"

Howells looked at him, tears in his eyes. "Marjorie was hysterical when she found out she was pregnant. I offered to marry her on the spot. I loved her and would do anything for her, even raise Stephen's child as mine. But she was too ashamed of what he'd done to her, and after she discovered she was pregnant, she couldn't get past the small town gossip and stigma this would engender for the baby, and she was not going to abort it. She felt that she would be dragging me into the middle of it by marrying me. I'd have left town, or done anything she wanted, gone anywhere with her.

"She had met Jerrod at college, and they had dated. She was about to graduate when this happened. Jerrod had already proposed to her. She rejected him, and he pressed her. She finally confided in him what happened. He was more stubborn than I, and offered to provide a place for her while she was ostensibly working on her master's degree in education, so that she could have the baby. He adored her and wanted to marry her. In gratefulness to him, and I think love too, she accepted.

"Marjorie had a dear high school friend here who had a son, and had tried for several years to conceive again. She wanted another child badly. Marjorie confided in her, and the friend and her husband agreed to take the child. They were of modest means, but proud people. They insisted that they wanted no financial assistance or interference, and that the child would be raised as theirs. Marjorie and Jerrod agreed, as long as she could be able to see the child growing up, to never divulge the truth.

"Mrs. Andrews went up to stay with Marjorie and help her through the latter part of the pregnancy, which would help give the lie that the baby was hers. I took Mr. Andrews and little Jeffrey with me. I delivered the baby, and brought the Andrews family and baby home.

"Three months later, Jerrod and Marjorie were married, and about eleven months later Monica was born."

Connor asked, "So Amanda still doesn't know?"

"No. Marjorie kept her word, even after Jerrod and Monica were killed, and after Mr. and Mrs. Andrews had both died. She wanted so badly to break the promise after Andy was gone, but realized that might be more than Amanda could bear. But she and Amanda became closer and closer, and I knew she loved her as much as she had loved her Monica. She wanted to do so much for the girl when Amanda was growing up, but respected the Andrews' pride.

"And I brought her into the world. I loved Amanda like she was my own, and loved Marjorie and despised Marks all these years."

"That must have been quite a burden to bear," Connor replied quietly.

"There have been good moments. It was funny to me to watch how Amanda would try to play matchmaker with me and Marjorie. She had no idea how much I wanted that. But I think Marjorie's secret and her shame were just too great a barrier. But at least I have been there for Amanda and Marjorie. Marjorie told me before she died how she always wished for me the happiness she had been able to experience. She didn't know that I felt the same pain and happiness along with her."

Howells pulled out a handkerchief and wiped his eyes. Connor said to him, "I believe you. You are an admirable man."

"No, just an old fool."

"Well, I hope to experience that love with someone one day. But for now I'm going to do what I can to protect your little girl."

"Thank you, young man," said Howells as Connor let himself out.

Connor was soon out of the hospital and back in his car. He realized that it was 5:30 and he had still not picked up the records from Barnes' office. Hoping to catch someone still at the office, he swung around to the back door of the office. He was relieved to see a small car in the parking lot next to the back door.

Running up lightly to the door, he knocked. Trying the door, he found it unlocked. "Is anyone home?" he called.

"Yes," a pretty petite blonde girl, not more than 19, with ponytail, fitted jeans and tight T-shirt, peeked her head from around the hallway. "Are you Mr. Thomson?" she asked sunnily.

"Yes, I am. I'm so sorry to be late, and glad you had not gone home," he replied, smiling at her.

"Oh, Mr. Barnes told me to wait for you, and if there was anything you needed, I was to help," she approached him, a hopeful look in her eyes.

Connor asked quickly, "I think you had copies for me?"

"Yes, there is a box full. Do you want me to tote it to your car for you?" she asked. Brushing close to him flirtatiously, she looked out the window. "That's a cool car. I'd like a ride in that."

"Perhaps some other time. I am late to an appointment, and have really kept you long enough. I'm really grateful to Mr. Barnes and to you for all your help. Now where's the box?" he interrupted, trying not to sound testy.

"Well, OK," she responded. "But I could show you around the place."

"That's a nice offer," countered Connor somewhat sternly, "but I'm here for the information Mr. Barnes had for me. If the box is too heavy for you, I will be happy to retrieve it. But with all due respect, I really must be getting on."

Pouting, she pointed. "Well, it's that box right there on the table by the door."

Connor looked at her, then the box. "Why didn't you say so?" Lifting the lid of the box, he scanned the pages, noting that it appeared to be what he was after. "Thank you very much for your time and effort in copying all this for me," he said, as he picked up the box and fled as gracefully as he could from the premises.

Once in the safety of his car and on the road, he made a call to his contact and made arrangements to deliver the documents he had collected during the day. At the rendezvous point, he made arrangements to meet with the contact and his team later, saying he had a promise to keep first.

Chapter 22

When Connor knocked on Amanda Childs' door that evening, he was burning with questions for her. There seemed to be so much ground to cover, and in his quest for the truth he was fighting the warring factions of the evidence they had obtained so far that implicated Amanda, buttressed by the statements made by Barnes, versus the hope, now fortified with Stephen Marks' confession, that she was innocent of the allegations. He knew that the sooner he asked those questions, the less time for other circumstances to intervene and cast more clouds over the investigation.

He wondered about the nature of her relationship with Barnes. Was Barnes telling the truth? Was Ralph right—was Andrew Amanda's only love? For the sake of his dead friend and the woman he had loved, Connor wanted to believe in her.

When he saw her, Connor was shocked at the picture of vulnerability she made. Her face, devoid of makeup, was ethereal, but he could see a pallor around the eyes that he had not seen on his earlier meeting. She looked young and innocent. She seemed defenseless. Although she readily answered his questions, he noted a wariness about her, no doubt caused or aggravated by Brownlee's accusations earlier.

His observation of her brought to mind an anecdote Andrew Childs had related to Jon just a couple of months before his death. The supervisor had called a staff meeting at the Atlanta bureau to share information and determine whether any of the ongoing investigations might have a connection. Andrew had walked into the meeting, his jaw swollen and bruised and his left eye blackened. He refused to divulge the cause of his disfigurement and bore the jibes of the other officers silently, commenting only, "You should see the other guy."

Later that day Connor had given Andrew a lift across town to retrieve some documents. Andrew had expressed his anger that he could not divulge Claude

Brown's escape to his wife. He confided that with Claude Brown at large he had been teaching Amanda some self-defense techniques in the days before leaving to fly up for the meeting. They had done some sparring before she had retired to bed while he stayed up late reviewing some field reports.

He could hear Andy recounting the events. "I came into the bedroom, and there she was, so innocent and childlike, fast asleep. She was dreaming, so I crawled into bed and kissed her, and just then she hit me in the ribs with a left jab, and an upper cut to the jaw. Then her fist made contact with my eye. Almost knocked me out. She woke up when I cried out, and was so remorseful she cooked my favorite meal the next night, and was so solicitous." Connor remembered Andy's sly smile. "The sex was extraordinary.

"But I learned not to make that mistake again. She's dangerous when she looks like that."

Remembering Andy's words, but sensing her exhaustion and hearing Dr. Howells' admonition in his ears, he reluctantly decided to cut short his visit, coming up with the plan of taking her to dinner later, which gave him more time to decide how to develop his line of questioning.

There again he was torn. The Bureau did not want its suspect tipped off, but Jon had made a promise to Marjorie Witherspoon. Marjorie had threatened that Amanda would be told everything. But just before her plane was called for her return home the day she died, Marjorie, obviously in agonizing pain, had extracted a solemn promise that Jon, who had accompanied her to the airport at her request, swear to tell Amanda and to protect her. And now he was trying to make good that promise, despite his superior's directive otherwise.

From Amanda's phone conversation with Petrino he gleaned that the car that had been used in the attempt to run her down had been located near the Witherspoon residence, and that the place had been burglarized. He resolved to question Petrino for the details.

He could not tear himself away, and kept asking questions, in spite of his resolve. But even as he remained, her pallor and obvious physical discomfort increased, and her movements became more erratic, until the point when she fled to the bathroom. As he saw the remaining contents of her glass spill over the table and floor, he realized that she was experiencing symptoms similar to what was observed of her the previous evening. Was Barnes right—was she under the influence of some drug?

His suspicions aroused, he strode to the closed bathroom door, where he could hear the sound of her retching, then of water running. He wondered momentarily whether she was anorexic, before he called out to her.

At first there was no answer, then the sound of water ceased and he saw the doorknob move. The door opened, and Amanda stood before him, pale as a wraith, attempting to smile, before falling in front of him. Without thinking, he swooped her up and carried her down the hallway and through the nearest doorway into a bedroom. He gently deposited her semi-conscious form on the bed, feeling her tremble, clammy and cold.

Amanda protested weakly, but he did not believe for one moment that she had the flu, and immediately selected Dr. Howells' number from his speed-dialer. Reaching the physician, he learned that Howells was only blocks away. Connor admonished Amanda to lie still, covered her shaking form with a quilt. When she mistook him for Andrew, his heart stopped a moment, and he realized she was suffering from some delirium.

He left the room quickly, his emotions at war within him. He picked up a tea towel from the counter and stopped to wipe up the spill on her table. As he did so, he noticed a small white residue where the liquid had spilled. Curious, he heard the doctor's car driving up and went to let the doctor in.

After showing Dr. Howells to Amanda's room and exchanging a few low words, he sprinted down to a corner deli. He hurriedly ordered soup and coffee, with which he quickly returned. Leaving the steaming cup of soup on the kitchen counter, he saw a pill bottle next to the kitchen sink. His heart sank. He quickly took the coffee to Amanda, then retraced his steps to the kitchen. He scowled and his face darkened as he looked at the contents of the open medicine bottle. He quickly scanned the kitchen cabinets, moving quickly through the room, then moved to the bar under the stairs. There he discovered another unmarked bottle of pills alongside a half-empty bourbon bottle. Frozen, he shook his head in disbelief, suddenly heartsick. From there he started a search of the living area. Under the cushions of the sofa he discovered another medicine bottle. Livid at her and at himself, he strode to the bedroom, bottles in hand, so angry he was heedless of preserving evidence.

As Howells was attempting to obtain information from the wan Amanda, Connor angrily marched into the room and dropped the pill bottles between them. He was not convinced by her denial, and was too untrusting of her and his own reaction to remain. He left the room to busy himself with pouring the soup into a bowl, finding utensils and arranging everything on a tray. Feeling somewhat guilty, he rummaged through her purse, careful not to dislodge anything, but found only a tube of antibiotic creme.

Connor entered the bedroom with the tray, in time to hear Amanda assure the doctor, "I would not take anything without consulting you."

Her words stirred his ire even more, as he proceeded to cross-examine her about the pills, until Howells cut him short and motioned for Connor to follow him outside the room. Howells quietly stated, "I was already on my way over here. Just before you called, Billy Barnes had me paged and said he had just left Amanda's, and that she just didn't seem right. He had asked me to check on her."

Connor demanded, "You are going to admit her to the hospital, aren't you? Doesn't she need her stomach pumped? She's a danger to herself, if nothing else. This explains last night."

Howells replied tiredly, "I believe what she is telling me. In any event, she appears to be past the worst of it. She refuses to go. I would hospitalize her if I felt it necessary, and will still do so. But with the wagging tongues of this town and the media crawling all over town in search of stories of the heiress-apparent, I think she's better off here. I'll get lab results quickly, and that will make my decision. In any event I'm not leaving her alone tonight. We'll go from there."

Howells returned to the room, leaving Connor alone arguing with himself. Meanwhile, he took the time to survey the contents of her cupboards and refrigerator, and checked the medicine cabinet in her bathroom. Finding no other evidence of drugs, he stopped and again checked the alcove under the stairwell, which held a bar, but all the other bottles of spirits were covered in a fine layer of dust from disuse. He scoured the shelves of the refrigerator and freezer, but found nothing suspicious.

Although her condition seemed to verify Bill Barnes' allegations, he could not rid himself of the look of Amanda, haggard and vulnerable, vehemently denying the usage of drugs. Neither could he rule out the response of Howells, who knew Amanda far longer and better than Connor did. However, if Howells was a father figure to Amanda, she would probably keep any drug usage from his knowledge, and would certainly not request drugs from him. And it was possible that Howells had a blind spot in his heart for the daughter he never had.

After a while Howells reluctantly took his leave, leaving Connor to watch Amanda until Howells could return from the hospital. Connor returned to the bedroom, still mentally scratching his head but with more questions than ever. He did not trust himself to ask them, and at the sight of her again suddenly felt sorry for her, as the thought hit him of all she must have experienced over the last week. Then his anger at the thought of her taking drugs again overtook him, and he challenged her, ending up searching her room while she looked on dumbfounded.

As he was leaving, he checked the refrigerator once more. Finding a pitcher of liquid, he decided on an impulse to pour a small amount in a jar to take with him for testing, and poured the remainder down the kitchen sink. Glancing through the kitchen drawers, he found some clear freezer bags. Taking three and a tea towel, he placed the container of tea in one. Striding through the house, he stopped to retrieve the bottle of bourbon and the glass on the coffee table, gingerly picking them up with the towel, placing them inside the bags and sealing them.

He drove to his team's rendezvous point, a motel on the outskirts of town. When he arrived, he found that the team had turned a suite into an operations' center. Some sorting had been done of the documents he had earlier provided, and his contact and three others were busy poring over documents and discussing between themselves.

The first guy he met said, "Jon, here are the pictures; I'm sorry, man."

Connor handed the bags to him. "Here, Bubba. Don't drink them—have them tested. There should be residue in the glass."

The man grinned, nodded and disappeared. He took a seat at the table and reviewed the photographs. "Looks like her, all right," he replied. "And yet . . . ."

"What?" the second guy, Kimball, asked.

"I'm not sure," Jon said. "This woman is shorter, curvier, and her shoulders slump. Our suspect has a very straight posture, and is slim. Yes, on first glance it looks like Childs, but I'm still not sure."

"You are kidding?" Kimball was dumbfounded. "Simpson is convinced, and wants her hauled in."

"Think about it a minute. If—just humor me—if someone was framing Amanda Childs, using her signature, wouldn't he or she perhaps go the extra mile to find a look-alike as well?" Staring at the photos, he asked, "Have we got any confirmation from Customs?"

"Checking it out," Zeke called. "Nothing back so far."

Connor continued staring. Without looking up, he asked, "What else do we have so far?"

Kimball replied, "I've listened to the tape of the Bishop's statement here, and Bubba," referring jokingly to the other man to whom Connor had handed the bags, "was there. Several angles we're already working on. We already knew about WWAC, Inc. Secretary of State's internet records show Amanda Childs as president, treasurer and CEO.

"Zeke scoped out WWAC, Inc.'s resident agent's address. It's a large warehouse in the old industrial park in Milford, about 45 miles from here. Same town as the bank. There's some activity out there, particularly at night."

"Do we have enough to scrape up a warrant for more wiretaps and listening devices?" Connor asked.

"Working on that," Kimball replied. "I've showed what I have to the U.S. Attorney, and we've got to peruse all these documents you got us today. If Bubba can finish linking the corporation and specific transactions, the prosecutor is willing to take it to the magistrate.

"But we're still trying to trace bank records to see what transactions were going on. Bubba has several leads on that. For some of these records, we need stuff with Amanda Childs' signature or handwriting—copies of pleadings, checks from her trust accounts, whatever we can get—for a handwriting comparison. You know, to test out your theory. The electronic stuff is more problematic."

Connor suddenly had a thought. "What about Barnes' handwriting?"

Bubba, who had returned to the room and was seating himself at a chair over which a white lab coat was draped, replied, "I'm ahead of you. Don't worry, I have a plan there. By the way, what's up with giving me spiked iced tea?"

Connor asked, "You sure? So soon?"

Bubba smiled. "I'm a connoisseur of Southern iced tea. But it's obvious it's laced with something."

"Xanax, perhaps?"

"Jon, I can't be sure, but there appears to be more than one agent floating in that liquid—the tea was cold when the stuff was introduced, and didn't take to mixing well. The bourbon I can't tell—don't see any particulates floating, but there's tinge of a salty taste. Zeke here will field test it before taking it in the run to Pensacola to the FDLE lab."

At Connor's questioning look, Bubba grinned again. "Got a friend of mine there to help us out with emergencies. I even got Simpson to agree, so we don't have to wait so long for results from our own lab. He's got a hard on to arrest Andy's widow, so I used that to our advantage. So what other information can you give me?"

Connor briefly filled them in on Barnes' statements and Amanda Child's most recent collapse. Connor stated as an afterthought, "You know, both times Bill Barnes was with her just before she became ill.

"But to get back to handwriting samples, I can get her exemplars tomorrow. I'm going to meet with Ralph Carmichael."

"Are you sure that's wise?" Kimball asked. "We don't know yet but what he could be involved too."

"I've got to get inside somehow, and Amanda Childs doesn't have that many doorways. Do you have anything to show that we should suspect Carmichael? The phone tolls have produced nothing substantial."

"Has Amanda kept in close contact with Barnes?" Zeke wondered aloud. "Maybe he's her co-conspirator."

"Actually, not much activity has occurred between them until the last few days," Bubba frowned. "I thought about that too, but it's not there. And she's had no contact with Brown that I can find."

"So she doesn't confide in her old buddy, or else she doesn't do it by the media we're watching," Connor concluded.

"No, but what about what you relayed about Barnes' saying he and Childs had a thing going?"

"The more I listened to Barnes, the more I suspected he has a motive for everything he said. I think he's marking his territory, and he considers Amanda in that milieu, or at least wants to world to think she's his. I'll tread carefully with Carmichael, but we also need to know about whether Amanda is a drug user, whether she has a reason to need the cash, whether she has a liaison with Barnes and/or Brown and/or Carmichael."

Connor continued to muse aloud. "We have just got to find the connection. Howells swears that Amanda doesn't take meds; someone with a problem who was just in an accident has a built-in excuse right now to possess some pain pills legitimately. So why the unmarked bottles of pills? And none in her purse, which is where I'd keep them if I was dependent on them. Why two bottles of the same thing lying around the house? It doesn't make sense."

"So now she's 'Amanda'?" Bubba teased him.

Ignoring the jibe, Connor continued, "I'll check out the drug and alcohol angle with Carmichael. I can go to the courthouse and pull some files where Amanda is attorney of record and get some pleadings copied for signature samples. Depending on my gut feelings after meeting with Carmichael, I can probably get more from him. We also need to check property holdings of WWAC, Inc., Barnes, Childs, and Carmichael for that matter. Bubba," he said, as the man winced, "you check the Milford courthouse here, and I'll check the one in Mainville."

"Guys, I know you are having fun at my expense, but my name is George," Bubba inserted plaintively.

"We really need to digest as much of these records as we can, and focus on the particular dates Marks stated for the money transfers to see if we can verify them," interjected Kimball, ignoring Bubba.

"And I want someone to check out this Brownlee's history. I still don't trust him," said Connor.

"Got it," said Zeke. "And this national treasurer dude? It seems that some of our buddies are already tailing him for some big-time fraud. They're pretty tight-lipped about it, but if I can dangle a statement—"

"Which is not that useful to them—it's only Marks' speculation mostly," added Connor.

"Nevertheless, I can probably wangle some cooperation out of them."

"OK," said Connor. "Get as much information on him as you can—it can't hurt. Bubba, do you know if the bugs I left in Amanda's house are working?"

"Think so. Not much activity going on there so that I can test them," Bubba called over his shoulder as he reviewed his equipment.

Conner switched gears. "Now, tell me about Claude Brown."

Kimball passed a photo to Connor. "History lesson recap first. Claudius Brown, raised on the streets. His dad apparently worked for Barnes' dad. As a teen Brown was selling crack on the street corners, until he got smart and became an entrepreneur. Then he got other kids selling the drugs for him. He graduated into forging prescriptions, and selling black-market pharmaceuticals. He distributed anything anyone could steal.

"Then came the internet. We haven't found yet who set him up in business, but he began selling his stuff on the internet, even pseudo-drugs. That's how

Andrew Childs got involved on the internet fraud side. And go figure—Amanda Childs represented the scum."

"Tell me, how is it that Amanda Childs represented him and Andrew was chasing him? That is too fantastic," Bubba chimed in.

"Well, neither of them apparently told the other his or her business, for one thing, because of their respective oaths of confidentiality, and they were dealing with Brown at different times. Andy didn't have a positive ID on Brown as his suspect until well after Amanda had represented him. And she got him as a client because he was appointed a public defender. Go figure, the man lied on his financial affidavit, said he was indigent, and got a free attorney. And as best I can determine, the public defenders have no control over whom they're appointed to, and what cases end up in their divisions."

Zeke said, "When I ran Brown's criminal history today, I could find no record that Amanda Childs had ever represented him before the one occasion, so she didn't know him professionally, from her side, so to speak."

"But why would he want a public defender? If he was making good and not blowing it all, he could get any attorney he wanted. Is there any connection between Bill Barnes and Claude Brown? And if so, why didn't he get Barnes to represent him?" Connor asked.

Bubba answered, "Well, let's use a little common horse sense, guys. Barnes is running with the country clubbers—he is not going to publicly dirty his hands with suspected drug dealers. Two, you said the other day that you had drinks with Alex Roberts, and he told stories about Amanda Childs' prowess in court. If she had a reputation for doing as well or better in court as the private bar, I'd save my money and go with her. Three, if it was a dead-dog loser of a case, most private lawyers don't want to touch it—they want to charge lots of money and win, thereby proving their worth. And four, if there is a connection between Barnes and Brown, neither is probably going to advertise it."

"Your points are well taken," grinned Connor.

"But get this," commented Zeke. "There's still no evidence of a connection between Barnes and Brown. Right now all we have is Marks' statement.

"One interesting tidbit. While I was digging up Brown's record today, I spent a little time with our friend Petrino at the police department. Seems that Brown attacked his attorney after his guilty verdict, and Charlie and some other cops had to pull him off the *femme* Amanda, right there in front of the jury."

"I remember Andy's relaying that story," Connor recalled. "Andy was livid that Brown had attacked Amanda in open court, and she didn't press charges. She was going to continue representing the guy, telling Andy to put himself in the guy's shoes, about to go to prison for the rest of his life. Andy was adamant that she was leaving the public defender's office and going into private practice."

THE WITHERSPOON LEGACY

He paused. "That information would tend to cast doubt on a conspiracy between Claude and Amanda."

Kimball spoke up. "Andy didn't get a real lead on Brown's involvement in the drug fraud scheme until after Brown escaped from prison. When Brown was seen by some of our informants on the street, then Andy was able to start slowly piecing the case together. He was about to make an arrest."

"And we all know he was snuffed out. But the top brass put a lid on the whole incident, so Andy's widow has no idea. What hell that must be, not knowing who killed your husband or why," Zeke added.

"That's why this operation is so important. We have to wrap this up and bring in Andy's killer," Connor charged emphatically. "He was one of our own, and we can't let his murder go unpunished."

The uncomfortable solemnity of the moment broke up the discussion, as they quietly resumed their review of the records, only interrupting the silence from time to point out some transaction to note.

A little after midnight, Kimball turned to Connor. "It's been a long day—we'll finish this up tonight and in the morning. Why don't you go get a little rest? You can sack out here."

Connor stretched. "I'm tired, but we don't have a lot of time. I need to make an appearance at my home away from home, to avoid attracting attention and in case I get any callbacks. I'll hit the courthouse early in the morning, and meet with Ralph Carmichael. I have a dinner date tonight with the beautiful Mrs. Childs."

Turning his back on the grins and smirks of his colleagues, he said his goodbyes and left, driving back to Mainville. In the dark with only some classical music playing on the radio, he ran through the events of the day. He thought back to Bill Barnes' statements. He wondered if Amanda was a closet junkie. Had she had an affair with Ralph? Was Amanda involved in this scam? Had Amanda indulged in an ongoing intimate relationship with Barnes? Connor knew that Andrew had little love for Bill Barnes, and somehow he just could not picture the Amanda of Andy's descriptions having a tawdry chronic affair with Barnes. And despite her vulnerable look, she seemed fiercely independent and aggressive, far from the picture of the dependent female Bill Barnes had painted. Was she a cunning schemer seeking to skim money off the church to support her drug habit, or to build her own nest egg? Was she the woman in the pictures? Had she exerted influence over Marjorie Witherspoon to inherit her fortune?

Reaching his hotel room and opening the door, Connor discovered an envelope lying on the floor, supposedly pushed under the door. Quickly closing the door and scooping up the enveloping, he noticed his name handwritten thereon. Opening the envelope, he found a handwritten letter, a post-it note attached:

'Mr. Thomson:

'I found this on the glass in the copy machine in Amanda's office this afternoon. I made a visit to the hospital to deliver it to the Bishop, but was informed that he had been transported to Pensacola. Malcolm Howells suggested that I entrust it to you to deliver to Bishop Marks.

'Fr. Colin Anselm +'

Attached was the missing letter Bishop Marks had received from the now deceased Marjorie Witherspoon:

Marjorie Stuart Witherspoon
500 Willoughby Lane
Mainville

PERSONAL AND CONFIDENTIAL

The Right Reverend Stephen Marks
555 W. Baylen Street
Pensacola
by hand delivery

Stephen:

I know that for many long years animosity has existed between us and our families. I only break the long silence because I have information of great importance to impart to you, and can only pray that you will read this letter in the spirit it was intended and heed my request to you.

You see, I realize that I cannot die in good conscience without letting go of my anger toward you. I must forgive you. And as part of that forgiveness I too must confess a great secret I've kept from you all these years. Although I did it from the best of motives, to protect a helpless child from the disapprobation of the community and the knowledge of the shameful way in which she was conceived, I realize now that perhaps in my withholding this news, in my belief that you had no right to this information, I have wreaked my own vengeance upon you. If so, I am sorry at this twilight time of my life.

If you have received this letter, it means I am gone, and must face my Maker and Judge for my part in this matter. Yet you have the opportunity to make amends, and I pray you do so. For you see, your assault on me 36 years ago produced a child, a beautiful little girl. I could not bring myself to destroy this life, for even though it was a memory of your assault on me, all life comes from God and must be cherished. Therefore, I had the baby in secret, and placed her in an excellent home, where she was sheltered and loved.

I have kept watch over her all this time, and she has no idea of her true origins. She has become a fine Christian adult. I have jealously guarded this secret until now—pretty much all those who knew, except for Malcolm Howells, my dear friend who delivered this child and helped me perpetuate this fraud, are dead. Malcolm is not to blame for his part—all of this was my idea, I coerced him into helping me, and he has already paid dearly for his protection of me. So please persecute him no more.

Now I come to the most important part. It has come to my attention that you are now part of a plan that would cause harm to and destroy my girl. You must not go through with this plan. I will no longer be there to protect her; I am charging you to save her, your own offspring, and yourself.

I have no idea whether my appeal as your once childhood friend or as the mother of your child will affect you. I have, therefore, prepared certain documents which I have entrusted to my lawyers, with specific instructions. If harm comes to our child, they will use the documents and the information of your past misdeeds to facilitate her best interests. I want to shield her from all knowledge of her true parentage, but if you fail to protect your own child I have given instructions for full disclosure, which in so doing would effect your own downfall, or discredit you sufficiently to prevent your further rise to power.

However, I don't mean to resort to threats with you—it's just that I am determined to protect her, and to give you the opportunity to do so as well. It is my fervent desire that this lovely child who has meant the world to me these last years be destined for lovely things. I hope you will see that preserving our child will redeem your own soul. May God give you the grace to do what is right, Stephen, and for all the right reasons.

Who is this child, you ask? You will know when you see her—you will see the man I thought you once were in her eyes.

Marjorie

Reading the letter, Connor felt that Marks' surmise could very well be right. If Amanda Childs was indeed the child of Marjorie Witherspoon and Stephen Marks, Marjorie would have had every reason and motive to name Amanda as beneficiary; Amanda would be the natural recipient of Marjorie's bounty. This letter could well be used as an acknowledgment that Amanda was the issue of Marjorie, which could easily be verified by Dr. Howells. Furthermore, she would be the sole heir and possess the entire fortune by operation of law if the will was disproved.

But Bill Barnes did not know that, he suddenly thought. Or did he? If the letter was found in the copy machine, it followed that a copy or copies were made. By whom? Where were they now?

He irrelevantly thought back to what Ralph had said: "Don't listen to the old biddies around here; Amanda has had only one love in her life, and there's no room for anyone else." If anyone had observed any illicit behavior between Barnes and Amanda, as Bill had intimated, it would have been Ralph. And so far Ralph's characterization of Amanda Childs had been nothing short of hero-worship; perhaps he was in love with her as well. Four years was a long time for her to nurse feelings for a dead man. Could Connor be sure that she didn't engage in a relationship with another man—Barnes? Carmichael? And to what extent would she manifest those feelings?

As he undressed, brushing his teeth and staring unseeing into the mirror, Connor realized that his thoughts had probably strayed too far from the crux of the issues in this investigation. He tried to shut out all thought of her golden green eyes and golden mane. Women, he thought irritably, they're all witches.

He fell into bed exhausted, but sleep came fitfully, his mind churning with more questions.

Chapter 23

Connor, thrashing about restlessly, gave up hope of sleep and rose at 5:00. He decided to go jogging and try to clear his mind for the day.

Leaving his room, he decided to run along the picturesque park in the downtown area. He ran past the courthouse and several landmarks of the small town. Busy in his thoughts, he subconsciously took a turn down the street on which Amanda Childs lived. Curious to see if a detail was watching the place, he continued running down the street.

As he came abreast of her home, he noticed that Howells' Lincoln sedan was no longer parked outside her house. He observed an older model blue Malibu parked on the street about two doors down from her home on the quiet street. Casually running down the other side of the street, he glanced in the car. The man leaning back with his head back and eyes closed was Claude Brown or his double.

Alarmed but continuing on down the street, Connor noticed about a block down a dark Crown Victoria with two men slouched down. Turning the corner, he noticed no other surveillance.

Continuing his run, he decided to stop in at the police department. Inside, he found Charles Petrino sitting with his feet propped up, cup of coffee in hand, watching the early morning news on television. Petrino, recognizing him, pointed to the coffee pot and offered him a chair. Other than a dispatcher in a nearby glassed cubicle, the place looked deserted.

Helping himself to a cup of coffee, Connor took the chair indicated. "Morning, Chief," he remarked casually, wiping his brow with the towel around his neck.

Petrino scowled as he muted the television. "Hello, Senior Special Agent Connor, or is it 'Mr. Thomson' today? I wondered when you were going to make an appearance. I talk to your fellow minions frequently."

"'Fellow minions'? Have you added to your vocabulary, Charlie?"

Petrino's frown only deepened. "I'm not in any mood to make nice talk with you, Jon. Have you told Amanda Childs yet how her husband was killed? Have you let her in on your being buddies with the deceased? It seems like you'd get around to it sooner than four years. Does she know Claude Brown is stalking her?"

Connor's face hardened. "You know I can't do that, Charlie. I didn't make the decision to keep the information under wraps." Rubbing his temple, he asked, "How are you doing?"

Petrino stared at the television screen morosely. "I always loved being a cop in this town. I felt like I did something valuable and protected my fellow citizens. Then you God-damned feds come in, and my hands are tied, while one of my friends is being stalked by the man who most probably killed her husband. And I can't do a thing about it. I can't even tell her how her husband died trying to save her, or that she is in danger. How the fuck do you think I'm doing?"

Connor, not surprised by his vehemence, understood his frustration. Sipping his coffee, he said quietly, "Brown is in front of her house right now, but a detail of feds is on him."

"And his ass should be hauled in here and locked up, not allowed to roam free. But I got one of my men watching her, Brown and your men."

Connor cut in, "You sure?"

"Yep—just left him. We're a lot less obvious that you G-men. You realize Brown almost cut her down yesterday?"

"I heard," Connor replied grimly. "We're working as fast as we can, Charlie, but not only do I have to prove who is running the show, I have to prove it isn't Amanda. We've got to have enough to make the whole case stick, else they'll remain free and we'll be helpless then."

"Helpless? I've never felt so helpless and out of the loop in my whole life," Petrino said, turning to Connor. "It's not just that if you fail I'm the one who has stepped on my hardware not protecting the public here, but Amanda's my friend. Hell, Andy helped me get the job here. I owe him. He and she both deserved better than this. I can't look at her without feeling utter shame that I didn't stop Andy's being killed that night."

"Charlie, what happened to Andy was not your fault," Connor matched Petrino's position, propping his feet on the table and sipping his coffee, his face a mask.

"If I hadn't been off screwing some bimbo, I'd have gotten his call, and I'd have been there," Charlie growled, planting his feet on the floor, leaning forward and slamming his coffee cup on the table.

"And if I hadn't been in New York at Tom's bachelor party I'd have made it back in time," Connor stated flatly. "However, we might both have joined him in death. And Andy was foolish; he didn't wait for back-up. He knew better. Why would he go in alone?" He fingered his coffee cup thoughtfully. "We'll never know, Charlie. But we still have an opportunity to catch his killer."

"Who is sitting outside Amanda's home right now," Petrino replied.
"We don't know that."
"His prints were all over the place. He had the motive."
"OK, OK," Jon nodded wearily. "You don't have to convince me. He's the prime suspect. Can I ask you about some things I've heard?" Connor asked. "I'm trying to tie threads together."
"Sure, why not? You're not going to let me blow the mother away," Petrino retorted angrily as he stood up to refill his coffee cup.
Connor planted his feet on the floor and faced Petrino, placing his elbows on the table. "You lived here all of your life, right, Charlie?"
Charlie sipped his coffee. "Yeah. Why?"
"Tell me the low-down on the Witherspoons and the Stuarts and the Barnes and the Marks."
"That's a tall order. Let's see, many years ago there were the Barnes and their relations the Marks. The Barnes were pretty ambitious, but didn't have lots of money like the Stuarts. The Witherspoon fellow didn't settle here until much later.
"Old Man Barnes was a lawyer, but also ran a mercantile store in Milford. He had three daughters, and a son he named William."
"Bill?"
"No, we're talking Billy's dad, William, Sr."
Connor looked at him surprisedly. "So Bill's a junior?"
"Yep."
"What happened to Sr.?"
"William, Sr., went off to Alabama to law school. Right after graduation he got himself appointed to the county judge position here in Mainville—one didn't have to be a lawyer, much less for a specified period of time, before qualifying for county judge then. All it took was some good ole boy politics. Barnes was also delegated much of the work by the circuit judge, who didn't have much interest in traveling to Mainville. Barnes was a judge for well nigh fifteen years or so.
"Bill Sr. was pretty ambitious, and had his eye set on Marjorie Stuart and her inheritance. But she was never interested in him—she and his cousin Steve were an item. Something happened there, and she ended up throwing Marks over for Jerrod Witherspoon.
"Then it gets interesting. Old Man Barnes packed Marks off to seminary. Bill Sr. went after Doc Howells. Not sure why. Dr. Howells was practicing in Pensacola, but pulled weekend ER duty in Mainville often, because there were not enough reliable on-call physicians here back then.
"Next thing anyone knows someone sued Howells for medical malpractice. Jerrod Witherspoon helped Doc get an attorney, some guy from New York City. This guy discovered that Bill Sr., who was hearing the case, suborned perjury, paying the Plaintiff to make the charges against the doctor.

"Well, the case was dismissed, and Judge Barnes was summoned before the Judicial Qualifications Commission. Through some shenanigans he made some deal to keep his license to practice law, but his judge career was over. Go figure. And all the records were sealed, so this is all on the Q.T."

"So who did know this?" Connor demanded.

"I don't know—Marjy and Jerrod Witherspoon, maybe Stephen Marks. I'm sure Bill, Jr., knows the story. My dad was sheriff back then—he made it his business to know everything, and he told me years later. But I think Monica and Amanda were shielded from most of the town's dirty secrets."

"Tell me about Amanda. What kind of lawyer is she? What does she do in her spare time? Does she have any vices?"

"Do you ask any easy questions? Short answers—I'd go to her if ever I needed a lawyer. Amanda's not afraid of cops, judges, other lawyers, the better-than-thous, or the riff-raff of this little town. She'll stand up to anyone, but she's extremely polite in her delivery, treats everyone with respect. She'll best you, then turn around and thank you and shake your hand like you had done her a favor. She's not snooty, but she's reserved, so some people might get that idea. Amanda is honest as the day is long. In her spare time—hell, she doesn't have any. Marjorie Witherspoon made sure of that. She works at the office, goes to court, practices the organ almost every night, and spent a lot of time with Mrs. Witherspoon. They always had something going at the church—boy choir, girl choir, teenagers' activities, adult choir, recitals. Marjorie had her representing these little punks in juvenile court *pro bono*."

"How did you know all this?"

"Man, she was always asking me to get involved. And I always ran into her with Marjorie and some kids or at court. And I—" Charles suddenly fell silent.

"You what? Come on, out with it," Connor commanded.

Red-faced, Petrino replied, "I used to slip in the church at night to listen to her practice. She had no idea I was there. She was a perfectionist. I never realized how hard the organ is to play or how really pretty it could be. She'd be playing away on some beautiful piece, and suddenly stop, work out some imagined kink I couldn't hear, over and over, and then play it again."

"How much time did she spend there?"

"Always an hour or two almost every night. Sometimes she would skip Sunday evenings, and sometimes she had outings or recitals at the church which took her away. But I could almost always count on her being there. I'd ride by the church on my way somewhere else just to check—I couldn't believe someone was that dedicated, with everything else she had. But of course she was trying to fill the void."

"What do you mean?" Connor asked.

"Well, at first, Andy was gone a lot and she was alone. She didn't complain, but I know that she missed him terribly. It was almost sickening—the two of them had eyes only for each other. When he was killed, she dropped out of sight for a while, then Marjorie brought her back. Marjorie kept her with a long honey-do list. It was Amanda's way of coping, I guess."

"Do you think Amanda ever tried to escape by drinking or taking any prescription or other drugs?"

Charlie started, turning to stare at Connor. "Where the fuck would you get an idea like that? She'd bite a bullet rather than take drugs. Now, I've seen her take a drink every now and then, but she was always concerned about setting an example for her kids. She was always reminding them to do all things in moderation, except drugs."

"Why would she be incoherent, out of her mind, two nights in a row? Why would I find drugs, alprazolam and hydrocodone, in her house?" Jon pressed.

Charlie swept the newspapers off the table in a fit of exasperation. "On the way home from the ER yesterday she handed me a bottle and a prescription for pain medication to throw away; if she was addicted to drugs, she'd have hung on to them. Furthermore, she had every reason to want some drugs after the tumble she took. Why wouldn't she take advantage of the opportunity?"

Connor shook his head. It didn't make sense, he agreed. "What about her relationship with Bill Barnes?" Connor switched tacks.

"Billy is pretty much the pursuer there. Yeah, sure, she once had a big crush on him in school, but she was too honorable to go stepping out with her best friend's guy. After Monica died, Billy wanted Amanda to continue to worship him, at least when he ran out of better things to do."

"Had you ever heard that they were lovers after Monica died?"

"Only in Billy's wet dreams," Petrino stated flatly. "Did he show you the picture on the wall in his office? I'll let you in on a little secret—that's not Amanda in the bikini. I took the picture when we were on a fishing/diving trip at Cayman Brac—Billy invited me and some of the other football buddies along. This was some looker he knew from past trips down there. He now passes off that picture as being of Amanda and him, in order to establish that she is his territory. Amanda has no idea. This girl looked so much like Amanda that Billy was blubbering one night that he was going to ask her to marry him. He likes to boast that he and Amanda were meant for each other."

"Really?" Jon was excited. He remembered the picture in Barnes' office. Out of his shorts pocket he pulled out a couple of the photos he had kept from the hotel. "I took a chance I might see you this morning. This the same girl?"

Petrino examined the photos. "That's her. Uncanny resemblance to Amanda, except that this girl's got bigger—assets," he finished lamely.

Petrino stood up to refill his coffee cup again. "You know I was in college with Billy and Amanda."

"No," Connor was surprised. "I didn't."

"I remember that Billy got some great kick out of lousing up Amanda's dates and sabotaging her love life, and would sit around with the guys drinking and scheming. He would sometimes have a betting pool on it. We were out one night at a student hangout, and Amanda and this study partner from her calculus class were out together getting a bite. He told me, 'Watch this.'

"He walked up to the table and started a scene. As Amanda and her date were leaving the place, he called her over, and kissed her on the mouth right in front of the guy. Amanda responded as if she was in a trance—it left no doubt in my mind how she felt about him then. That's when I knew she had a serious crush on him. I think Billy may have even been surprised. Then she pushed away and slapped the crap out of Billy, but not before embarrassing herself. Her date walked away in disgust and left her there. Billy was gloating, and offered to take her home and 'tuck her in'. She walked off, mortified and angrier than hell at him. She wouldn't even let me walk her back to the dorm.

"She was scarce on the scene for a while, wouldn't speak to him or have anything to do with him for a couple or three months. He finally convinced her he was truly sorry, that he had been drunk and not himself.

"What she didn't know was that the few times she ever dated a guy more than once, Billy did something to nix it—threatened the guy, or told him some outrageous story about her having some disease, just anything. I never understood his obsession over Amanda. I tried to talk to her about what Billy was doing, but she just laughed it off. She couldn't see that she was an attractive woman, and she never seemed to take Billy seriously.

"You know, when she started dating him, Amanda only had eyes for Andrew Childs, and I think that burned Billy up. But he wasn't able to stop it by that time—somehow Amanda made the break from Billy, and the spell was broken. One night before that we were out drinking, and Billy said he was going by Amanda's apartment to 'make her night'. I don't know what happened, but Amanda never had anything to do with him again until she moved back to Mainville. She's friendly with him now, but keeps her distance."

"They looked awfully intimate at the wake," Connor interposed.

"And who was making the moves? Billy was, wasn't he?" Petrino snapped.

Connor thought a minute before nodding. Deciding to change the subject, he queried, "What about you? What did you do after college?"

Petrino sipped his coffee. "I played football, majored in criminal justice, and did two summer internships with the Florida Department of Law Enforcement. After graduation, I was offered a job, and even attended the FBI Academy training program at Quantico. I stayed on with them about four years. But as you notice we all ended up back here. My dad bought a farm, and I missed home. So I came back to help him out and took a job with the sheriff's department for a while as an investigator. Billy was destined and educated to take his place in Mainville society. I just liked small town life where I knew everybody. It's not as much excitement, to be sure, but there are compensations. Amanda escaped for a while, but when her mother got cancer, she came back. I think she would have left again after Mrs. Andrews' death, but by then she had forged stronger ties with Mrs. Witherspoon, and just stayed on."

"What about Ralph Carmichael?"

"Ralph graduated from high school with Monica, Marjorie's daughter. He got a full basketball scholarship to Duke, quite a feat. Then he managed a fellowship or something to law school there, so he was skimming up the ladder. He did a summer clerkship with a big law firm, and told me he wasn't going to work at that speed for the next ten to fifteen years for some silly partnership offer.

"He was dating a majorette in the Florida A&M band—what a great band to watch in action. She majored in nursing and education. He followed her to St. Petersburg, where she was getting a master's in educational leadership or something. He took a job as a prosecutor, was doing great, then out of the blue decided to come home. He talked Claire into taking a job teaching here at the community college, but hasn't married her yet."

"Ralph and Amanda seem pretty close."

Charlie eyed him as he leaned back in his chair. "Yeah—what's that supposed to mean? Ralph adores Amanda, but she doesn't see him that way. She's been trying to get him to pop the question and marry Claire. But there are still racist pockets in this town, mostly on the lusher side of the tracks. If ever a white woman is nice to a black man, tongues wag.

"No, Amanda and he are business partners, and friends as much as she let anyone but Marjorie be. But there's a point at which none of us, even Marjorie Witherspoon, got past with her. Only Andy penetrated that shell, and she's paid dearly for it. OK, what other scuttlebutt must I dispel?"

"Tell me more about Bill Barnes."

"Billy? I've known him all my life, and played sports with him. He runs hot and cold. He's a very political animal, likes to be in control. One minute he's your best buddy, and the next he doesn't have the time of day for you. He is charming, very competitive, and doesn't mind much what he has to do to win. He's a fascinating bird, but can be very cruel.

"You know, once when we were kids, Amanda had a cat that she adored. Billy was playing rough with it one day, and it bit him. A couple days later the cat showed up dead and mangled on the doorstep. Mr. Andrews found and buried it—Amanda never knew. She cried and looked for her kitty for weeks. Billy had a great laugh over killing it.

"Billy can be the greatest kind of guy until his dad gets to him. Barnes, Sr., is just an ugly, evil guy, and Billy would do anything to win his dad's approval. The dad knows how to push all Billy's buttons."

"Does Bill still have power over Amanda Childs?"

"I really don't think so, man. I have seen her wipe the floor with him in court a couple times. If I didn't know her better, I'd think she got a great deal of enjoyment out of it. I can tell you it wasn't good for Billy too. But I think he is in his pursuit mode for her again. And I worry about her—she's all alone right now, very vulnerable, more so than she's been since our college days."

Switching gears, Connor asked about the accident, and Petrino filled him in on the details, adding what was known about the burglary. Connor inquired, "Does Bill know or has he ever known Claude Brown?"

Petrino's eyes narrowed thoughtfully. "It is a small town—we all knew of Claude Brown. We were all aware of what he was doing. His dad worked for Barnes, Sr., for years.

"You know, your question just reminded me of an incident several years back, before Brown escaped from prison. I was interviewing some inmate at the prison a couple miles above town. As I was going through security to get in, I met Billy coming out. He nodded but did not speak to me. I was curious, so I asked the security chief why he was there. Chief said he was there to visit Brown. The sign-in sheet was strangely empty. I don't know why—had no idea there was any connection between them, and didn't know Claude had been transferred to this prison."

There was a moment of silence, then Petrino added, "You know, Claude was not a product of some slum environment. His dad was pretty well taken care of by the Barnes for decades of loyal service. They lived in a nice house, dressed well, were well liked. The other two kids grew up, were good students, popular, graduated with honors and went in together and started a florist shop. They hate even having their name associated with Claude."

Connor looked at him thoughtfully. "That is interesting, Charlie. You know, you have been a great help this morning."

Standing up and turning to leave, Connor added, "And your tail on my detail is just between us—I would consider that assistance, not interference, with a federal investigation."

Petrino snorted. "Fuck you—sue me. If anything happens to Amanda Childs, I'll be leading the tar and feather brigade, and Ruby Ridge will seem like a sputtered-out marshmallow roast for you guys."

Connor stared at him. "Andy was my friend too. There's not a day goes by when I don't relive seeing his body riddled with bullets and wish I had made it in time to save him. I realize how dangerous this operation is, and I don't agree with my supervisors on leaving the enemy out running loose this long, and not having more men surrounding Mrs. Childs. But my bosses still list her as prime suspect. I don't believe it. Until the noose is tightened around the real culprits, I'm going to do all in my power to protect her."

"Me, too," mumbled Charlie, glaring as Connor walked out the door.

Connor quickly jogged the shortest route back to his hotel, showered and changed. Dressing in a gray suit, black shirt and silver tie, he made his way to the courthouse to do some research. On the way, he made a call.

"Kimball here," the voice came on the line.

"Connor. We need to review Marks' statement and maybe get some clarification. Remember Marks said 'Billy' instead of 'Bill' every now and then? It didn't hit me at the time. There are two Bill Barnes, a senior and junior. Marks is cousin to the older Barnes. Therefore we will need to clear up which Barnes he is referring to. This may also pose a complication, an added suspect."

"Roger."

"Also make sure Bubba knows that when he does his property checks."

Connor briefed Kimball on the information received from Petrino. Kimball let out a low whistle. "This is better than 'Peyton Place'. Good work—some real evidence to support your theory. Fabulous news about the Amanda 'double'. Stay in touch."

Ringing off, Connor made a call to Howells' cell phone to check on Amanda's condition, leaving a message.

Connor arrived at the courthouse at 8:00, just as the clerk's office was opening. Allowed in the computer area, he ran a few searches on the property records and did some quick grantee-grantor traces. He also ran a search in the public records for cases where Amanda Childs was listed as attorney of record. Approaching a pleasant-looking young female clerk, he asked to review some of the files, and quickly found what he was looking for, ordering copies of pleadings as well as some deeds and mortgages. Paying for his copies, he was leaving the clerk's office when he spied Ralph Carmichael, the latter frowning as he hung up a cell phone.

Calling to him, Connor walked over to Ralph and shook hands. "I was wondering if you might have the time to renew that talk today. You could probably be some help to me in my search for information. Hey, is something wrong? I wasn't interrupting anything, was I?"

Ralph smiled distractedly. "Well, I am chauffeuring Amanda, alias Hopalong, this morning. She's upstairs prepping a client for a hearing at 9:00. I just got back from the office where I retrieved messages. You want to walk up with me? I want to see if Amanda is on her game this morning. And I'll see if I can find some time for you while we're on the way up."

"Sure thing," Connor said, as they walked to the elevator and Ralph pushed the 'up' button. The latter flipped out his cell phone and hit his speed dial. In a moment, he was saying, "Sheila, what's the rest of the day look like for me? I'm trying to work in an appointment," smiling and winking at Connor.

A minute later, he said, "Today? Yes, I do need to see him, and he will take some time. We haven't heard back about the mediation this afternoon, have we? What about tomorrow? What about mid-morning? Just a minute." Turning to Connor, he said, "I'm booked today with a new client, an old one and a settlement conference, but have some time mid-morning tomorrow. How does that sound?"

As Connor nodded, disappointed, Ralph spoke into the phone. "Write me in a 10:00 tomorrow there at the office, please. Connor Thomson. Yes. Thanks—I'll see you as soon as I deliver Amanda from the forces of evil, or vice-versa."

The elevator opened, and they stepped in. Connor asked again, "Is anything wrong? I don't meant to intrude, but if there's anything I can do—"

Ralph grimaced. "No, I'm just miffed at Amanda. She was in an accident yesterday, and I'm just now finding out that it was a little more serious than she made it out to be."

Connor wanted to ask more, but they reached the fourth floor and stepped out. Ralph spoke quietly to a bailiff, then turned to Connor. "Court just got called into session, and she's first up to bat this morning. Sarge here will let us in."

They slipped quietly into the courtroom and took a seat on the back row, as Amanda was arguing her case. Connor was amazed at the transformation from the vulnerable woman he had seen the previous night, to the calm, icy, self-assured advocate before him. She looked pale, but seemed relentless in her quest for relief. Within minutes the hearing was concluded, and she had received everything she asked for.

Ralph and Connor stepped outside the courtroom as the next case was called. Walking down the hall Ralph looked at him and grinned smugly. "That's my girl. A little more edgy this morning than usual. She wouldn't normally take a shot at the prosecutor like that. But her philosophy on child cases is the opposite of the state's. Traditionally prosecutors, and judges for that matter, hire in starting at the juvenile division and work their way 'up', so to speak. Mandy always advocated that juvenile court was more important than just a hated bottom stepping stone for careers of civil servants, so she is generally meaner there. They all know her, and have their ducks in a row or else. That prosecutor is a little green around the gills. She'll whip him into shape."

Connor had observed Ralph's apparent concern and intent concentration during Amanda's court argument, and decided to confide about Amanda's sudden illness the previous night. "Has she told you she passed out again last night at home?"

It was like Ralph had been hit with a thunderbolt. "What?" Ralph's head jerked around as he heard Connor's words. "How do you know this?"

"I happened to stop by to see her a moment with a few questions. I ended up calling Dr. Howells. Ralph, I found an open unmarked bottle of Xanax in the kitchen, and some other drugs in the house."

"Shit," said Ralph softly, his shock apparent from his facial features. "I don't believe it. That's not like her at all."

Amanda walked out of the courtroom. As the two men looked on, they saw Barnes accost her, engaging her in earnest conversation as he backed her against the wall. Connor noted that Barnes looked around and saw them, then turned back and grabbed Amanda's wrist, kissing her and smiling at her loss of composure as he released her. Barnes waved, a triumphant smile on his face, as he turned and followed her to the men. Jon casually stuffed his papers in his jacket pocket.

"Good morning, counselor and counselor," Bill said breezily, ignoring Amanda's embarrassment as her face suffused with color. Turning to Connor he asked, "What brings you to the courthouse this morning?"

Jon was affable. "Just visiting and admiring the architecture." His eyes moved to Amanda.

Ralph looked on as Bill turned to Amanda. "Yep, court against Mandy is like facing the hurricane. I'm sure she won." Grabbing her arm and brushing her lips with his again, he murmured, "I'll see you later, darling." Whispering in her ear and winking at Connor, he said meaningfully, "If I can be of any service to you, just let me know. Good day, gentlemen."

Amanda made no response, her eyes following Barnes as he strode away.

Ralph looked at her severely, but recovered his equilibrium quickly and bantered with Connor. Connor requested copies of the recital series fund records from Amanda, and again reminded her that he was picking her up at 7:00 that evening, then excused himself, leaving them free for the skirmish he could sense, from Ralph's expression, was on the horizon.

Reaching his car, Connor sped away, his mind racing. So was there something between Amanda and Barnes after all? Or was Barnes just trying to stake his claim? Spotting a cop parked alongside the road, he forced himself to slow down, and soon pulled into the parking lot of Childs & Carmichael.

"Hello," Connor greeted Amanda's assistant as he let himself in the back door. "I believe the bosses are right behind me. I've come to obtain some copies of documents Ms. Childs has graciously agreed to provide."

"Hello, Mr. Thomson," Sheila's manner was brisk but friendly. "Could I offer you a cup of coffee while you wait?"

"No, thanks. I believe I hear them pulling up now."

A moment later, the door opened behind him, and he heard Amanda's voice saying, "One minute he's threatening to sue me; the next he is making out with me in public. Today he wanted to elope."

Her eyes widened as she came face to face with Connor. As they exchanged greetings, she looked past him, her eyes disbelieving. Turning to see what had caused her reaction, he noted the large arrangement of white lilies and red roses.

"They just came," Sheila remarked, seeing her response. "There's a card attached."

Amanda snatched the card, read it, and discarded it angrily, mumbling an epithet. Connor saw Ralph retrieve the card, read the message, and drop it. Connor surreptitiously retrieved the card and envelope from the garbage, concealing it in his jacket pocket.

Amanda explained to Sheila Connor's need for the recital series records, then stalked out of the office. Ralph looked at Connor and shrugged. "What a persistent cuss he is," he remarked as he followed in Amanda's wake.

While Sheila was copying for him, he pulled out the card and read the message. Noting that the flowers were delivered by Felicia's Florists, he made a note to himself and placed the card in his pocket. Thanking Sheila, he made his way to the car, called in to Kimball, and reported he was making his way back to the motel with additional documents. He also asked that an operative remain on stake-out and watch the comings and goings at WWAC, Inc.

"And Kimball," Jon added, "I just lucked into a possible handwriting sample from Billy Barnes. Didn't Claude Brown have a sister named Felicia? I think I know where you can find her. Just on a hunch, check with Felicia's Florists on Magnolia Drive. See if she's had contact with her long-lost brother recently."

Chapter 24

Connor was on his way to pick up Amanda for dinner that evening. His cell phone rang. "Yes?"

"Wanted you to know the wires in her house are working. She apparently has just found out that Claudius is at large. She's wondering why Petrino has kept the information from her. Her partner was wanting her to call the chief, but she apparently suspects Petrino now. Apparently she must have caught sight of Brown, and it raised her suspicions. She told the story of representing him. She was genuinely surprised that he had escaped, and there's no evidence of any contact between her and Brown, much less a conspiracy."

"Good work, Bubba," Connor praised him. "Anything else?"

"I'm not sure of the placement of the bug in the living room, but Ralph was talking to her about getting out of town. However, I can't hear everything. She did say she's very interested in having dinner with you tonight." Jon knew Bubba was smirking.

Connor rang off as he wheeled into Amanda Child's driveway at 6:50 pm sharp. He pulled beside Ralph's car. As he rang the bell, the door opened. He was surprised at her promptness, but recovered and invited Ralph to join them. He could sense some hesitation on Carmichael's part as he declined.

As Connor pulled away with Amanda in tow, he saw Carmichael scanning the street warily. OK, so they suspect that Claude Brown is close at hand, he thought. But have they discovered any of the others tailing her?

Amanda gave directions, and soon they were at the restaurant and seated at their reserved table. Based on his friend Alex' stories about Amanda's once fun-loving nature and upon Bill Barnes' thinly-veiled insinuations, he was taken aback when she ordered only water. His inquiry produced a reasonable response. Funny, he thought, would an alcoholic pass up a drink?

After encounters with her where he observed her in anger, wariness, and in steely control in a courtroom, he was further surprised by her wit and humor, and could tell, from her brief remarks regarding the association with Alex Roberts, that she possessed many fond memories of those times and still held her old friend in high regard.

As he asked her questions and began to draw her out, he concurred with his old college roommate's assessment—she was indeed an interesting conversationalist, full of witty or poetic phrasings and literary allusions and twists. As she talked openly and innocently about Stephen Marks, he found it hard not to continue gazing at her to determine whether guile lay there.

He could find evidence of none, however, and was mesmerized as she relayed the story of Monica and Jerrod Witherspoon's deaths. It was as though she had forgotten he was there, and was reliving the event in intimate detail, although attempting to mask the pain the memories brought. Her account of Marjorie Witherspoon did nothing to disguise her extreme affection for the woman.

The history lesson of St. Catherine's brought up some very interesting leads. He resolved to have the team check out the previous treasurer, the story of the loss of trust funds, and the treasurer's untimely death.

Jon felt rather than saw Amanda's pain and withdrawal when he mentioned Andrew. When he broached the subject of Bill Barnes, he felt her answer to be honest, yet sensed her reticence and unwillingness to open any doors of revelation. *So there's something she's not telling me, but what?* he wondered. As he challenged her story, her temper flared, and she blazed into loveliness in her denial.

Connor carefully brought up the subject of the recital fund, and decided to test her reaction to information regarding the discrepancies in the records. Her total shock and complete lack of knowledge regarding the subject, before she recovered with an iciness he had encountered earlier, convinced him that she was ignorant of the use of the fund as a laundering tool or transfer of funds. Her complete refutation of the solicitations of funds seemed credible. However, his delving into the subject was taken by her as accusation, and acted as a douse of ice water on the interview. He found himself sad to cut a fine evening short and bring it to an anti-climactic ending.

When she abruptly rose from the table, he realized that his opportunity to glean more from her that evening was at an end. He felt her shrinking from him warily as he took her arm and opened the car door for her, and soon was on his way to take her home. However, he sensed her palpable fright when she spied the blue Malibu parked in front of her home. Although he realized she was trying to cover her terror, her actions and remarks to Ralph on the phone, particularly her comment that "I'm afraid it's that Brown business again," confirmed to him that she was indeed aware of Brown's presence in the community and of her danger.

As she started to exit the vehicle, he grabbed her wrist, unwilling to allow her to completely slam the door of communication with him and hoping to wrest from her some remark or admission that would provide a toehold to her confiding in him. But he saw with dismay that she had again isolated herself, fearing and distrusting him, counting him with the enemy.

Frustrated and reluctant, he drove out of sight, then parked where he could view the driveway to Ralph's home. He called his team. "What's up? Are you on surveillance?"

"Yeah, and Malibu is here. Where's alpha?" Zeke's voice was reproachful. "You shouldn't let her get away, not if you disclosed about the fund discrepancies."

"I just dropped her off at her partner's house. She knows Claudius is out there—her reaction to seeing the car gave her away. She was terrified."

"Where are you?"

"Just down the street from the partner's house. I'm keeping my eyes on them. You need to stay with Brown. I'm calling Petrino to ask for some assistance."

As he rang off, he noticed the black Lexus pulling out of Carmichael's driveway. Recognizing the car as Carmichael's, he decided to follow at a discreet distance. He watched as the car doubled back and parked a block away in view of the Malibu. He looked for the surveillance team, but did not see them.

He called the police station, but was told he would have to hold because Petrino was on another line. As he was on hold, he saw the Malibu drive off, then his quarry. Ah, they are aware of Brown and are following him. His call waiting beeped.

"Why are you here, man?" Zeke demanded.

"I'm following the partner; he's following Claudius," he replied. "Hold a moment." Pushing the button he could hear Petrino asking if anyone was there.

"Connor here. We got a problem."

"Damn straight. Ralph just called and said he saw a car with a man matching Brown's description in front of Amanda's house. He says he doesn't know where Amanda is."

"I just dropped her off at his house minutes ago. I am following him now, and believe Amanda is in the car with him. Why wouldn't he tell you where she is?"

"I don't know, but I was tied up here. I'm leaving now to find them. Where are you?"

"Not far from the law office. Still behind Carmichael, who is tailing Brown as we speak. We're heading south on—Beeler Street. Wait a minute—" Connor watched as the Malibu pulled into the parking lot of the law office and the other car kept going, speeding up.

"Brown has alighted at the law office, and Ralph has just taken off. I'm going to try to keep him in sight. Call you back." Pressing the call waiting button, he said, "You there?"

The voice replied, "Yeah, we're behind you."

"Don't let Brown out of your sight. I'm after the Lexus myself."

Passing the parked Malibu, he also speeded up, watching to make sure he was not in turn followed by the Malibu. But it remained stationary, and he turned his attention to trying to tail Carmichael. He knew that he was at a disadvantage because they knew the area better than he did, so his best bet was to intercept them. However, after several minutes of driving he realized that he had lost them. In panic, he called back to his men.

"Eyes are still on Brown, but we're more exposed in this section of town."

Calling the station, Connor again tried to reach Petrino, saying it was urgent. He was placed on hold, and in the meantime realized that Petrino was probably on his way to arrest Brown. Jon drove tensely, trying to guess at a shortcut to intercept Petrino. He felt that he had to reach the police officer before the latter did something rash.

About two blocks from the law office he saw a police car. On a hunch he pulled his car sideways to block the car, and quickly exited the car, running to the vehicle. A gun appeared outside the driver's window, and a voice was heard saying, "Stop right there."

Connor stopped, but realized with relief that the voice was Petrino's. He identified himself, "Connor here," and walked up to the window.

Petrino held his gun on the man. "Remove your car. I'm going to arrest Brown right now."

"You can't do that—you have no charges to press."

"I can and will—he's stalking Amanda, and he attempted to run her down; he's a fugitive from justice. I'm not going to let him remain loose on the streets. This is no longer some of your federal cop games—we're talking about a woman's life here."

Connor held his hands up to show he was holding no weapon. "Charlie, listen one minute. Ralph is gone, and my men are still on Brown's tail as we speak. I'm sure Amanda was in the car with Ralph.

"Don't blow the cover—we are so close to making this case. I'll call in extra reinforcements, and I'll personally arrest Brown for you if you'll let me do my job. Instead, check Carmichael's place and make sure he didn't leave Amanda there. Do you have a number for him? Call him back. Let's ascertain Amanda's location—we can't protect her if we don't know where she is. And let's get out of the road. Someone is likely to see us and wonder what's going on here. I'll follow you back to the station."

Connor retrieved his car and followed Petrino back to the police station. Upon arrival, Petrino got out of his car scowling and cursing. Connor asked, "What is it?"

"Ralph says he doesn't know where Amanda is, and that he is looking for her."

The truth dawned on Connor. "He's lying to you. Amanda is with him. He's taking her somewhere away from here, somewhere safe. Where would they go, Charlie?"

Charlie was apoplectic. "How the hell should I know? Why would Ralph lie to me? There's some place Amanda used to refer to as 'Marjy's cabin', but it is out of state somewhere, I have no idea where. Why wouldn't he tell me? Don't they trust me? God damn it, man, what are we to do?"

Connor said, more to himself, "Amanda knows about Claude Brown." At Petrino's stare, he continued, "She knows he's out there looking for her."

Petrino clenched his jaw. "And she blames me for not telling her. She knows I must be aware that he's been an escapee all this time. God, she thinks I'm in with him or something."

Connor was also frustrated. "Well, we at least still know where Brown is for the moment. We need to keep our eyes on him. I'll find Amanda, if I have to camp out all night at Ralph's place and office."

Pulling out his phone, he dialed his contact. "Kimball? Subject discovered Claudius on her tail and has booked. Zeke still has Claudius under eyes, but alpha has given us the slip. Yes, I take full responsibility.

"I need someone to keep eye on the Witherspoon place and Carmichael's house. I intend to watch out at the office myself.

"Have Bubba review those documents and deeds. I need a list of places we can check to find our alpha. We are getting warm, and cannot afford to make mistakes now. I'll stay in touch."

Petrino came up to him. "My man just reported that Brown has left the law office. He's heading back in the direction of Amanda's house. We'll see where he stops."

Connor informed him, "I've ordered eyes on the Witherspoon and Carmichael homes. I'm going back to the office and stay there. You know Ralph or Amanda will call in there tomorrow. I have men working on other leads. If you come up with some, let me know."

Petrino said, "I'm coming with you."

Connor responded, "I appreciate the company, but we don't need two of us, when it's unlikely that they'll show before morning. Let's take shifts—you get some sleep and I'll stake it out. Then you can relieve me."

"OK, but I'll take the shift tonight. Ralph may show back up—it's not likely, but if he's mad enough he may come back ready to blow the stalker away—and I can't sleep right now not knowing where Amanda is. I'll call Carmichael again in a little while."

Connor looked at him, then shrugged his shoulders. "So be it. I'll go back and get some rest, and relieve you. And Charlie, I keep my promises. Don't do anything rash."

On his way back to the hotel, he called in to his contact. "I want to talk to Bubba this time," he said shortly. When Bubba came on, he asked, "Where would our girl go? I've stepped in it big time. I need some answers, and tonight would be good."

"Well, we can't find any reference to any place listed in Marjy's will that would meet a description of a 'cabin', and of course we can't get in touch with Feinstein's office until business hours. I also ran some records checks and checked the material you sent me, and much of Marjy's real property in this state consists of the house and some commercial rental properties. We got an expert poring over the handwriting samples."

"Talk to me," Connor implored. "Give me some ideas—we're running short of both ideas and time."

"There's always this warehouse in Milford that is in the company name—I've sent Randall to scope it out per your instructions."

Connor was terse. "Bubba, I need ears on that place now."

Bubba replied, "I'm ahead of you. Got info to the U.S. Attorney after you left this afternoon. Will have another packet to him. He may call you. Meanwhile, Randall and Zeke are trying to figure out how to get in and plant bugs if we get the go ahead for wiretaps."

"Good," said Connor. "Let's spike the place and quick."

Bubba offered, "Well, my gut is that Ralph is taking her out of state, or maybe hiding her out long enough to fly her out. She suspects Petrino now."

Connor grunted. "Yeah, Petrino guessed as much just now. Did you get anything from the wire that would be a clue to where they might be going now?"

"Ralph told her she was crazy to go out if Brown was after her, but she was curious as to why you were asking questions of her. She wanted to make her date with you. Part of your animal magnetism, I guess.

"There were a few minutes they were talking so low I couldn't hear all the words, but it sounded like he said that no one would ever look for her there."

"But where?" Connor was insistent.

Bubba hesitated, then offered slowly, "There's one other possibility about where partner took alpha, but I think it is a long shot."

"What is it?"

"Andy and Amanda owned a place out of town—it's never been sold that I can tell from a records check. We have a legal description, and can get a GPS pic or two, but it's out in the woods somewhere. There's an easement in favor of a Fred Vaughan for access rights. Unless Petrino knows where it is, I can't help you tonight on that one."

"What was that name again? The easement holder?"

"Fred Vaughan. Ring any bells?"

Connor grunted. "Sounds familiar. A face comes to mind, an older guy, was in Secret Service or something—maybe CIA. Can you check and see if you get any hits on that name?"

"You know how CIA protects that info. I'll see what I can do, though," Bubba promised.

"And Bubba, do you have any contacts in New York? The Witherspoons had holdings and property up there. That's a long way, but Ralph may be trying to get her on a plane to hide her out up there."

"Do you want nuts on that ice cream sundae? Damn it, man. I'll see what I can do."

"Let me talk to Kimball," Connor cut him off.

When Kimball came on the line, Connor asked, "Can you get us some backup?"

"You must think you work for a Democratic administration. We're stretched thin, and we have to tread carefully, or some of these blue-bloods will be complaining about encroachment on their civil rights."

"I know, but see what you can do, OK?" Connor rang off, irritable for hitting a brick wall. He wanted to call and ask Petrino about the property owned by Andy and Amanda, but having experienced Charlie's temper, he hesitated. He knew Ralph would be back or contact the law office. They would not remain incommunicado. But would they be safe in the meantime? If their theory was correct, Claude was more than likely not in this alone, and his cohorts might just be privy to Ralph's and Amanda's hiding spot.

He finally decided he would drive back out to the law office and talk to Petrino. Looking around at the deserted street, he did a U-turn, and headed back to Amanda Child's office. Driving slowly, at first he could not find Petrino. But after doubling back he finally found Petrino's patrol car half hidden in some hedge behind the office parking lot.

Pulling his car nearby into an alleyway, he exited and made his way to Petrino's car, letting himself in the passenger door. Petrino glared at him while munching a pretzel. "Yeah, what is it?"

"I figured you were already missing me," Connor said lightly.

"Like hell. I know you want something," Petrino snarled.

"Do you have any idea where Amanda and Andy's 'farm' was located? The place they lived together?" Connor hardly dared to breathe.

"Yep. But I don't think Amanda would consider going there. She's avoided that place since right after Andy died. Got her neighbor to keep the place mowed, but acts as if it doesn't exist. Some great fishing out there, if I remember correctly," replied Petrino.

"It's a long shot, but it's not too far from here, right? And no one would guess she would go there because of her apparent aversion to the place, don't you think?"

Petrino looked at the dash a minute, drumming his fingers against the steering wheel, deep in thought. Suddenly cranking the car, he quietly pulled out of his sheltered spot.

"Where are we going?"

"Might as well check it out," Petrino was curt. "They are not coming back here tonight. I can let you out here."

"No, it was my idea, so I think I'll ride along."

Petrino blustered, "Do you want me to dog-slap you and cuff you to a tree?"

Connor repeated stubbornly, "It was my idea—I'm going too. I think I can take you in a fight, but I need you right now because you know where the farm is. You need me to protect you from going off like a bomb. So just drive."

Petrino muttered under his breath, but cautiously pulled out and left the area, making sure they were not being followed. Soon they were on a county highway leaving town. Connor and Petrino were silent, each intent on his own thoughts, as they traveled on through the night.

After several minutes, Petrino pulled up to an old forestry fire tower. Switching off the ignition, he turned and reached for two sets of binoculars and got out, heading toward the tower. Connor quickly followed, catching up to him. "Where are you going?" Connor was piqued.

Petrino answered, "The only entrance to the farm is through the neighbor's pasture. If we come driving up without invitation, he will blow us away. We can tell if there's activity at the place with these," pointing at the binoculars, one manufactured for night vision.

Petrino quickly jumped the locked gate to the stairwell leading up the tower, and Connor followed suit, climbing up with him to the top. On the tiny porch outside the roofed tower, Petrino quickly scanned to the west with his binoculars. Jon stopped to catch his breath.

"We're in luck," Charlie finally spoke, handing the night-vision scope to Connor and pointing at an angle in front of them.

Looking through the binoculars, Connor could make out the movement of a dark small car and its headlights along a tiny trail.

Petrino said quietly, "I'll place money on that being Ralph Carmichael's Lexus. No one else is going to be driving a little car like that on that trail this time of night, not even kids going parking for a little action, not with Fred around."

"Fred?" Connor echoed.

"Amanda's neighbor, former Special Forces, Fred Vaughan."

Connor's memory sudden focused, and he remembered meeting Vaughan years before. A quiet, reserved man, known as a loner. His classification was inaccessible—no one much knew what he did.

"Let's give it a few minutes, and see if lights come on at the place," Petrino spoke.

They stood in silence, both breathing heavier from their climb. After what seemed like an eternity, Petrino breathed, "Bingo."

Connor followed his gaze. "Can't we go after them?"

"Do you feel like dying?" Petrino was blunt. "If Amanda and Ralph don't trust me or you, I'm not letting Fred spill my blood tonight. They're safe for the moment. Let's go back."

"How do you even know Vaughan is there?"

"Because he rode with me in the funeral procession to the graveside the other day," Petrino asserted. "He's home."

"Then you know him. Wouldn't he let you through?"

"Not if Amanda told him not to," Charlie replied through clenched teeth. "He'd shoot now and ask questions later."

They slowly felt their way down the stairs of the tower and drove off back toward town. After a period of silence Petrino asked, "What's next? I have to grab a couple hours' sleep because I need to relieve my guy."

Connor announced, "I'm going to be at the office early waiting for Ralph Carmichael. We have a 10:00 appointment—he'd better keep it, or I'll go in after them myself."

Petrino's jaw was tense. "I want to be there too."

Connor looked at him and said quietly, "There's no need. I need your help, Charlie. I'm short-handed, and from here on out you're in the loop. Let's make a pact here and now—we share information, and neither of us acts without letting the other know."

Petrino was grim. "Do I have a choice?"

Petrino let Connor off at his car. Jon drove back to his hotel, arriving around 1:30. He knew that the next day would be a critical one. He fell on his bed, and slept fitfully, dreaming about a girl with flashing gold-green eyes.

Chapter 25

Connor arose the next morning, again at 5:00, with even less sleep than the previous night. He gauged that he had time for a quick run before showering and staking out Amanda Child's law office.

A few minutes later, he was off, his cell phone on vibrate but clipped to his side. He decided to take a straight route by Amanda's house to see who was on lookout. He was surprised to find no one there. Doubling back in order to determine if he could spy anyone on lookout, he stopped under cover of a tree several doors down and made a call.

"Where's Claudius?" he asked a sleepy-sounding Kimball who answered.

"Zeke reported he left alpha's house about a couple hours ago. He made his way to Milford, and guess where he ended up?"

"Industrial Drive?" Connor asked.

"You got it. My men are sort of exposed out there, so one is on foot and the other is parked behind one of the businesses in the front of the park. We've asked for a team if we get the warrant, and some local backup. Everything is quiet right now. Foot patrol reports Claudius went inside the WWAC warehouse, and his car is still outside."

"Keep an eye out," Connor advised. "What about other units?"

"Petrino has a cop patrolling in the residential neighborhood where Marjorie Witherspoon's house is. I am trying to get some others. We have one guy trying to keep an eye on both Carmichael's and Child's house, and trying to watch the law office in that circle. With so much other ground to cover, we couldn't spare an extra of ours, and Petrino's guys are stretched thin. I'm waiting for business hours to call and ask the sheriff to up the patrol in that area."

"I'm going to the law office in a little while and wait for Carmichael to show," Connor announced, "and will see where Petrino is. He's not far away."

Hanging up, he jogged by the police station, but didn't see Petrino's car. He decided to try him once he returned to the hotel. Calling, he only got an answering machine. That's odd, he thought, but left a message.

Showering, he was just drying off when his phone rang. Going into the next room and answering it, he heard Petrino's voice. "You rang?"

"Yes," Connor said. "Where were you?"

"I went home," Petrino confessed. "Big mistake, because the wife was mad. I've been spending some long hours at work, and she felt neglected. She cut off my phone. I don't know about her, but I feel much better."

Connor laughed. "I'm so happy for you. What's on your agenda this morning?"

"I want to be at Amanda's office when one of them calls or comes in."

Connor said, "That's not a good idea, if they don't trust you right now."

Petrino muttered curses under his breath.

Connor told Petrino that they sorely needed someone to trail Bill Barnes. Petrino assented to take on that detail, and they agreed to check in around noon.

Dressing for the morning, he decided on a more casual appearance, and chose some khaki trousers and blue oxford shirt without tie. He knew there was a chance he had a long wait, but he also knew that Amanda's assistant would be Amanda's and Ralph's key contact.

Driving to the office, he parked in the back parking lot. He was in luck, for there was already a white Toyota Camry parked there. He remembered the same car in the parking lot on Monday. He walked up to the back door of the office. It was unlocked.

Walking in, he heard a sharp intake of breath, and found himself face to face with Sheila Turin, who was picking up papers from the floor. Realizing he had startled her, he found himself saying, "I'm so sorry. I knew it was not time yet for the office to open, but saw your car. I hope you don't mind."

Sheila, recovering herself, remarked quickly, "Mr. Thomson, you gave me a fright."

Connor smiled his most disarming. "I really didn't mean to. But I do need your help. You see, I have a 10:00 appointment with Mr. Carmichael, and it's urgent that I see him. Have you heard from him yet this morning?"

Sheila paused. "I'm sorry, but Mr. Carmichael called early this morning and asked me to cancel all his appointments today." She stood up, papers all gathered in her hands.

Suddenly the door opened, and in walked Charles Petrino. "Hi, Sheila. How are you?"

"Hi, Charlie," reciprocated Sheila soberly.

Petrino, noticing her expression, exclaimed, "What's wrong, Sheila?"

"I don't know if I should wait for Ralph to get here before telling you," she said uncertainly.

"For what?" Petrino frowned.

"Someone was in this office again last night," she replied unsmilingly.

"What?" exploded Petrino. "And what's this 'again'?"

"Monday morning I noticed some papers out of place, stuff in Mrs. Childs' briefcase strewed about. She noticed it too. We found the bathroom window unlocked. This morning, things look rifled through again, and this time," she hesitated, biting her lip.

Petrino prompted her, "This time?"

"The bathroom window was broken."

"Anything missing that you can tell?" Connor interrupted.

"Not that I can tell. Whoever it is was being careful, but looking for something in the document stacks, inboxes, briefcases."

"Have you informed Ralph or Amanda?"

"Not yet," Sheila informed him.

"Have you heard from them?"

"Ralph left a message this morning and asked me to cancel all appointments today."

Petrino, frowning, asked her, "About that coffee?"

"Sure, coming right up. Mr. Thomson, would you like some?"

"Yes," Jon said automatically. "Black will be fine, thanks."

As she left the room, Connor hissed at Charlie, "What the hell are you doing here?"

"I realized that you as a stranger probably wouldn't get far with Sheila, but we do this coffee thing once or twice a week. And now I'm glad I came by—she'd never have told you about the break-in."

"OK," mumbled Connor uneasily, as Sheila came back with three steaming cups of coffee on a tray.

As they sipped the coffee, Petrino asked several questions about the alleged break-in. Then Charlie broke the ice.

"Sheila, Mr. Thomson here has some urgent business with Ralph. Do you think Ralph will come in today?"

Sheila shrugged. "He cancelled all appointments, but said he would see me later today. He is good about checking in. He does have the settlement papers to sign off on, and they have to go out today in order to cancel the trial, so between you and me, he'll drop in before noon. He's a morning person, you know."

Charlie leaned toward her and spoke quietly and conspiratorily. "Can Mr. Thomson wait for him? This is a matter that concerns Amanda and her safety. I know I can trust you to be discreet."

Sheila, alarmed, interjected, "Is she OK?"

Charlie was smooth. "Yes, but this is strictly off the record. I believe someone is trying to implicate her in a scheme, and that's where Connor here comes in. It's vital that he talk to Ralph.

"If at all possible, Sheila, you've got to encourage Ralph to come in if he calls. Don't tell him Connor is here until he gets here. He needs our help to protect Amanda, but he doesn't know that yet. Can you do that and keep this hush-hush?"

Sheila nodded, concern written on her face. Charlie pressed her hand and said, "Thanks for the coffee and your assistance. I'll talk to you later."

As Charlie left, she turned to Connor. "Mrs. Childs is in danger, isn't she?"

Connor, looking at her stricken face, admitted, "I think she is safe for the moment, but yes, she is. Ralph is trying to protect her, but he can't do it alone. I appreciate your help. I've got to talk Ralph into trusting me this morning."

Sheila said, "Charlie's a good man. If he trusts you, then I do, too. Mr. Carmichael's office is the second door on the left. I don't think he'll mind your waiting there. Make yourself at home, and I'll send him in as soon as he gets here."

Connor thanked her and entered Ralph's office. Walking around, he noted the well appointed and neat masculine office. He looked at the pictures on the walls, and noted a picture of a pretty younger woman on Ralph's desk.

Unable to sit still, he paced for a while, then decided to call in to his contact. "What's the latest?"

Kimball replied, "Several things. Barnes showed up at the hospital here, and was mad as hell that the Bishop was moved without his knowledge. He was told that the Bishop is in critical condition. Petrino got there a few minutes ago, in time to follow Barnes to the interstate, and it looks like he is headed toward Pensacola."

"Our man on foot in Milford said that Claudius left the warehouse and Man #1 is trailing him. He's at the Waffle House. We're waiting for word on the warrant so that we can spike the place with bugs.

"The Pensacola office highly recommended a handwriting analyst, and we've already delivered the copies of the corporate documents and the pleadings to her. We'll hopefully have a report on that soon, but we won't have the degree of certainty with copies that we would with originals.

"A small surprise—the national treasurer, Carroll Coughlin, is a lot older than Bill Barnes. However, he and Barnes, Sr., were law school classmates and frat buddies at University of Alabama. Our counterparts on the Coughlin investigation have discovered a busy telephone trail between the two, as well as some possible embezzlement by Coughlin that may result in an arrest soon. They want us to stay away from their suspect, of course.

"Bubba is working on New York properties. He says no 'cabins' have come to light under the Witherspoon name, only a Park Avenue penthouse and some business holdings. He is trying to get a location of the Childs' farm."

Connor interrupted. "Tell him the latter is one less thing for him to worry about—I've found it."

"Great," said Kimball, relaying the information to Bubba. "And Brownlee is clean so far—we've found nothing. Our people in Pensacola have reported that he is back at the diocesan office, awaiting instructions from the hospital on when he can see his boss. They're keeping watch on him. They are still giving out that the Bishop is critical and not able to see anyone."

"You need to tell them that Brownlee is likely to feed information to Barnes, so they need to keep him screened from any information that will compromise this case. And if Barnes is heading that way, they need to be tipped off to keep him and the Bishop apart."

"Our white coat is right there—no problem," remarked Kimball. There was the sound of a scuffle, and Connor asked, "What's going on?"

Bubba's voice came on, excitedly. "I had to wrestle the phone from him. Guess what? I just found something interesting."

Connor, his excitement matching Bubba's asked, "Tell me."

"I ran the corporate name in some computer databases for Florida, New York and Delaware corporations' divisions of the Secretary of State or equivalent for those states. The name hit matches with a company in Delaware, one in New York, and another one in Florida. All list Amanda Childs as president and CEO.

"In researching the Delaware corporation I found that a 'William Witherspoon' was the original organizer of the company, and signed the original documents registering the corporation. I'm after those signatures as well. It may be a long shot, but with those initials and Amanda Childs' name, I'm bound to find a connection. A 'W. Witherspoon' is listed as registered agent at the Milford address.

"I've asked agents at each of those capitals to attempt to get signature cards, if on file. Delaware may not keep signatures on file, since it is the easiest state in which to incorporate.

"Good idea, Bubba," breathed Connor. "I smell a promotion coming out of this."

"Keep the promotion, but send me all your money," Connor knew Bubba was grinning.

"Did you get my present?" Connor asked Bubba.

"Barnes' love note to our alpha? Thanks—I already passed that on to the expert. Competition for the lovely Amanda must be keen."

"I wouldn't know," Connor heard himself denying, to which Bubba laughed.

"And did you realize that Bill Barnes just happens to do a thriving business practice in Milford? I took the liberty of getting copies of his signatures on some pleadings over there, and have submitted them to the handwriting analyst."

Hearing the hum of a sports car, Connor looked out the window of Ralph's office and saw Ralph's familiar vehicle pulling into the driveway beside the office. "Gotta go. My 10:00 has just arrived."

Hanging up, he went to the door of Ralph's office and cracked it so that he could listen. He heard the back door open, and Ralph's voice greeting Sheila. "Any problems with cancelling the appointments?"

"One," she informed him hesitantly. "Mr. Thomson still needs to see you. He was insistent, and is waiting in your office."

"Damn!" he heard Ralph exclaim, then Sheila's quick apology. He heard Ralph quickly soothe her, "No, it's not your fault. It's OK. I'll see him."

He turned and faced the door as Ralph opened it. Forcing a smile, Ralph extended his hand. "Connor, it's good to see you. I hope I didn't keep you waiting long."

Connor was ready. He pulled out his badge and flipped it open, placing it in Ralph's outstretched hand. "Ralph, Amanda's in grave danger, and I need your help."

Ralph blanched as he took in the import of the badge in his hand. He walked to his chair and sat down heavily. "So that was you following us last night? I demand to know what charges she is facing, and what evidence you think you have. I will be representing her in any proceedings. She's innocent." His jaw clenched reflexively. "I'm telling you, Connor, it's not her."

"No, you don't understand. I'm not here to seek her arrest. We have evidence that tends to show she has been implicated, I think innocently, in a major fraud operation. Yes, she was a suspect, but I believe I will obtain the evidence which exonerates her. But she is in danger from others in this conspiracy."

"I have reason to believe she is very safe right now," Ralph said evenly.

"Maybe so, but if Charlie and I could find out where you were last night, so can those who are after her," replied Connor.

Ralph's eyes narrowed. "You think you know where she is?"

"Yes, but you're going to need more than just Fred Vaughan to protect her."

Ralph closed his eyes and prayed, "Oh, God."

Connor continued, "It is much bigger than you think. We are investigating major discrepancies in the diocesan funds that have been transferred to overseas accounts. Amanda's name has been used in this scheme, so she was an obvious suspect. She is listed as a CEO of a Florida corporation called WWAC, Inc., through which most of these funds have been channeled."

Ralph protested, "Never heard of it. That cannot be true. How would she have access to these funds?"

"It was made to appear that Amanda was the church treasurer, and that funds were disappearing via the recital series fund she controls, as well as capital outlay gifts from the diocese. Bill Barnes alleged that she was slipshod in her record keeping of the fund, and was not good at figures or accounting."

"That's simply not true," blustered Ralph. "She has never been church treasurer. She does keep our firm's trust accounting records, and they are correct to the penny each month. She makes me sit down each month and reconcile them with her. She's had me help her reconcile the series fund also. Once a month she barrages Bill with questions about contributors, amounts, and information to complete her report. There's no more anal person about that than Amanda."

"Would you mind my having copies of documents containing Amanda's handwriting and signature, perhaps some redacted trust account ledgers, for comparison of handwriting and her accounting practices to the diocesan and church records?"

Ralph replied, "I'll see what I can do for you. Mind you, I cannot violate the attorney-client privilege."

Leaving his office, in minutes he was back with copies of documents, handing them to Connor.

Connor thanked him, then asked quickly, "Why would someone want to break into your office twice? What would he or she be looking for?"

Ralph's eyes grew big. "Twice? I knew about Monday, but we really couldn't find anything missing."

Connor informed him of Sheila's suspicions. "Could it have anything to do with the will and documents Feinstein left?"

Ralph replied, "If so, they didn't find anything, because Amanda gave me the papers for safekeeping. I've had them in my briefcase with me all this time."

"You have been around Amanda as much as anybody, other than Marjorie Witherspoon." Jon hesitated. "Ralph, there's a drug connection to this criminal activity. Have you ever suspected her of being under the influence of drugs or alcohol? Could she perhaps be skimming money to supply a habit? Could she be involved in criminal activity without your knowledge?"

Ralph looked at him as if he had grown another head. "Who would give you such a crazy idea as that? The only time I've seen her act weird was Sunday night when she passed out at the church. Amanda is as straight as they come."

"What about her relationship with Bill Barnes?"

"He comes around from time to time hanging all over her."

"They are close. She wouldn't be involved with him? Be willing to cover for him?"

"No. I know he's putting big pressure on her to marry him right now, but the only reason she's considering it is because she's all alone and tired of fighting him. And I think the only reason he's doing it is because she is an heiress. She admitted to me that she doesn't love him, that the past is just that: history," Ralph protested desperately.

"What about what we saw yesterday at the courthouse? The flowers?"

"That's Billy playing his head games with her. He's never let up, even when he was married to Celeste."

"What about you and Amanda?"

Ralph's eyes widened in surprise. "Me and Amanda? Amanda would be a fabulous catch, but I already have a girl. In fact, Amanda just this morning talked me into asking Claire to be my bride. If it hadn't been for Mandy, I'd have let her walk away."

On a hunch, Connor asked, "Do you know a William Witherspoon?"

Ralph hooted with laughter, then the laughter died as he saw Connor's eyes.

"What is it?" Connor demanded urgently.

"That's what we used to call Billy in high school when he dated Monica. We told him he would have to change his name to marry into that family," Ralph clarified.

At Connor's serious expression, he questioned, "What is it? Tell me."

Connor said quietly, "Oh, shit," and pulled out his cell phone. Hitting the speed dial, he waited. "Kimball, I know who William Witherspoon is. It's Bill Barnes, Jr. I think we have our connection. We need to gather the net."

"Tell Petrino that we cannot afford to let Barnes out of our sight."

Outside in the reception area, they could hear the telephone ring. Ralph quietly walked to the door and listened to Sheila. "It's Amanda," he whispered to Connor. "I told her to call in by noon." He called out to Sheila. "I want to talk to her NOW."

Picking up his extension in the office, Ralph hit the button. Connor reached over, covered the mouthpiece in his hand and whispered, "Don't tell her anything about what I've told you. She deserves to hear it in person."

Ralph said into the receiver, "Messages? Don't you ever give up? There's a plethora of messages here, but I'm dealing with it, OK? How do you feel?"

He nodded to Connor that she was well. "It's good to hear you're cooking—how long has it been? You bet I'll be there."

Running through the messages, he informed her that Charlie had called with no luck on catching the suspect, and that Ralph had given out that she was at "Marjy's cabin" a few days, that Jonathan Connor wanted to meet with her again, that Bill had called and was taking care of the audit business, that next week's trial was settling, and that Bill had called this morning looking for her. After listening a while, he said, "I will. See you between six and seven," and rang off.

"What did she say?" Connor wanted to know.

"She is cooking dinner tonight, and wanted me to come out."

"I'm going with you. I need to talk to her, Ralph. And we need to get her to safety in New York and brief her tomorrow. If Barnes is antsy, he may suspect something. And he's definitely looking for her. How long before he decides to check the farm?"

Ralph was obviously shaken, but responded irritably. "Can't it wait until after dinner tonight, OK? She sounded more like her old self. I think she got the first real rest last night she's had in some time."

"How do you—it's none of my business," Connor interrupted himself, embarrassed.

Ralph replied to his unspoken question. "I was with her last night, but not like that. I sat by her bed with a loaded shotgun. She was out like a light before we got to the farm, and didn't stir all night. But she still dreams of him."

Connor didn't ask. He knew about whom Ralph was referring. He felt a sudden inexplicable urge to go to her immediately, but knew he had work to do and that Ralph was right.

"Ralph, I need a little time to try to tie up all the loose ends and pull together what evidence I have so that we can prepare affidavits to present a magistrate. I have to check in with my people. I want to be able to move quickly, maybe within the next couple hours. If the least thing goes haywire, I can't wait. Can you be ready, say on a few minutes' notice?"

"Sure. I'm going to contact Fred to be on the lookout for anything suspicious, to let me know the minute anything happens, and that I'm bringing you out. I'm going to the airport and lease her a SUV, something with power and four-wheel drive in case we need it. All she has is Andy's old pickup truck. We can take it out to her. And I'm in charge of dessert tonight," he said, a tight smile appearing. "We'll have you drive out the rental, and I'll take my car so that we'll have a way back."

"OK. I'll call you. Can we meet at my hotel? I'm in Room 142. I'll leave my car there, and anyone who might be checking will think I'm in for the night."

Connor shook Ralph's hand gravely as he walked out, copies of the Witherspoon trust account in hand. Noticing Sheila's worried look, Connor assured her, "We're going to take care of her," as he left the office.

Chapter 26

Connor strode into the motel room in Milford. "Here's the tape from my dinner conversation with Amanda, in case you didn't get it on the wire." He dropped the microcassette in front of Bubba. "What do we have?" he asked. Spying Kimball, he added, "What did you find about Felicia's Florists?"

Kimball responded, "The shop is run by Claude's brother and sister. I went out there, flashed my badge, and said I was doing a routine follow-up on all escapees due to the new statute, some bull I made up. Interesting thing—the place was burglarized a couple weeks ago—only the money in the till was taken. But it was not reported. The brother was obviously frightened, but the sister was pretty vocal. She insisted it was Claude, and the only reason was to send them a message that he was in the area. She hasn't seen him, and pretty much hates his guts. Per Petrino, she has reported seeing him before, but they could never find him. But the brother confessed that he thought he had seen Claude from a distance a few times recently, and is definitely frightened of the man. They weren't able to help us any more than that."

Connor digested the information momentarily, then turned to Bubba. "What about you?"

Bubba didn't even pause from typing on notebook computer, "Got a preliminary report on the handwriting exemplars. The handwriting is very similar to Amanda Childs, but the analyst says no. But this is where it gets funny. Childs used to be a public defender here, and I sent Zeke for some samples of her pleadings from those days. The analyst says that these on the corporate documents are clever forgeries, close to her handwriting from that time period. However, sometimes our handwriting evolves and certain aspects change while other characteristics remain the same. Childs' apparently changed the way she wrote the A beginning her first and maiden names at some point, but whoever has been signing this stuff doesn't seem to know that.

"Most of the signatures our expert says she thinks could be done by Bill Barnes as our good Bishop stated, but some, the better forgeries, are by someone else, and don't fit his or Amanda's more recent exemplars. Since the items are dated, Childs has been eliminated as the originator. The analyst went to the courthouse herself and actually reviewed Barnes' original signatures on pleadings, and is ready to swear that certain of the forgeries were by him. I just don't know about the others."

Connor suddenly thought out loud. "Didn't Claude Brown's criminal history include charges of forging prescriptions, among other things?"

Bubba snapped his fingers. "You're right, man. It's going to be hard to get exemplars from Brown, but between the state attorney's office and the court files I'll see if I can find something. We might be able to prove a connection between Barnes and Brown if we can establish the other forger to be Brown."

"A buddy of mine gave me a tidbit of unofficial information a few minutes ago," Zeke walked into the room. "Seems they're serving arrest warrants on the Coughlin guy, the national treasurer, as we speak. He's being booked on federal racketeering and laundering charges. I told him we had a cousin of a case over here, and asked if they found out anything that would help us to let me know. And I asked them to keep it under wraps a day or two if possible, because of the possible connection."

"Don't we have enough to make an arrest?" Connor asked. "If we can pin the forgeries on Barnes and Brown and prove the signatures are not Amanda's, what else do we need? What else do we have? I've got Marks' sworn statement, and we have what circumstantially we have gleaned from Mrs. Witherspoon before her death, Dr. Howells, Petrino, Carmichael and Barnes himself."

Bubba replied, "I have been able to retrace paper trails on three different large transactions, two from the diocese and one from the recital series fund, to the Caymans' account. It's a start, but the connection to Barnes is still weak."

Connor slapped a diskette down in front of Bubba. "Let's go for it. Bubba, here are my notes. You and Zeke get the affidavits and warrants ready. We need those bugs on the warehouse, and fast. The U.S. Attorney is ready to review what we have, and I want us to move on what we got. Kimball, what about the U.S. Attorney?

"Working on it right now," Kimball countered. "Prosecutor wants you to call him. As soon as we get the affidavits typed—I'll need your signature on some of them—we're on our way,"

"I'll wait, but hurry. We're running out of time. I'm checking on Amanda Childs tonight. We need more protection on her," Connor insisted. "I'm awaiting word from Dr. Howells on final lab results, but he is sure her drink was tampered with on Sunday evening. That's hard to trace, but could point to Barnes. Again on Monday night—that circumstantially points to Barnes."

Bubba nodded. "Lab results on your jar of liquid was sweetened ice tea laced with a hefty dose of GHB AND alprazolam—some seriously bad stuff," Bubba informed Connor.

"Both?" Connor asked.

"Both," Bubba confirmed. "And get this: the Wild Turkey was full of GHB. No alprazolam, but GHB is in liquid form—wouldn't necessarily show up during cursory examination. Sometimes it gives of a bit of a salty taste; one might notice it or not. I, as a connoisseur of good bourbon who drinks it straight, noticed. One drinking it with a sour mix might not. And if ingested, it is out of the system pretty quickly, after a few hours."

Connor paused, taking in this information. Bubba continued, "We've evidence to point to Brown as the one who tried to run her down. So the bait of the simultaneous death clause in the Witherspoon will may be flushing out our quarry, but we're at a dangerous point now, and cannot afford to make mistakes."

Connor suddenly interjected, "She's been drugged twice that we know of, and almost run over. We have to do something now. I want to bring her in and provide her protection now. I want to accompany her to New York and make her invisible until we effect these arrests."

"Simpson thought you'd recommend that, and he vetoed it. He says we cannot compromise the mission by doing that—we need to leave her out there a little longer," Kimball intentionally avoided looking at Connor. "He's not convinced, even with the statement from Petrino, that Childs is not our suspect."

"Simpson doesn't have shit for sense. I made a promise to a dying old woman that, in exchange for her cooperation in setting the trap in her will, I would not let anything happen to Amanda Childs," Connor argued emphatically. "I want to catch them as badly as anyone and don't intend to compromise the mission. I have a vested interest in taking down Claude Brown," his meaning was clear to the men, "but neither am I one to renege on a promise, particularly at the expense of the life of my best friend's widow. So you had damned better come up with a plan yesterday, or I will, Simpson or no Simpson."

Angry, he walked out. Kimball looked at Bubba, shrugged, and picked up the phone, hitting his speed dial. "Yeah, you tell him it's time to fish or cut bait. We need a team and we need it tonight. I'll have the documents ready, and the U.S. Attorney can see us on short notice."

Connor paced outside the motel room, wishing that he smoked. The men inside working feverishly as he called the U.S. Attorney and outlined what they had.

Hanging up, he walked back into the motel room. Bubba turned from the printer, shoved a sheaf of papers into Connor's hand, and returned to a desktop computer. "Proofread those," Bubba ordered, resuming typing furiously.

Connor asked, "The U.S. Attorney has a magistrate lined up if we can finish and fax him copies for review. Someone will need to drive over the originals, and our guys need to be on stand-by to install the bugs."

Connor reviewed the papers meticulously. Satisfied, he signed the affidavits and handed them back to Kimball.

Bubba called over his shoulder, "Childs has a ticket to LaGuardia leaving at 10:30 in the morning."

Connor said, "I have a feeling that if we know that, Barnes may too. If so, they will be looking for her, so do everything you can to get this in place."

Connor walked out. Once in his car, he punched a button on his cell phone's speed dial. "Where are you?" he asked.

Petrino's voice came through, the connection scratchy. "I'm on my way back from Pensacola behind the man."

"Barnes?" Connor couldn't believe his ears.

"Yep. They didn't have anyone else, so I volunteered to tail him. He apparently didn't get in to see our hospital friend, but went by the diocesan office. He didn't stay long, came out with some folded pieces of paper. We're on Highway 90, not the interstate. I think I know—"

Then static took over. Connor kept hearing his voice in and out and heard the words, "dead spot" and "later" before the line went dead. He tried to redial the number, but received no answer.

He wondered what Petrino was trying to tell him. Looking at his watch, he decided to return to his hotel and shower and shave. He called Ralph and set a time to meet.

Standing in the shower, he let his thoughts turn to Amanda Childs. He could not explain why he was so drawn to her, and why he wanted so badly for her to be innocent. That's simple, he thought, it's because of Andy and his faith in her.

But Connor could not explain away his attraction to Amanda, and why when he saw those flashing eyes something in his cold heart melted. He had watched her as she painted the word-pictures of the past, and strangely wanted to wipe away the hurt and pain he saw in her eyes. Around her he was suddenly inept, and he was not used to possessing such emotions. He was inundated with guilt for feeling this way toward his friend's widow, remembering the moments of sheer jealousy he had experienced at Andy's relationship with his wife. He castigated himself for letting this unfamiliar longing distract him from the mission at hand.

He knew that they needed to work quickly to finish the job and bring the culprits to justice, because his objectivity was slipping, an alien experience for him and one with which he was ill equipped to deal.

Deciding again on casual attire, he dressed in dark slacks, a dressy knit shirt open at the neck sans tie, and tweed jacket. There was a knock on the door. Out of habit he checked his 9-millimeter, placing it behind his back under his jacket.

Checking the peephole, he saw that it was Ralph, and let him in. Ralph quickly surveyed the room and Connor, then said, "You ready?"

"Just a minute," Connor hesitated. "Why didn't you tell Petrino last night you had Amanda with you?"

Ralph looked at him suspiciously. "I'm not sure it's such a good idea that you accompany me tonight."

Connor held up his hand to silence Ralph. "Petrino is on our side. He had both Brown and our men under surveillance. He wanted to arrest Brown for stalking, but my boss vetoed that. But you told him last night that you were looking for Amanda, and all that time she was with you."

Ralph looked at him long and hard. "We did a little sleuthing on our own last night. We were in the car behind Claude when I called Charlie about a suspicious car in front of Amanda's house. Within a minute of that call Brown was pulling off, leaving the scene heading straight for the law office. We came to the conclusion that Charlie must be tipping him off. That plus the fact that Brown was at large all this time but Charlie never notified Amanda of that fact made her less than trusting of Charlie."

Connor, visibly relieved, nodded. "I might have jumped to the same conclusions, but Brown's leaving the scene was pure coincidence. And Charlie didn't notify Amanda all this time because the feds ordered him not to."

"But why wouldn't the feds let her know she was in danger?" Ralph demanded.

Connor replied, "Damned if I know why the goons felt the investigation was more important than protecting a victim. But I do want you to know that Charlie was the one who led me to you last night. If he had been dirty he could have had you both taken out before we even knew you were missing.

"He's been tailing Barnes today for us, and he's already threatened the feds with bodily harm if anything happens to Amanda."

"So this investigation includes Billy?"

"Yes, if Bill is actually 'William Witherspoon'. We have reason to believe Barnes and Brown are connected, that Bill has been defrauding the church and diocese out of large sums of money, doing some drug dealing and laundering in the meantime, and using Amanda's name as a foil."

"The bastard! Is she still a suspect?" Ralph asked hopefully.

"My superiors have not removed her from the suspect list, but I have," Connor gazed at him solemnly.

"Well, let's not keep her waiting. The more I talk to you, the more nervous I get."

As they stepped outside the hotel, Ralph threw Connor a set of keys and pointed to a shiny dark-green Toyota Four-Runner. "I'd have rented a Cadillac Escalade for her, but she's more into Japanese vehicles. Why don't you drive and drop me off at my house so I can pick up my car?"

Connor said, "Sure, but let's try to make sure no one follows us."

They pulled out on the road, Connor watching carefully. They were both silent, as Connor tried to concentrate on familiarizing himself with the vehicle and put on some classical music in order to shut out his thoughts of Amanda Childs. He tried to organize his thoughts about the investigation and what questions remained unanswered, and what other avenues they should check.

Dropping Carmichael off, Connor wondered where Charlie Petrino was; pulling out his cell phone and trying the number, all he got was a recording that the cellular customer had left the calling area. He worried about Petrino—where was he?

After about fifteen minutes' driving, Ralph pulled off the main highway, and onto a dirt road. Connor followed suit, and soon they were in a wooded area following the ribboned trail deeper into forest. After some driving, they arrived at a clearing, dominated by a log cabin with a fenced pasture. Ralph exited, punched a code into a keypad by a locked gate, which opened. They drove through, Ralph exiting his car to re-close the gate. They continued down a two-rut trail for a couple more miles until they reached another clearing, where stood a lit two-story white-framed farmhouse with porches and dormers. A full moon was just peeking through the dusk above the horizon. Connor could see the gleam of water down behind the house, and an inviting dock overlooking the pond. The air was full of the sound of crickets, frogs and birds.

Ralph pulled up to the house, and Connor did likewise. They alighted to the sound of a dog barking, and Ralph said, "Welcome to what was Andy and Amanda's home. Oh, I forgot something," and he turned back and retrieved a confectioner's box out of the car. "Dessert," he explained.

Connor followed Ralph onto the porch and into the house. As they entered, they could hear Amanda and another man discussing Scotch, and Ralph joined in. As Amanda turned, his breath caught in his throat. He was dumb, drinking in the sight of her; the flowing yellow dress made her fair skin and golden hair glow, and she resembled a goddess. He understood Andy's falling for her, and felt a stirring within him. As her eyes met his, he heard her sharp intake of breath and muttered imprecation, before she murmured a greeting. He saw her withdraw fearfully, and knew that she felt threatened by his presence.

As banter was made over the Scotch, Amanda went to the basement door, took a flashlight and made her way down. Ralph, looking at Connor, urged him to follow, saying, "Go after her, man. Don't let her be breaking any fine bottles of Scotch."

Connor, feeling even more an intruder, found a flashlight on the shelf by the door and followed her downstairs carefully. As they shined the lights around the small room, he could smell the fragrance of her washed hair. She stumbled in the dim light. He caught and righted her, and could feel how rigid and tense she was. He said softly, "You smell nice."

She laughed nervously. "If you like the smell of fish."

"Amanda, I'm sorry for the way I broke the news last night. I want you to know I believe you."

She found the Scotch, and he knew immediately that it was the case he had sent Andrew for an anniversary gift. Reaching down, he noted the yellowed gift card and surreptitiously slipped it in his pocket, retrieving two bottles. Turning, he bumped into her. When her flashlight hit the floor, he fought an inexplicable urge to kiss her in the dark, and instead handed her his flashlight.

He followed her gingerly back up the dark stairwell to the light of the kitchen. Reaching the room, he held aloft the bottles of Glenlivet triumphantly, as Ralph cheered.

The dinner was delicious, and Amanda seemed to gradually relax during the conversation. He tried not to stare at her, but it was hard for him not to watch her face light up when she smiled at a joke or added her own. Andy, he thought, you know I wouldn't look twice at your woman if you were still here. I can't help myself.

Just before dessert, Ralph announced the need for music, and left the room, followed by Amanda. Connor stood up, ostensibly to help serve the dessert and coffee, but spied Amanda and Ralph talking earnestly in the next room, with Amanda showing Ralph some papers. Although he tried to get close enough to overhear, they caught him watching them from the doorway. Amanda returned to the kitchen to complete serving coffee while Ralph found some music.

When Ralph asked Amanda to dance, Connor and Fred followed them into the living room, Connor sipping his coffee as he roamed and looked at photographs on the walls and watched the dancers. Connor picked up the album cover, noting an autograph: "To Andrew and Amanda—may the rest of your lives be as lovely as you look together tonight. G. Benson."

Connor tried surreptitiously to see the documents Amanda had shown Ralph, but was unable to without arousing suspicion. He noticed a familiar picture on the mantel, and approaching it recognized himself and Andrew at the helm of a boat, laughing. Startled, he realized that Amanda must not have recognized him.

Noticing the piano covered in the living room, he remembered the recording Andrew used to carry and play over and over, classical piano music Amanda had recorded for him. Jon asked her to play. As he listened to the Debussy, he felt again a longing for her. He moved to the other end of the piano, as though the instrument itself might provide a sufficient barrier from giving in to his feelings. He could see that her mind was far away as though she had traveled to another plane.

"Debussy and Sibelius—like a spring breeze."

When he acknowledged that he recognized the Sibelius, using Andrew's words, he saw her violent start. Connor knew he should not have resurrected that memory, but something in him wanted to leave clues for her, to prepare her for the shock of who he was and his past acquaintance with her deceased husband. Upon seeing the sadness in her eyes, he felt ashamed and walked out on to the front porch, his face to the moonlit scene as he cursed himself silently. He could hear the voices of Ralph and Vaughan talking and laughing, cajoling Amanda.

Connor returned inside to find Ralph and Vaughan washing dishes. When he offered to help, Ralph nudged him outside, saying, "We don't need any help. Now's your chance to talk to her. She's sitting on the back porch."

Moving outside to join her, he realized that she was deep in reverie, and it was a few minutes before she noticed that someone was with her. As he began to draw her into conversation, he realized how hard it had been for her, always portraying a cool and tough exterior to hide the vulnerability and sadness. Again he was mesmerized by her as he was able to get her to talk about Andrew and the past.

But as quickly as she dipped into the past, she withdrew. In reaction to his voicing what she seemed to think was sympathy, she recoiled, and her anger brought her beauty into full flame. He also discovered how close she was to the truth of who he was. He wondered about her remarks about e-mails from dead people and corporate treasurers she did not know, and realized that she was relaying new information to him regarding the case at hand. He watched her stalk off to the dock, her goddess regalia fluttering around her, oblivious to her effect on him.

Quickly walking inside, he brazenly walked to her desk and picked up the papers she had shown Ralph. Damn, Connor thought as he scanned the pages quickly. He suddenly understood Amanda's meaning, and that she was lashing out in fear and distrust. He looked out the window to her form on the dock in the moonlight, and knew that for her safety's sake he could not let the matter rest any longer.

Making his way to the dock, he could sense the turmoil, anger and fear she felt. Taking the information about the deposit into her account as an accusation, she responded in rage and panic. Losing her balance, Amanda almost fell into the water. Reaching out instinctively to catch her and pull her back, he felt her nearness and his feelings overtook his reason.

Connor crushed Amanda in embrace and kissed her savagely. Feeling her swaying toward him, he was unable to resist, and kissed her again, this time longer and more intense. As she murmured protest, he found her body belied her objections and molded to his, and a feeling of passion the intensity of which he had not felt before made him want to protect her and never let her go. She suddenly responded to him fervently, cradling his head in her hands as he continued to hold her mouth captive. They clung to each other, drowning in each other.

He finally and reluctantly released her mouth, and gazed at her upturned face. "I'm sorry," he said, "but I couldn't help myself. I look at you and want you more than anyone I've ever known. I feel so guilty for feeling this way, but I do know one thing. Andy would not want you to keep up a shrine to him. He died saving you. He loved life but loved you more, and would want you to exorcise your demons and go on with life. You deserve to love again."

She stared at him as though he had poured cold water on her. As he vainly tried to keep her from withdrawing again, and to tell her of her danger and his desire to protect her, she slapped him, a hard stinging slap.

"How dare you—what do you know about Andy—"Amanda began, but he refused to let her go, trying to explain. She succeeded in pushing him away and escaping to the house.

Just then his cell phone rang. Rubbing his stinging face and cursing his ineptitude, he reached for it and answered it. "Connor here," he spoke hoarsely, impatiently.

"Kimball here. Carroll Coughlin has been taken into custody, and is squealing like a stuck pig. Our friends up north want to know if you want to get up there and question him about our case."

"Yes, of course. When?"

"Tonight—we can have a plane at the nearest airport to pick you up."

"Tonight? Now? The timing sucks. We need backup here. I have a bad feeling about this. Can't you go without me?"

Kimball replied, "Boss' orders—we both go."

Looking at Amanda's retreating form, he shrugged helplessly. "OK, yes. But not until you get me that backup."

Kimball added, "And we got the warrant for the wiretap and listening devices at the warehouse. Our men slipped in, and got away just before Barnes himself showed up."

Watching Amanda run up to the house, Connor was only half-listening, realizing that he had fallen in love with her, that he could not have chosen a worse time or subject, and that he had botched his chances with her badly. Cursing in frustration, he trekked up the hill after her.

"Did you hear me, Jon? We've finally got proof of a connection. We got Barnes at the warehouse with Brown. This is the breakthrough we've been waiting for."

"I'll call you right back in one minute," he replied into the phone.

Chapter 27

Running after Amanda, Connor was in time to hear the bedroom door slam as Ralph called out concernedly, "Mandy, what's wrong?"

Connor strode in. "Ralph, how far to the airport?"

Ralph sputtered, "What did you do to her, man?"

Connor interrupted, repeating, "How far?"

Ralph responded, "There's an abandoned airstrip about a twenty-minute drive from here. It's an hour to the commercial airport. What's going on?"

Connor spoke rapidly. "I need you to get me to that strip ASAP." He flipped open the phone and hit a button, speaking into the receiver. Breaking off to ask Ralph for directions, he relayed them into the phone. ""I'll be there as soon as I can. Have a plane waiting in thirty. Get some surveillance here—how many times do I have to say it? We cannot leave her unprotected—she's a target. There have been at least three attempts on her in the last 72 hours, and they're on the lookout for her. If nothing else, tell Simpson she is a material witness so we can bring her in. It's imperative you get a team in place pronto."

He rang off, then looked at Ralph and Vaughan, who were gaping at him. "I don't have time to explain it all to you. You are going to have to trust me. But I need Amanda in New York—she needs to be on that plane in the morning. I'll meet her at LaGuardia—we've got a key witness ready to talk tonight. She's in grave danger, so be careful—the ones behind this operation will be looking for her, and they could make the connection to this place. And you must keep all this to yourself—no one knows yet but my men and Chief Petrino. It's imperative that we not blow the cover until the operation is complete."

The bedroom door was suddenly wrenched opened, and Amanda stood in the doorway, a Beretta in hand and pointed at him. "Who the hell are you? You don't think I'm going to just let you walk out of here without an answer? This is my life. You know what happened to Andy, and I demand to know what's going on—I've been in the dark long enough," she demanded, her voice quavering.

He turned and walked toward her, taking the gift card out of his breast pocket. He heard the safety on the gun click off as she said, "No further, please."

Ralph quietly implored, "Mandy, for God's sake, put the gun down. Jon is a friend, not the enemy. He's on our side. He's a federal agent."

Jon continued toward her, and slowly handed the card to her as she continued to point the gun at him. He calmly said, "The Glenlivet was from me. Shoot me if you wish."

She took the card with her free hand and read it, then stepped to the mantel. Pulling a photograph down, she looked at it, then at Connor.

"You? You're Andy's 'J.M.'?" she whispered incredulously. "Why didn't you tell me?"

"Yes, I'm Jon Connor, Amanda. Andy and I were working together at the Bureau when he was killed. It's a long story, Amanda, and I want to tell you everything, but we've no time, and you ARE in danger."

As Ralph and Fred looked on, he crossed over to Amanda and gently took the gun from her, laying it on the mantel and taking both her hands in his. She stared at him dumbly, and he addressed the two men, "I need your help, both of you."

As they looked on, Connor continued authoritatively, "Ralph, I need you to get me post haste to this airstrip. I'll explain on the way what is going on. And Vaughan," turning to the older man, "Ralph will have to fill you in on who I am later, because I don't have time. I know who you are, and will need your help until some reinforcements arrive. You've got to protect Amanda.

"Suffice it to say that under no circumstances can Amanda go back to town or have contact with anyone until she gets on that plane tomorrow morning. I'd take her with me tonight, but I've been vetoed on that. We don't know yet who all the collaterals are, and until the net drops we cannot do anything that might warn them."

His eyes rested on Amanda. "I don't want to leave you behind. I'll be back as soon as I can. But I have a team on the way. Until they arrive, I'm counting on Ralph and Vaughan."

Vaughan stood up. "You got it."

Connor thanked him, then said to Ralph, "Let's go."

Turning to Amanda, he released her hands, saying, "I'm sorry to leave you like this. Rest assured I'll be back, and I'll tell you everything." Wanting to kiss her, he touched her cheek, then quelled his desire and abruptly walked away. Ralph followed him out. As they reached Ralph's car, Connor looked back at the house, hoping for a glimpse of Amanda, but she was no longer in sight. He reluctantly climbed in the passenger seat.

Ralph's mouth was tight as he backed out of the driveway and sped down the trail. Without looking at Connor he spat, "Well, she's been seduced, maligned, abandoned, and run over, but I don't think she's ever had to pull a gun on a man before. You take the cake—just what kind of son of a bitch are you?"

Connor looked out the window at the moonlit woods. "I love her," he said simply.

Ralph hurled angrily, "You need some lessons in how to show it. What is this about you and Andy?"

Connor continued looking out the window. "We were at the FBI academy together. Our first assignment was in Maryland together, but then we ended up on different details. He was sympathetic when my wife left me, and I was there for him when he was away from Amanda. We drank Scotch and swapped stories after work hours."

"Then he was sent out West a while on a big case. When he came back, he was working on loan to DEA as liaison on some drug cases. Just before he was killed, we ended up working different ends of the same case, although we didn't know it at the time. He was investigating Claude Brown and the ring there, and I was working on the white-collar embezzlement which ended up involving the Episcopal Church and some deep pockets there. I had just traced some threads to Mainville and the scam here, when Andy was killed."

"Why didn't Amanda know you then?" Ralph asked, his hands gripping the wheel.

"Amanda and I never met. I was called out of the country on a family emergency—my sister eloped—and didn't make it to the wedding. I knew Andy's time with her was limited and precious, so I never accompanied him home on breaks. And after Andy was killed, I went after Brown, who we suspected was Andy's killer, and who had fled to Mexico. I was already on the assignment by the time of the funeral. Andy was the best, and I felt I could do more for him and her out in the field than here."

"So Brown is Andy's killer?" Ralph inquired. "And Amanda was never told? And she didn't know he was at large all this time? What kind of operation are you guys running?"

Connor countered irritably, "Don't you think I've hated every minute of this? I have argued against this tactic—it flies in the face of all the statutes and the protections for victims put into place. But I've had the larger mission of trying to solve this case, find Andy's killer and exonerate his widow. It's been a long four years."

"Why four years?" Ralph demanded.

"The trail went cold as ice when Andy went down. I tracked Brown as far as Mexico, and he disappeared. We had no questionable transactions, nothing going on for about a year or more. I refused to let them file this away as a cold case. Then the investigation started heating back up again as the perpetrators got greedy and monies started flowing again.

"We saw an opportunity this past year, when Marjorie Witherspoon requested that the Presiding Bishop conduct an audit, and voiced her own concerns. I interviewed her, and we talked a great deal. She apparently knew the new Presiding Bishop well, and was changing her will. Of course, her telling him that made the National Church sit up and take notice. The Presiding Bishop was already suspicious of the national treasurer, and we were called in on the quiet.

"So we came up with the idea that I could perhaps pose as an auditor in order to obtain evidence, while ostensibly helping the diocese reconstruct missing audits and save face with its public in light of recent scandals in several major church denominations. No problem, with my background. It put the suspects on edge, although it avoided putting them on notice that the FBI was investigating them. They weren't edgy enough, I thought. Barnes was just too cool through all this, although Bishop Marks was certainly acting nervous."

"So what do we do now?" Ralph wanted to know.

"The arrest affidavits should be ready for taking to the U.S. Attorney before I take off. I'll review them on the way. The national treasurer is talking and may help nail the case for us, as well as some wire taps and bugs in place. I'm on my way to take his statement tonight.

"Ralph, I've got reinforcements on the way to protect Amanda. I'm hoping to have word on them when we reach the plane. You're going to have to take them in to her. Once I get Amanda in New York I can better protect her, but I have limited manpower out here. So I desperately need your help."

"We're here," replied Ralph, pulling into the tiny deserted airstrip. They could see a private jet near the terminal. As he pulled up to the parking area next to the runway, and they disembarked, suddenly there were two men in black, one with a rifle pointed at them.

Kimball came up to Connor. "Glad you made it," he said.

Connor responded, "Kimball, this is Ralph Carmichael. Ralph, this is Senior Special Agent Chuck Kimball, one of my team. He's the best."

As the second man put down his rifle, Kimball nodded toward him and told Connor, "Dan's our pilot—he's the best too."

Connor asked Kimball, "I have a feeling something's going down tonight. They will be looking for Amanda to keep her off that flight tomorrow. What about my requested backup?"

"I got two men flying down and should arrive here in less than thirty minutes. Simpson wants me with you, even though we are shorthanded here. I figured the sooner we get there, the sooner we are finished and back here."

Connor frowned. "I don't like leaving Ralph without reinforcements. Ralph is going to have to show the men in. He can be trusted. You got the final affidavits?"

Kimball patted a large envelope he was carrying.

Connor spoke to Ralph. "I hate to leave right at this time, but I have no choice. I want badly to wrap this case up and get the arrests made. And I want to make things right with Amanda—she deserves to know the truth. Can you hang out here long enough for the men to arrive? They'll know to expect you. They're experts, so you can trust them. And I'll remain in contact with you and them."

Connor asked for Ralph's cell phone number and wrote it down on a business card provided by Ralph. "Don't forget to have Amanda on that plane in the morning. I'll be checking in with you. And, Ralph," he added, reaching behind his back for his weapon, "you may be needing this. Have you ever fired one of these?"

Handing Ralph the gun, Connor heard Ralph's swift intake of breath as he said simply, "Yes." Connor slapped him on the back, then the three men jogged to the plane. Connor watched Ralph standing by his car as the plane began taxiing down the runway.

Kimball was on the phone to the incoming plane and the two operatives, describing Ralph as their contact.

Connor, uneasy, said, "I don't know why it takes both of us on this. You could have just as easily taken this interview."

Kimball looked at him, surprised. "I thought you were chomping at the bit to nail these guys. You wouldn't miss this for anything."

"But I've got a charge down there with bad guys looking for her."

Kimball said, "You're getting too close—you've got to back off. We're about to complete this arrest."

Connor pulled out the sheaf of papers from the envelope and coughed. "I know."

In silence he studied the documents. Kimball stared at him a minute, then sat back and closed his eyes as the plane made it into the air. They continued in their respective postures for several minutes while Connor carefully studied and signed the affidavits, changing and initialing two small typos. He placed the documents back in the envelope and handed it back to Kimball, who remarked wryly, "Always meticulous."

"Have you checked in with Bubba and the men in the field?" Connor asked.

"There's nothing much happening at the warehouse. The equipment is working. Brown has come and gone again—nothing but a little chit-chat so far. He said something about 'the old man'. We've lost touch with Petrino, who was shadowing Barnes. I'm worried there. I've got Zeke on lookout for him around the town and environs. I've got someone waiting for these documents to take them directly back to Bubba and the U.S. Attorney as soon as we land. I would rather one of us was there, but you can't always get what you want."

THE WITHERSPOON LEGACY

Connor paced the deck of the small jet. "Something isn't right."

Kimball said, "It's all going to be fine—we're so close now."

Kimball's phone rang, and he spoke into the receiver. "Kimball here. You're on the ground—good. What? Are you sure? A black Lexus sports car there? Nobody? Shit!"

Connor asked excitedly, "What is it?"

Kimball looked at him. "Carmichael is gone. There's no sign of him on the ground. The car is still there, keys in the ignition, and the gun in the seat."

Listening into the receiver, he repeated what was being told him, "Sign of scuffle, blood on ground, a spent casing."

Connor picked up the cabin phone and said tersely, "Turn around and take me back, now, and make it quick." Turning to Kimball, who was protesting, Connor ordered, "Tell your men we're coming back, to wait for me. They need to fan out and search the area.

"We'll get Bubba to meet me and take this to the U. S. Attorney now and brief him, and you can fly up and get Coughlin's statement. I'll take responsibility for disobeying orders, but I'm not going to let them get away, and I'm not leaving that girl unprotected. I'm the only one who knows how to reach her, and I've pulled Ralph into this."

"OK, OK," countered Kimball, talking quickly into the phone to his contact on the ground, arranging for Bubba to meet them to receive the documents and have a vehicle for transport from the airport.

Connor waited until Kimball completed his call, then reached for his own phone and dialed Ralph Carmichael's cell phone number. He heard it ring, then nothing. He tried the number again, but received only a recording.

"No luck with reaching Ralph," Connor was pacing the floor angrily.

The pilot's voice came on over the intercom. "We're landing in about five—please put on your seat belts."

Kimball grabbed Connor's arm. "You know, Jon, we really don't know who to trust. Ralph is missing—there was no one at the airstrip when we left. And Petrino can't be located now. You think Amanda is innocent, but what if she is in on the scheme?"

Connor looked at Kimball's hand on his arm angrily, and said flatly, "You think Ralph called someone and left the scene and his prized Lexus? I was with him. He didn't have time to marshal any forces. I led him straight into danger. And I know Amanda could not have been acting. She was shocked at the information I gave her. What are you trying to say?"

"Only to be careful and trust no one," Kimball warned softly.

They both braced themselves as the plane touched ground, then Connor stood up and reached for the intercom, speaking to the pilot. "Do what you have to do, but you'll be taking Kimball up north without me; I'm getting out here."

When he stepped off the plane, Bubba was waiting with Connor's car and the two agents. Connor walked up to Bubba and handed him the envelope. "I'll need you to get this to the prosecutor and walk it through. I'm available by phone, but I'm going with these men back to Amanda Childs."

Turning to the two men, he asked, "Find anything?"

One walked up with a small cardboard box. "Found this at the far end of the runway. There was a small parachute, and another parachute at the halfway point without a box."

Inside were plastic bags with various baggies of powder and pills, vials and hypodermic needles. Connor looked at them. "Does anyone know what these are?"

Bubba said shortly, "Not sure about all of it, but those small pills look like MDMA."

Connor started. "Ecstasy?"

"Yep," replied Bubba. "We're guessing that perhaps someone is dropping packages out here at night for pickup, maybe part of the local distribution."

"No prints in the car other than what we think are Carmichael's," the second man said. "A 9-millimeter casing outside the car about six feet away, with some blood on the ground, none in the car." The man paused a minute. "I checked the clip—don't think it came from the gun in the car. The clip is full. We'll send off samples. Not much else to find out here but the car tracks and foot prints. Looks like two guys."

"OK," Connor said. "Bubba, here's your wet dream come true—you get to drive Ralph's sports car. You two," addressing the two operatives, "come with me."

Bubba said, "Wait a minute—you'll want this," and handed him the 9 millimeter Beretta. "Kimball said you gave it away."

Thanking Bubba, Connor climbed into his car, he and the operatives were off at high speed in the direction of the farm. Arriving at Vaughan's gate, he jumped out to open it, then stopped as he saw the gate hanging open, and heard a dog on the porch barking.

"Wait a minute. That's Vaughan's dog, and he was at Amanda's earlier tonight. Let's check out the place."

The operatives nodded and exited the car. One went around in back of the house, as Connor went to the front, soothing the growling dog and petting him. The dog sniffed him and calmed down, wagging his tail.

"Good boy," Connor crooned. "Where are your friends?" Trying the front door, he found it unlocked. Connor cracked it open and listened intently. There was nothing but the sound of a clock ticking and a low buzz. As his eyes adjusted to the dark, he could see the glow from a computer screen. Carefully he opened the door, raising his gun.

Checking out the house thoroughly, one operative coming in behind him and taking the other side of the house, they satisfied themselves that they were the only ones there. Connor walked up to the screen and touched the "enter" button. Up came the message received by Amanda earlier from "Marjorie".

Noticing a Navy blanket on the floor next to the sofa, he picked it up and smelled it. Recognizing Amanda's perfume from earlier that evening, he said to the agent, "She's been here."

The second man came up. "There's a pickup truck in the barn. Engine is still warm."

"Something's wrong," muttered Connor. "Let's go."

They left and reentered the car, Connor taking break-neck speed down the two-rut trail to Amanda's house. Again they split up, Connor taking the front and the other agents the back. After checking the house and grounds, they admitted defeat—Amanda and Vaughan were nowhere to be found.

Suddenly, Connor's phone rang. Connor picked it up. "Connor here."

Petrino's voice greeted him. "I'm gonna need back-up. Get here quick. 355 Industrial Drive, Milford."

The phone went dead.

Connor said, "Let's go."

They ran out to the car, and again hurtled down the trail, making it to the highway in minutes. Connor called his contact phone, praying that someone was there or had the phone. A moment later, a familiar voice answered.

"Zeke? This is Connor. Tell me how to get to 355 Industrial Drive, Milford."

After listening a few minutes, Connor looked grim. "I know the place," he said tersely and accelerated down the highway.

"What about our surveillance there?"

Zeke informed him, "The bug and wire are working. We've got eyes and ears. Sounds like they are interrogating someone. I can hear some conversation. I could hear three sets of voices, one wanting to know where 'she' is."

"Put our people on alert," Connor said. "Petrino just called, requesting backup, so he has to be close at hand. Carmichael is missing. Alpha and her bodyguard are AWOL too, and may be on their way there. There's no sign of them here, and bogies apparently got in contact with her. Hopefully I'm right behind them."

He disconnected, and the agents were silent for several minutes. Then Connor asked the other men, "How much have you been told about this operation?"

Connor tersely briefed the men. After giving instructions and history, Connor again fell silent. His thoughts turned to Amanda—where was she? He felt raw fear now, and tried to beat it down. He could not allow her to fall into the enemy's hands. And from the evidence at the airport he felt that Ralph was injured, if not dead. He was personally responsible for leaving Ralph alone, and for leaving

Amanda before backup arrived. And Petrino was there, but apparently alone. Where were Vaughan and Amanda?

Picking up the phone, he dialed the contact number again. Zeke again answered. Connor spoke. "What's going on at the warehouse?"

"There's been some recent activity. Barnes, Jr., left in his Cadillac a little while ago, and returned about fifteen minutes ago. My man could not get close enough to see who was in it before it pulled into the garage. Right before that, the older model blue Malibu came in with two men, one dragging another inside. There were drops of blood on the ground leading up the steps to the loading dock door."

"Listen very carefully. Chief Petrino is on site somewhere. They probably have Carmichael. I'm on my way there. Tell your men there to watch for Petrino and Fred Vaughan with alpha. Don't let anything happen to them. If you get anything, ANYTHING, to prove up Carmichael's in there, rush the place."

"Got it," Zeke assured him.

Connor looked down and noticed that his speedometer was exceeding one hundred miles per hour.

Chapter 28

Amanda felt herself lifting out of a fog. Her eyes would not focus. The lights were blinding, and she was shivering. She could not swallow. She tried to lift her hand to shield her eyes from the light, but her hand refused to budge. Her head and heart were pounding and she felt nauseous, but she could not move. Closing her eyes against the light, she felt herself drifting, her head heavy, her stomach and throat on fire.

After a while she could hear voices, and tried to concentrate on them. At first she could not understand what they were saying, even though they seemed nearby and loud. And then she wished they would go away so she could sleep.

Suddenly icy liquid was thrown on her face. She began coughing, and could feel bile rising in her throat. Feeling someone help raise her up and bend her head over, she vomited. She recoiled as someone slapped her, then heard a man's voice murmuring to her and wiping her face gently, and could smell and taste bourbon, although she couldn't figure out why.

"Andy, help me," she whispered pleadingly, opening her eyes. The lights were not as bright, and she began to focus. The man's face came into view, coming very close to her. She reached for him, but froze as she realized it was not Andrew. A chill went through her as she recognized Bill Barnes holding her and forcing liquid into her mouth. She coughed as the bourbon burned her throat, choking her.

He suddenly spoke angrily to someone in the doorway. "Good, she is coming to. Damn it, Claude almost killed her. Get out of here—leave us alone."

"What does it matter?" a male voice said. Amanda was trying to remember that voice. She couldn't see the man.

"What has she done to you? You've always looked down on her."

"Because she is white trash from the other side of the tracks. Your plan has always been nothing but a pipedream. Sure, get your kicks with her, but for God's sake I'll kill you myself before I let you marry her."

"You're wrong about her," Bill rejoined, throwing two folded pieces of paper in the direction of the figure.

"What's this?"

"Copy of a letter from Marjy to Steve—got this from your buddy Brownlee. There is a next generation, and you're looking at her."

There was a long pause. "All the more reason not to leave your DNA all over her."

Barnes held up his hands encased in latex gloves, then turned his back to the figure, continuing to enfold and rock Amanda as he addressed the figure. "Haven't I done your bidding all these years? I'll get you Marjy's money. Now leave us alone."

"Don't forget who you're talking to, boy," the voice warned. "Make it quick. We have clean-up to do." The figure disappeared, as Amanda felt everything go dim.

Some time later, she awakened, and tried to mentally take stock through the fog. She was on a bed in a small room. The walls were a dull red brick. She felt wet and clammy, and started shaking violently. She felt very cold, and realized that she wore nothing but her underwear.

She didn't know how long she had been unconscious, but found herself again in Bill's arms. He was holding her close, rocking her slightly and kissing her ear and the nape of her neck, whispering, "Don't leave me now, Mandy."

She felt feverish and continued shivering. She began remembering where she was when she collapsed, and suddenly the sight of Ralph bruised and bleeding filled her consciousness. Her body went rigid with the memory, and weakly tried to push away from him.

"Don't push me away," he spoke against her hair. "Damn Claude—he poured a bucket of cold water on you after you went out on us. I thought I had lost you." Noting that her teeth were chattering and pulling her closer, he continued. "Your clothes were soaking wet. You're freezing, and you need me to warm you up. And you know I can do it, too." His right hand cupped her breast under her bra as he nuzzled her ear. "Feel that? Andy can't do that for you. But I can keep you alive and warm. We belong to each other, Mandy, and I can save you. And all you have to do, sweetie, is just go along with my plan."

Hearing his words, Amanda was suddenly more frightened than she had ever been in her life. She could feel the panic rising and the room spinning, and fought to stay calm. As his hands moved over her, she stiffened and chattered, "Save me from what?"

Bill engulfed her in his warm embrace, his body covering hers. Amanda, shivering violently, clung to him desperately for warmth and tried to look out over his shoulder at her surroundings, her head throbbing at the light. They were sitting on an army surplus iron bed. The remaining furnishings consisted of a rustic bedside table and a plain wooden chair. There were no windows, and only one door. As she tried to adjust to the light and view the room, which didn't seem to remain still, she saw Andy's gun, her gun, lying on the chair, and felt her mind and body begin to thaw. She knew only that she needed to find out his plan, and to formulate one of her own. She had to reach that gun somehow.

Swallowing convulsively, she asked quietly, "What is going on, Billy?"

Bill pushed away, held her by the shoulders and looked at her. "Marry me, Mandy. Don't say no—your life depends on it. Baby, I can take you far, far away. We can run away, you and me, and leave all this behind. I could protect you, get you stashed away in a non-extraditing county, set you up in a little cabana on the ocean breezes. You'd be sitting there waiting for me like you used to do when we were kids. I could keep you barefoot and pregnant, with little bastards running around to keep you company. We could be happy, carrying on the Witherspoon/Stuart legacy. I could even let you continue to run some of the business from down there—hate to waste all those smarts. It's not like you have a choice."

"Are you W. Witherspoon?"

"Yes, that was Dad's idea. It's what the guys in school used to call me—pissed Dad off in those days. And since we're the figurative heirs to Marjy's fortune, I needed her financial records, so I had Claude take the laptop and diskettes. Claude tried the safe—I wanted the original previous will if it still existed. But no go there. I tried to get Alex to get me the trust accounting ledgers, and had Claude search your office for the probate documents and the will."

She suddenly realized who the figure in the doorway had been. "Billy, what has he put you up to do? Don't give in to your dad. You're better than that."

"Am I?" laughed Bill harshly. "Do you really think that? If so, prove it and marry me. Save me and yourself. I can keep my old man in check—I can protect you, Amanda. But it will cost you—Dad has me in too deep to dig myself out. I want to prove to him that my plan for us will work—he's been hell-bent to just off you." His face turned dark as he scowled. "You'd have to renounce your fortune and let me hole you up somewhere where they can't extradite you."

"Extradite? I haven't done anything . . ." said Amanda blearily, trying to keep him talking and comprehend what he was saying.

"Oh, but you see, Dad's plan is going to make you take the fall, one way or the other. What's so bad is that you don't even know what it's all about."

"Tell me, Billy," Amanda pleaded, knowing she had to buy time.

"You see, ever since he was defrocked as judge, Dad has been a gambler and free-spender. He gambled and lost until he has run through his money, Grandad's fortune, and then Celeste's millions. He and Steve concocted the idea of draining the church trust fund, but then the treasurer started developing a conscience. Dad took care of that, and then I hired on as treasurer.

"All this time we were pretty comfortable with the monies coming from the diocese and the recital fund. And I've multiplied that several times with Claude's and my little drug business, a gold mine of a business. But the theft of the church funds is about to be uncovered, to your detriment, I'm afraid.

"Celeste found out about her sudden poverty and the diocesan scheme, and confronted me about it. Dad really liked Celeste—the merger of her money and our family name was all his idea—but her confronting him was a mistake and cost Celeste her life. So you see what I'm up against.

"All this time Dad had eyes firmly set upon the Stuart-Witherspoon millions. We lost that once when Monica was killed, but with the will giving the diocese the funds and Steve Marks as bishop, it seemed like all was going our way. Then damn it if Marjorie didn't change her will.

"So," Bill continued relentlessly as he stroked her hair, "Dad decided that you wouldn't make it the first thirty days from Marjy's death, so that the inheritance would pour over into trust for St. C's. I told him no, you'd marry me, and if charges are pressed against you, you'd renounce the inheritance. Either way, I would control the money. Just to be on the safe side, he was going to make sure that there was enough suspicion on you to make people think you'd influenced Marjy, thereby ensuring the plan worked. I figured if worse comes to worst Claude and I could get you out of the country quickly." He paused, a smirk on his face. "Claude volunteered to take you over the border himself."

"But Dad insisted that we plant enough evidence to make sure his plan had a fool-proof backup. Claude provided the drugs and I planted them on you, and slipped enough in your drinks for others to conclude that you were out of it, drowning your sorrows at Marjy's passing. That gave you a motive, and dampened your credibility. Dad's plan was, if you didn't go along, Claude could stage your demise to look like the suicide overdose of a disconsolate woman."

Fear again gripped Amanda, as she sucked in air. "I'm sorry," he taunted her gently, "I've frightened you, baby."

"Drugs? You gave me drugs? Why? What has happened to you, Bill? I cannot believe that you'd let your dad steal your soul. You are never in too deep to turn around and do the right thing. I promise to stick by you and defend you."

Her words ebbed her tiny reserve of energy, and she felt spent, breathing heavily from the strain. "That's my girl, the fabulous defense lawyer, cheering me on to righteousness and godliness," crooned Bill as he crushed her to him and kissed her. She limply tried to resist him as the room started whirling again. She struggled to concentrate. She needed to act.

He continued to hold her to him and ran his hand down the length of her body, and rested his hand between her thighs, a finger running along the hem of her panties. Amanda, although terrified, tried to keep him engaged in conversation, trying to take in what he was telling her. "What kind of life do you think we could lead together?" she whispered.

Bill murmured in her ear, "Why, our family business, of course," as she felt him caressing and moving his hand closer. She froze, and tried to pull away, but he held her in a vise. She asked, "I'm so cold. Where are my clothes?"

He said softly, as he lay her down on the bed, "You don't need them. Don't fight me—just say yes. This can be good for you too."

Suddenly he was on top of her, and she cried, "No, Billy." She pushed at him, but he caught her hands and imprisoned them above her head to keep her from pummeling him, as she tried to writhe away from him. She screamed as he held her and fumbled with his fly. As he was lowering himself to her, she jammed her knee into his groin as hard as she could, and he doubled over in pain. Rolling off her, he let her go, and she scrambled blindly toward the gun on the chair. But he managed to grab her by her hair and haul her forcibly back down on the bed, imprisoning her with his body.

She screamed, a weak sound, and the room was going black again, his weight smothering her. Bill slapped her back into consciousness. She struggled in vain as he rasped, "I guess Dad was right—all you Stuart women are Frigidaires. I guess that's the price we men pay if we want the money."

Looking at her in disgust, he continued, "I just wish I had known about your relationship to Marjorie before today. All this time I was lusting after Marjorie's own. I could have had you any time—wouldn't Dad have had a stroke? To succeed where he failed."

He raised himself painfully, stumbling over to the chair and grabbing the gun. He pointed it at her, as Amanda, more alert, grabbed the damp covers and wrapped them around her. She struggled to catch her breath, and found her voice. "But you forget—I'm not a Stuart."

"Oh, but that's the beauty of it," Bill laughed, despite his pain. "All this time Dad thought you were white trash, and you had Marjorie's blood running through you."

Amanda, uncomprehending, just stared at him. He smiled at her confusion. "Yes, Marjy's bastard child."

"You're lying," Amanda whispered, her body cold again but her face aflame, now shivering with dread.

"Oh, no. And you will never guess who your daddy is. It's just too funny. A man of the cloth having his way with dear sweet Marjorie, and out you come. Here we are, kissing cousins."

Amanda muttered, "I don't want to hear any more. Just tell me what you mean to do with me."

Bill looked at her sympathetically. "You know, in that moment of denial you even look like Steve."

At the horrified look on her face as she gasped, he continued, happy he had gotten the response he wanted. "Baby, if only you had given me some years ago, we could have skipped all these steps. I was always enamored with you, and wanted to keep you all for myself. It pissed me off that you found someone else, but I at least had the use of your name."

"What do you mean?" Amanda said, closing her eyes, rubbing her temples, and trying to make sense of his riddles. She inched her way toward him and the door. She knew she had to keep him talking until she could get away, for she realized in a second of cold clarity that she knew too much, and he meant to kill her.

"Well, thanks to Dad's scheme, my smarts and Claude's entrepreneurial ability, you own all this, girl," Bill said, waving the gun around the room. "The warehouse, the whole operation. You're the president. You should be proud. You're pulling in and distributing a fortune, from drugs and synthetics, to cold hard cash from the church. If it was legal, you might make the cover of Fortune Magazine."

Amanda shook her head. "You know that dog won't hunt, Billy. No one is going to believe that. I hate drugs."

"Oh, and Dad insisted on my spiking your drinks and planting the drugs. He said we had to make others think you were a lush and using the profits on your own habit. It'll go down that Marjorie's death and the truth of your parentage just screwed you up too bad. Dad wanted to make sure there was enough evidence lying around that corroborated your turning to drink and drugs in your grief, so that the suicide makes sense."

"No one will believe that," Amanda repeated, desperately trying to look past him.

"Yes, I think so. And all this time you were working in concert with your old pal and client Claude Brown. Who would have guessed that? After he attacked you in court that day, and killed your husband in cold blood."

At the mention of Andy, Amanda's blood froze. "What?" she cried.

"Well, that's the police's theory, and the one I am satisfied with personally. Why should I take the fall? Oh, that's right—you never knew. I killed Andy myself, strung him up right in the next room. Of course, Claude had already shot him, angry that you hadn't landed in the trap he sprung for you. Glad I was there to intervene; would have messed up my plans for you. That was tricky business, killing a federal agent and covering the trail. But Claude was fingered and didn't mind, because he didn't plan on ever getting caught again anyway.

"Don't worry—I promised Andy in his last moments that I would service you myself, and do my best to keep Claude's hands off you."

"You bastard," Amanda protested, her eyes brilliant, the tears unchecked.

"You know, that's just what he said," Bill countered, as he moved toward her again.

Suddenly gun shots rang out from the next room. Startled, she cried out, as Bill, gun in hand, bolted through the door ahead of her. They were in time to see Claude Brown lying on the floor not far from where a motionless Ralph lay. Claude had been shot in the chest, and was looking confusedly at an elderly figure standing over him as he gurgled his last breath. Amanda gasped as she recognized William Barnes, Sr., who looked at Brown in cold fury and said, "You won't be denigrating any white women ever again," waving the gun in Amanda's direction.

Turning back business-like to face Amanda, Barnes, Sr., laid the gun on the counter with a gloved hand. He addressed her, "Surprised to see me? Probably even more surprised that I would defend your honor, I guess. But I always had this thing for Marjy, and after all, you're the offspring of her and my good buddy Steve. I'm sorry we must meet again under these circumstances, Amanda."

Bill was livid. "What the hell are you doing?"

Looking at Brown's body, the elder Barnes shrugged. "He was gloating, hoping you were 'going to leave him some'. He was too disgusting—he just had to go. He was too 'high maintenance', like Celeste, and too much a liability to keep on. I never agreed with the pre-eminence of the drug division of our little business—too trashy. It was time that ended."

Bill shouted, "You fool. You really don't think that all our money was coming from the skimming of church funds, do you? Claude and I were turning that pittance into a fortune in the internet drug market, and laundering for other dealers. Claude was our major liaison, the chief rain-maker." Bill stuck the Beretta in his belt behind his back as he knelt before the dead Brown. "Come on, Claude, don't die on me," he pleaded to the still form on the floor.

William Barnes, Sr., retorted coldly, "You forget who you're talking to. And there's nothing you can't handle without that piece of trash who constantly forgot his place."

Ignoring his son, he turned and gazed at Amanda's shivering form, and laughed harshly. "It's funny, but I guess you can thank me that you exist. I wanted Marjy, but she didn't have the time of day for me. I hated her for ignoring me. She was so sweet and virginal, and her dear fiancée Cousin Stevie wasn't getting any.

"I persuaded him to have his way with Marjy, explaining how Southern women liked a forceful man, and he had to thaw and tame the Stuart icicle in order to win her. Of course, we didn't count on Marjy becoming headstrong and throwing him over after that.

"Then Steve came home one day and said he was afraid Malcolm Howells was stealing Marjy from him. After Papa packed Steve off to seminary, I decided to get rid of Howells. But that plan backfired and cost me big." He paused, Amanda regarding him as though hypnotized by his words. "I lost my judgeship. But Malcolm just dotes on you. Guess I'll have the last laugh after all."

Turning to his son, he snorted. "Billy had a habit of drinking too much, and couldn't keep his mouth shut. Together we went through Celeste's money—she didn't know it was all gone. Steve and I concocted the plan to relieve the church and kept Celeste afloat while enjoying the proceeds. We even solicited large contributors to your fund. It was too easy.

"But Billy had a row with Celeste and told her the whole story. She wanted a divorce from Billy, and was going public with the story. So I had to step in and clean up that mess, just like I'm doing now."

Addressing Bill, he continued, "It will look like Claude kidnapped Amanda. Her partner came looking for her, and Claude took him out. Then Amanda in rage killed Claude, then took her own life by overdosing. Why? Brown was getting his vengeance on Amanda and Ralph got in the way. Or maybe Claude had already shot her up, Ralph burst in on him, and he and Ralph killed each other. Maybe people will think they were locked in a jealous duel over Amanda. Besides, once white trash, always white trash. It will be so confusing they may never figure it out.

"She," the elder man pointed to Amanda, "has to go too. Don't cross me on this, boy. Your crazy pipe dream would never have worked. You can't keep her quiet and in line."

"No," Bill objected angrily, as he stood up and moved back toward Amanda. "I'm telling you. We don't have to kill her."

"You heard me," the elder Barnes commanded. "Stop thinking with your hardware, Son. Look at her. She's poised for flight. She is never going along with your plan. And you don't need to take the chance. The trail needs to end tonight with her and Claude. Otherwise, they'll come looking for you. We can't let that happen. We're so close to the inheritance now."

Picking up a hypodermic syringe, Barnes withdrew fluid out of a vial lying on the counter. As Bill advanced on her, Amanda looked at them in panic, clutching the bedclothes around her. Her eyes darted about, trying to gauge how far the door was and if she could get away. She tried to bolt toward the warehouse door as the elder Barnes approached.

"Don't let her get away," he warned his son. He gazed with satisfaction at the hypodermic. "Ecstasy and heroin—a deadly combination. Claude's last contribution."

Bill grabbed Amanda's wrist, tears in his eyes. "I am so sorry, Amanda." His voice grew hard and brittle. "But Dad is right, as usual."

"No, Bill," she cried. She tried to snatch away from him, but he was too strong for her muddled senses, and his grip tightened painfully. She screamed and struck at him wildly with her free hand as he jerked her toward him, dragging her back toward Barnes, Sr.

Just then, the door swung open, and she heard glass crashing behind Barnes, Sr. Bill's hold loosened as he whipped out the Beretta with his free hand and fired wildly toward the door. Suddenly off-balance, she tripped and fell headlong to the floor as the loud report of guns filled the air.

Stunned, she felt an enormous weight crash on top of her, and everything went black.

Chapter 29

Amanda again felt herself traveling through a thick mist. This time she felt no pain, no nausea. She heard someone calling her name, but could not see anything. She felt at peace, without anxiety and worry.

Again she heard her name, and realized that there was someone just ahead of her. She peered forward. At first she could not make out his features, then she recognized Andrew.

She started to speak, but he touched her mouth with his fingers. It was a pleasant gesture, like he used to do to silence her during one of their debates. She smiled at him, and he smiled back.

He took her hand and led her to a picnic blanket. He pulled her down beside him, and cradled her head in his lap. She remembered a time like this by the stream only days before he was killed, and she smiled happily up at him, simply glad to be with him again.

They remained like that for a long time, then he said, "Amanda, I have something to tell you."

"You've found another woman?" she said, and remembered they had used these same lines down by the stream.

"No," he said, smiling that wonderful smile that melted her heart. "But this is hard. I'm here to tell you that it's time—you've got to let go of me."

Amanda, confused, wanting only to prolong their time together, said, "I just got you back. Don't talk to me in riddles. Make love to me. I need you."

"No, you don't, Amanda," he said in that mellifluous voice she had loved so well, that she had tried to coax into the choir.

"But I don't want to be without you any more. We belong to each other, together," Amanda said gazing at him, drinking in the sight and sound of him.

"It's time you moved on. You don't need anyone's approval anymore, not even mine. And you're safe now."

"But I'm all alone," Amanda's eyes filled with tears. "God wouldn't take you away again?"

"You've never been alone. And it's not your time," Andy soothed her, kissing away the tears.

"But was it your time?" she argued, but he again placed his fingers over her lips. They remained silent for a while. Then Andrew spoke.

"Life is like fly fishing, Amanda, except that sometimes you are the fisherman, sometimes the fly, sometimes the stream, sometimes the pebbles in the stream, sometimes the fish, and sometimes just the water that moves it around."

She laughed, "No more riddles, please," as he laughed too and kissed her on the mouth, again silencing her. She reveled in the kiss. Then he was gone. The fog receded and she was alone in the darkness. She was no longer afraid, and she slept, a long dreamless rest.

She didn't know how long it was before she heard voices. She couldn't make out the conversation. Gradually the other voices became closer and more distinct. She recognized Dr. Howells' voice. He was saying, his voice distant, "I really thought we were going to lose her yesterday, but her vitals stabilized during the night. We're waiting and hoping."

Howells watched Amanda's face intently. He suddenly took his small penlight and opened her eyes, one at a time, flashing the light in them. "Amanda, can you hear me?"

Amanda, consciousness now flooding around her, opened her eyes. She looked up and saw Dr. Howells, tears streaming down his face. She weakly squeezed his hand in hers.

Petrino was standing by his side. She tried smiling, but felt like her muscles were frozen. Petrino asked, "How are you feeling?"

"Like a fossil in an icecube."

Petrino said huskily, "I'll tell the others you're awake."

"Ralph?" she croaked.

"He's going to be fine," Howells told her. "He looks like hell, but with you back in the land of the living and his own personal nurse taking care of him, he's going to be back to normal."

"Nurse?" she echoed.

"Claire is here," Howells told her, watching her reaction.

"Thank God," she said hoarsely, her voice sounding far away. "Has he proposed yet?"

He broke into smile.

"What day is it?" she managed to say.

"It's Saturday," Petrino replied, appearing again.

"What happened?" she asked.

"Later," Dr. Howells interrupted. "Everyone out."

She felt someone squeeze her hand, as she drifted into unconsciousness. Howells hovered, reading the monitors.

Later she awakened, and as she moved, suddenly Jonathan Connor's face appeared. He smiled as he inquired, "Have you decided to rejoin us? How do you feel?"

She shook her head groggily. "Where am I?"

"You are still in ICU at the hospital."

"How long have I been here?"

"Let's see—today is Sunday, so about three days." He asked gently, "What do you remember?"

"I remember—" she echoed, then grimaced as the picture flooded her mind. "Mr. Barnes killed Brown—I watched him die. They were coming after me with a needle."

Howells, standing behind Connor, began, "Amanda Katharine, this can wait," but she insisted, "No, I want to know."

Connor took her hand. "Vaughan met up with Charlie at the warehouse site. Charlie was staking out the place, and had seen someone else stalking. He felt they had Ralph and were trying to find you. Charlie didn't think he could get Ralph out without help. So when Vaughan found him, they hatched a plan."

Petrino quietly entered the room and stood across from Connor looking down at Amanda. He took up the narrative. "Next thing Fred knew, you were inside and disarmed. We had to alter our plan somewhat to try to save the both of you. He inched up to the rooftop and the windows. When we heard the gunshot and heard them talking, we knew we had to move and couldn't wait, and I charged the door, at the same time Jon arrived."

Petrino paused. "Jon pushed me aside and charged in first. He shot Bill, but Bill was crazy. My shot took him out, Amanda." He looked sadly down at her.

Howells added quietly, "That vial contained a lethal dose of heroin laced with MDMA. You would not have survived."

Petrino's eyes held a glint of tears as he said, "You're safe now. Bill's dead. The old man is in custody—he didn't stand a chance against Vaughan." Charlie blinked back a tear. "You know, Bill was brilliant, and could have committed the perfect crime. But he was so supremely self-confident. He had a superhuman complex: he could be so meticulous and thorough, then become over-confident and sloppy. That was his failing as a quarterback. Thank God for it, because without that God-complex and his desire to explain it all to you, we would not have made it in time."

Amanda was silent, trying to swallow the pain as the memories crowded back.

Petrino continued. "You hit the floor hard and were knocked out when Bill landed on top of you. When Jon got to you, I thought we were going to have another patient—he turned white as a sheet."

Howells said softly, "You almost didn't survive as it is. We're glad to have you back. Now everybody out—let's not overtax her."

Petrino squeezed her hand and walked out. Connor gazed at her, and she found she could not return his look. He said reluctantly, "I have to leave for a while. There's a lot of work to do to wrap this case up. I'd like to look in on you when I get back."

"I'd like that," she breathed. "I have lots of questions."

Connor squeezed her hand and replied, "And I promise to answer all I can."

He left, and Howells checked the monitors attached to her and listened to her heart with his stethoscope. As he raised up, she took his hand. "I know about Marjorie and Bishop Marks," she said simply.

Howells looked at her sadly. "That was a part of history Marjorie never wanted you to know. She loved you so much, and wanted you to have a normal life with a normal family. She did not want you to be stigmatized by the pain of your conception."

"I'm so sorry for the secret you've carried all these years. I know you loved her."

"Yes," Howells murmured, tears in his eyes.

"Does Marks know?" she whispered, looking away, breathing hard from the exertion of talking.

"Yes, but only after Marjorie's death. He was a willing participant in Bill Barnes' scheme, but when he received a letter from Marjy just before the funeral and guessed you were his daughter, he confessed to authorities and begged for you to be protected. I think he's living his own personal hell right now, in protective custody."

"It's hard not to hate him," she muttered, suddenly very tired and pale.

Howells, alarmed, ordered, "Put this out of your mind. Let's get you well. You have the rest of your life to work through all this, so we can let it rest until later. Are you in pain?"

"No," Amanda replied. She swallowed convulsively. "Doc, I need to know something." She suddenly had trouble framing the question, embarrassed and terrified of the answer. "While I was—at the warehouse," tears formed as she looked away, "did Billy—did he—" she found she could not ask.

Howells gazed at her, trying to fathom her question, as she refused to meet his eyes and the tears fell unchecked. He suddenly understood.

"Did he sexually assault you? Is that what you're asking?" Howells whispered.

Amanda, mortified, nodded.

Howells took her hand and turned her face to look at him. "The physical examination showed no evidence of penetration, of any trauma or semen," he told her quietly, pulling out his handkerchief and wiping the tears from her face. "Personally, I think Billy was so egotistical that he would not have forced himself upon you unless you were conscious. He wanted you to be aware of his mastery over you."

Amanda nodded in agreement. "Thank you," she whispered gratefully.

"Please get some rest. I'll be back to check on you soon."

"Give Ralph and Claire my best."

A nurse came in, and Howells whispered to her. Amanda closed her eyes, but the memory of Bill's assault on her, of Claude Brown's eyes as he died, of Ralph beaten up and laying on the floor, kept coming back. She knew the nurse was giving her something in the IV, and she didn't want to see, because she remembered the needle in Barnes Sr.'s hand and shuddered.

She realized with startling clarity how Bill Barnes had spent a lifetime assaulting her, using her vulnerabilities and affection for his own purposes, attempting to seduce her, and in the end introducing drugs into her body, something as heinous to her as the sexual assault. She tried to seek satisfaction in the fact that he was dead and no longer able to manipulate and hurt her, but she only felt hollow. She wanted to hate him, but realized, as though a voice from the darkness was still talking to her, that giving in to the anger and hatred was just another way that Barnes, though dead, could still affect her.

She tried to turn her thoughts elsewhere, to shut out the horrible pictures that kept flashing in her head. She thought of the blessings she had received: friends who had saved her from death, the love of two mothers and two father figures, her time with Andrew, her abiding friendship with Monica and Marjorie, the memories of the faces of young people with whom Marjorie had involved her. She thought of the church, of Father Anselm and the organ and the children. Then she thought of Ralph and Claire, and smiled to herself. It might be the one success I might have in matchmaking, she thought.

She started feeling drowsy, and the last image before sleep was the face of Jon Connor.

Chapter 30

By Tuesday, Amanda had improved, and after noon was moved to a private hospital room. At that point, she was showered with flowers and cards. She was overwhelmed by the response of people in the community, particularly those from the church. Over the years she felt some of the members had disliked or resented her; now they made known their appreciation, and she was humbly grateful.

Ken came to see her that afternoon, to tell her all about the Sunday service and bring her the bulletin. She smiled wanly, propped up in bed, as he told about the crucifer dropping the cross while putting it away during the recessional, and almost breaking the beakers of extra wine and water in the middle of the postlude, the 'Allegro' from Charles-Marie Widor's Sixth Symphony. He regaled her with the story of hitting a piston to bring it to full organ where it would not otherwise be, in order to cover the noise of the crashing about by the hapless youth.

"I felt there for a minute that I was playing for a silent movie," he concluded, as Amanda held her head weakly, tears streaming down her cheeks from laughing.

Dr. Howells walked in. "It's a jungle in here," he complained good-naturedly. "Ken, why are you making my patient cry?"

Ken was apologetic, but the doctor cut him off. "As long as you don't wear her out laughing, it's good exercise. What, are you telling her about the dance of the falling cross at church Sunday?"

Ken nodded, and Amanda wiped the tears from her eyes. Ken turned to Amanda. "I've got Vierne's Third Symphony ready, and the rest of Widor's Sixth is just about under my fingers as well. I thought I'd break the movements up into prelude, postlude and maybe even do the 'Adagio' during communion. The congregation doesn't sing as well during communion without you anyway."

Amanda looked at him admiringly. "I love them both. You've been working hard. You have to wait so I can be there to hear it. Do you like your new organ teacher Professor Jones?"

Ken replied, "I love her, and my piano instructor Kynaston too. Thanks so much for recommending me to them. They're putting me through my paces."

"It was my pleasure," Amanda told him warmly. "It was time you had a few master classes under your belt before heading off to the big league, and they're excellent teachers."

Looking at Dr. Howells, Ken stood. "Well, I gotta get out of here. I got rehearsal of your boys and girls singing together for vespers next week. See you, Amanda."

He bent over and she kissed him on the cheek. "You don't know how much I appreciate you. Break a leg," she whispered.

As Ken left, Fred Vaughan poked his head in the door. "May I come in a minute?"

As Dr. Howells frowned, Amanda held out her hand and beckoned to him. Vaughan walked in hesitantly, aware of Dr. Howells' disapproving stare. But Amanda told the doctor severely, "This man helped save my life. If you don't like it, you shouldn't have moved me out of that horrid ICU."

Howells laughed at her. "Amanda, if I hadn't moved you, you would have incited a riot in there. It was a matter of preserving my hospital."

Vaughan sat in the chair next to Amanda's bed. He asked, "How are you feeling?"

"Much better, thanks."

Howells frowned. "She's not eating yet," he informed Vaughan.

"Well, no matter how good the cook, hospital food is not conducive to good appetite," Amanda retorted. She looked at Vaughan, and her eyes misted. "Thank you and Charlie for my life. I thought I was ready to join Andy, but I'm really glad I'm here."

Then lightly, she added, "I've been thinking of selling the farm. You have right of first refusal. What do you think?"

Vaughan looked at her hard. "Mandy, you planned and built that place. It was first Andy's place, then Marjorie redecorated it. Why don't you make it your own? Where else are you going to find the perfect spot in the deep South to hone that four-count rhythm? Besides, the old momma cat has just this morning had four kittens in the barn, and is looking for a home for them."

Amanda looked at him soberly. "Maybe I will stay."

The door opened again, and a man was wheeled in a wheelchair by a beautiful well-dressed black woman. "Ralph! Claire! How good to see you!" Amanda exclaimed.

Vaughan stood and moved the chair as Ralph came up close to the bed and grasped Amanda's outstretched hand. "I'm sure glad to see you," he responded fervently.

"I'm glad you're alive," breathed Amanda shakily, her eyes wet with tears. "I just knew you were dead on that floor, and I couldn't live with the thought of that."

"No, but I was in and out. Claude had caught me unawares at the airport, and shot me. Later at the warehouse he pummeled the crap out of me. Thankfully his blows didn't hit anything vital. I got a few good licks in, but I'm not the street fighter he is. Next thing I knew, Brown was kicking me and asking where you were and what was I doing out at the airstrip. I told him I had just seen you off. I don't remember much else, except seeing you with a gun and Bill behind you."

Claire, behind him, said, "Thanks, Amanda, for calling me about Ralph. I had given up on him, and had decided to move back to Ohio, when you called. I came back down here as fast as I could."

Ralph reached back and took Claire's hand. "And I took the plunge and asked her to marry me," he grinned, "but she says I need to prove I am worthy of her."

"Good for her," Amanda smiled.

"We're both so happy, and owe it to you," Claire said, her sunny smile raining down on Amanda.

"I love you two," Amanda replied. "I'm so glad you're together, and that Ralph did not lose you by trying to be my savior. I would like a few godchildren running around, but I'm not pushing you."

They laughed, and Ralph looked at Dr. Howells. "How long does she have in here?"

Howells responded, "I've got an MRI scheduled for her in the morning. I want to see if we have any residual effects from the drugs and the fall. Amanda complained of a bad headache last night, which we think could be withdrawal. So far she hasn't had a recurrence today, and that's good. I'd say within the next few days she'll be able to go home."

"What about me, Doc?" Ralph wanted to know. "You know, I got a law practice to run and a woman to win," he quipped, grinning at Amanda and Claire.

"Ralph, those ribs are going to be tender a while, and you're going to need a little therapy with that leg. The gunshot thankfully was only a flesh wound. However, we'll see. The fact that you're up and in a chair is good."

"Aw, Doc, this is no different from the aftermath of a normal rugby game," Ralph grimaced as he shifted in his seat and touched his ribs.

Claire winked at the doctor. "You should punish them by putting them in the same room."

Dr. Howells snorted. "If I put them together, they'd have a class action lawsuit ready to file against the hospital in no time. Meanwhile, I'd have some sort of food fight. No, that's not a good idea. Get him out of here—they've been together in the same room too long for one day."

Ralph grinned as Claire backed his wheelchair out the door. "I'll be back," he promised Amanda, as Vaughan followed in their wake.

Howells, alone at last with Amanda, sat down and took her hand. "How are you feeling?"

"Much better, although I do feel a headache coming on."

"I have called in a neurologist for consultation. We don't want any long-lasting effects on that pretty head of yours. You're sure you've not had migraine symptoms before?"

"No," indicated Amanda. "And I hope not to."

"Do you want me to give you something?"

"No, Doc, I think I've had enough," said Amanda firmly.

"Well, I know that people will be clamoring to see you, but how about I give you a cold cloth for your head, cut out the lights and put a 'do not disturb' sign on the door for an hour or two, to let you regain your strength?"

"OK," nodded Amanda gratefully.

She must have fallen asleep. She dreamed about the warehouse, and of trying to get away from Billy and the hypodermic. She awakened with a start. The whole room was dark except for the couple of monitors still hooked to her. As she stirred, someone in the chair beside the bed said quietly, "Amanda? Are you OK? Can I get you anything?"

"Connor?" she murmured, recognizing the voice. "How long have you been here?"

"Oh, I don't know," he replied, and she could hear the weariness in his voice. "I knew you needed the rest, but I just wanted to be here with you. I hope I didn't disturb you."

Amanda was touched. "Thank you." They were silent. She finally stammered, "Th—Thank you for saving me that night." Her eyes adjusted and she could see his outline as he stood beside the bed.

Connor took her hand. "I was just so afraid that we wouldn't get to you in time, and I feel that I failed Andy, Marjy and you, for putting you through all this. When I saw you on the floor in that warehouse—"

"No, don't feel that way," Amanda stammered. "I was willfully blind about Bill Barnes. I thought he was my friend."

"Do you feel up to talking about it?" Connor asked tentatively.

"Yes, if you will answer some questions for me," Amanda replied firmly.

"Do you want me to turn on the lights?"

"No, I think I prefer the dark, if you don't mind," Amanda said.

Connor, surmising that she did not want him to see the pain some revelations might bring, respected her wishes.

"What happened after you left the farm?" she began.

"I was taking a plane to interview the national church treasurer, who had just been fingered on embezzlement and racketeering charges. He and Barnes, Sr., were buddies, and Coughlin had information for us, hoping to get some leeway with the prosecutors if he provided substantial assistance. I left Ralph at the little abandoned county airport to await the backups and bring them in to protect you. However, when my backups landed, Ralph was missing."

He continued relating the story to her, as she listened in silence. "About that time, Petrino, who had been tailing Barnes all day, called me and told me to get to Milford to the warehouse right away. We made it as fast as we could, but in the meantime, the worst happened. Thank God Vaughan and Petrino were there, and we were in time to save you and Ralph. My surveillance team swarmed in as soon as they heard gunshots on the tape, but because the area was exposed, they were about a half-mile away and using a relay on the bugs. And I had just pulled in front of the warehouse and saw Petrino about to rush the door.

"We got the conversations on tape and the old man in custody. I'm so sorry for what they did to you." The anger was unmistakable in his voice as he squeezed her hand.

"It's over now," Amanda whispered. She willed herself not to cry.

"What other evidence do you have?" she queried, strangely comforted by his hand in hers.

"Well, Kimball got a statement from this Coughlin guy that links both Barnes' men to the transactions. We have a handwriting analyst who has linked Barnes, Jr., and Brown to your forged signatures. Several other witnesses have been able to corroborate or discount some theories. Stephen Marks gave a statement that he had seen Barnes forging your name to documents and checks, and as to his own involvement. I know he's the scum of the earth, but he was really concerned about protecting you."

"What else? Am I exonerated?" Amanda pointedly ignored his last remark.

Connor, noting her refusal to acknowledge Marks, continued. "Yes. We have been able to finally trace the transactions from the diocese and recital series funds into WWAC, Inc., accounts, and then to other accounts. We're in the process of recovering what is left of those funds now. And our man in the Caymans has found the girl who posed as you.

"We realized after the fact that Stephen Marks was implicating both Barnes, Sr., and Jr., in his statement. Stupid me—I didn't realize he was making a real distinction between "Bill" and "Billy", didn't stop to check out Williams, Sr., in fact. One of my guys went back and clarified the matter with Marks, who is willing to testify against Barnes, Sr."

He was silent a moment. "I promised Marjorie that I would not let anything happen to you, and look what happened."

"You knew Marjy?"

"Yes, we met. She had called the Presiding Bishop with concerns about the financial matters at St. Catherine's. I was preparing to go in, ostensibly as an auditor to conceal the Bureau's involvement, and she insisted on meeting me.

She had talked to Feinstein about what she could do to bring the perpetrators to justice, and we came up with this simultaneous death clause. The real will has no such clause. But we were going to spring it to see if we could flush out Barnes.

"Marjorie balked at using you as bait. She made me promise to protect you with my life. However, just as the plan was to go into effect, her health spiraled downward and she died. I've tried to keep my promise to her."

"You did. You could not have chosen a better bodyguard than Fred. And I'm happy to know that Charlie was a good guy. Ralph and I suspected him of being in with Brown."

"Marjorie was a fine woman, and she was devoted to you," Connor said. "She made me take her to the opera one night, and had dinner served at the penthouse. She talked about you incessantly."

"She was probably just playing matchmaker, trying to set you up with me. She was chronically guilty of that."

"It worked," he said softly. "I'm hooked."

Amanda withdrew her hand slowly. "You still haven't told me what happened to Andy."

Connor, realizing that what lay unspoken between them hung heavily in the air, plunged in. "Andy and I were at the academy together, and served our first stint together in Maryland. Then he got called away out West, and I traveled, working on cases trying to trace down financial information, bank accounts, things of that nature. We ended up both working this case, although our paths diverged and we didn't realize it was all the same case at the time. He was working on Claude Brown's drug enterprises and contacts, but didn't know it was Claude until just before he was killed. And I was working on the Caymans' accounts, trying to trace monies in conjunction with the IRS and our fraud division.

"Brown hated you, Amanda, and he knew Andy was on his trail. He thought you had ratted out information on him to your husband. He sent a note to lure you out to the warehouse that night four years ago. We think he was going to use you to draw Andy out. But Andy intercepted the mail. He made sure that you didn't know about Brown or the note.

"Andy went out to the warehouse that night early, hoping to catch Brown. It used to be a run-down deserted place titled in Barnes' maternal grandfather's name. Apparently it was an old mercantile distribution center years ago. The property was part of the grandfather's estate, and ended up being apparently 'sold' to the corporation, which kept Barnes' name out of the transaction.

"Andy generally used Petrino as a source and back-up, but Petrino was out of pocket that night and Andy couldn't raise him. So Andy called me. I was on my way back from New York, and tried to talk him out of going alone, told him I was on my way. But he insisted, because of the imminent threat to you, and he didn't trust what backup he could get on such short notice. Vaughan was on a mission to Iraq. Andy said that he wanted Brown alive, and was afraid Claude would disappear again before backup would arrive.

"I caught the first flight I could. I called a friend agent in Pensacola to meet me, and we sped there. We were too late. When we found him, he was already dead."

"How did he die?" Amanda asked, her voice muffled. "I need to know—don't spare me."

Connor hesitated. "He was shot at point-blank range in the head and heart, and strung up. Apparently Brown or the killer had used him for target practice."

Amanda said, her eyes closed in the dark, "Billy admitted to me that night that he killed Andrew. They never liked each other, but I never thought Billy was capable of such cruelty. But now I understand all the target practice and self-defense lessons Andy gave me.

"I remember Andy taking me to the shooting range one day, and wanting me to shoot a round straight at the head at twenty paces. He told me to imagine that the guy was coming to kill me. I laughed and said, 'Like Claude Brown sprung from prison?'

"Andy took his gun and emptied it perfectly through the target's head. He didn't smile, but said, 'I'll feel much better when you can do that.' It all makes sense to me now."

Connor countered quietly, "Andy was such a good cop, but his only kryptonite was you. The note to you was a blow to his soft underbelly, to what he cherished most, and he made the mistake of not waiting. He refused to let a threat to you remain out there, even long enough for me to get there. You seem to have that effect on men," Connor added meaningfully.

Her voice was small. "I wondered about you on and off all these years," she admitted. "You were to be Andy's best man, and didn't show. I never met you. And then you didn't come to the funeral. Andy talked so much about you, but . . . ." her voice trailed off.

He hesitated, aware of her pained silence. "I couldn't bear to break the news to my best friend's widow, and was furious that the superiors were keeping the circumstances of his death from you. I took off tracking Brown down to Mexico immediately. I felt I could do more good that way. I might have killed him myself had I found him. But the evidence trail dried up. He dropped out of sight.

"But then we started picking up leads on Barnes' involvement. Of course, he had carefully kept two sets of books, and had implicated you by use of your name and signatures. Then not long ago, there was another major transaction. That coincided with the time Marjorie Witherspoon spoke to the Presiding Bishop, and we decided I would go undercover.

"Marjy suspected Bill Barnes, Junior. The Bureau confronted her with suspicions of your involvement. She was adamant to me that you were innocent, and my superiors convinced her this plan was the only way to prove that and catch the others. Even then, she threatened to tell you everything, and extracted a promise from Feinstein to disclose everything to you, Bureau be hanged. She didn't get to tell you herself; she succumbed before making good her threat. That's why Feinstein was so anxious to get you to New York, away from here and the danger."

Amanda was silent for several minutes. She finally found his hand and squeezed it. "Thank you for telling me about Andrew. Not knowing what happened was harder than I thought possible, because I always felt that because no one told me how he died and I didn't see the body he might come back to me any day. Now after all that has happened I can finally close that door.

"You know, it sounds so silly. I had never understood my parents' horror of cremation—maybe it's something from our Southern Baptist fundamentalist background. But Andy's wish was to be cremated. When the time came, I almost didn't go through with it. Marjy tried to comfort me, to tell me that the body was not him, and I latched on to that thought, although not in the sense she meant it. She meant his soul was gone in the Christian sense, but I believed he was still alive out there somewhere, maybe in witness protection. I don't know—I was crazy with denial. But since that body wasn't him, it was OK to cremate it, give it to science, whatever. I didn't care—he was out there somewhere.

"One day I found the program from his funeral service. I just sat there a moment, then started to throw it away. But I couldn't, and I threw it on the coffee table. I had a session with the psychologist that day, and he saw the program.

"He started talking about closure, and I got angry. He got that look in his eyes like those guys do when they're about to commit you to the locked-down CSU. In fact, he took out a little notebook and started making notes, which scared me, because he never took notes during a session.

"So I mouthed the words I thought he wanted to hear about acceptance and going on with life. He knew I was lying, but I guess he reasoned that if I said the words maybe in time I would come to believe them.

"I was so angry at Andy for not being there. I just knew in the back of my silly mind that he would move heaven and earth to be with me. When the Peace was exchanged at Marjy's funeral, it was the final blow. Suddenly I realized that neither he nor Marjy was coming back ever again. Your telling me today actually helped—an eyewitness account, for what it's worth."

Connor held on to her hand as he wiped the tears from her face with his other hand. "I didn't want to tell you, but if it helped, I'm glad.

"One more thing. I'm sorry I came on to you the other night. But you were so beautiful out there, and I felt this overwhelming desire to cradle you and protect you. I had never seen a goddess in the moonlight before, and there you were. I lost my head, and I apologize. But I wouldn't trade that kiss for anything.

"I know you're still hurting over Andy, and so much has been handed you. You don't need one more entanglement. But I'd like to be there for you, if and when you're ready. My timing couldn't be worse, and perhaps knowing what you know, you may not forgive me for my part in the past. But I've fallen for you. I'll give you as much or as little as you want. If it's only friendship, then I'll try to be happy with that."

He couldn't see her eyes, but he knew she was looking at him in the darkness.

"I think I like you, Jon. But I'm pretty much damaged goods. I'm not sure you're up to the challenge of me. So let's just take it slow and see if anything develops, OK?"

"I'm rusty on relationships, too, but I'm an excellent student," he said, reaching over and kissing her fingers. She laid her hand on his head, and they were silent a while.

Connor finally broke the silence. "I'm flying out tonight. I've got to finish up my report for the U.S. Attorney, and we still have some accounts to trace and loose ends to tie up. We found Mrs. Witherspoon's laptop and diskettes when we searched the warehouse. They're being processed for the evidence. I'll be on the road a while, but I'd like to call you, and to see you when I get back. Would that be all right?"

"That would be all right," whispered Amanda, and he knew she was smiling.

"May I kiss you goodbye?" Connor asked.

Amanda's heart flew to her throat. He leaned over her, gently probed her mouth with his. He cradled her head in his hands and kissed her eyelids, then moved back down to her mouth. He murmured in her ear, "I'll be back, Amanda Childs—you can count on it."

Then he was gone. Amanda still felt weak at the effect of his kiss. You know, she told herself savagely, you're such a pitiful sex-starved creature. It was just a kiss. But the feeling lingered, warm and pleasant.

Chapter 31

"Why Ralph and Claire had to pick this weekend to get married, I'll never know. They waited six whole months—one more week wouldn't have hurt. What with Holy Week and Easter, then the spring break, and the wedding this weekend, it's almost too much."

Amanda, lightly tanned and casually dressed in shorts and tank top, was good-naturedly ranting at Sheila, who was the only victim present to hear her tirade. Sheila smiled knowingly. Amanda's eyes were dancing with delight, as she smelled the fresh blossoms just delivered by the florist and read the card: "I'll be there in time for the rehearsal. Love you madly. Jon".

Amanda, unsuccessfully trying to suppress her pleasure, turned to Sheila. "Well, at least we had the foresight to close down the office this week. You don't know how much I appreciate you coming down to the beach and helping to chaperone these teenagers with me."

Sheila replied, "I wouldn't miss it for the world. I always thought of spring break before with dread, but this was a great idea."

Amanda had decided to rent a large beach house on the Gulf of Mexico and bring the teenagers from the church down. It was a way to provide them a place to stay for spring break, and to try to provide a fun alternative. She had talked Petrino and his wife Jill into coming down as chaperones, and Vaughan had come along to take a group of kids surf-fishing. So with five adult chaperones and twenty kids they had a full complement in the huge house. They had set up the largest adjoining bedrooms on either side of the house as male and female wings, and set down the rule of no drinking, drugs or sex on the premises. Amanda knew the adults probably couldn't keep all the teenagers from those temptations while the latter were out on the beach with friends, but felt they could provide other options to keep them otherwise occupied. They planned activities such as shopping trips, a dance, and a final karaoke talent contest the evening before Ralph's and Claire's rehearsal dinner.

The week had gone really well, and Amanda was able to commute back and forth to town during the day when necessary to help with the last-minute wedding arrangements and for fittings of the obligatory bridesmaid's dress. Ken, now a full-scholarship student at MIT and studying privately with the organ professor at Juilliard, was flying home after his finals to play the wedding. Claire had asked Amanda to be the matron of honor, and Jon Connor was Ralph's best man. The two men had become fast friends.

Amanda's thoughts turned briefly to the church. She had thought about leaving, particularly with the discomfort of Bill's death and the questions it raised. The Bureau had agreed to hold off on any public announcement of the resolution of the case. But Amanda was conspicuously absent from Bill's funeral, having left the service in the hands of Ken and gone to New York to meet with the Feinstein firm. She did not see Connor during that trip, he having been sent down to the Caymans to deal with the banks there in recovering funds. Since then, she had made three trips back to New York on business, and he had taken her to dinner once, out on the town sight-seeing, to the zoo, to the opera and the gala ball put on by the Metropolitan Opera on New Year's Eve. He had come back to Mainville during trips to meet with the U.S. Attorney's office regarding Barnes' impending prosecution. Amanda had felt more and more drawn to him. So far he had kept the relationship light and had not pressured her, although she had caught him looking at her and holding her hand a little longer than usual. But though she felt she was clearly falling for him, she was afraid deep down of again living with the anxiety of being a law enforcement officer's wife.

When she came back from her first meeting with Feinstein, a committee of the church, with Father Anselm, Ken and several other members came to her and pleaded with her to stay on, citing the work she and Marjorie Witherspoon had done with the music and the youth of the church. She at first tried to decline, but they were insistent, and apparently had been told by the Presiding Bishop (apparently omitting the details of the one at fault) that certain funds that should have gone to the church had been diverted, and that whatever was recovered was theirs.

The church committee had later approached her and asked about the possibility of buying Marjorie's spacious home and making it into a private girls' group foster home. She had told them she would think about it. She knew that Marjorie would be thrilled with such an idea, but that just the right person would need to be found to organize and run such a home well. Feinstein, retiring from the firm but still handling Marjorie's estate personally, called her weekly, and argued with her good-naturedly about spacing out her charitable contributions and not giving her inheritance away.

In light of the events that transpired, the probate of Marjorie's will had gone smoothly, and in consequence Amanda now owned three homes. She was planning to donate Marjorie's home to the church for the purpose of establishing the girls' home, and was busy trying to help the church by having Malachi negotiate with the diocese regarding the recovered funds, and to prepare the documents for the endowment of funds deemed St. Catherine's to cover the operating expenses. She had agreed with Father Anselm that the vestry's plan seemed appropriate. She had engaged Feinstein to create a 501(c) entity for the home, and had made her own generous pledge of contribution to the endowment.

In the meantime she had done a little renovation of the farmhouse, doing some painting and rearranging herself. She had to discard some things in order to make room for the furnishings she wanted to keep from Marjorie's home. She realized that if she was going to live there, she had to transform it from a shrine to Andy to a place where she could comfortably live in her new life.

Amanda's reflections were interrupted by Vaughan. "I'm taking some kids to the store. Do you need for me to check on anything for dinner tonight?"

Amanda smiled at him, amazed at how young he looked in a shirt of impossible print, khaki shorts to his knees and a floppy straw hat. "No, I'm calling to confirm that the caterer is delivering everything about 5:00. Ralph and Claire are coming, and some of the kids asked if they could bring their friends."

"I think there will be plenty of food," Vaughan growled. "You're fattening up these anorexic girls to where they actually look good in a bikini."

Amanda laughed. "I'll tell them you noticed."

He waved at her and yelled to the group of teenagers on the deck, "Head 'em up and move 'em out."

Amanda sauntered into the large Florida room where Sheila was setting up the karaoke machine, testing mikes and programming the teenagers' selections for their night's talent contribution. Amanda saw two girls practicing on the back deck, two of the boys sitting in deck chairs and coaching them. A volleyball game was in progress on the beach.

Sheila pointed to the group on the back deck. "Love is in the air," she remarked.

"Teenage love is a powerful thing," Amanda nodded. Shanna, the girl she had rescued in court, ran in with a tall lanky youth, and they each grabbed one of Amanda's arms. "We need you on our team," the girl cried, as they dragged her away. Amanda let herself be captured, and was soon in the middle of the volleyball game.

Sheila was watching her through the French doors when Connor appeared. Standing watching her too, he said, "She's doing well, isn't she?"

Sheila started. "You scared me, Mr. Connor."

"Jon, please," he said, smiling at her.

"She is doing well. The pace has not slowed, but Mrs. Witherspoon's legacy has allowed Amanda to carry on and expand the projects the two of them envisioned. She seems content. She doesn't get that faraway look, and she's a whole lot less mean in court."

"No! Get out of here," Connor said in surprise.

"She hasn't called the prosecutor a scum-bucket in weeks, and she has not marched into chambers and argued with a judge. I had Judge Jones call me last week and demand to know if something was wrong with her—she apparently complimented him on a ruling the other day. She doesn't storm and rage as much as she used to."

"You don't say," Connor said in amazement.

"It's frightening," Sheila said. "And she gets this really goofy smile on her face when she gets your flowers or cards."

Connor grinned. "Oh, yeah?"

Sheila looked at him. "You're good for her—keep it up."

Connor sobered. "I almost despair sometimes of winning her. She is not one to leave the door cracked. You have given me renewed hope." He watched as she cavorted with the kids, until they grabbed her up, ran and threw her into the water. She came up sputtering, and he laughed. "I'll be back," he said.

Sheila stared at him. "You're not staying for tonight?"

"She doesn't know I'm here yet. It's a surprise. Don't tell her."

He left, and minutes later Amanda came in, all wet. As she did, Ralph and Claire walked through the room. "My God, girl, can't you stay out of the water?" Ralph declared, as he lightly kissed her on the cheek.

Amanda took both of Claire's hands in hers. "I'd hug you, but I'm all wet. You look beautiful, like a bride-to-be should look."

Claire looked at her in concern. "Here, let's get you into the shower and dressed up. Your guests are arriving."

Amanda called out as they walked out, "Ralph, look out for the caterers and set up on the big table in the dining room. We'll do buffet style, very informal. Hope you are ready for your talent tonight. Tell the kids that they need to come in and get ready for dinner."

Ralph waved them out of the room, and helped Sheila finish up the preparations for the night. They could hear Claire and Amanda giggling like school girls. Soon several of the teenagers appeared and went to ready themselves for the evening's festivities.

As Amanda was getting dressed, one of the girls ran in. "Miss Amanda, I can't get in front of these people and sing."

"Of course, you can," soothed Amanda. "Everyone is a friend, and this is fun. What's your favorite song? I'll help you." Soon they had selected a piece, and Amanda handed her a CD to take to Sheila to set up.

Wearing a light blue cotton knit wrap dress and sandals, Amanda's tanned and relaxed look made her appear even younger. As the kids, chaperones and guests arrived, they mingled and drank punch. Then Amanda announced dinner, they said a prayer, and the kids went mad, serving themselves and laughing.

Claire asked Amanda, "Is Connor going to make it?"

Amanda said, "I don't know, but he promised to be here by tomorrow's rehearsal."

Ralph came up behind them and kissed Claire on the neck. "You know, six months ago I was frightened at the thought of what I'm about to do with this woman. But now I cannot wait. I cannot imagine life without her."

Amanda looked at them, and she felt their happiness. Ralph then nudged Claire, and Claire gave him a dirty look. He nodded in Amanda's direction, and Claire cleared her throat.

"Amanda, I've got a friend coming in for the rehearsal and wedding, but I hate to put anybody up in a hotel, where it's so cold and sterile. I was wondering if you could—"

"Put her up with me? Sure," smiled Amanda.

Ralph grinned. "There, now, I told her she'd say yes." Claire looked at him with a conspiratorial look.

Sheila was making the announcement. "Tonight is our grand finale, and we have a karaoke/talent show lined up. This is how our charges pay their rent for the week, by entertaining us tonight. First we have Cindy and Maria."

The room was filled with the latest hip-hop thriller music, as the two girls pranced and sang, and the other kids whooped and hollered in delight. One by one and sometimes in groups, the teenagers got up, some to dance, some to sing, a group of four to do *a capella* music of the style of Take 6.

Finally Sheila announced, "And now Corrie and our fearless leader Amanda will do a Sheryl Crowe number for you."

Amanda took the first verse, and everyone joined in on the chorus, and Corrie, emboldened, sang the second verse impeccably, with everyone cheering and joining in, "Every day is a winding road".

As they were arm and arm and singing the last verse, Amanda looked up and saw Connor standing there, looking handsome in polo shirt and khakis. A flush of embarrassment and excitement stole upon her cheeks, as he joined in the clapping and singing.

The song over, she left the stage, and stood there somewhat out of breath. Silly, she told herself, go up to him. But she stood by the machine as one of the teens got on stage and announced, "This one is one of Miss Amanda's favorites, from her grass-smoking days."

She protested and looked at the teen with mock indignation, until he laughed, pointed at her and said, "Got ya." Everyone laughed as he launched in a rendition of "Rocky Mountain Way", as the adults sang along.

Amanda stood there, aware that Connor had come up and was standing next to her. His hand rested lightly on her waist. She felt feverish. You're not a schoolgirl, she told herself sternly.

Next Claire came up, and her clear soprano voice rang out with the kids oohing and ahhing, giggling at Ralph as he swooned in mock ecstasy. Then he followed suit, with the Temptations, "Get ready", doing gyrations and words, while the girls squealed in delight and Claire doubled over in laughter.

After all the others had gone through their turn, the girls turned to Amanda. "Your turn."

Amanda smiled. "Actually, you all are going to do mine for me," she winked at Connor. "You know what I want."

"Ah, Ms. Childs, no church music," a freckled-faced young boy, looking not more than 12, whined good-naturedly.

"But it's my favorite," she insisted gently. "And you do it so well. And there's no dessert until you do."

The kids lined up and she gave them a note. A girl began a solo, and the others joined in singing Ralph Vaughan Williams *O taste and see*, as Amanda listened, tears in her eyes.

When they were through, she smiled tremulously. "A little rough around the edges, but very nice."

"Aw, that's what you always say," Shanna cried, as they laughed. Two of the girls ran up to Connor. "OK, now, what are you going to do?"

Smiling at them, he went and handed a CD to Sheila, and took Amanda by the hand. "We'll need a little space here," he said, looking at her enigmatically. When a Sinatra number came on, she smiled at him as he twirled her to him and they danced. The teenagers clapped. The next she knew the whole room had paired off and everyone was dancing.

Connor steered her out of the room and on to the deck, then took her hand and led her to the beach. Bending down, he took off her sandals and his boat shoes, and they walked along the water line, hand in hand, as the half moon soared overhead and lit the white sands.

She said simply, "I'm happy to see you again."

He responded, "I'm happy to be with you again."

"Where are you staying?" she asked.

"Oh, I thought I might crash here if there's room on the floor, and take you back to town tomorrow after we close up shop here. I think Ralph and Claire have made arrangements for me."

She said tentatively, "I had a spare room, but Claire asked me to allow some friend of hers to stay over."

Smiling, he teased, "Would you have wanted me to stay with you?"

Amanda, embarrassed, murmured, "That might have been nice."

Connor, his heart leaping, turned to her, held her to him and kissed her long and gently. "Does that mean you've grown any fonder of me?"

Amanda looked down. "I love you, but I'm afraid."

"Afraid of what?"

"That you're a cop. I've lost a cop. I'm over Andy. But I couldn't face that again. If I give myself to you and lose you, I don't know if I'm strong enough to weather it a second time."

"Well, I have something to tell you, but it's going to have to wait until tomorrow. Maybe I can allay your fears."

Amanda asked, "Tell me now—" but he silenced her with a kiss, then turned and walked back with her silently to the house, hand in hand. As they arrived back to the deck, they were greeted by a row of faces watching from the window and cheering. Laughing, Connor held Amanda to him and kissed her again for their audience.

The next morning, everyone was up early, and pitched in to clean up and close the house. They had planned to make it back to town by noon so that everyone could unpack and prepare for the rehearsals. The boys, girls, and teeenage choirs all had music to run through with Ken before the final rehearsal and dinner.

As they were loading the van, Vaughan said to Amanda, "Why don't you go on with Jon? There are four of us chaperones left, and none of us are in the wedding party. So get on back, so you can get your hair and nails done and all that female stuff."

Amanda kissed him on the cheek, and joined Connor at his car. He squeezed her hand, and they took off, the kids screaming and waving at them. As they sped down the road, Connor asked casually, "Would it be a great inconvenience if I showered and shaved at your place? I have some business to take care of this afternoon, and will be out of your hair shortly."

Amanda responded lightly, her voice even, "Sure, that sounds fine to me," although she felt extremely light-headed at his nearness.

They sped along the causeway, Amanda oblivious to the birds and boats sailing through the channel. All too soon they were pulling up at the farmhouse. Connor opened her door for her, and reached in and grabbed a suit bag and small carryon bag. Walking her up the steps, he looked at the interior in admiration.

"This place has changed. You've done a fabulous job with it."

"Thanks. The guest bedroom and bath are in there. Make yourself at home."

She went idly into the kitchen and made a pot of coffee. Fiddling with things and tidying in the kitchen, she was jittery at being in the same house alone with him. She knew that she wanted him.

She sat at the table, fingering her cup of coffee and trying not to think of him in the next room. After several minutes, he came in to the kitchen, dressed in suit and tie and smelling faintly of soap and aftershave. Pouring himself a cup of coffee, he turned to her. Reaching for her, he raised her from her chair and held her, kissing her lightly as he said, "Are you going to wish me luck?"

"Don't you want to stay?" she murmured plaintively.

Looking at her face, he drew in his breath sharply. "Shit, Mandy," he said as his coffee cup went on the counter and he drew her to him. Shamelessly she held him and kissed him hungrily, as his hands explored her curves.

Finally he pushed her away. Embarrassed at her reaction, she apologized.

"Don't apologize. I've been wanting you to do that ever since I met you. It's just that the timing couldn't be worse. This meeting is important, Mandy, or there's nothing that would tear me away from you. I wanted to tell you later, but I'm meeting with a Pensacola firm that has a branch office beachside. They are needing someone to do tax and estate work, and of course with Bill Barnes gone, they are hoping to get some of the business in this area as well. I've already talked to them, and was looking at the office and negotiating with them today. If so, I'll leave the Bureau and go into private practice."

Amanda protested, but he silenced her by putting his fingers to her lips. Remembering the gesture from her days with Andy, she was compliant. He said, "I love you and want to spend the rest of my life with you. I don't want you worrying about me while I'm off on a case, and I don't want to be away from you on long stretches. I really think I like this firm, and I wouldn't take the job otherwise. I plan on being around for a very long time. That is, if you want me."

Amanda, tears in her eyes, hugged him hard as he wrapped his arms around her. He traced the tears with his fingers and laughed at her. "Let's hope the firm and I can agree, now that I've told you my secret."

Releasing her, he started to the door and left. A moment later, he was back, with another carryon. As Amanda looked at him in surprise, he replied, "By the way, I'm Claire's friend who needs a place to stay with you tonight. I'm glad you approve. I'll see you at the rehearsal, since you'll have to be there early for the kids' practice. Wear something sexy."

"Why, do you think it's your lucky night or something?" she asked playfully.

He crossed the room in great strides and pulled her to him, kissing her long and deep. Satisfied with her response, he said, "Yes, I think I'll have a lifetime of lucky days and nights from here on out, if you'll consent to marry me."

Slipping a box out of his pocket, he slipped a three-diamond engagement ring on her finger. She looked at it and him. He faltered. "I'm not moving too fast, am I?" he asked.

"No, it's just right," she purred, kissing him. "I love you, Jon Connor. Hurry back to me."